C000325721

B
UNI\

Mary Whelan

The Whistleblower's Secrets

© 2021 **Europe Books** | London
www.europebooks.co.uk – info@europebooks.co.uk

ISBN 979-12-201-1393-9
First edition: November 2021

Distribution for the United Kingdom: **Vine House Distribution ltd**

Printed for Italy by Rotomail Italia
Finito di stampare nel mese di novembre 2021
presso Rotomail Italia S.p.A. - Vignate (MI)

The Whistleblower's Secrets

Index

I would like to dedicate this book to my basketball coach, mentor and dear friend Sean Treacy who was a major inspiration and who had a profound influence in both my personal and sport's life. Sean was instrumental in contributing to my playing and refereeing career and was a key motivator in helping me to make history by achieving my Grade 1 and FIBA International Basketball Refereeing awards. I would like to thank Sean for all the fun, laughter, torture and good times we had together, the valuable lessons he taught me and for the wonderful memories that we shared which I will treasure forever.

Sadly, Sean died last year, January 23rd 2020. He is sadly missed by his loving family, friends and sports colleagues and by everyone whose lives he touched. I would like to thank his daughters, Eileen and Caitriona for their support in writing this book and for their invaluable loyalty and friendship that we shared throughout Sean's life.

Thank you, Sean, for being you, the unique and wonderful person that you were. You will forever remain in a special place in my heart. All my love Mary.

Coach Sean Treacy

TESTIMONIALS

This is a compelling and heart-rending story which creates a fascinating picture through its brilliant descriptive images of a fiercely driven woman who fought and boxed her way through many battles to overcome what seemed like insurmountable obstacles, to succeed in rising to the top, breaking through an all-male dominated field of referees. Perseverance permeates the book from start to finish. One of the telling characteristics is her ability to transfer her skillsets from one area of her life to another as her life continues to evolve. I love the way this book paints a nuanced portrait of the relationships which influenced her on her journey in particular her dynamic relationship with her main basketball coach. I found it to be a truly inspiring book which can change your life and one I couldn't put down. Fascinating and brilliantly insightful, it is a book which transcends trailblazing in sport and offers a blueprint for those interested in striving to achieve in any walk of life.

Mick Dowling
Former Irish national, international and Olympic boxer.

This is a remarkable book about a remarkable woman. One of the most inspiring books I have ever read. A must for anyone interested in achieving success and realising their dreams in life. I particularly love the twist in relation to the 'positive principle of perfection' that permeates the book. It is a book that displays true courage, self-belief, honesty and ambitions and reveals the secrets of how to become successful, overcome life's traumas and shows how to turn adversity into triumph.

Emily Hopkins
Sportsworld Running Club, former Irish International

athlete and member of Dublin City Harriers. Dublin City Marathon Winner 1981

Mary's story is a fascinating read and one of the most honest, open and emotive books about sport and life I have read. A compelling true tale of facing the challenges of growing up as a child with a disability in 1960's Dublin, to excelling at sport and rising through the ranks of basketball to become Ireland's first female referee. Wistful and inspiring, this book is also an engaging look at how our experiences shape our perspectives, succeeding against the odds and the mental and physical resilience of the human body, mind and spirit.

Fiona Oppermann, Sports Therapist, Former Irish 400m Athlete and founder of The Dublin Sports Clinic.

This is a wonderful, heartwarming story of a brave woman who overcame severe childhood trauma and went on to become a champion basketball athlete and the first international Irish woman Referee, then endured car crash traumas and healed from those to become an excellent counsellor herself. A great inspiring tale of courage, determination and endurance!

David A. Lillie, Trauma Therapist SEP (Somatic Experiencing Practitioner)

Pain and suffering have their own rewards and can be worthwhile in the end. An extremely thought provoking and uplifting book full of insight which will speak to people in all walks of life.

Deirdre Collins, Counsellor & Psychotherapist, (IPP)

A really impressive story about an extraordinary woman. The positive side of the principle of perfection is both intriguing and fascinating. Mary shares her unique outlook on the extraordinary rewards that perfection has yielded for her. I found her story to be particularly motivating and her novel outlook on perfection will resonate with people of all ages. It highlights modern day issues in society in relation to gender equality and sexism in sport. All in all, The Whistleblower's Secrets is an extremely thought-provoking and uplifting book leaving us with nuggets of gold and sparkling gems to hold on to and bring into our everyday lives.

Claire McGlynn CMG Fit Coach & Personal Trainer – Olympic Weightlifter, Powerlifter, Former 400m International Athlete.

CHAPTER 1
Tick ... Tock ... Tick ... Tock ...

Tick ... tock ... tick ...tock .... My partner gives me the eagle eye! A look that's loaded with a ton of information. Tick ... tock ... tick ...tock .... Those steely eyes bore into me with a penetrating warning look. Tick ... tock ... tick ...tock .... A huge roar emerges from the crowd, the supporters of the home team screaming wildly because their team have scored to go two points ahead. Tick ... tock ... tick ...tock .... 70-68. The home team cheerleaders are jumping up and down, waving their pom-poms in delight. The atmosphere is electric. You can feel the spectators moving closer and closer to the edge of their seats. I don't have to look. I can sense it! I can feel it! Another penetrating glare from my partner. I say my mantra to myself. Stay focused. Stay in the zone. No cock-ups. This is *NOT* the time to make a cock-up. Concentration! Concentrate, stay cool and calm, don't react.

An even bigger roar from the crowd erupts and disturbs my thoughts. This time it's the away team supporters, the away team have scored to equalise. Tick ... tock ... tick ...tock.... 70-70. We are running like crazy now. Pitter patter, pitter patter, clop clop clippity clop, thump, thump, you can hear all the feet. The screech of the runners on the wooden floor and the noise of the bouncing ball pierces our eardrums. Up and down, up and down we go. Swish this end, basket good. Swish the other end, basket good. Both teams are hot now, swishing like mad, each responding to one another's scoring. Suddenly there is an almighty hush. You can hear a pin drop in this over packed stadium. The ball is thrown in the air and it slams off the backboard. The backboard reverberates violently. Tick ... tock ... tick ...tock.... The ball rolls around the ring, six or seven times, before it finally bounces back out of the basket. Huge sighs all around. Sighs of relief. Sighs of frustration. Massive moans and groans. Someone roars, 'Jesus, shit that was close.' Another penetrating glare from my partner. I glare back. Tick ... tock ... tick ...tock.... The clock is running down. This game is going to go to the wire, no doubt about it. I remind myself to concentrate!

The crowd are up on their feet now, no one is sitting down. They are shouting, screaming, singing, cheering their teams on. The only thing they are short of doing is running onto the court to help their team. Tick ... tock ... tick ...tock.... The players are dripping with sweat now, the sweat is rolling down their backs from the pressure they are under. They are fighting, tooth and nail to win this match. It's anyone's game. In fact, neither team deserves to lose, but one of them is going to lose, has to lose. Tick ... tock ... tick ...tock.... 60 seconds left. 80-80. Are we going to have overtime? That's the big question now. It's highly possible, highly likely. The pressure! Jesus! The pressure is immense. I can feel it. My partner can feel it. The players can feel it. The table officials can feel it. The crowd can feel it because they are responsible for it. The crowd are pumping up the pressure more and more. We are all up on our toes now, the players and us two, the referees. A long shot by the home team. It scores. All hell breaks loose in the crowd. Tick ... tock ... tick ...tock.... 82-80. 30 seconds left on the clock. The away team are frantic to score, the home team are doing their damndest to stop them. My partner calls a foul on the home team. The home team supporters boo him. Sideline possession. Tick ... tock ... tick ...tock.... 10 seconds left on the clock. Can the away team score? They must if they want to stay in the game.

One of the tall girls drives to the basket, gets fouled in the act of shooting. It is my responsibility to make this call, the foul is in my area. If I make this call, I'm going to be both very popular and extremely unpopular. The home team are going to hate my guts. I don't dither. Boom! I make the call; my integrity won't let me do anything else. No chickening out. I blow my whistle loudly and fiercely. I have to sell this call! As a FIBA referee it's critical that I sell it! I run towards the player who fouled, point clearly to her to indicate it was she who fouled and I shout loudly and clearly, 'Foul on 6 yellow, on the arm, 2 shots to come.' I stand on the spot, firmly holding my position.

She reacts very strongly. She does not want to be the one to give the other team the opportunity to equalise. She does not want it to be her fault that the game goes to overtime. She is immensely frustrated and she is kicking herself because she knows in her heart and soul that the offensive player fooled her and she was slow to move and as a result was late to the spot. She knows my call is 100 per cent correct. She glares at me and decides to throw a tantrum. I glare back with a look and a nod of the head that says, 'Ah ah, no tantrum here lady.' My communication stops her in her tracks and she eyeballs me like nobody's business. I don't move. I eyeball her back. Our eyes are locked together. She desperately, desperately wants me to rescue her and to change my call. Her eyes are pleading with me, begging me to save her. Her emotions and body language are captivating. I don't waiver. Her look changes to a forlorn look, equally as pleading and begging as the first one. I stand firmly, holding my position to let her know I am not going to change my mind. Then I change my look. I decide to align with her emotional state. I give her a look that shows my sympathy for the awful situation she is in. I empathise with her. My look communicates that I am putting myself in her shoes and I am sorry I have to make this call. A flicker of yet another emotion flashes across her eyes. I catch it! I hold her gaze. My empathy has reached her, has touched her. I wait! I can feel the door of the impasse between us unlocking. Suddenly, she responds. One last look of resignation before she finally surrenders and raises her hand high, straight as a rush, for everyone to see. She acknowledges the foul call, takes responsibility for her mistake and lets everyone know that my call is correct. I give her one final look that communicates my respect and appreciation for her honesty.

I run out into the middle of the floor, away from all the players, into a clear space where everyone can see me. I now must sell the call a second time to everyone else in the audience. She has made my job easier. I shout clearly the information again, letting everyone know that there are two shots to come. Now it's time to resume the game again. Another eagle eye from my partner, only this time it's a look of relief and commendation. I respond with a look that says, 'No need to worry, I'm not a shrinking violet.' He is relieved no end because if he was forced to make the call on my behalf from the lead position, it would have been disastrous for both of us.

He hands the ball to the free-throw shooter who is gathering herself to take the shots. Tick ... tock ... tick ...tock.... One second left on the clock. The poor girl! She must score both shots for the game to go into overtime. What horrendous pressure she is under. I remember this feeling from my own playing days. She steps up to the line. The sweat is pumping off her. We have to dry the ball for her. She wipes the sweat off her brow, takes a deep breath and shoots the ball. Clean as a whistle, it swishes through the basket. 82-81. The home team are clenching their teeth, the crowd are biting their fingernails, the coaches and substitutes have their hands over their faces, afraid to look. The player shoots the second shot. No swish this time. The ball hits the ring, bounces back and hits the backboard. Dead silence! Everyone is waiting with bated breath. It's 50/50. Please miss. Please go in. The ball stays on the backboard for what seems like an eternity. Nobody is breathing now; everyone is holding their breath. Finally, it happens. The ball goes from the backboard back into the basket. The score is good. 82-82.

The reaction from the crowd is momentarily halted until the penny drops, just like that final shot drops into the basket. The crowd goes wild. The away team's supporters are leaping and jumping out of their seats, going mad and I mean mad, with delight. They are in pure and utter ecstasy. The home team supporters are sitting down or kneeling with their heads between their knees. The players are jumping on top of their teammate for scoring. High fives all around. The coach and subs of the away team are hugging each other and jumping up and down. The home team coach is standing, his hand on his chin, pensive. The home team's subs are sitting in utter dejection. Tick ... tock ... tick ...tock .... One second left on the clock. Can the home team score? The home team coach calls a timeout. Everyone thinks it's futile. My partner and I have a quick conflab to discuss our plan of action. We are ready! The game restarts. The home team throw the ball to a girl who is standing on the halfway line. The minute she receives the ball she throws the ball at the basket. A high trajectory throw, which looks like a *Hail Mary* shot. The ball is in the air, the buzzer to end the game sounds. It can't possibly go in! Gasps galore! It is most definitely a Hail Mary shot! However, it is travelling in the right direction and the line seems quite good. No, it can't. It can't. It can't possibly go in! Can it? The closer the ball gets to the basket the more the question looms. What the heck? The crowd are now literally standing on the edge of the basketball court. Everyone is frozen to the spot, feet rooted to the ground, hands on heads, hands on faces, you name it. Some are holding on to their partner's shoulders for dear life, squeezing the daylights out of them. The tension is that unbearable they can't feel the pain of the squeeze. All eyes are on that ball travelling to the basket. The ball travelling through time and air in what seems like slow motion. It's cruel the way a ball and a basket can torture you! Tick ... tock ... tick ...tock.... Tick... The ball is travelling, travelling, travelling. At long last, it arrives straight at the basket, doesn't touch anything, sails straight through and before everyone's incredulous eyes, enters the basket.

The shock is palpable. The silence is deafening. Everyone in the stadium is trapped in the disbelief. Eventually, it is the cheerleaders who break the silence. The home team players, subs and coaches dash over to the hero and lift her up and give her the bumps. The poor hero is dumbfounded. She can't believe it. She just can't believe her Hail Mary shot actually went into the basket.

Now it's the turn of the spectators to join in the celebrations. Mayhem, that's what it is, pure and utter mayhem. But it's a good mayhem. So many happy and smiling faces, so many handshakes of congratulations, so many pats on the back, so much enthusiasm and praise floating everywhere. A match to remember! What a climax to an amazingly well contested match. A horrible way to lose and a fortuitous way to win. These kinds of shots, while they are extremely rare in basketball and you could count on one hand the number of times they occur, they actually do happen.

My partner and I, like everybody else, enjoyed soaking up the wonderful atmosphere. It was a pleasure to have been part of such a unique occasion. Then a lovely thing happened. When the jubilation eventually died down, the players shook hands with us and thanked us for reffing. The player who I called that awful foul on, came up to me, shook my hand fervently and thanked me for how I handled the situation with her. She said she had learned an important and valuable lesson from me. She said she desperately wanted to hang me and put the total blame on me for her silly mistake. I laughed and said, 'Yes, us poor referees, we are always to blame, it's never the players fault.' She laughed back sheepishly and admitted that this was indeed the case. She told me that it was a new experience for her to have someone being that authoritative with her and yet sympathetic and understanding of her predicament at the same time. She was touched by this experience. She went on to say that it took her by surprise and it really moved her. She commended my integrity and courage and declared her respect for me. She had a big broad smile on her face as she said, 'I can't believe we won the match with a fluke shot like that, after my big mistake. I don't feel so bad now.' I replied, 'Well, maybe the win is your just reward for working through your emotions to allow your wisdom and integrity to take over. After all, taking responsibility for your mistake is also a demonstration of integrity.' 'Yes,' she said, 'That's exactly the valuable lesson you taught me today. You helped me to realise it's never the referee's fault. I lost my concentration and that was the problem. Thank you so much. I wish you the best in your future refereeing career and I sincerely hope our paths cross again.'

My partner shook hands with me, winked and said, 'How can I follow that? Well done. Superb job Mary, I thoroughly enjoyed refereeing this match with you.' As I left the court with my partner, I knew that this match was one of the matches that would be etched in my brain forever.

Sitting in the airport in Rome, on my way home, my flight delayed by a couple of hours, I was able to take the time to think and reflect on my refereeing career to date. My partner and I had received extremely positive feedback on our performance in the match from the commissioner and the assessor. I had been highly commended for having the guts, courage and integrity to make that vital call in the dying seconds of the game. The assessor was suitably impressed that I had kept my cool, held my nerve, kept my concentration, and hadn't frozen under the extra fierce pressure we were under at that particular point in the match.

Sitting in the airport I felt like a happy camper. I had thoroughly enjoyed the match and had loved reffing with my partner. He was a topper. I mused on how lucky I had been with each of my co-officials to date. Pure gentlemen, great fun and extremely proficient and talented people. I spent some time grinning to myself as some of the funny memories came tumbling in. Who would have believed or ever thought, that it was possible to arrive at this international level of refereeing, coming from the background I came from?

CHAPTER 2
Living With Deafness

I went to the doctor with hearing problems
He said, 'Can you describe the symptoms?'
I said 'Homer's a fat bloke and Marge has blue hair'

Despite being two weeks overdue and small, weighing only 7lbs, I was born on Friday, 7th June 1957, a perfectly healthy beautiful bonnie baby. Little did I know that my perfect healthy body was going to be ambushed before I turned four years of age. Little did I know that the formative years of my life, from the ages of four to fourteen, were going to be a torturous nightmare, riddled with pain, suffering and trauma. Little did I know, how harrowing it was going to be to endure what this trauma was going to cause me.

I had a nasty accident at home at 3 going on 4 years of age, where my mother dropped me and I fell down the stairs. It was an extremely bad, awful fall. I banged my head off the wall and stairs as I tumbled and bumped the whole way down from the top to the bottom. I went unconscious and when I woke up I couldn't hear anymore. My hearing didn't return in the following days and months and I ended up deaf. I distinctly remember being severely disorientated after this accident. For weeks and months afterwards, I went around constantly running the taps and flushing the toilet over and over again knowing I should hear the sound of the water. Not being able to, distressed me to the point, that I walked up and down the stairs and banged my head off the wall thinking, if this is what caused me not to be able to hear the sounds that if I banged my head enough times off the wall, it would make my hearing come back. The innocent logic of a child! However, unfortunately I remained deaf despite my best efforts. This led me to attending Crumlin Children's Hospital, where I had to undergo constant treatment over many years. My parents were given a choice by the doctor, between a long slow cure, or an operation that was 60-40 against success and would render me permanently deaf if it failed. They chose the long slow cure. The doctor explained that because I was such a small child for my age and because my ears were tiny, he could do many operations at each stage of growth and if these were successful I would eventually, in ten years' time regain my full hearing. A long journey of treatment began which initially was extremely intensive, attending the doctor in the hospital every day. As progress was being made this was reduced to every second day, every third day and so on. The hospital became my second home.

At home, however, living with deafness was a pure nightmare for the family. My mother couldn't cope with the effects of my disability. While she followed the doctor's instructions, she did it in an angry, impatient and intolerant way. She was physically rough and aggressive in her handling of me and couldn't bear it when I didn't answer her because I couldn't hear her. This became a huge bone of contention between us, as prior to that I would *hop to it* when she called me. Now it appeared as if I was ignoring her, which of course was not the case. The frustration that ensued on both sides is indescribable. My mother couldn't tolerate being ignored and I couldn't understand how she couldn't understand that things had changed because I couldn't hear her anymore. She became quite desperate with the whole situation and she went to the bother of bringing me to Lourdes in the hope of a miracle cure. This was no mean feat, as package holidays and cheap frequent flights simply didn't exist at that time. It would have been costly and unusual for a child to have a passport back then. It was a very different Ireland.

I was four years old and I remember those freezing cold baths like it was yesterday. The shock of the cold waters was so severe that it ripped the air from my small lungs. The busyness, the hustle and bustle of the sick and the infirm being brought to the baths was frightening for me as a young child. When the baths ended for the day, the next stage of the healing ritual was the celebration of mass, followed by a procession. This mass was celebrated in Latin, a language revered by mass goers, but alas this was lost on my deaf ears. This was followed by a pilgrimage candlelit procession, where everybody had to carry their own candle and walk in silence. The stillness and the meditative quality of the procession, appealed to my silent world. The silent stream of moving lights was like a beautiful flowing river against the backdrop of the dark skies of night. The atmosphere was filled with a sense of peace. We attended the baths, the mass and the procession on each day of our seven-day trip, during which my mother desperately held on to the hope of a miracle cure for me. Unfortunately and sadly, there was to be no miracle! Disappointingly, everything went back to the way it was before the trip, my parents not being able to cope with the reality of living with a deaf child.

My whole world changed overnight as a result of this accident. I was accused of *pretending* not to hear. How could I be sitting that close to someone and not be able to hear them? This was their logic. I often felt like shouting; 'You bloody eejits, it's because I'm DEAF. Do you know what DEAF is? Deaf means you cannot hear, even if I'm up your jumper I still won't be able to hear you. IDIOTS! STUPID, STUPID, THICK PEOPLE!' This is undeniably one of the life experiences which sowed the seeds and became the roots of me turning into an angry person. My anger was constantly bubbling away in the background, which eventually turned into a pure rage at being unfairly and unjustly accused in the wrong and my disability not being understood. There were times when I wished I could bang each and every one of them on the head with a frying pan, with such force, that I could make them go deaf and then they would understand the pure agony and torture that I was going through.

Being deaf is NOT a nice place to be I can tell you. There was no special assistance or help of any description for me either at home or in school outside the hospital visits. I had to cope all alone. Neither my parents, nor myself could cope with my deafness. On top of that, I couldn't cope with their inability to cope. As a young child of four, I desperately needed and wanted my parent's help and love. My world became a lonely, isolated place. Nobody wanted to be around me. It was draining and tiring for them having to permanently repeat themselves to no avail. Eventually everyone gave up and stopped trying. It was too much like hard work for other people, trying and trying to communicate with me, especially when there was no return for it. What they didn't realise was, it was equally difficult for me having to permanently repeat myself also with no return. Their withdrawal from me caused me to withdraw, further and further into myself. I remember sitting on the floor on my own, away with the fairies, in my own little dream world, minding my own business. Someone would come up behind me and I wouldn't hear them. I would jump out of my skin and get an awful fright when they would touch me, or I became aware that they were there. This happened countless times. I had to change my sitting position and put my back against something, a press, a wall or whatever, in that way at least I had some chance of seeing them advancing towards me.

While I loved school on the one hand, school was also a difficult and frustrating experience for me. In school I was put sitting in the front row which was miraculously supposed to make me hear better! There was no such thing as lip-reading or sign language in those days. I'm sure I was always the child with the most bewildered face in the class. Most of the time I had no clue what was going on around me. The fact that my teacher's teaching methods were innovative and creative, helped me no end, as her way of teaching required a lot of visual learning. At least I could guess and figure out some of what was going on by reading her body language, facial expressions and hand gestures. Only for this I don't know what I would have done. This was my saving grace at least to some extent. Sometimes I was that desperate I pretended I could hear. When someone laughed, I copied them and laughed too. I had no clue what I was laughing at, but it gave me an illusion of being included and part of what was going on. Feeling different to everyone else made me feel like a freak and an alien. I always remember when I saw the film 'The Elephant Man', I could identify with the cruelty and suffering that he endured. My heart went out to him - I felt terribly sorry for him. I wanted to wrap him up in cotton wool, protect him and take him home with me away from those horrible people. Of course, I was looking at myself and what we had in common with each other. The infliction, caused by a problem outside our control. The infliction, leaving us vulnerable and wide open to be badly treated, tortured and hated by one and all.

Making friends proved to be difficult for me. I tried and other children tried. Because children are primarily interested in playing with each other and having fun, rather than talking to each other, once I made an effort to play with them, at least I could mingle amongst them, albeit under false pretences. While I was mingling on the one hand, on the other, I couldn't engage properly because I couldn't hear and therefore couldn't understand or grasp what was going on around me. If somebody shouted at me to give me instructions, to warn me to move or sidestep, to tell me to watch out because I was in danger, I would of course, remain where I was and wouldn't move. This used to drive my playmates mad and they would be frustrated as hell with me because of this. To look at me you wouldn't know there was anything wrong, I looked as normal as they did and they would forget that I was deaf and couldn't hear them. This situation used to frustrate me too and I would end up feeling hopeless. There I was, trying my best and they were too, but it didn't make any difference to the situation we found ourselves in. Despite continuous efforts for me to be included, I always ended up eventually being excluded. Children don't have patience with other children when they can't respond and keep up with what's going on. It created awkwardness and no one knew how to handle that or what to do next.

As an adult I realise that not only was I robbed of my hearing, but I was also, in ways, robbed of my playtime. Play is natural and vital for children but more importantly, for children who come from troubled backgrounds in helping them to cope with their difficult family life. It provides them with an important survival mechanism to overcome the circumstances outside their control. Playtime is one of the core developmental stages for children. Along with the fun and joy it brings, it teaches them how to make friends, how to deal with enemies, to negotiate, to share, to problem solve, to compromise, to take turns, most importantly, to build and create ideas together which evolves into a new life taking off spontaneously.

When I look back now, I understand the magnitude of my loss. I missed out on a lot of this developmental milestone and the significance of missing out on the developmental stages between four and fourteen, had serious repercussions on my psychological, emotional, mental and social wellbeing. Missing out on this type of spontaneous play, irrespective of my ardent attempts to be included, had a crushing blow on my sense of self. There were times during this ten-year period my spirit was broken. This caused me to feel extremely down and I wished I hadn't been born. I had many recurring dreams about being tortured and being killed and imagining what my funeral would be like. I used to wish that I could go to sleep and never wake up just like 'Sleeping Beauty.' I would be bitterly disappointed when I did wake up and feel dejected at the thought of the day ahead, which would be full of problems and tortures. I didn't want a prince to come along and wake me up, because I knew if that happened, he would just leave me anyway when he discovered I was deaf. That would be the end, he wouldn't want to have anything to do with me, just like everyone else. During those ten years of deafness, I more often wanted to be dead than alive and deaf. Everything was a struggle. Life was a struggle. Life was hard, mean and cruel. It felt intolerable. Everything in life was overwhelming for me. It seemed like the bad always outweighed the good and any break from my torture was short lived. I can see that this today would be labelled as depression, whereas at that time it was not visible. Friends were few and far between when I was young. It was only when I regained my hearing that I could make any genuine attempt to make friends.

After many operations and much treatment, the idea was that my hearing would gradually and slowly begin to return. This did happen in tiny increments. At first, I could begin to hear minute sounds but not clearly. It's hard to explain. It felt like I was imagining things because I could never identify where exactly the sound was coming from. I was totally unsure. This left me feeling more confused and frustrated rather than anything else. Did I or did I not hear something? It was an ever-present question. At this time, I was far too young to understand the significance of this, it just seemed like more of a hassle rather than anything else to me. The doctor was delighted with this progress, but I could never understand his delight. It didn't have the same impact on me in the slightest. For me, the change was insignificant. It didn't change my deaf world. As a result of not being able to hear, my visual senses became more heightened and more alert. I became totally dependent on using my eyes to read people's body language, to learn things and to see obstacles that others could hear but I couldn't, like cars on the road, the sound of the traffic lights changing, the doorbell ringing or bells on bicycles ringing. I had to be extra careful particularly when out on the street, because the expansiveness of the outside world was far more dangerous for me. I think this is one of the reasons I don't like big places even now. I always preferred small more enclosed spaces and places where I was less likely to get lost because I always felt lost in my deaf world. Smaller felt safer and bigger unsafe.

My way of learning became twofold, on the one hand visual and on the other hand, the practical learning of being shown how. To watch someone else and to copy them yielded results for me. When people had the patience to sit down beside me, show me how to do something, have the tolerance to repeat it a few times, observe me doing it on my own and patiently correcting me, this was best for me. Learning from manuals and instruction booklets were of no use to me because I could never understand the words that were written there. Diagrams were fractionally more helpful, but I still couldn't understand the words attached to the diagrams.

When I became older, around ten, eleven and twelve and I began to hear words for the first time, my problems increased even further. You would imagine that this would have been an asset to me, but it wasn't. People had unrealistic expectations of me as they assumed I could hear properly again. As this was not the case, this put more pressure on me and alienated me even more. It was at this point that I really started to get into trouble with everyone and exams and schoolwork became an absolute nightmare for me. The reason for this was, while I could now hear somewhat better than before, I still couldn't hear properly. What happened next was, I would hear the words incorrectly, thereby picking up everything wrong. The words that I would hear would have no resemblance whatsoever to the words that were being spoken. As someone once said, 'She's hearing everything arseways.' That was exactly it. An example would be, if someone said *dying* I would hear *dieting* or I would hear *suck* instead of *sock*. There are many funny examples when I look back now. To the question, 'Do you want Exit 11?' I might answer, 'Eggs at eleven? No, I prefer them for breakfast' or there's the ad about hearing loss where the confusion is *sand wedge* or *sandwich*. This is one of the reasons why exams were a nightmare for me. I couldn't recognize the words that were written down on the exam paper, they would be alien to me, because I would hear something totally different altogether. My mind heard *eggs at* which meant I missed that opportunity to learn the word *exit.* This kind of confusion is normal in language acquisition but with my hearing impairment it became more intense and more significant. The problem was magnified as I was now a teenager trying to catch up and not a child at the age of two or three, where people more readily accept it. There I was, poor old me, thinking I was great hearing these spoken words properly for the first time only to find out I wasn't at the races at all.

You can imagine how devastating and frustrating this was. I honestly don't know how I got through school, especially secondary school. It was a pure miracle. Secondary school is a completely different ball game to primary school. This new partial hearing made people angry with me again, just like when I was younger and they accused me of pretending not to hear.

When I could hear fully again it felt like I was back to square one. There was a huge amount of rehabilitation that had to be done to reinstate me into normal living conditions. I had to redeem everything from scratch and had to be reintroduced to a high volume of various sounds again such as bird song, the noise of the kettle boiling or door bell ringing, the noise of hall doors and car doors opening, closing and slamming, taps running, the gas being turned on, the jingle-jangle of money or jewellery, fire and house alarms going off, the pitter patter of feet, the birds pecking on the window, the buzzing of bees and many, many more sounds, too numerous to mention, the sounds of everything in life. I had to learn how to speak properly and I was sent to elocution lessons which I hated. I had to unlearn a lot of what I had learnt incorrectly due to mishearing and had to do major catching up in my education. I felt like a baby starting from scratch again, only now I was a *Big* baby.

It was like the stories you hear and films you see about people who have been institutionalised, for example, people who have been in prison for years and when they come out, they can't integrate back into life again because everything has radically changed while they were incarcerated. The film 'The Shawshank Redemption', captures this brilliantly, when the man who was the librarian of the prison for years leaves prison and goes to work in a supermarket, packing the groceries for the customers. He can't keep up with the pace and speed of the groceries coming at him and people start shouting at him to hurry up and telling him that he's too slow. He ends up committing suicide due to overwhelm of the readjustment into everyday life.

I heard a radio documentary one time about the Birmingham Six and the Guildford Four who, when eventually released from prison had similar experiences. Technology had advanced in the sixteen years while they were imprisoned and when they came out, they couldn't adapt to these technological changes. It put a terrible strain on their marriages and family life so much so, that several of their marriages broke up as they couldn't cope and fit back into society. This is exactly how I felt when I had to emerge from my own insular institutionalised world of being deaf. Just like those men, I found it extremely traumatic trying to fit back into society, a society that had moved on while I was stuck in my silent world. It's like being trapped in a slow ancient time zone while everyone else is in a modern, fast moving time zone and you have been left behind, but now have to propel yourself forward at lightning speed, in order to catch up. The jump from so far back to so far forward is terrorising and seems impossible. I was shocked when I heard the details in this documentary because the joy of being reunited with their families was promptly destroyed. It never occurred to me that such a thing could happen. It was a sad and harrowing realisation for everyone concerned and yet one I could identify with and relate to in myself.

CHAPTER 3
The Doctor – My Saviour

The doctor, Dr. Johnson, was an elderly man, awfully gruff and cranky, but luckily enough for me an excellent doctor. For some unknown reason to the nurses and everyone else concerned, he took a special shine to me. He would sit me up on his lap, while he treated my ears, chat to me and I would hug him and thank him for all his help. We became good buddies. I got a terrible slagging from the nurses because he didn't do this with any other child and they were mesmerised by this. Whenever I had an operation, I made him promise to be sitting beside my bed holding my hand when I woke up. This he always did and never once did he let me down in this regard. The nurses were gobsmacked. What charm did I possess that the other children didn't possess, that I could penetrate my way into this obstreperous man's heart! He was impatient with the other children and often gave them and their parents a good telling off when they didn't do what they were told to do. But never me. He was forever patient, kind, gentle, caring and loving with me. My mother was a narcissistic attention seeker, always needy of praise, looking for confirmation that she was a class above the other mothers and that she was the only mother who followed the doctor's instructions. So, my mother cooperated with him in order to gain this praise. Maybe this was partially due to the unspoken guilt she may have felt!

The first day I met the doctor he scared me he was so grumpy, but I was also nervous about going to the hospital. That was because my mother was up the walls about it herself. While he scared me, I was also somewhat preoccupied with my own thoughts in relation to my mother and myself. His grumpiness didn't affect me in the way it might otherwise have. On the second day I took more notice of him. He had grey hair which was a lovely snow-white and a snow-white grey moustache, which was not skinny but somewhat bushy and short in length. I loved playing with his moustache and I loved tickling him through it. I could see the twinkle in his eyes. He had beautiful big blue eyes which twinkled in two ways, one in amusement and one mischievously. When he smiled which was rare, he had the most beautiful smile. A smile which made my heart melt. It was then that I knew that this gruff, grumpy, impatient man had a heart of gold beneath his rough exterior. Often, I would tickle him and mischievously he would tickle me back – I had loads of tickles. We had great fun tickling each other over the years and hours of fun and laughter enjoying this mischievousness. This was great for me because it didn't involve any communication which required me to hear him. It most definitely helped me to become relaxed with him and helped me to develop trust in him.

The doctor was amused at my fascination for his moustache. No one else must have shown interest in it the way I did. I had never seen a moustache before. No one in my family had one. It looked like it was inviting me and begging me to explore it. Because my hands and fingers were so tiny, when I touched it, my finger would disappear into it and I thought this was great craic. Tickle tickle tickle and his mouth would twitch in a real funny way. This sent me into peals of laughter. My laughter was that infectious he too would end up laughing. My mother wasn't a bit impressed by my behaviour. She was mortified and didn't like being made a *Show Of*. She would glare at me and tell me to stop, but the doctor would tell her to leave me alone, I wasn't doing any harm and he was enjoying it. Luckily enough for me he did this. This reassurance was crucial for my mother, otherwise she would have killed me when we got outside. Our little game continued for many years and became an important part of our relationship. Funnily enough, it was a game I never grew out of and he never stopped it either. It was our special little connection that was unique to both of us and it drew us closer together.

In the early years of my deafness and for many years afterwards, I had excruciating pain in both my ears. I remember it being constantly unbearable and I spent a lot of time holding my hands over my ears in an attempt to reduce the pain. I often felt that I was going mad with the feelings of thunder in my head from the pure pain and agony I was permanently in. My ears and my head felt like they were going to explode and I wished they would because then maybe the agony would be gone with the explosion. However, I was an excellent patient and I didn't grumble or complain too much considering the levels of pain I was enduring. The main reason for this was, I was downright terrified of my mother. I didn't want to discommode her because when she got angry you wouldn't know what she would do. She was capable of anything and the fact that she couldn't cope with my deafness added fuel to the fire. I was a big disappointment to my mother because she wanted a boy. You can imagine the extra and bitter disappointment when I developed this disability. A girl! A deaf girl!! I most certainly was not the flavour of the month in her eyes. Having to attend the hospital every day and so regularly in the early years, took its toll on her and increased her stress levels enormously. When I was being operated on and I had to stay in overnight this doubled her stress. Of course, this was overly time consuming and had to be followed up with quite intensive home treatment, carrying out the doctor's strict instructions.

The doctor and the nurses wondered why I never wanted my mother to be beside me when I woke up from the operations. It was more natural and common for children to want their mammies. But not me. I only wanted the doctor. From a young age I was quite intuitive and had good wisdom to know a good thing when I saw it. In my eyes the doctor was the best and safest choice. After the operations I needed a calm and reassuring influence, not one of hysteria like my mother would have been. I felt safe and comforted with the doctor holding my hand and rubbing my head and forehead which he did very gently, tenderly and lovingly. When I opened my eyes, I was always greeted with a warm, welcoming, big broad smile which immediately made me feel better. He fussed over me in a loving and caring way and if I was well enough, we played our little tickling game to get me smiling and laughing again. He always made sure that the nurses treated me with something nice, jelly and ice cream for example. I loved jelly and ice cream and he always praised me and rewarded me for being such a good, brave patient. Who would trade a hysterical mother for that? I might have been deaf, but I wasn't stupid. The abundance of love and attention from the doctor was so precious to me. I absorbed it like a sponge and lapped it up every chance I got. Young as I was, I had deep appreciation for how lucky I was to have someone to make up for what my mother wasn't capable of giving me. I attended Crumlin Hospital and this doctor for over ten years at this critical stage of my development, between four and fourteen years.

Ten long years later, when the day came that my hearing was 100 per cent back and my deafness was cured there were great celebrations all round. The doctor and nurses were delighted for me. It was a long hard slog and a long road to recovery, but on this final day when success was ours it felt worthwhile. Of course, I was inconsolable that I wasn't going to see the doctor anymore now that there would be no more hospital visits. I was also going to miss the nurses and miss going to the hospital itself as it had become my second home. I loved it there and I had lovely memories of it. After the excitement was over, I began to cry and the more I cried the more I realised that something special and precious that I had treasured very much was coming to an end. The doctor too was sad. I asked him if I could keep coming to the hospital to see him because I was going to miss him terribly and I was going to have a big hole in my tummy from missing him. He decided that I would have to come back for check-ups once a month just to keep an eye on things and make sure that everything remained okay. Gradually over time this was extended to bimonthly and then every three months. I did this until he retired, I think within four or five years.

After he retired, we kept in touch by telephone and I eagerly awaited my precious phone calls with him. Our conversations were never short, they were always long and interesting and fun filled. One of the things we talked about was my basketball career. He took a particular interest in my development as a player and he loved hearing every morsel of news about it. The fact that I was as small as I was fascinated him, because basketball players are notorious for their height and being tall is of great importance. I told him the funny stories of how I could duck and run between the other girl's legs with the ball because I was small. He thought this was both ingenious and hilarious. As he got to understand the game better through our talking about it, he gave me some good ideas himself that I could try out. My love for basketball was immediate and he enhanced my love for it even further with his genuine interest and willingness to learn more about it. He was extremely proud of me whenever I reported back to him that I was top scorer in the games. We talked about anything and everything, there were no holds barred. He shared his life stories with me and I shared mine with him. I never got tired talking to him, nor he with me. We always found it hard to say goodbye and hang up the phone. But in the end, we had to of course. Then I would just savour our conversation and hold on to it, eagerly awaiting our next one. That was especially nice too, having that spark to hold on to.

The doctor's treatment of me played a vital role in sustaining me through those extremely traumatic years and helped me at a primal level to survive this ordeal. Without him, I most definitely would not be where I am today. His love became part of me and fostered an ability to take the risk to trust. He was a positive male role model, a man of integrity and true to his word.

Whenever I see a man with a moustache it always reminds me of him. I always think of him and the deep sense of love we had for each other. He was the first person who taught me what love truly meant. He gave me my first lesson in unconditional love. This I am truly grateful for. His influence had such an imprint on me that it shaped me into the loving person that I am today. Mysteriously and magically and difficult as it was, I was able somewhere, in the depths of myself to hold on to this incredible experience and not destroy the seeds that this unique and special man had sown in me. As a child growing up, people always described me as adorable, lovable and affectionate. The doctor's influence on me no doubt had a huge bearing on this. His love gave me the sense of having a base. His consistency in being ever-present and keeping to his word, laid a solid foundation in developing genuine trust and love between us. The fact that he was always there and had never let me down deepened our relationship and made the love grow even more. I was able to love sport, love basketball, love refereeing and many other things as a result of this experience. Transferring the feeling of love to other things came naturally because the foundation was solid. Sustaining the relationship after the treatment was over was pivotal in this regard. It always felt like we were two souls that came together, two souls that went on a journey together, soul mates to the end. Our love always seemed to be in rhythm and in tune. It flowed evenly and freely between us. It was a unique and precious experience and one that I will treasure forever.

It was no accident that in future years men would play a significant role in propelling me towards my sporting successes. By the same token, it is ironic that men were my stumbling block when it came to breaking through the male-dominated world of refereeing in basketball. The doctor's influence on my life, however, was a foundation for the former and probably significant in reducing my fear of the threat of men in the latter.

Unfortunately for my doctor, when he got older, he ended up in a nursing home. For me this was great because I was able to visit him there and resume our contact. It was just like old times as it had been in the hospital as if we had never been apart. We were able to play our little game again. I had missed it in those intervening years, in fact I had missed it terribly. We couldn't play that over the phone, although we did try to imitate it through our talking, but it wasn't the same as playing it in the flesh. Playing our little game made the years roll back for both of us. It felt like we were right back to where we had started. This was a lovely feeling.

It happened immediately and spontaneously. It is amazing how a simple thing can bring so much joy and intimacy into life. I went to visit him in the nursing home as often as I could, at least once or twice a week until he eventually died there.

I remember when he was dying, I tickled his moustache and even then, it brought a smile to his face. This was a memory I always treasured after he died. When I was in the throes of grief for him, it would comfort me to know, that at least he left the world with a smile on his face as a result of our little game and I trust that it gave him some comfort too in those final moments.

It was an honour and privilege to have him in my life until he reached the ripe old age of ninety-three. His death was one of the most significant deaths in my life. I felt the bottom had fallen out of my world. I thought he was indispensable because he was in fact, indispensable to me. I was broken-hearted and inconsolable when he died. However, I will never forget him as long as I live because he gave me the greatest gift of all time, the gift of love. Oh yes! and my hearing.

CHAPTER 4
Primary School Teacher

St. Clare's Primary School was the obvious choice of school for my parents, as it was a mere ten minutes walk from both my own house and my grandmother's (Nana's) house. My nana was my mother's mother. I had just turned four years of age in the June preceding the September of my enrollment, which meant I was quite young.

I loved school and I loved St. Clare's. I was exceptionally lucky to have the most wonderful lay teacher whose teaching skills and innovative and creative teaching methods, made learning fun and enjoyable. It was obvious she loved her job and took great pride and satisfaction in teaching us. She was definitely ahead of her time.

My teacher, Miss O'Flynn, was a lovely easy-going person, extremely friendly and had a kind, caring, loving nature. She was a small woman, about 5' 4" (1.62m) in height with fair curly hair and a skin tag on her cheek, which made her cute looking. Her eyes were blue and she had a lovely pleasant face and she was motherly and warm. I can still clearly remember her face to this day despite the passage of time. She wore a tweed suit, skirt and jacket, with a nice blouse underneath. She had shoes with a slightly raised heel. I honestly can't remember a day that she was in bad humour. Her loving, gentle, warm, smiley, welcoming face was the first thing we saw every morning when we went into school and this is how she always greeted us. She was an incredibly kind person and seemed to have time for everybody, but yet made you feel you were special to her. With me she had to go to extra lengths because I was slower to pick up what we were doing because of my deafness. She was unbelievably patient and understanding with it. She did her best to include me in everything and made extra-special efforts to have little chats with me whenever she could. When she spoke to me, she made it her business to sit close to me. She did this in a tender and compassionate way as she had to make eye contact to ensure I could get a sense of what she was helping me with or showing me. She tried to enter into my silent world. She would put her arm around my shoulder and point to things in my book or an object she'd be using to explain something. She would use finger pointing, sensory touch, drawing shapes, numbers and pictures to try and explain the lessons to me. I could see she would be thinking about how she could explain something and get through to me. I loved this quizzical expression on her face because I could see she went to extra effort for me and didn't give up on me, like many others did.

I loved her so much – she was such a sweetie pie. Everybody idolised her. She really tuned into children. She knew how to listen to them, how to go at their pace, how to meet their needs and to dispel their worries. She was extremely kind and empathic. She had a great sense of fun and could break the tension that arose at times in the class with children struggling with their learning by telling a joke or saying something funny. She showed that she accepted somebody struggling, it was ok, part of the learning process. For me this was extra important because of my double struggle of ordinary comprehension plus deafness.

Her constant presence and dependability gave us a sense of safety and a feeling of security. She built our confidence and self-esteem. She made us feel worthwhile as children and treated us like proper human beings. She didn't show favouritism and treated everyone fairly and equally. While the whole class idolised her, she equally made us feel idolised by her. She taught us manners and etiquette and how to respect her and each other. She disciplined us in a good way and never punished us by slapping or hitting us with rulers and sticks, which was common practice in that era.

Irish was a subject that everybody in the school hated but our class was the exception. We loved Irish and we excelled at it. I learnt so much Irish from my teacher that it carried me the whole way through secondary school – first year right through to sixth year. I could use loads of proverbs which gave my Irish a higher quality and standard when it was used correctly in an essay. Unbelievable but the gospel truth. Unfortunately, my secondary school Irish teacher was not a patch on her and it was a real pity because I didn't progress any further as a result.

First thing every morning, Miss O'Flynn would get us to say our prayers in both Irish and English. She would divide us into various groups and we had to act out the parts of the prayers. There were scarves and clothes to dress up in. It was like we were putting on a play. We loved this and had great fun choosing and fighting over the parts. Over the weeks she got everyone to rotate the parts, therefore we each got a chance to play the different parts. Every group had to perform their little play in both Irish and English, which made learning Irish easier. The fact that the prayers were repeated so many times and because we were so absorbed in the variety and quality of acting, helped us remember the words in a fun and enjoyable way. There were other times when we had to speak only Irish for a certain amount of time and this was done through playing different types of word games. There were always little rewards for the winners. This increased individual participation and encouraged everyone to make a great effort. We also had group games of a similar nature.

Miss O'Flynn incorporated funny and comical stories in her teaching and in turn she asked us to bring in some of our own and to create and invent stories to stimulate our imaginations. We had many hours of fun and laughter which often caused the nuns to knock on the door wondering what all the hullabaloo was about. She also had great tricks for teaching sums, as a lot of children struggled with what was called arithmetic in those days. We did a lot of creative work such as artwork, making cards, toys and other different projects. These were created through both Irish and English as a parallel teaching method. Knitting and sewing were thrown in for good measure but not in the traditional way. First, we played games with the wool and progressed through the game to putting stitches onto the needles. After this our tables were recited and we would knit the tables we recited on the needles. When we were playing games, she would teach us and get us to do it her way. She'd be egging us on, heavily involved, encouraging us, her face lit up, incredibly expressive and animated while spurring us on – go on, you're doing great, don't give up. I still do that when I am working with kids nowadays.

Miss O'Flynn taught us to sing and recite poetry at a very young age. Much of our learning of geography, history and the various other subjects were learned through singing, poetry and nursery rhymes. She also had musical instruments which we had great fun playing and these too were incorporated into her teaching techniques. Unfortunately for me I had no idea what the music sounded like because I couldn't hear it. From watching and observing the children singing and playing instruments in the classroom, I could see by the animation on their faces that it was something enjoyable. The expression on their faces was totally different to when they were learning something in a more serious manner. Their faces, instead of being glum or frowny, were bright, cheery, smiling, their eyes twinkling, alive and alert and they appeared to be having fun. Their body language was also different because when they were serious their bodies were more still and heavy, but with the music their bodies were moving and jigging freely around the place and they were much lighter in themselves. While I didn't understand what was going on, I could see and feel from the atmosphere that it was something I most probably would like. After all, if the other children were enjoying it so much, why wouldn't I? While at some level, I enjoyed watching it, because it looked lively, I also felt frustrated at not being able to hear or understand exactly what was going on and I always felt left out. I was acutely aware that no matter what Miss O'Flynn did, I couldn't be part of it in the same way the other children were.

In the same way that I couldn't understand music, I also couldn't learn the words of songs or hear the tune and sound of the music. I was reliant on my visual senses to try and pick up what was going on. Sounds were alien to me and there was no way of learning them. When singing in the classroom, Miss O'Flynn had the children divided into groups and she used her hand to conduct the singing. I could see that she was waving her hand around, moving it up and down, to the right and left, sometimes circling her hand. When I looked closely at the surrounding children, I could see their chests moving as they breathed in and out. I became aware that when she moved her hand up, their bodies would also move up and when she moved her hand down, their bodies would drop. I didn't understand why this was happening and it was years later that I discovered the up movement was for the high notes and the down movement was for the low notes. Miss O'Flynn drew pictures for me to try and help me to get a gist of what was going on, but in this situation it was more difficult because it was much more complicated than trying to show me a simpler picture of something like an animal and unfortunately, I didn't get it. I couldn't understand the message she was trying to convey to me.

Even though I struggled to follow the music and felt apart from the rest of the children, I didn't feel alone because I could sense Miss O'Flynn's compassion for me and her eagerness for me to take part. I couldn't hear a word that was being said, but at least visually I could get an idea of something that was going on. I don't know if she used these techniques with music and rhythm because of the deaf girl in the class or if she always worked like that, but I found it penetrated into me somehow and it enabled me to be involved. I was part of the class and I could participate in a big crowd. I consider myself blessed and lucky to have had her for the duration of my years in primary school. This fostered my love of music and I continued to enjoy it as a subject throughout my school years.

No amount of describing or explaining gives the true picture or reflection of what it was like to be deaf. It's like everything in life, you would have to go through it yourself before you could fully understand the effects of it. My homework was never right when I brought it into school the next day because I hadn't a clue what was going on in the classroom. Miss O'Flynn always had to write my homework down for me every day so that I could show it to my parents. But as I've already mentioned, my parents couldn't cope with my deafness. The homework became an absolute nightmare and caused much fighting at home. Neither of my parents were as tolerant and patient as Miss O'Flynn and they traumatised me instead of helping me. This undid some of the good work that Miss O'Flynn was trying to do for me because their impatience caused me to shut down and feel miserable and hopeless. It would take Miss O'Flynn a long time to shake me out of this the next morning in school. From what I remember things got that bad she had to eventually stop giving me homework. While this was good on one hand, it was also detrimental as it caused me to fall further and further behind the other children when I was already miles behind them in the first place. Poor Miss O'Flynn, she had her work cut out for her trying to teach me.

I think it was through her that I developed a deep love and appreciation for colours and beautiful things. She often used the scarves and clothes as a method to help me to understand better. This increased my visual awareness and nourished my appreciation and love of colour and beautiful things. She deepened my aesthetic values, which I still treasure today. She used the vibration of the musical instruments to help me to learn my counting and tables. When everyone else was reciting their tables, I had to play the instrument and sense the vibration while she got the rest of the class to tap their desks in conjunction with the tables they were reciting. The rhythm of the tapping matched the numbers and when I eventually got the hang of it, I could learn the easier tables at least. Therefore, I got basic learning regarding the sums which of course was better than nothing. Had I been left to my own devices and ignored I would have learned absolutely nothing at all. In those days there was no help available, no hearing aids, no sign language, no lip-reading and no Special Needs Assistants (SNA) like nowadays. The class numbers were huge. Thirty-six to forty children in the one classroom each one clamouring for her attention and needing to be taught, doesn't leave much room to give special attention to a disabled child in need of extra help. Unfortunately, despite her best and greatest efforts learning was still an immense struggle for me but she gave me a chance and a fighting chance at that, to hang in there. She never caused me to feel awkward or stupid and I loved and appreciated the love, help and attention she gave me.

When I think about Miss O'Flynn it brings a smile to my face. She conjures up memories that I will never forget and will treasure for a lifetime. Her even temper, her forever jolly, pleasant, smiling face, her sense of humour, sense of fun and her childlike qualities which were infectious were a treasure to behold. She was a vibrant and colourful character. I loved her dearly as did my classmates. She was just one of those admirable, adorable people that you couldn't but like. Her kindness, her generosity, her friendly easy-going and outgoing personality and her high-spiritedness left its mark on all of us.

Her love for her job and her dedication and commitment to us, her children, was so steadfast and consistent that she gave us a sense of security and we felt safe in her hands. I don't know what her personal life was like, but if she had any troubles, worries or difficulties in her own life, she was a master at containing herself and her emotions. She never projected her woes on to us or took her problems out on us and I'm sure she must have had plenty. There is no doubt she was a special, unique woman and teacher. I have friends who had horribly bad experiences in school, especially primary school and they envy my joyous experience with Miss O'Flynn. How lucky was I, my classmates and the innumerable children who passed through her hands?

She most definitely was a perfect role model of someone 'Who walked the talk.' She led by example and yet had superb control over the forty children under her wings. She commanded respect and got it easily. She was a person of integrity. Her caring and loving ways yielded far greater results than the brutality that was commonly applied in teaching in those days. What commanded our respect and love for her, was her ability to love us unconditionally and to treat us equally and fairly while at the same time making us feel we were individually special to her. This is a rare quality in a teacher in the Ireland of the 1960's.

When I look back now, I appreciate what I know and remember about her. I feel honoured and privileged to have been one of her pupils. I feel lucky to have been exposed to her knowledge and wisdom, her creativity and her broad expansive mind. Like my ear doctor, she influenced my life in a way that made the torture of being deaf more bearable. To this day, Miss O'Flynn has a special place in my heart and she will always remain there until the day I die.

This poem is a dedication to Miss O'Flynn, with deep love, thanks and gratitude from 'Little Mary.'

To Miss O'Flynn who I loved so dearly
You're every child's favourite quite clearly
There was no competition you were loved by one and all
The best, the most adored, from your pedestal you could never fall

Everything about you we loved so much
Your beauty and your tenderness our hearts did touch
Always keeping our best interests in sight
Forever and always shining your light

That sparkling light matched the twinkling in your eyes
Those beautiful eyes that made our hearts rise
Thank you so much for just being YOU
Unique and special with an integrity so true

You shaped us, you moulded us, you gave us confidence to grow
Seeds for our future you most certainly did sow
You taught us respect, you taught us how to trust
You taught us that in life taking risks is a must

You taught us to make friends and that you too were our friend
When we fought and fell out you showed us how to make amends
Your sense of humour and fun made everything alright
Your smile and your laughter were a beacon of light

I needed you to shine your light onto me
And you did! It was there for everyone to see
Your light broke the darkness of my barren silent place
That secret deaf place hidden behind my tiny little face

You showed us the importance of enjoying the here and now
That each new day brings gifts to which we should bow
But the greatest gift of all was the gift of yourself
Your knowledge, your wisdom, your unrelenting help

I don't know if you realise how precious you were and are
The angels from heaven sent us one magnificent big star
Sirius is the brightest shining star in the sky
You were our Sirius and you taught us to fly

If I had a hundred wishes to make
I would wish for every child in their wake
To have a hundred experiences of a teacher like you
Because people like you are far too few!

So thank you Miss O'Flynn for everything you gave us
You enriched our childhoods without any great fuss
Our learning you made easy you stayed through thick and thin
The end result for us was an overall win

Your attributes and talents are too many to mention
One thing's for sure we never lacked your attention
Words cannot express the gratitude I feel
For the memories I'll treasure they are so surreal

How lucky was I, all those many years ago?
How lucky was I, that you shaped me so?
How lucky am I now, to look back and to cherish?
How lucky am I now, that you didn't leave me to perish!

CHAPTER 5
Play

I spent a lot of time in my nana's house, where I had hours and hours of fun playing out on the street with the other children in the neighbourhood. I much preferred to stay in my nana's house than my own because there was greater scope to mix and play there with other children. My mother was unbelievably strict, a tough disciplinarian. My younger brother and I were not allowed out on our street to play, as ours was a dangerous busy road with cars, motorbikes and bikes speeding around a sharp corner in front of our house. In addition to that, my mother wanted to have full control over us, whereas my nana's road was safer and she enjoyed watching us playing and having fun.

The only time we were indoors in my nana's was when we had to go in for our meals and go to bed at night-time. We never got bored or tired playing and we couldn't eat our meals quick enough so that we could go out to play again. Heaven knows how we didn't develop ulcers and other digestive ailments from the speed we used to eat. Gobble gobble gone – was our motto and everyone stuck to it like glue.

Again, when I look back on this time, this laid the foundation for my development of coordination skills, spatial awareness skills, balancing skills and competitiveness through the many games we played. Games we played were skipping, football, hopscotch, ball games, swinging on the lamp post and many more. Our creativity was stimulated and nurtured through the creative imagination of inventing and creating new games to play with each other. These assets, accumulating over numerous years of childhood, stood to me in later years and were instrumental in shaping me into the sports person I was eventually to become.

I particularly loved playing Beds and Hopscotch, which involved kicking a shoe polish tin which was filled with clay from one number to the next, up one side of the numbers and down the other side of the numbers, going from one to ten. We drew the patterns and numbers on the ground with chalk. Hopscotch had the numbers laid out differently with a combination of single numbers and double numbers beside each other. When you became good at beds you could progress to hopscotch. In both games you had to hop on one leg, balance yourself, kick the tin into the next square without touching the lines or the tin and jump into the next square until you completed every square. It started by throwing the tin into the number one square. Next you kicked the tin for the whole round. When you successfully completed round one, you threw the tin into number two square and kicked the tin from there the whole way around. The winner was declared when the rounds one to ten were completed. To make the game more challenging you could either reverse it backwards or play it on your opposite leg, your non-dominant leg.

I can see now how these two games were perfect for developing skills I needed later to play basketball. Playing on both legs allowed you to become ambidextrous in your legs and developed the muscles, tendons and ligaments equally on both sides of the body, thereby bringing an extra overall equality of strength and balance into the body. This promoted extra suppleness and agility which in basketball terms enhanced players' skills in the ability to change direction and change pace at speed. Hopping on one leg not only developed strength but developed great balancing capabilities. In basketball this was useful because when heavy contact by an opponent is made it allows you to hold your ground and not be knocked off balance easily. As a player having this skill makes you harder to defend. Throwing the tin and having to get the tin exactly into the square developed hand-eye coordination, precision and spatial awareness. In basketball these skills are extremely important for catching the ball, shooting, team passing and bypassing opponents through small spaces. The jumping in the games of course, were vital as in basketball there is a lot of jumping for catching to receive the ball, to intercept passes by the opponents and jumping to shoot.

Another firm favourite I loved, were the ball games. You started with two balls throwing them to the action of nursery rhymes and sang the rhymes as you went along. Everyone's favourite was 'Plainy a packet of rinso.' These games were played against a wall or in the air if you didn't have a wall to play against. The games started by doing each of the actions once until you completed the cycle of the rhyme. You progressed to two of each of the actions, then three until you got to ten of each action. The first player to complete round ten without dropping the ball won the game. When you became proficient with two balls you could progress to juggling with three balls and continue further to juggling four balls. The next challenge was to play the two balls with one hand only. Hardly anybody managed to progress to four balls or two balls with one hand only, but because I loved a challenge I practised and practised until I could do it.

These games developed hand-eye coordination, spatial awareness and dexterity in mobility and movement through the hand throwing and catching and the manoeuvring of the body for the more complex actions of the game. It strength-ened the fingers, wrists, hands, arms and shoulders and flexibility in the upper and lower limbs. The singing of the rhymes of course was good for the larynx, neck and throat muscles. These skills are vital and critically important for basketball. Communication amongst team members is par-amount in basketball due to the speed of movement and the fact that there are players behind you whom you cannot see when you are playing defence. Players have to instruct and talk to each other in order to maintain the shape of the de-fence and keep the defensive structures impenetrable. The crossover of the natural universal rhythm in the singing of the nursery rhymes, combined with the movement of the ball, mirrors the natural rhythmic flow and movement of the skills in the basketball game. The primal nature of rhythm as part of the human condition expresses itself naturally. Rhythm is essential for the movement of the muscles, ten-dons, ligaments and joints in the body.

In a documentary called 'When the Moment Sings' two women and a child work rhythmically in sync to turn the corn into bread. The child is five or six and is sitting on the ground with her legs crossed in a yoga position and she has a bowl in front of her. The two women are standing, one on each side of the child, with tall thick tree trunk like poles. One of the women pounds the corn with the pole, the child folds the bread with first one hand, the second woman pounds her pole and the child folds the bread with the other hand. The three are working rhythmically and in total uni-son. By sticking to the rhythm of the movement, each one knows that no one is going to hurt the other. Sticking to the rhythm keeps them safe. This is amazing and beautiful to watch. The unison and harmony between them was exqui-site. They make it look effortless and are relaxed and tuned in to the rhythm. Our games too had the same tempo, the same rhythm. I now realise that we were doing exactly the same thing rhythmically that these people were doing. The games promoted freedom of movement which prevented us becoming inhibited in how we expressed ourselves and instead fostered and nurtured our natural abilities to flow and flourish rhythmically.

We also played a variety of hide and seek games, one of the favourites being 'Queenio-who-has-the-ball? Is-she-big-or-is-she-small? Is-she-fat-or-is-she-thin? Does-she-play-the-violin?' which of course we sang. For this game everyone was standing behind the person who was throwing the ball. The child with the ball had their back to everyone and threw the ball over their head. Someone had to catch the ball or pick it up if it fell on the ground and everyone had to put their hands behind their backs. Everyone would sing the rhyme and the person who threw the ball had to turn around and guess who was holding the ball. If s/he got it right they got to throw the ball again, if they didn't, the person with the ball became the thrower. The mischievous antics of the children was great fun as the objective of the game was for the catchers to outwit the thrower and equally for the thrower not to be outwitted by the catcher. Queenio instigated a lot of fun and laughter and brought out the rascal and mischievousness in everyone. This game was excellent for developing the senses, reading body language and facial cues. It was also good for fine-tuning intuition.

These skills are important in basketball as the better players are the players who read the manoeuvres of their opponents. On offensive plays the more skilled players can take advantage of the defensive players by reading the body language and facial cues of their opponents as a way to beat them one-on-one. In defence however, the opposite applies. It's important for the defensive player to stay focused on the torso of the offensive player and not be drawn into his/her body jerks in fake moves and facial expressions, in order to prevent the offensive player beating them one-on-one. Strong intuition is vital in basketball in order to determine the timing of the game plays, knowing when to and when not to take an action, when to make a move or when to make a decision. Given the quick pace of the game the demand to act, react quickly and intuitively are both critical.

Skipping was another favourite. Using our own ropes we played skipping games together. We also had big fat thick ropes. Two children held and turned the rope, one at each end. Everyone else got into a line and one by one we had to run into the middle of the turning rope, jump and count starting with one then two etc. and each child had to do it one after the other. This game was more of a team effort. The game would progress to running in and two children jumping together, three children and so on. Sometimes the skipping was played to singing rhymes. This game developed timing, jumping ability, judgement skills and rhythm and it taught us the importance of teamwork, again, vital skills in basketball.

Another game we played was Paths. This involved the children standing on each side of the road facing each other. You threw the ball, usually a football, from one side to the other. The ball had to hit the edge of the path and come back to you. Each successful throw was one point scored. When you missed, it was the other child's turn. The winner was the child with the highest number of points or you could decide a number to play to before the game began. This game was great for developing precision. It sounds easier than it was. Aiming the ball at the edge of the path with the correct amount of force so that the ball bounced back to you was no mean feat. Precision in basketball is of course, as everyone knows, extremely important, a skill which separates the good from the very good, from the excellent and outstanding players.

When we got older, around nine or ten, a new game called Chinese Elastics was introduced to us. This was a unique, innovative and interesting game. There were loads of elastic bands tied together in big, long strips. Stepping inside them you would face your partner and place the bands around your ankles. Together you would jump, twist and turn, cross and uncross your legs, manoeuvring the elastics, making different shapes and designs as you moved. The idea was to work in conjunction with one another to make the shapes and designs, without knotting or breaking the elastics. You could move the elastics from the ankles up to knee level and play a game from this height which was totally different from this position. Chinese elastics remained the rave for many years as it was fun, exciting, challenging and different to other games. The elastic bands were a mixture of different colours, this made the shapes and designs look more magnificent. This game stimulated brain function and the thought processes which were required to figure out the patterns and designs within the strict regime of the game's rules, just as in basketball where the players are required to implement complex, strategic offensive and defensive plays.

Other games we played included chasing, football, rounders, roller skating, kick the can and swinging on the lamp posts. This last game was great fun and was most definitely one of the more daring and adventurous games. Not everyone had the courage to play that one, but I loved it and played it every chance I got.

An indoor game we played, which was a favourite with everyone, was Musical Chairs. This game was reserved for birthday parties only. There were two rows of chairs back-to-back against each other in the middle of the room. If there were eleven children, there was ten chairs, always one chair less than the number of children playing the game. The children had to run around the chairs and keep running until the music stopped. Once the music stopped, you had to find the nearest chair to sit on. One person was knocked out each time. At the end of each piece of music another chair was removed. This went on until there was only one chair left with two children chasing each other to fight for the chair. Of course the child who sat on the last chair won the game. This game provoked much hysteria, with children running like crazy, yelling and screaming, wailing and throwing tantrums when they were knocked out and squealing with delight when they grabbed a chair. There was plenty of pushing and shoving in the desperation to gain a chair. None of the other children were as good at pushing and shoving as me, thanks to my tomboy disposition. When I was deaf, I couldn't hear the music, therefore I was always the first one to be knocked out. This didn't appeal to my competitive nature, which meant I had to devise a way to know when the music had stopped. I eventually began to realise that if I used my eyes more diligently and started reading the other children's body language and facial expressions, while also throwing an eye at the record player and the person operating it, I could get a clue as to when the music was going to stop. With much practise I became quite proficient and astute at using this technique. This combined with my tomboy disposition helped me to stay in the game much longer. I even won sometimes! When I eventually regained my hearing, I couldn't be beaten at this game. The observation skills I had acquired when I was deaf, in addition to being able to hear again, were an added bonus and advantage. This turned out to be a winning combination, lucky me! I absolutely loved this game as did the other children – I'm not sure about the adults though. The noise level of it I'm sure was anything but appealing it was so boisterous. There was no such a thing as ear plugs in those days!

When I look back at these games now, I realise and appreciate how precious they were. When you are young and carefree you just play spontaneously and the importance of what you are doing is not understood or realised. From the competitiveness perspective they were exceptionally good because they developed competitiveness in a healthy and natural way. As children, because we played nonstop, we were forever practising and rehearsing these skills without even realising it. The constant repetition made everyone highly skilled at playing the games. Nobody was left out and everyone was encouraged to play. The level of competition in the play itself was inadvertently extremely high due to everyone's abilities and enthusiasm to play. It was genuinely accepted that the winner was the winner. Someone had to win and when they did win, they deserved to win. We enjoyed beating each other and egging each other on. There was no jealousy or envy or resentment towards the winner. Instead, the winner was applauded and appreciated in the winning and everyone was delighted for them. It was all part of the game and a valuable life lesson. This nurtured an innate healthy competitive streak in everybody and is another important factor which I was able to bring to the basketball.

The fun, pleasure and enjoyment we got out of playing and playing together is indescribable. I had a great sense of fun, a lot of courage and I loved a challenge. These characteristics proved to be extremely beneficial in my basketball career. It fostered a genuine love of training and working hard in order to get results that made playing basketball more enjoyable. Of course, playing these games for hours and hours at a time and every day developed great stamina, fitness and persistence in us as children. I feel sorry for the children of today because they miss out on this extremely valuable type of playtime due to computers and mobile phones.

I heard a radio programme recently which discussed a medical report carried out on fifteen-year-old children. The results of the report indicated that the heart function of these fifteen-year-olds, was equivalent to the age of an adult between fifty-five and sixty. This is an alarming statistic. These children's hearts are four times below what the norm is for their age. This doesn't auger well for the health prospects of these children for their futures. I was shocked beyond belief to hear this disturbing statistic.

The children from my era developed into healthy, fit people with incredible heart and lung function and incredible stamina. This in turn provided them with an overall strong body constitution, with a robust immune system which was efficient in fighting against sickness and illness. This exercise and energy was brilliant for relieving stress, anxiety, frustration, anger and worry. Children were that happy in their play, they never wanted to be sick and miss out on their playing time. It was a precious part of childhood.

I think that nowadays children feign sickness in an attempt to seek attention. I remember a particular incident one time, when I was an adult, coaching basketball in a primary school. It was a mixed class of six to seven-year-olds and I was teaching the children how to pass and catch the ball. One little girl was having difficulty with the exercise and she ran over to me, grabbed me around the legs and told me she had a pain in her tummy. I immediately realised what was going on, gave her tummy a little rub and took her to one side and showed her how to do the exercise. It took a little while because her coordination wasn't as good as the other children and she was feeling insecure and inferior to them. I brought her back to the group and stood beside her to help her and by the end of the exercise she had improved considerably and was delighted with herself. I gave her an exercise to practise at home and explained to her that if she practised every day, until the next week, she would be as good as the other children. She did this and the next week, hey presto, she was able to do the exercise without any problems. The extra attention, the practise and repetition were precisely what she needed to resolve her problem at the physical level.

After a few similar incidents I tackled her problem from an emotional perspective. I took her aside and explained to her that the problem wasn't actually her tummy, her tummy was just reacting to her anxiety of not being able to do the exercises. I further explained to her, that the best thing to do, was to say that she wasn't able to do it and to ask for help. I told her it was better to do this, because then she could get her need met and learn what she needed to learn, rather than losing out by withdrawing from the exercise. It took a while for her to fully grasp and do this because she was embarrassed, but with patience and encouragement I got her to practise doing it with me. By the end of three months, she had successfully overcome her shyness, fears and inhibitions and the pain in her tummy had disappeared. I had many experiences like this one, especially in the primary school, but also with the older children in the secondary school. Recognising and understanding their need for attention and meeting that need, always, in my experience, cured the problem.

Another issue facing children and teenagers nowadays is increasing obesity levels. Fundamentally this is due to lack of exercise and eating unhealthy food or overeating. We didn't have problems like this back in the 60's. The constant movement in our play and creativity left us with a sense of satisfaction and fulfillment despite whatever other problems might be going on around us. Eating was based on fewer food choices as there was much less variety available. Portion sizes were smaller than those of today and food was considered purely fuel for the body. Our activity kept us lean and fit, in a way that our focus and attention was much more on progressing our skills, which then opened a gateway to greater opportunities as we transitioned into adulthood. Many of the children I played with in my nana's went on to become great athletes in various sports such was their foundation of skills development from our playtime. One girl became an international soccer player, while others went on to excel in Gaelic football, tennis and basketball.

CHAPTER 6
My Father

You are probably wondering where my father is through-out the story so far. Well, my father was a typical man of the times, more often absent than around. My father worked hard and enjoyed his work. He worked in C.I.E. Railway works in Inchicore as a Fitter five days a week. Every day he took the bus to and from work.

He was an extremely creative man along with being a proficient handyman. He could turn his hand to most things, a placid, laid-back, quiet, patient easy-going man with a great sense of humour, but a chancer, forever chancing his arm. He was a charmer to beat the band and a friendly outgoing, generous charismatic person. A loveable rogue. He was a simple down to earth man who took great pleasure in the ordinary things in life and he was easily pleased.

He was popular amongst both men and women and of course women were always hypnotised by his charm. To cover the fact that he never remembered people's names, particularly women, he would do that old-fashioned etiquette of pulling out the chair, holding the door open, holding the woman's coat for her to put it on, 'Here you are my darling, (or pet). Let me hold your coat for you,' and they were delighted and thrilled by him. He would give up his seat on the bus for a lady to sit down. A pure gentleman!

As a child I didn't take too much notice of this, but when I became an adult his over the top charm made me squirm. When I would tell him, he would just laugh and wind me up even more. I would genuinely feel sick and would make the pretend gestures of puking all over him. This would only amuse him further and make him continue some more.

As a boy he lived near the canal with his parents and had one older brother and one younger sister. His father was a stocky, burly man, a lockkeeper and a shipwright on the canal barges. My father worked with him as a youngster and it is from my grandfather that he learned and acquired many of the useful skills which were a great advantage to him and which stood to him in later life. My grandfather was a strict man who took his work seriously. From different accounts of my grandmother, she was a lovely, gentle kind soul, but I never knew her because she died at quite a young age before I was born. She and my father were quite close. When my uncle, the eldest, went to work in England at the age of seventeen, my father then only seven years old was left with the extra responsibility of taking on the male jobs. He became the assistant man of the house to his own father, who was of course the main man of the house.

My father liked fishing and reading the newspaper. He had a relaxed way of doing things. He didn't fuss about things and never got worked up either. He took everything in his stride. He was a perfectionist in a good way i.e., he loved to do a job properly and with pride and he got great satisfaction from a job well done.

He was a carpenter and his ability to be meticulous in his work and pay attention to detail made him outstanding. In the garden he had a large shed where he carried out his carpentry work. No one was allowed into his shed only me because I respected his tidiness and didn't mess it up. His tidiness and organisational skills in arranging his tools were second to none. This always fascinated me. I could spend hours looking at his tools, deftly and neatly stacked, hanging and arranged in lines in a way that he could put his hand on anything he needed in seconds. He had loads of little boxes for his nails and screws and these too were neatly stacked, placed and kept in line. Everything was orderly and easily accessible. I loved the tidiness, neatness and sense of order in his shed. I looked at his tools in awe at the perfection the way they were displayed. My father always cleaned his tools properly and tidied up after using them. They were always shining and gleaming and put back in their proper place. There was never a mess. It was like he had measured everything to a tee. No space was wasted and yet nothing was cluttered or in the way of anything else. There was no disturbance. Everything was exactly perfect.

This positively excited me. I can't explain the effect it had on me. All these amazing tools - large ones, medium ones, small ones, with weird and wonderful shapes, immaculately gleaming and glistening and laid out to perfection. Every bone in my body and every muscle used to tingle with pleasure at the mere sight of it. The utter perfection of it enthralled me. It gave me a magical, wonderful feeling, a feeling that would last for ages afterwards.

He treated his shed the same way as he treated carpentry, with respect and adoration. There was a running joke in the family that Da's shed was the most important thing in his life and meant more to him than his wife and children. In some sense I think this was true. It was an honour and privilege for anyone to be allowed to put their nose inside that door. He always kept his shed locked and had the key, so no one was able to intrude into his personal special place. It was his private sanctuary. He worshipped it. The famous temples around the world wouldn't hold a candle to my Da's sanctuary. To him his sanctuary surpassed all these temples, the sanctuary of sanctuaries. Woe betide anyone who dared to enter uninvited. They would be cursed. Strangely, amazingly enough, in his lifetime his shed was never broken into. I would say the energy of his prohibiting curse was enough to keep potential and unwanted intruders away!

We used to call my father Da. He loved sweet things and smoking cigars, cigarettes and the pipe. He had a special fancy for Silvermints and in later years Polo mints, 'The mint with the hole.' The Silvermints were a good decent size and if you held them on your tongue, they would crumble and melt in your mouth. I think he particularly liked these because they helped to reduce the smell of smoke on his breath and the taste of the mint lingered in his mouth for a long time afterwards. He never went anywhere without his Silvermints. Despite his craving for them he was good at sharing them with my brother and me. So of course, we too developed a fondness for them. They became one of our little connections with our Da.

I had a close relationship with my Da growing up. I was his favourite, *Daddy's girl* and I used to sit up on his lap every chance I got. I had him on a pedestal for years and years and years. As a child I was desperate for one of my parents to love me. I saw no fault in him whatsoever, so desperate was I for his love. There was no way he was going to be knocked off that pedestal.

Although I was always a black and white, realistic person, I somehow managed to delude myself in relation to my Da. His inappropriate behaviours, mannerisms, bad temper, lack of responsibility as a father, either escaped my notice or were noticed and neatly dispatched into the recesses of my mind, never to be retrieved. As an innocent and needy child, I loved my father unconditionally as children tend to, no matter what their circumstances. He was the better parent but even this notion I fluffed up to be better than it was. As I have already mentioned he was unable to deal with my deafness. He abandoned my brother and I by hiding behind his newspaper and retreating to his shed when the going got tough and things became unbearable and overwhelming for him. He was afraid of my mother although he would never admit this and wasn't manly enough to stand up to her. While he was a hard worker and a good provider for us, he was emotionally absent. In adulthood I was lucky enough to be able to talk to him openly and challenge or confront him regarding some of his behaviours. Eventually, of course he fell off his pedestal and our relationship went through some turbulent, challenging and painful times. Despite everything however, we managed to face our important issues, to resolve what mattered and let go of what was necessary to let go of.

My relationship with my father offered me personal growth and played a vital part in shaping me into the person I am today. Some of his positive attributes were critical to my later sports development. I wonder was my skill in dealing with the organisation required in basketball, for instance, in shaping and training for set plays, affected by the organisation I admired as a child in his shed.

My father's family were of similar nature and temperament, mostly very even-tempered and calm and they rode along on a nice even plateau. Nothing seemed to phase them. They took everything in their stride and there was no drama – drama was for the theatre not the family home! They never got overly excited about anything. No highs, no lows, life was life and they just accepted life's many challenges with grace and ease. Every problem was resolvable in some way or another. My aunt, daddy's sister, was probably the most unbelievably laid-back of the bunch. One day the ceiling fell in on top of her. She just calmly looked up, surrounded by the rubble and said, 'Oh dear, the ceiling has fallen in. That's a nuisance, I'd better ring Bill and get him to come down and fix it,' and this he did. No hysteria, no panic, no drama and, of course, my Da would toddle down at his leisure and fix it in the same calm relaxed way.

My father's family, despite their simple view of life, were excellent at everything they turned their hand to. My aunt for example, was brilliant at painting and wallpapering the house, making and hanging curtains, fixing and doing odd jobs in the house, growing flowers, sewing and needle work and she was a fantastic cook. Everything she did was done at snail's pace. There was no rushing or fussing and it didn't bother her in the slightest that it took her double or treble the time it would take others to do the same job. I loved my aunt dearly and I was very close to her throughout my life. She had a calming influence on me and she was like a constant steady rock in the background that couldn't be removed or overturned. I could always call in to her whenever I needed to. I remember for my twenty-first birthday she bought me my first bicycle, a Triumph Twenty, with small wheels, the latest fashion of the time. I loved and adored my bike; it was to be one of my fitness companions for many years into the future. I thought I was *Kingpin* and *Queen of the Castle* flying around on my yellowy gold Triumph Twenty.

Being a Gemini, the twins, I have two distinct sides to my personality. I most definitely inherited my father's family traits into one of my own Gemini sides. Like his side of the family, I can deal with trauma and crises in a clinical, practical, matter of fact non-emotional way. I am good at finding solutions to problems and can be quite creative in this regard. This was extremely useful in taking on the challenges of the male-dominated basketball refereeing world. It helped me not to give up when the odds were stacked against me, to stay calm under pressure, to persist until the job was done and to direct my energy on to the job at hand in a positive, calm and determined way just like my aunt dealing with the ceiling falling down around her. I have my Da to thank for my tidiness, my astute organisational skills, my love for precision and perfection and the easy-going side to my nature that has carried me through, not only my sporting successes, but many difficult times in my life.

CHAPTER 7
My Mother

My mother was born in Charlotte Street, just off Camden Street, where she lived with my granny, grandfather and her two siblings. She was the youngest child. According to reports she was an attractive and good-looking woman in her young adult years. She worked from a young age and trained to become a hairdresser which she worked at until she eventually got married. As a wife and mother, she was a reasonable cook and had a couple of dinners that were particularly tasty. She was good at her job or at least that's what she said, but you couldn't believe the *Our Father* out of her mouth.

My mother, from my experience of her, was different to her two sisters. She was overly wrapped up in herself and she was the black sheep of the family. She got on better with her older sister more than her middle sister, as the eldest one was a bit of a softy. This appealed more to my mother because maybe she was spoilt as the youngest and she couldn't bear being challenged or confronted either about herself or in relation to topical issues up for discussion. Her middle sister was both confrontational and somewhat hard-hearted and she didn't like this. She was jealous of her two sisters as they were both extremely creative.

The middle one was my godmother and she was a fabulous seamstress and used to make my mother's and my clothes. My mother, when in a positive mood, like her sister, had a sharp eye for combining colours and had excellent dress sense. My godmother was my favourite aunt and her being my godmother as well was an extra bonus. She only had one child herself, which gave her plenty of time and space in her life to lavish her affection on me. This she did whenever she could.

My mother's nature and temperament were different to her sisters'. She was far more hot-headed, stubborn and impatient, got easily riled and ruffled under pressure. She was a disorganised procrastinator and quite chaotic in every aspect of her daily life. She was temperamental and oversensitive and took challenges too personally. On the positive side she was thrifty, good at saving and had a great eye for a bargain when shopping.

From a financial perspective she ran a tight ship. My mother's family in general were an argumentative bunch. They argued and fought over everything from politics, religion, current affairs to two flies climbing up the wall. No one ever gave in during these arguments. Everyone was always right! A narrow-minded and tunnel visioned bunch. Man, nor heaven could not change them from their fixed ideas. They acted like know-all's which gave them a sense of superiority in relation to others. The atmosphere was always tense and electric and voices were raised – I would say they liked to hear the sound of their own voices – and it always felt like it could get physical at any moment.

As children sitting in the midst of the chaos, we had to stay quiet, sit on the sofa, cross our arms and legs and were warned not to utter a word or make a sound. This we did because we were terrified to do otherwise. Obviously, I couldn't hear this melee, one of the few advantages of being deaf. My poor brother! It's a wonder his ears didn't fall off! They must have been truly assaulted by the whole thing. Anyway, we just did what we were told in order not to get into trouble.

More often than not the arguments went on for a long time. It always amazed me that the adults never seemed to get exhausted from it. Instead, the opposite occurred. They kept getting more energised the hotter the argument got. My brother, my cousin and I were exhausted just looking at them. We couldn't wait for it to be over. What a relief it was when it finally ended and everyone was still standing and in one piece.

My mother would come away from these arguments yacking her head off, giving out yards about her family and we would have to listen to her ranting and raving as we walked home. As if that wasn't bad enough my poor father's peace would be disturbed and he would have his ears chewed off with a further rendition of the whole story when we arrived home. If he didn't side with her against the others, she would start a big fight with him. It could take my mother days to wind down from these events. She was a tenacious character and couldn't let things go. To say she got fired up in these situations is putting it mildly.

From the stories my mother frequently told us as children she had an intense adoration for her father. She clashed with my nana more because she was an authoritative and strict mother. According to the stories her father was a nicer, softer person and was more lenient on the girls and especially on my mother. She maintained that she was his favourite child. When I became an adult, I often wondered did she idealise her father in the same way that I idealised mine. My grandfather died when my mother was in her early twenties, so I never met him. My mother was distraught and when I look back at her, I feel she never got over his death. It threw her into a terrible spin, which in turn catapulted her into a major depression. My mother expected my father to replace her dead father. This was an unfair, unrealistic and impossible task and I don't think he measured up to it. The responsibility to replace her father then fell on to my brother's young shoulders.

Before my mother met my father, she had met another man with whom she had fallen madly in love. She often spoke to us about this man when we were children. This man stole her heart and was the 'Bee's Knees' in her eyes. She went out with him for quite a while. Her two sisters got married before her and this became a bone of contention for my mother. In those days there was a stigma attached to 'Being left on the shelf.' She was desperate beyond desperate not to have this happen and the fact that both her sisters were married increased her desperation. When she met this man, she thought her dreams had all come true. The relationship ended reluctantly upon her discovery that this man was an alcoholic. However, it never truly ended as he always had her love and her heart, tragically for us her family.

At some point she met my father in her late twenties and married him on the rebound despite not having recovered from her broken relationship. This, coupled with her father's death, goes some way in explaining her deep unhappiness and disappointment in life that was constantly displayed in her parenting. Nobody could meet my mother's expectations. She was a suffering, tortured soul. My father, her family, her friends, my brother and myself – no one could fix it, could fix her. Everybody tried their best, but no one succeeded.

Strangely however, this tortured soul was a secret she kept indoors. Outside in the world she pretended to be happy, to be happily married and to love her children. She was the pillar of society in people's eyes always described as a loving, happy, carefree, generous and a kind person, extremely sociable and chatty. She never wore her heart on her sleeve. Indoors however, she retreated into her shell, into her inner world of bitter disappointment because of the cards life had dealt her and unfortunately never resolved the issues within herself. She developed cancer later in life and died at the age of sixty-four.

Her death was a terribly sad one because the cancer reduced her to a skeleton of nothingness. It seemed that the pure pain, bitterness, disappointment, unresolved grief and rage that were festering inside her and eating her alive manifested on the outside through this terrible disease. Her vulnerabilities were exposed. The disease exposed her hidden secrets. Observing her in those last days of her life, it appeared that her inner torture and this terrible disease shrunk her into a pool of insignificance. Her past caught up with her and she could no longer play the game. I remember feeling truly sorry for her on the day of her death because the expression in her eyes revealed, even then, her disappointment and the shock and the shame of how her body was betraying her and letting her down. She was forced into a humble place. No longer in control, despite her best efforts to desperately try to hold onto control. It was a sad ending. An ending without an inner peace or the peace of a life well lived.

CHAPTER 8
The Marriage

My parents weren't young when they got married, they were in their late twenties. In those days, people were younger when they married. My father most definitely fancied my mother and found her attractive. Some people described him as handsome and attractive in his charm. I never saw him that way. I guess as a child you don't think of your parents in those terms. My father was nine months younger than my mother which she wasn't overly happy about, but she had to put up with it. Another stigma of the times. A woman had to be younger than the man. They courted for some time, got engaged and then got married.

They had one interest in common. They were both members of a variety club and that's where they met. The variety club hosted many performances which had various types of acts. My mother was a singer. My mother's style of singing didn't appeal to me – she sang sombre, mournful songs - but I loved my father's songs. My father was also a singer, but his style was more specific, his was much more creative, dramatic and exciting. He imitated Al Jolson who was considered the world's greatest entertainer of his time. My father dressed up in a special suit, blackened his face, painted white around his eyes and wore white gloves - not so politically correct these days. He also imitated Jolson's voice in the singing and sang his songs. His two most famous songs were 'Mammy' and 'Baby Face.' My father always sang 'Baby Face' to me as a child. It was one of our special little connections. Being deaf I couldn't hear him, but I could see him preparing himself, transforming himself into someone entirely different. It was only later in my mid-teens when I got my hearing back and watched the Al Jolson films with my father, I then could hear my father through Al Jolson.

There were other styles of singers in the shows as well as a comedian, a juggler and sometimes circus acts. The shows were amazingly entertaining and as children we were brought along to both the rehearsals and the performances as my parents had to be there for the whole time.

My mother insisted on them buying a house before they got married. It was unheard of in those days to buy one's own house, this was not the norm. To live with one's parents was the done thing. This put an enormous amount of financial pressure on the relationship and marriage as they were way out of their depth taking this risk. Both my parents' families came from a poor working-class background, with no financial help available to them. It was considered by everyone at the time as an act of madness. Everyone tried to advise them and talk them out of it, but my mother wasn't having any of it. She was getting what she wanted. I presume because one of my aunts was already living with her husband in my nana's, was another part of the reason. Nor did she want to move in with my father's father and sister who were living together. My father wasn't keen on buying the house because he knew that realistically it was not financially viable and was well out of their grasp. Foolishly however, he succumbed to my mother's wishes. This was probably a fatal mistake as it started the marriage on a rocky road.

They trucked along ok for a while and it was three years before they had their first child – me! My father didn't want children, but again he succumbed to my mother's wishes.

This added more pressure to the relationship and when my brother was born one year and 8 months after me, the pressure increased even further. It wasn't long before my mother began to feel the strain of everything – extra mouths to feed, extra clothes to be bought, nappies, extra everything. She went into complete overwhelm and my father wasn't there to help her. He was out working and his was the sole income as my mother gave up work when we were born. The burden of only one income was extremely stressful.

Fatality struck. My father developed Dermatitis in his hands and fingers. He couldn't work and had to stay at home, but he couldn't do anything as his hands and fingers were bandaged. My mother had to change his dressings several times a day, depending on the amount of poison that would leak out. The pus, redness and swelling in his hands and fingers were disgusting to look at. The pus, deep yellow in colour, used to flow out of his fingers. I will never forget it. His poor hands and fingers were badly infected. The doctor prescribed special cream called Betnovate but when he was extremely bad the cream didn't work too well. It transpired that my father was allergic to the oil in his job, which meant he could no longer work as a Fitter. This was a big blow to him.

The house loan went into arrears as now there was no money coming in. You can imagine what this did to my mother and the relationship. An extremely unfortunate turn of events. My father was out of work for a long time but he was lucky that the job transferred him to an office position. So at least he still had a job. He was devastated to lose his original job because he loved that work and wasn't suited to office work. However, he had to be grateful and appreciate it and make the most of it, despite hating it due to the mounting financial pressures at home. When this disaster struck my father wanted to relinquish the house, but my mother point-blank refused. She wasn't going to let people see that they had failed and that everyone's advice was correct. She didn't want to face the wagging fingers and the, 'I told you so.' Her pride and snobbery wouldn't allow her to give in. They trundled on. My mother started to take people into the house to resume her hairdressing as a way of earning money. This caused huge disturbance to the household and pushed my mother to further breaking point. Already at her wits end before the shock of my father's illness this was the last straw. A happy marriage? Definitely not! My mother resented my father's illness and blamed him for everything that went wrong for years afterwards.

I don't know how the hell they managed to stay married. There were many dodgy moments, many fights and many threats of leaving but somehow, they survived and managed to hold on. They were probably the most incompatible pair you could ever imagine, chalk and cheese doesn't describe it, certainly not a match made in heaven. On the other hand, however, it might have been a case that opposites attract, I honestly don't know. At some level, as we say, 'My father must have been a saint.' His placid easy-going nature and his ability to take things in his stride and accept things obviously saved the day.

For us as children these events had a huge impact on our lives. It seemed that life was never on an even keel. There was always some drama going on. We could never feel secure, as all hell was constantly breaking loose around us. Chaos and more chaos were the order of the day, our constant companion. Whatever small amount of love that might have been there between my parents at the beginning went out the window in two shakes of a lamb's tail. Our house was not a replica of 'Little House on the Prairie', which I used to watch on the telly.

From my mother's side her ego probably ran the show. Her pride in considering herself the best wife and mother would have been shattered if the marriage broke down. Her need for status, her worry in relation to what others thought about her, her fear of failure, being unsuccessful in comparison to her two sisters were the driving forces behind her hanging in there. It was better and safer to be unhappy and miserable than to suffer what I think would have been to her an emotional annihilation. Crazy as it may seem, for her, it was the lesser of two evils. Protecting herself from this unimaginable personal slaughter was the overriding motivator in her secret decision making.

From my father's side, he felt trapped. He couldn't see a way out. It was the done thing in those days to stay together and uphold the marriage vows. Despite feeling helpless and hopeless, he had a deep compassion for my mother's state of being. He blamed himself a lot for both his and her unhappiness. Playing the game became automatic to him because it kept the peace and he just wanted peace regardless of the cost and would do anything to achieve it. He revealed this to me in later years after my mother died. My mother always called him a coward. He told me he just couldn't be bothered. It was too much of an effort to take her on and it was easier to let everything go over his head and turn a blind eye. He became ultra-proficient in implementing this strategy and developing it to perfection.

When I look at my parents, both individually and collectively as parents, I can now understand how it just wasn't emotionally possible for them to love anybody unconditionally. They were terribly fraught with their own inner broken worlds, more particularly my mother, that it was impossible for them to have the capacity to either love each other or us their children. There was no space for anyone only themselves. They were trapped in a quagmire of deep unhappiness and unresolved emotional issues. They did their best under the circumstances of the times, though unfortunately this fell short of what was vital to us as children. Our needs were quite demanding and sometimes became overwhelming through neglect. My brother and I were lucky to have experienced love from other people in our lives. They say that once children have one good experience it can keep them on the right side of the line.

CHAPTER 9
My Brother

When my brother was born both he and my mother nearly died during his birth. It was a difficult birth, so much so, that my mother was advised not to have any more children after him. They both were extremely lucky to survive. My mother was elated that the baby was a boy. She desperately, desperately wanted a boy. He became her favourite and the fact that the birth was so difficult and that they nearly died made the bonding extra-special to her. The bond between them was cemented and deepened from the get-go. My brother was the most adorable and cute little baby. He was absolutely gorgeous – I could understand my mother falling in love with him. Everyone did. He had the pudgiest cheeks you ever saw and big, beautiful eyes. His eyes were expressive from soon after his birth. Everyone just wanted to pull his pudgy cheeks and cuddle him to death. He just had that effect on people. Due to his difficult birth, he had some health problems in his early years. His bones were brittle because they didn't develop properly. This was quite a serious problem because the least little knock would cause his bones to break. As a baby he broke his leg one time and it had to be put into plaster of Paris. Unbelievably, the hardness of the plaster hitting against his other leg broke the bones in that leg too. He ended up with his two legs in plaster of Paris at the same time and had to be carried everywhere. You can imagine what a nightmare this caused my parents. He had to be watched like a hawk to stop him from bumping into things, stop him from falling and being touched by anything hard. The good side of this for him was that he couldn't be smacked or beaten. He had to be practically wrapped up in cotton wool to keep him safe. I used to dream of brittle bones!

As a result of this, me being his Big Sister, I had to become his protector. Whenever I felt he might be in danger I would hide him in various places, under the bed, in the hot press, in the wardrobe, other presses and under the stairs. One time I hid him in the bath and covered him with towels – but that wasn't such a good hiding place. My brother and I shared a room as babies. In bed at night-time, he would rock his cot and rock it so violently I thought he was going to overturn the flipping thing. This used to make me extremely nervous because if he fell out of it, he could break all his bones, so I would climb into his cot and hold him in my arms and rock him until he fell asleep. My brother's problems with his brittle bones continued for many years.

As we grew older and when we stayed in our nana's house, he kept me on my toes fighting his fights for him with the other boys because he couldn't fight them himself. I would come home from school and he would say to me, 'Hey Mer, I have another fight for you today.' He always called me 'Mer.' He would say this with great pride like he was doing me a great big favour. Wasn't he the thoughtful little brother to find me a fight? What a rascal! So, muggins here would have to fight the poor other fella that caused the barney. This is definitely one of the things that turned me into a right little tomboy. My brother always wanted me to win because he used to feel that me winning was the same as him winning because I was fighting on his behalf. Maybe this is one of the reasons he became a Walter Mitty in later years. Of course, because it meant so much to him, I would give it my best effort and knock the stuffing out of the other chaps. It wasn't long before I became very good at the fighting and more often than not came out the winner. I was never afraid of my opponents. I just got on with it and would do anything I had to do to win and stay in one piece myself. There were no holds barred. Heaven help the boys that were foolish enough to get into a fight with my brother. Ironically enough, it was a strange thing, none of the other boys ever took advantage of my brother or tried to hurt him at this time. It was understood and accepted that he had to be left alone and that I was his knight in shining armour. I was my brother's protector which went on for a long number of years.

This resulted in a strong bond developing between us. We swapped roles. I was the tomboy and he was more like the girl. Because of his brittle bones my brother got away with murder with my mother. He was a bold, mischievous little divil and used to do terrible things, things that I would have been killed for. We always had cornflakes for breakfast and he loved spraying the cornflakes out of the box all over the kitchen. The toilet rolls never stayed in the toilet. He would pull it into the bathroom, which was separate to the toilet, down the stairs, everywhere, like the Andrex ad you used to see on telly with the Labrador puppy. My brother would put the plug in the sink in the bathroom and turn on the taps and of course the water would come flowing down the stairs everywhere. My mother had to bring him to the hospital for my appointments with the doctor. The nurses would put him into the playpen to occupy him and give him lots of toys to play with. When they came back into the room to check on him the toys invariably would be strewn about the place where he had great fun throwing them out of the playpen. The poor nurses! He loved wrecking the place!

My mother had a friend who came over every week to visit, just so that she could hear about the constant mischief and pranks he would get up to during each week. She thought he was hilarious and always got a great laugh out of the different stories and antics that he got up to. She used to call him 'Dennis the Menace.' I quivered with fear and nearly had a nervous breakdown, afraid of him getting into trouble when this was going on but because my mother's friend reacted in the way she did, that seemed to put a different perspective on it for my mother.

My brother was extremely intelligent, much cleverer than me. He was talking before I was, despite being much younger than me. Even if I had not been deaf, he would have surpassed me in everything – no doubt about it. Of course, my deafness gave him an extra advantage and he made full use of it. He sailed through school and was always quicker and sharper to understand things than I was. I had to go to him a lot when we were older to get him to explain things to me that I didn't know about. He often thought I was just having him on, because he assumed that as I was older, I should know the things I was asking him about. Naturally, as a young child he didn't understand the affect being deaf had on me and how I was always behind everyone else in my learning. It didn't matter to me that he was in disbelief or if he slagged me, my desperation to get the information would force me to swallow my pride, not give up and keep chasing him until he told me what I needed to know. I didn't mind feeling thick or stupid in front of him. I was always being compared to him; I was well used to that. I distinctly remember, one day we were watching a programme on the T.V. There was a pig having piglets. Of course, I hadn't a clue what was going on. He ran into the kitchen to my mother and said, 'Mammy there's a pig having piglets and Mer doesn't know that they came out of the pig's tummy.' My mother replied, 'That's because you're my clever boy and she's very stupid.'

Due to my brother's brittle bones, he didn't get to play the games we played until he was older, as a result he never took an interest in sport. Instead, he followed in my parent's footsteps and went into variety acting. He became a comedian, an excellent one at that. He joined the Harold's Cross Musical Society and did some super shows with them. I was so proud of him – I thought he was the greatest thing since sliced bread. Despite our closeness as children, it was interesting that we ended up being different in our interests and hobbies when we became older. In fact, we were like chalk and cheese. However, I used to love going to his shows and equally he used to enjoy coming to my basketball matches. Our personalities were also completely different. My brother was seen as a soft, gentle character with a good sense of humour. He was also a charmer like my father but in a more subtle way. My brother and my father didn't get on too well, particularly from the teenage years. My brother was like my mother, untidy, messy and he took short cuts at every given opportunity when doing jobs of any description. My father detested him for this, it drove my father mad and they had many fights and arguments because my brother never did anything properly. Nevertheless, in people's eyes my brother was the *lovely one* with a soft, kind, gentle nature and I had the reputation of being the hard, stubborn bitch. The fact is that we were both equally stubborn in our ways due to our upbringing. My hard stubborn side was much more to the fore than my soft gentle side, so he was generally favoured over me.

How did my relationship with my brother influence my adult life and my success in sport, you might wonder? Well for one thing, fighting his fights and turning into a tomboy developed my physical strength so much that I played basketball more like a man than a woman. I could handle strong physical contact by opponents despite being small and if people tried to hurt me – which they did, because I was so good – I was able to ward if off and fight back within the spirit of the rules. Taking responsibility for my brother by being his protector trained me into being able to step-up and take the full responsibility on my shoulders to be the player to win the game for my team. Minding and protecting my brother developed mental, physical strength and toughness in me, so that no challenge phased me. Fighting his fights taught me to maintain my composure while under pressure and to use my intelligence as well as my physical strength in combination with each other as a means of outwitting my opponents. The long years of practise facilitated me in sustaining the ability to remain steadfast in the face of responsibility. Remaining faithful and loyal to my brother for the length of time he needed it, developed my patience and understanding and taught me an important lesson in consistency. One of my strengths and gifts as both a basketball player and a basketball referee is my ability to be consistent in my performances. This is one of the most vital components in achieving success at the top-level.

My love for my brother and being a tomboy has given me an appreciation for men. In general, I love men and their male energy. I love the strength and power of male energy and I love the force from their testosterone that ignites male competitiveness. Male energy has a unique life-force. It is vibrant and emits a sense of aliveness, a strong sense of engagement in life. Men scream and shout at each other when they are playing sports but when the game is over, they don't hold any grudges and everything is forgotten immediately afterwards. I like this. Sometimes women can be bitchy and hold grudges against each other. The contrast of the soft feminine side to men, I also love and find this quite fascinating. Males who are balanced in their yin and yang energy are, in my opinion, generally interesting men. In my basketball career I was lucky to attract into my life the right men, who were paramount in positively influencing my development as both a player and an international referee.

My brother and I were very close growing up during our childhood. Our relationship, while we still loved each other, drifted when he married. Unlike me, he married young which lucky for him, meant he was able to escape from the family home. Despite everything, my brother managed to move on and live his life in his own way. He finally settled on becoming a landscape gardener having tried his hand at many other jobs. Unfortunately, he gave up his interest in the musical society and being a comedian. He and his wife had two sons who are fully grown men now. His marriage was going through a difficult time just prior to our mother's death. While she was alive, he tried to save her from the embarrassment of his *failed* marriage. As was typical of our mother, his failed marriage would have been viewed by her as a bad reflection of her as a mother. She would have perceived his broken marriage as him making a show of her in front of the entire neighbourhood, her friends and peers, as usual all about her with no care for my brother. We didn't know the word for it back then, but nowadays we do, 'Narcissistic.' Narcissism at its best. Even though he was her favourite, she still treated him badly in relation to this. Soon after his marriage broke up, he met another lady whom he is happily married to for many years now.

I'm so happy to say that in more recent times my brother and I have re-established our original connection. We make a point of going out, just the two of us, at least once a month for a meal and a catch up. It's lovely to have his enthusiastic and heart-felt support.

CHAPTER 10
The Seeds Of My Love For Perfection

As a child from a young age, as far back as I can remember, I had a love, a passion and real appreciation for the beauty of perfection in everything around me. I admired so much and was mesmerised by the intricacies and delicacies of things and artificial objects perfectly designed to the minutest detail. I loved the vast range of different colours that surrounded me and I loved the colours of the rainbow. The rainbow held an extra-special fascination for me. I could look up in awe and wonder at the rainbow, at its magnificent colours stretching out across the blue horizon of the sky, the definition and distinction of its seven colours - red, orange, yellow, green, blue, indigo and violet. A sight to behold. On those rare occasions when a double rainbow appeared in the sky, I thought all my birthdays had come together.

There are many things in nature that are specimens of perfection - the sea, sky, clouds, mountains, rivers, lakes, hills, fields, trees and flowers. Stalagmites, stalactites, caves, glaciers, icebergs. Extraordinary. The relationship between the elements in nature transforms the landscape into a beautiful scenery which was captivating to my naked eye. Switzerland for example, is a country that is often described as 'Picturesque as a postcard.' The Swiss Alps are so stunningly spectacular, magnificent and breathtakingly beautiful that they look every bit as perfect as they do on a postcard. They are also a good example of what is perfect in its imperfection. While this sounds contradictory, the erosion of the rocks in the Alps and the movement of the tectonic plates cause indents and curvatures in the stone which give the mountains their unique peaks and shapes, which in turn is what makes them visually beautiful.

The beauty and perfection in nature sent shivers up my spine. I was always amazed at the cycle of nature. The ground being prepared and dug out, the planting of the seed, the nurturing of the seed through feeding and watering and eventually bit by bit the seed growing into a beautiful colourful flower. When I was a child, I would wait with bated breath for the flower to open and blossom and my excitement would be ignited when this finally happened. I was always sad when the flower eventually had to die even though I understood the process of life and death. The paradoxical nature of life and death is interesting. The process of birthing and dying is one and the same for both the flower and a human. Just like the flower, the human life goes through the same cycle, the seed being sown, the gestation period, the birth of a human being, the span of life, with the life cycle ending in death and the remains of the physical body being returned to the ground. I could relate to this process as my life carried this paradox too, on the one hand my passion for such beauty in life and in the world around me and on the other, my struggle with deafness which brought me close to wanting death to end the struggle.

The joy flowers bring into people's lives by their colour and beauty is enchanting. Flowers brighten a room, lift the heart, cheer people up when they are sick and down and are mood altering when one is having a difficult or bad day. If you look past people's faults and misbehaviours, human beings, just like flowers, can be beautiful. When you get to look closely you realise flowers have perfection in them, this I find fascinating. The rose for example, when you look underneath, its bud has a five-pointed star in its sepals. This star is so perfect it is unbelievable. Many other flowers have characteristics of a similar nature. The rock rose for example when in full bloom looks like a dancing ballerina in its splendour of yellow. The complexities of flowers are like a sculptural brilliance, works of art! Go up close and inspect fritillaria or fuchsia or the amazing iris or even the common daisy and the buttercup.

I don't know how I developed an appreciation for nature and beautiful things. My parents didn't introduce them to me as they were constantly firefighting their own lives and didn't have time. My mother's sister undoubtedly had an influence on me due to her creative expression in her work. My primary school teacher also influenced me with her colourful and creative teaching methods. Being deaf more than likely had a big influence, as I needed some form of escape from my isolated, insular world. My eyes naturally were the obvious choice in adapting an interest and fascination for everything visible. My eyes compensated for my lack of hearing. Objects and beautiful things probably became my survival mechanism against the traumas that I was enduring. They were significant in distracting me from my feelings of loneliness by giving me something to be involved in and an external focus to direct my attention onto, in order to occupy my mind differently. It aided me in not becoming overly self-absorbed or self-pitying. It encouraged me to come out of my shell and gave me a reason to go on living. As I've already explained, I was often dying inside and felt life wasn't worth living. It gave me a break from this inner torture. Because my deafness was preventing me from making friends, these objects of beauty became my imaginary friends. Children love playing make-believe and inventing friends when they are lonely and I was no exception to the rule.

When I was a child, I used to spend a lot of time in my aunt's dressmaking shop. In those days she used a Singer sewing machine. Again, I was fascinated by the operation of the sewing machine. The fine-tuning of setting up the threads around the bobbin into the needle and the tiny little stitches, perfectly straight and close together, that came out when the foot pedal was pressed was amazing. I could never understand how the stitches remained in such a straight line with the intense vibration of the machine and the needle moving up and down as quickly as it did. Of course, the material being sewn had to be kept firmly held and perfectly taut and straight with the correct amount of tension applied to it to keep it from curling up or slipping out from under the needle, while at the same time also applying the correct amount of pressure to the pedal underneath the machine. The absolute perfection of this whole mechanical process at work was astounding to my eyes. There were different types of stitches that the sewing machine could produce, back stitches, herring bone stitches and overlap stitches and these were each perfect in their own way. I used to love examining the detail of these stitches when a garment was completed and the incredible perfection of the stitches would send me into what felt like ecstasy. I was amazed by them and excited and always questioned how they were so perfect, so unique. My aunt used to be highly amused by these reactions.

Another thing that I loved in my aunt's shop were the bales of fabrics and materials. The designs on the fabrics were all shapes and sizes with many different textures and no shortage of colours. I loved running my tiny little hands up and down the bales feeling the materials. I particularly loved the feeling of velvet, fur, satin and suede. These were my favourites as they were smooth, silky and warm to the touch. They had a comforting effect on me. Some of the other materials were plain and others had different types of patterns. Again, the patterns attracted my attention as the shapes and designs were perfectly laid out on the material. I used to wonder how it was possible, if it was squares for example, to have them identical in size. How did the manufacturers do that? My curiosity was stimulated and I just couldn't get my head around it. I was dying to know how they did this. Between the variety of colours of threads, the materials and patterns, I was in my element observing these wonderful examples of perfection. It was like being in an enchanted garden of beautiful, scented flowers only this was an enchanted dressmaking shop with the beautiful smell of fresh new fabrics. I think that this is where my love for colours was fostered and nourished and to this day I adore colours and wear them with ease and pride. I have no inhibitions around wearing or mixing and matching colours and as a child I was liable to wear many colours at the same time whether they matched or not.

As a youngster I started collecting dolls. The people who came to the house to get their hair done used to bring me back dolls from their foreign holidays. The dolls generally represented the national costume of the relevant country. They were the most amazing, magnificent dolls you have ever seen. The perfection of the intricate details of both the doll itself and the dolls costumes were spectacular. I don't know how they were made as perfectly as they were because there wouldn't have been the fancy, fangle dangle machinery that they have nowadays. Some costumes were handmade and the others I just don't know. We had a glass china cabinet in our sitting room and this was where my adorable, prized dolls were kept and displayed. In what seemed like no time at all, my cabinet became full and I had to use the outside and put my dolls on top of it as well. I adored and loved my dolls with a passion. I spent hours looking at them in admiration and examining the intricate details of their costumes bit by bit. Of course, the colours too were magnificent. I had some favourites, although this was particularly hard because each of them were so beautiful. One of my favourites was a replica of Annie Oakley the cowboy girl. You would have to see her to believe it. She literally had everything and I mean everything, that the real live cowboy had. The suede boots with the fringes, the suede skirt, the blouse with the cravat, the belt with the holster and the gun in it, the cowboy hat and her blonde curly hair hanging down to her shoulders. The gun and holster were incredibly real looking and you could take the gun out and play with it. I used to love imagining shooting people with my gun – only the people I didn't like of course! She wasn't a big doll; she was in fact quite small which made the magic of the perfection even more awe-inspiring. Talk about needing nimble hands, nimble fingers and good eyesight to create that magnificence – it was wow! A big wow!!!

In my collection I had a variety of Spanish dolls, both male and female. These were striking to look at due to the magnificent colours of their dresses and costumes, different shades of reds, pinks, yellows, blues, greens, oranges, you name it, I had it. The designs of the dresses varied greatly with interesting trimmings of lace or teenchy-weenchy flowers, dots or other designs. Frequently beautiful silk ribbon was used for bands around the waist and around the hats. The costumes would vary in accordance with the different villages they were representing. Each village had their own unique costume. Some of the female dolls had long tight-fitting dresses which clung to the body of the doll and went down to the ankles and tailored off like the fishtail of a mermaid. They had silky black hair tied up in a bun with a lovely coloured ribbon to match the colour of the dress. They even had perfectly made miniature castanets in their tiny hands. The male dolls were smartly dressed in white shirts, tight black trousers widening into bell bottoms, black waist-coats, a tie or cravat, a black hat and castanets in their hands. They too generally had black shiny hair. These dolls were a perfect replica of the real-life dancers that you would see if you were in Spain. They were so lifelike that looking at them would transport you to Spain the country itself, and you could quickly imagine and visualise yourself sitting in the middle of the *real thing*, the Spanish flamenco dancers dancing in a live show. These dolls were gorgeous, colourful and captivating to my eyes. They were a great eye-catcher and source of conversation to the many visitors to my house. People were intrigued by them and would always state that they had never seen anything like them. If you gazed at them long enough it would spark a desire in you to want to learn flamenco dance.

Another doll I had was a black African lady wearing a long tight yellow dress down to her ankles. The dress had different coloured sashes wrapped around it and she had a bowl of fruit on her head. To my child eyes she looked tall, elegant and graceful with great posture and poise like African women you would see on the T.V. She had black curly hair and a smile that showed pearly white teeth. In her ears were big gold loopy earrings. I loved these earrings. I also had a black male African doll who was sitting on a stool playing a timpani double drum. He looked focused and concentrated while playing the drums. The detail on the drums was magnificent even down to the membrane of the drum-head which looked so authentic.

I also had these two most amazing small rubber dolls. They were twin Native American Indian girls, dark brown, with pudgy cheeks and both were in a sitting position with the soles of their feet touching each other. They both had green sleeveless waistcoats, red headbands around their heads with a red feather sticking out of the headbands and a shiny beaded necklace hanging around their necks. So, so, cute! The interesting thing about them was, they were like two sides of the same coin. One was happy and smiling and the other was sad and crying. The sad one had two white tears painted on her cheeks. I had a special relationship with these two dolls. They always reminded me of myself. The pretend happy smiling child that presented to the world on the outside and the sad unhappy child that was on the inside who lived behind closed doors. My star sign is Gemini – the twins –these dolls were my twins – they were me. The twins were amongst my favourite dolls and I still have them to this day.

I don't know exactly how many dolls I had altogether, but I definitely ended up with a full china cabinet and more, with dolls from many other countries in addition to the ones I've described, each one as beautiful and unique as the next.

I went to see the film 'The White Crow', which tells the story about the rise of Rudolph Nureyev, from his peasant origins in Russia, to achieving international fame following his defection from Russia whilst performing in Paris. It was his lifelong ambition to be the best ballet dancer in the world. He had an immense interest in art and he loved paintings. While he was training in Paris, he would spend hours each day thoroughly inspecting every solitary detail of the works of art in the museums. He was trying to gain a deeper understanding of the artist's artistic expression and technique. The film depicts this extremely well and highlights his enormous appreciation for art. One gets the impression that he is trying to get into the mindset of the artist in order to get a true sense and feeling of what the artist was trying to convey in his work. He used what he absorbed from the paintings to give another dimension of feeling into the expression of his dancing. It is fascinating to watch him doing this in the film. Rudolph Nureyev was a perfectionist and he admired the perfection in others, those artists and colleagues who embraced perfection like himself. He was unique in the way he studied art and incorporated it into his dance. It made me realise that this is exactly what I was doing as a deaf and virtually mute child, soaking up and absorbing the perfection and beauty in everything around me. I didn't have the art to appreciate like him because I was never introduced to it, but I had nature and everything else around me that I myself could lock my eyes on, to adore and treasure, in the same way that he did with the paintings and sculptures. I never thought about it before, but people who watched me playing basketball in later life, often commented on my fluidity of movement, particularly when I was accomplishing the more complex skills of the game. Nureyev too, included in his choreographies many complex ballet moves which made him standout in comparison to others. This type of in-depth appreciation of the perfection and beauty of art enhances the commanding presence one can have on stage or indeed on the basketball court. When Nureyev stepped onto the stage to perform, he commanded the stage and the audience. As David Hare, screenwriter of the 'White Crow', stated in relation to Nureyev in his interview prerelease of the film, there were only two people he ever met and saw in his life, that, once they stepped onto a stage, commanded the stage with such authority that the audience only had eyes for that person and couldn't look at anyone else and Nureyev was one of these two people. While I'm not putting myself on the same level as Nureyev, when I stepped onto the basketball court, either as a player or as a referee, I commanded the court and the game with my presence. In my case, this was extra important because of my lack of height and my being a woman.

I think I was a magpie in a previous life. I love, love, love shiny things. Shiny spoons for some reason had an extra fascination for me. I have no idea why! I remember as a child looking into the spoon like it was a mirror. I had great fun twisting the spoon from side to side, making the shine jump and the light catching the reflection making the spoon shine even more. This thrilled me to bits! Shiny things that appealed to me were cutlery, tin foil, silverware, brass, glass, mirrors, patent leather and jewellery. Again, it was the perfection of the objects and the materials that made them shine and dazzle that enchanted me. How was it possible to create such a shine? How do you do that? Of course, the various objects I mentioned are pretty delicate, except for the cutlery and I used to wonder how such delicate and fine objects didn't break or lose their shine by big maulers mauling them. I loved washing or cleaning the objects when they got dull and I remember the joy I used to feel when they would transform again into gorgeous, shining, sparkling objects. Sometimes, with glass, colours would run through the glass like a prism if you washed them when the sun was shining. Colours of the rainbow would emerge as the bubbles from the washing-up liquid cleansed the dull and dusty glass.

When I was an adult my mother started collecting Waterford cut glass and of course, who ended up cleaning it? Only muggins. The only reason I didn't mind, was because I got such a kick out of seeing the transformation that occurred and the excitement of watching the colours form through the glass. Like the spoons, if I twisted and turned them

97

while drying them, colours would spin around the glass and even sometimes reflect onto the kitchen walls where I was washing them. They looked regal and proud when they were returned to their shelves radiating a sparkling energy in the room. Each piece, standing in its glory and splendour, displayed to perfection. Once cleaned, the dank, lingering, musty smell disappeared and was replaced by a fresh clean fragrance. The change in the energy in the room was palpable. It was like the advert you would see on T.V. for the Fairy Washing Up Liquid, where the fairy comes and tinkles the glass with her magic wand and the special effects on the T.V. would produce a sparkling star over the glass. The effect of the washing-up liquid and the fairy's magic power made the glass look taller, more noticeable and eye-catching. The Waterford glass looked just like this on these occasions. I would stand back and gaze in admiration at this glorious sight before my eyes. It made the hard work cleaning them worthwhile.

Patent leather was another shiny thing that equally fascinated me. I always wanted a pair of black patent leather shoes because they were the shiniest. You could look down and see your face in them and I thought that was so cool. It was easy to keep them shiny, they held their shine no matter what punishment they got. I was raving about them so much that eventually my aunt bought me a present of these black patent leather shoes. I don't have to tell you the ecstasy I was in. You couldn't get them off my feet. A JCB wouldn't have extracted them from me. I loved them with my whole heart. They became my most beloved best friends and went everywhere with me. I was only short of sleeping with them on. When I took them off, I would put them standing up at the wall facing me at the end of my bed, they were the last thing I saw at night going to bed and the first thing I saw in the morning. It was like they were talking to me saying goodnight and smiling good morning to me. Equally while I was dying to put them on, they too would be dying for me to put them on. We clip-clopped everywhere together. We were a right pair!

When my feet eventually grew too big for them, I used to squeeze my feet into them and didn't care if they hurt me. Luckily, I had them for a long, long time before that happened. It was a sad and miserable day when I had to say goodbye to them. My mother wanted to throw them out and of course I didn't. When she did, I sneaked to the bin when she wasn't watching and took them out and found a special hiding place in my room where nobody would find them. I just had to, HAD to keep them. They were special to me and brought me much pleasure and happiness for many years. They were my perfect little shoes, perfect in every way and their shine exuded perfection till the end.

My mother entered me into the Girl Guides when I was about eight years of age. There were no Briginis in those days, only Girl Guides and you had to be eight years of age before you could join. I loved the Girl Guides with a passion. It was right up my street because there were many activities and things to do and we had no time to feel bored and discontent. I always loved being occupied and on the move. I never felt isolated or excluded because everything was done in groups, small groups and big groups, depending on the task at hand. We met in a hall every Friday evening. Every week we were given tasks to learn and do and often there were games to be played that were considered Girl Guide games. One game that we played was Bean Bags. The bean bags were small and square in shape and were filled with beans so that they had weight in them. There were two rows of girls facing each other but facing the gaps between the opposite girls. This gave a zigzag effect up and down the line as people had to throw the bean bag from one person to the next making its way down the line and back up again. You weren't allowed to drop the bean bag and you had to throw it at speed. After this you would do it with two bean bags and progress to three and four when you became more skillful. I was brilliant at this game thanks to my hours of practise at the other games I already mentioned. Everyone wanted me on their team. In an instant I was super popular! If you let the bean bags fall, you were out of the game. We played this game in competitions against other Girl Guide units. We always won; we were ultra-proficient at it. I loved winning. I loved the exhilarating feeling that winning gave me and everyone else. We would be buzzing around the place like bees from the exhilaration and euphoria of winning. It spread through the group in a contagious and infectious manner. We were as high as kites, thoroughly enjoying ourselves.

Every week was packed with both serious and fun-filled tasks. The serious tasks came in the form of earning badges to sew on the left-hand sleeve of your uniform. The badges were circular and colourful and were sown on in rows of three. There was a picture on the badge which corresponded to the relevant task that the badge represented. For example, a badge for cooking might have a picture of a pot with a flame lighting under it. You name it and they had a badge for it! Even unusual things like birdwatching, astronomy, and campfire lighting. I loved attending the courses and learning about the novel and interesting topics. It transpired that I earned all the badges in the book and I had more badges than anyone else by the time I left the Girl Guides. In an effort to fit them on I attached them to my sleeve in rows of five. Whenever we went anywhere where we mixed with other units, I always stood out as a result of my badges and no one ever matched me or came close to having as many as I did. It always caused a great stir and instigated conversations amongst the girls and leaders in the other groups. I was very proud of my badges and I loved the attention that they brought to me. They always made me feel special and good about myself.

Then of course there was the outdoor activities. We went hiking for the day up to the Pine Forest on many occasions and had to gather the relevant materials to make and light a fire.

We had to cook food on the fire such as sausages, rashers and beans. When we finished eating, we would gather around the fire and have a campfire singsong. This entailed learning the words to multiple Girl Guide songs. The favourite song was, 'We'll make a bonfire of our troubles and burn them all away.' These days were great fun and used to feel like a little holiday away from home. They were great for teaching discipline, obedience and the importance of respecting and adhering to rules. If you stepped out of line you were stopped from attending the next hike. It was rare for someone to be penalised in this way because everyone enjoyed the hikes and day out that nobody wanted to miss one.

We also went on weekends away with the Girl Guides, but these were more sporadic than the hikes. Whenever a weekend away was coming up the excitement that built up was electric. Everyone worked as a team like eager little beavers to prepare and get everything ready for the trip. On the preceding Friday night to the trip, we would have to meet in our depot and the leader would have a list of things that had to be gathered and ticked off the list. By the end of the night, we had to have everything ready to go and the list fully ticked off. Normally we travelled on a big bus and the babbling of excitement would reach fever pitch. Sometime after the bus took off, we would eventually calm down and settle into our journey. The leaders and the organisers were always meticulous in their preparation for these trips. We were put into special groups and the messers were separated from each other. This was good because none of us wanted our trip spoiled by the messers. On the bus we would sing the Girl Guide songs. The unfortunate driver had his poor ears blown off by the noise, but at least it was proper singing! Better than unruly, screaming and shouting I suppose! Of course, being deaf I couldn't hear the singing properly, maybe he would have liked to have traded places with me. I was so geared up with the excitement that not being able to hear didn't make me feel excluded.

When we arrived at our destination we had to split up into our groups and each group had to set up their tents. This was fun and we did this with great eagerness and pride. Everyone had their own sleeping bags which we had to bring with us and our own haversacks with our belongings that we would need for the weekend. It was compulsory for everyone to have their clothes and gear labelled with their names. After this we would have to set up a fire and cook our meal and each person in the group had to take part and contribute to the cooking, everybody brought food of their choice. This was super because we got to taste each other's favourite foods. I always brought pork sausages because I loved pork sausages. You can't beat good ol' Irish pork sausages!!! Some of the girls had mothers who were great at baking cakes (mine wasn't) so these girls would have gorgeous cakes to share and my! were they yummy yummy! My sweet tooth always got a great feast and treat with these wonderful cakes. After eating we would have to wash up and clean up and leave everything ready for the next morning. It was early to bed because we had to rise at the crack of dawn.

Next morning, we would arise like the lark and we always had to do some kind of exercise before breakfast. After breakfast the real action began. Each group started with an activity and the groups rotated to the next one and so on, until every activity was completed. This depended on the number of groups, the more the merrier. Then we might have a nature trail and learn different things about the trees, leaves, animals etc. There was always a stream nearby where we would paddle and fetch our water from. I wasn't allowed to go into the water because of my deafness, for some reason I wasn't allowed to get water into my ears. I don't know if there was a medical reason for this, but my mother drummed this into me from the beginning. I was never allowed to learn how to swim or do any sports or activities that involved water. This was a pity, but I had to accept it although I didn't like it. When I was older people couldn't understand why I couldn't swim and thought it was odd considering the fact that I was such a sports fanatic.

After all this, each group would cook their lunch and afterwards we would set off on more adventures. The day ended with the groups gathering around the big campfire for our usual singsong. We slept soundly at night-time as exhaustion set in from the constant excitement throughout the day and night. There was method in the madness of the leaders!!! Of course, all good things come to an end and we had to go home again. Nobody wanted to go home. We had so much fun, got on so well and became quite united in our little groups and indeed united as a whole unit. We grew fonder of our leaders and got closer to them as a result of these trips. Dejection would set in and we even cried when it was time to say our goodbyes. Our parents, when they collected us after the trip, couldn't understand why we cried in the way we did if we had such a good time. They didn't understand the kindred friendships that had been established and the depth of the intimacy and the emotional connection that developed through spending and sharing this quality time with each other.

Upon reflection, when I compare school which I enjoyed, to my experience in the Girl Guides, while both were structured in their own way there was a freedom in the Girl Guides that didn't exist in the school environment. In school I was the deaf girl. I was alienated from my classmates and the learning process. This was purely due to my deafness and was no reflection on my teacher. In contrast, the Girl Guides offered me a sense of belonging through their ethos of inclusivity. Despite my teacher's attempts to reduce my stress levels in the classroom, school however remained stressful for me. On the other hand, the Girl Guides provided a stress-free welcoming environment which enabled me to blossom and grow despite my disability and its limitations. This was every little girl's dream. While I benefitted from my time in the Girl Guides, my fellow Girl Guides also benefitted from learning how to deal with deafness and difference. The naturalness of the environment facilitated this in a relaxed, non-threatening way. The contrast being that in general the learning in the school environment was more passive whereas the learning in the girl Guides was more action based.

When I look back and evaluate my time in the Girl Guides, I realise how lucky and privileged I was to have been part of such an amazing organisation. I learnt so much from them. When I examine in close detail the various activities we took part in and the things they taught us, no question about it they set us up for life. The biggest revelation was the level of perfection that was taught to us and demanded from us in a non-obtrusive way. Everything had to be done perfectly and I mean perfectly. The importance of perfection was taught to us in a steady, consistent, patient way. It was an extremely positive experience. The reasons for perfection were explained and demonstrated continuously. A safe fire for example won't light unless everything is in place and arranged. The leader would demonstrate the negative result in not doing it correctly, to make us understand the importance of doing it properly and perfectly. This was the case for everything we did and the same principle applied for each badge I achieved. You could only pass and receive the badge if you fulfilled the requirements perfectly. The difference between *Making* or *Helping* somebody to do or understand something is vitality important. *Helping* can result in the person not ending up doing or understanding, whereas *Making* ensures that the doing and understanding gets done. The intent behind the *Making* for *The Good* versus *Making* for *The Bad* is crucial. Unfortunately, nowadays *Making* can be misconstrued and in its extreme perceived as bullying. However, we didn't feel we were being *Forced*, for us we knew that the extension of *Making* stopped us avoiding and challenged us to reach our potential. *Making* versus *Helping* requires a lot more perseverance, patience and refusal to give up on behalf of the person who is *Making*. This misperception can cause people to lose out an awful lot in their life. So, the end product is *Delight* in the achievement versus *Disappointment* in the failure.

It was exceptionally good training for us. We worked in harmony to do everything perfectly and to do things right.

We would correct each other and between us get to the point of perfection when completing our various tasks. It taught us the importance of teamwork, the power of unity and what we could achieve as a collective. The beauty in perfection was highlighted to us in a loving and caring way and we were taught to be proud of doing things properly. We were taught that it was as easy to do something properly and in a methodical way with care and attention as it was to be sloppy and careless and produce something of no worth. Being productive versus being non-productive. Whenever we completed our tasks perfectly and to the satisfaction of the leaders we were acknowledged and praised and sometimes rewarded for a job well done.

The leaders helped us to channel our energy and emotions positively rather than negatively. For example, they taught us how to channel anger in to doing something useful as opposed to misbehaving and expressing our anger in a destructive way that would end up getting us into trouble. This was a lifesaver as I often felt angry as I've already explained. The leaders explained the importance of releasing and expressing anger versus the detrimental effect of holding anger inside and letting it fester until it eventually had no option but to explode. Expressing a little and often was the motto. Angry children were sent off to chop logs into firewood. Working to perfection became a natural state of being for us and became a natural part of our mindset.

I am quite sure that this experience of perfection moulded me to such an extent that I viewed perfection as something wonderful and beautiful. In later years this positive experience and attitude to perfection was to stand to me in my endeavour to reach the top-level of my sports. What I realise now is, this conditioning made my achievements in sport more easily attainable, in a somewhat effortless way. Aiming high and achieving the perfection I had to achieve was a normal and natural aspiration to me which is probably the vital ingredient that turned that breakthrough into a reality. While I felt nervous of course during the refereeing exam, this conditioning quenched and expelled any overriding factors that could have presented themselves, potentially leading me into making mistakes causing me to fail the exam. It is only through writing about this now that I have a greater understanding and appreciation of my giftedness and ability to not only perform well under pressure, but to be able to surpass the expectations of the demands put on me and to maintain my composure when under this extreme pressure. This is a quality which enabled me to sustain my consistency over my entire national and international refereeing career.

The Girl Guides gave me the tools which enabled me to develop and nourish these qualities within myself. The foundations of the core qualities of resilience, confidence, self-esteem, problem-solving, creativity, leadership skills and the ability to look beyond myself to see the bigger picture were birthed and fostered through the ethos and the teachings of the Girl Guides. This process, through those formative years of childhood, then gestated through to adulthood.

CHAPTER 11
The Beginning

My basketball career began in sixth class in 1967, when Sr. Patricia, one of the nuns in St. Clare's Primary School in Harold's Cross, started up a basketball team for the children in the orphanage and the outside schoolgoing children. The girls in the orphanage were known as the House Girls and we were known as the Outsiders. This was purely for differentiating purposes. Sr. Patricia was a tall, quiet, ladylike nun. She had many lovely qualities and we revered her. She had a nice face, big brown eyes and her face became expressive and animated whenever she became enthusiastic or excited. When I think of her now, I don't know how on earth she became interested in the game. Basketball is an explosive game for a quiet person like Sr. Patricia. But by Jove did she become interested! She was as eager as we were once she got us in to it. I wonder now where she learned about the skills and rules of the game. There was no internet or Mr. Google in her time!

She headhunted us one by one to join her team and she had a good eye for spotting talent and potential. She was interested in me because even though I was deaf and extremely small for basketball, she spotted my ability to run fast and recognised that I had a good level of fitness. Basketball is an exceptionally fast game and you need people who can run fast on your team. From the time I entered first class I walked to my nana's house for lunch and walked back to school from there. This I was able to do on my own. When I look back on it now, the foundation of my fitness development probably started with this experience of walking to and from school, four times a day, five days a week. There were few cars in those days, we had to walk everywhere. I loved running around and I never got tired, I was bubbling over with energy. She loved this as she was the same herself when teaching us how to play.

From the get-go she taught us the important skills of the game. The first thing she taught us was how to score a lay-up. She made us do hundreds of lay-up shots during every practise session. This was extremely important because the lay-up is considered the most important shot in the game. It is deemed as the easiest and most frequently used shot in basketball. There is a specific technical method for shooting a lay-up and Sr. Patricia taught us this to perfection. The lay-up is the shot taken closest to the basket, you can either use the backboard, which is the easiest option to score or shoot the ball straight into the ring, which is technically more difficult. The backboard has a small black square on it, the purpose of this square is to assist the shooter in achieving the most accurate shot. In order to do this, you have to the aim the ball at the top right-hand corner or left-hand corner of that small square and a fraction towards the centre of the board, depending on which side of the basket you're standing on. To miss a lay-up in basketball would be the same for Sr. Patricia as committing a mortal sin. We loved doing our lay-ups and didn't mind doing hundreds of them because we felt great when we scored them. Sr. Patricia also incorporated lay-ups into little competitive practise games against each other and this was great fun.

The next two technical skills she taught us were dribbling and passing the ball. Dribbling is considered important because you have to be able to dribble at high speed without losing the ball yourself or having an opponent snatching the ball away from you. The lower you dribble the ball the easier it is to protect the ball and to prevent opponents stealing the ball from you. We were like little beavers dribbling around the basketball court trying not to lose the ball. She moved on to the passing skills – chest passes, overhead passes and javelin passes. We especially loved the javelin passes because these were more difficult and challenging. You had to put the ball on to one hand, lean back, put your weight behind you and throw the ball the whole length of the basketball court, just like throwing the javelin in athletics. This type of pass is especially important for running what is known as the fast break moves in the game. The advantage of this pass is that it gets the ball from one end of the court to the other quickly and in the shortest amount of time, outwitting the defenders so that they can't catch up and stop you scoring.

She also taught us how to catch the ball properly because for obvious reasons it's not good to drop the ball. We became proficient at this because if anyone was angry or frustrated and they threw the ball hard at you, if you didn't catch it properly, the ball could knock your head off, put a dent in your chest or hit you in the face. A basketball is big and extremely hard. If it hit you in the face for example, it would draw tears from your eyes and give you a good ol' red and swollen nose. As nobody wanted that, it is amazing what can motivate you to become good at catching!

The primary school had an outdoor basketball court, which made it easy for us to run out to play and practise after school. We could also use it at weekends or during school holiday periods. It wasn't long before I fell head over heels in love with basketball. I couldn't wait to have my own basketball to go down to the court whenever I wanted to practise. Sr. Patricia used to keep the basketballs in the convent and I had to knock on the door there to borrow one to practise with. I took to basketball like a duck takes to water and before long I became quite proficient at it. I used to call in to my friends or the house girls and drag them out to practise with me. We had a good team. Sr. Patricia organised competitive matches for us and entered us in a basketball league to help us improve. We loved playing the matches and we always wanted to win. She was delighted when we played well and she could see the benefits of her and our hard work. Sr. Patricia always told us that results happened over time, not immediately or overnight. She told us to work hard, stay consistent and most importantly to be patient. She taught us the importance of individual excellence and how to incorporate that into teamwork, a vitally important element of the game.

The people who play basketball now have it easy in comparison to when we played. Now the game is only played indoors in heated gymnasiums and most venues have lovely changing rooms and showers. We didn't have changing rooms never mind showers. We only played outdoors and if you were lucky the court was made of tarmac. We had to practise and play games in the pelting rain, freezing cold and in the wind, seldom in the fine or sunny weather, as basketball is a winter sport. I remember once we even played a match in the snow and the court was full of ice. We were sliding and slipping around like I don't know what, falling about the place and doing the splits. The winner was the team that could handle the conditions the best. That of course was our team because we thought this was great fun. It didn't phase us, we got into the spirit of it, whereas the other team were afraid, kept holding back and whinging and whining. We just got stuck in and kept going, it was like playing ice-hockey without the skates and the padded gear. That was a particularly memorable match, one of those rare occasions that happens once or twice in a lifetime.

Playing on the tarmac was not easy because when you fell, which we frequently did, your poor knees would get badly cut and you would end up digging the tiny little gravely stones out of your knees for weeks afterwards. However, this was something we had to get used to, it was part of the game. In one way it was a good thing because it toughened us up. Whenever we fell, we just jumped up again immediately and carried on playing, bleeding or not. It was only when the game was over that we attended to our cuts and bruises.

Another time we played an away game on a court that wasn't flat like it was supposed to be. This court was concrete and had a hill on one side of it. It was most peculiar. I had never seen one like it before and haven't seen one since. I got the brainwave to roll the ball down the hill towards our basket, sprint down the hill after it, pick it up and score. It was too difficult to try and dribble the ball and keep it under control while sprinting down the hill. This turned out to be a great idea! It worked! It helped us to overcome the problem of the hill because the home team had a home court advantage over us as they were used to their court and we of course were not. I remember that game being very close, nip and tuck right the way through and it was only in the dying minutes that we snatched a victory. We were one of the few teams to be triumphant as an away team on this court.

But in those days, that's the way it was. You just had to make the most of everything and do your best. The circumstances were the circumstances and you quickly learned that the circumstances were not going to change. You had no choice but to get on with it and do your best. This made us strong versatile players and toughened us up a lot. It taught us to have a clinical and pragmatic approach to the game and not to make excuses for playing badly or losing. We weren't allowed to succumb to the old saying, 'A bad workman always blames his tools.' We were encouraged to be creative, overcome the problem and deal with it whether we liked it or not. We were taught about the importance of focusing on the game itself and implementing the skills instead of focusing on the potential problems. The game had to be played – that was the bottom line!

Sr. Patricia was fantastic in this regard. She taught us so well, how not to be phased or easily put off by obstacles. John Quincy Adams said, 'Patience and perseverance, have a magical effect before which, difficulties disappear and obstacles vanish.' I think Sr. Patricia followed the same philosophy. With much practise we adopted this approach and it rendered us successful in winning matches and leagues that otherwise we would not have won. Sr. Patricia taught us that talent and hard work alone were not enough, there were other qualities and levels of intelligence, that also had to be applied to playing the game if you wanted to become a good player and a good team.

Thanks to Sr. Patricia I got a good start and a good foundation in the basic skills of the game. By the time I finished that year in primary school I was one hundred per cent sure that I wanted to go to a secondary school that played basketball. Sr. Patricia gave me the bug to continue and encouraged me not to let it go because she saw how good I had become. She didn't want me to lose what I had worked so hard to gain and she didn't want me to waste my talent. I was sad leaving Sr. Patricia and Saint Clare's school. Apart from my deafness and the difficulty in learning that my deafness imposed on me, I had a good overall school experience there. I left with memories to cherish and that final experience of playing basketball with Sr. Patricia unknowingly to me, paved the way for my sporting career to flourish in the future.

I got it into my head at the age of ten, that when I grew up, I wanted to become a primary school teacher. Miss O'Flynn's influence on me probably birthed this idea. I was quite adamant about it and this led to my mother making enquiries about the best route to take. The head nun in St. Clare's informed my mother that when I left secondary school, I would have to go to Sion Hill College in Blackrock. It was the only teacher training college in Ireland where you could train to become a primary teacher at that time. As a result of this, she advised my mother to send me to secondary school in Dominican College, Eccles Street, because Sion Hill was run by the Dominicans and I would have an extra advantage. She thought it might be easier for me to get into Sion Hill because it wasn't a big college and numbers were limited there. The head nun suggested that my mother take me over to have a look at Eccles Street and see what we thought. This we did. My first impression was one of shock and I felt daunted by the size of the school. In comparison to St. Clare's, it was huge! To my little eyes I was convinced I would get lost in it and never be found again. There were stairways and staircases everywhere – straight ones, winding ones, you name it. The corridors were long and wide and had many other corridors off the main one. From the outside it was a tall and long building, it was the whole length of Eccles Street, many floors high with a basement below. It had a back entrance from another side of the road altogether and this is where the basketball courts were. Two lovely big full-size basketball courts, beautifully tarmacked. They looked quite new with lovely rings and the baskets themselves were made from chains. That was it, there and then! I was hooked and I was going to go there no matter what! My mind was made up! I had never seen baskets made from chains before. The ones I was familiar with had nets on them. The chains intrigued me. In time I grew to love those chains because they made a cool sound, a special jingle-jangle swishing sound when the ball passed through. There was no such sound from the nets. My hearing was beginning to return and this sound was one of the first I remember. I think the fact that I loved the sound so much is one of the things that enticed me to become an excellent shooter.

Dominican College it was! Thank heavens my mother liked it, otherwise heaven knows what would have happened. I certainly wouldn't have been given my own way. As it was, I had to curtail my excitement when I saw the basketball courts because my mother was the one making the decision, not me! It came across as a lah-di-dah school which of course appealed to my mother's high ideals and this is what probably clinched her liking it. The biggest problem was its distance from Harold's Cross. It was far away, on the north side, the other side of the city. This was a bit of a stumbling block but luckily both the 16 and 16A buses went straight from the end of my road directly to Dorset Street and stopped right outside the school. The head nun from St. Clare's informed my mother that one or two of the house girls would be going there. That made my mother feel better, now she felt she had someone who could keep an eye on me and report back to her if I misbehaved.

One thing led to another and the decision was finalised. I had to enroll, sit an entrance exam, get kitted out with a school uniform, schoolbooks and everything else that was on the to-do list. On my first day in secondary school my mother didn't come with me and I had to go alone. I remember being scared stiff and feeling extremely nervous. I was leaving the small school and going to the big school, the really big school! There was a primary school across the yard from the secondary school and when I went into the secondary school, I was met by a nun who was directing the children to their various classrooms. When she saw me, because I was tiny, she thought I was enrolling for the primary school. She kept telling me I was too small for secondary school and was ushering me towards the primary school and insisting on bringing me over there. I nearly had a heart attack because I didn't want to come across as cheeky, especially on my first day and I didn't know what to do. If I got into trouble on the first day my mother would have killed me. This added further to my anxiety. I was close to tears and feeling helpless when one of the house girls came along and saw me. She said hello to me and was able to confirm to the nun that I was indeed meant to be starting in the secondary school and that we were both coming from St. Clare's Primary School. Phew! What a relief! I could have hugged her to death for saving my bacon! Hurdle number one crossed! It took me a good while after that to settle in because my nerves were fairly frayed by that stage. Can you imagine me ending up in the wrong school and having to explain that to my mother! Not on your nanny! It would have been my first and last day in secondary school!

There were no first year classes in Eccles Street. Classes were numbered from second year to sixth year. I was put into Class 2S. There were a lot of girls in the class and once again, I was put sitting in the front row because of my deafness. I had just turned eleven and was at the stage where I was beginning to hear bits and pieces, but I was still a long way off from hearing properly. At this stage I was no more interested in the lessons than the cat, I just wanted to go out to play on those magnificent courts. They were calling me and I couldn't wait to respond. My longing and yearning were so bad that it was palpable to everyone around me. Eventually, one of the girls offered to bring me down at the lunch break. I was delighted and excited, I didn't want to eat my lunch and I gulped it down quickly so that we could hurry out.

When we got out, there were some of the older girls already playing on the courts. The P.E. nun, Sister Isnard, was also there and my classmate introduced me to her. She told her I was an avid basketball enthusiast and that I couldn't wait to get out to play on the courts. Sister Isnard was delighted, she was always looking for girls to join her sports and she quizzed me up and down about my interest in the game. I told her about Sister Patricia and the basketball I had played in primary school and the leagues. This sparked her interest in me immediately. She asked me if I would like to join in with the girls who were playing, even though they were older, so that she could see me playing a bit. Of course, I was that eager to play it didn't bother me about the girls being older and I just got stuck in like good ol' Sister Patricia taught me to and played with them. The girls at first when they saw me were a bit put out and thought I was far too small to be able to play. It wasn't long however, before they changed their minds! They could not believe how good I was. Not only could I play but I was as good as and maybe even better than them. Sister Isnard standing on the sideline, rubbing her hands in glee, was smitten with me instantly. I suppose when I stand back and look at the scene now with adult eyes, I can understand Sister Isnard. It's always so cute to see a tiny girl being able to hold her own in a competitive environment amongst bigger and taller girls. It pulls at the ol' heart strings and people always tend to side with the underdog. The girl from my class also standing on the sideline was awestruck when she saw me playing. On the way back to the classroom she said to me, 'You never told me you were that good. Where did you learn to play like that? By golly you're some player.' I told her the story and told her she should try it, it's a great game. She told me she wouldn't be any good as had she never played it before. I explained to her that I thought the same but what you have to do is learn it and practise a lot to become good. After that Sister Isnard was all over me like a rash and she kept me playing with the older girls and started a second year team. I encouraged the girl who helped me to join because loads of other girls didn't know how to play either. I told Sister Isnard about the house girls and she got them to join as well. We had a right little team in no time. I really got to like Sister Isnard because like Sister Patricia she was extremely enthusiastic and encouraging. The older girls nicknamed her *Izzy Bizzy Belly* behind her back because they considered her to be a real nosey parker. I thought this was hilarious. Poor Sister Isnard if she only knew! I'm sure she wouldn't have been impressed at all, at all, at all !!! Unfortunately for her however, the nickname stuck.

There were other games in Eccles Street that I learned to play – Volleyball, Badminton and Athletics. They were one of the few schools in Dublin who had professional coaches hired to train the girls in running, basketball and other athletic events. Because of my prowess in basketball, Sister Isnard told the athletics coach about me. He came to watch me playing basketball and asked me to try out for some of the running events. As I loved running, I did and I also proved to be very good at it. I ran a few races for the school team and did very well in those. After a certain length of time, the athletics coach approached me to have a serious chat. He wanted to know if I would be interested in training to become an international runner. I was too young to understand the implications of this and I told him that while I loved running, I also loved playing basketball and I didn't want to give that up. He told me that I didn't have to give up playing basketball, that I could do both and the two sports would complement each other. I was running races goodo and playing away at basketball. It got to the point that the athletics coach saw my true potential and decided to talk to my parents about his proposal to turn me into an international athlete.

My father wasn't bothered one way or the other and it fell on my mother to make the decision. The coach explained what was entailed and the talent and potential he thought I had. He was convinced I could most definitely go straight to the top in the athletics world. He told her he hadn't seen such good talent in a long time. On one hand, my mother's head was turned by this and on the other hand she had her own ideas of what she wanted me to be in the future. He made this sound extremely attractive to her and pointed out the advantages it could have on her life in the future. I could see she was struggling to let the idea in because it was in major conflict with her own original idea. The poor man, he worked desperately hard trying to persuade her and made her an offer which seemed irresistible. He explained the importance of giving the idea a fair trial period before deciding anything concrete one way or the other. My mother asked him to give her time to think about it and discuss it with my Da. The coach agreed to this and off he went. My mother no sooner had the door closed behind him, when she immediately told me that if I was going to be a primary school teacher that I couldn't attempt to entertain this notion of being an international runner. She didn't even bother discussing it with my Da, not that it would have mattered, as he wouldn't have challenged her decision anyway. Becoming a primary school teacher was much more important and would lead me to a permanent, pensionable job which would secure *her* financial future and would make *her* look good as a mother. To become an international runner would never hold the same status. It would be an extremely short-lived career, whereas teaching would take me up to retirement age and the pension. The decision was made and I was to get the hoity-toity nonsense out of my head and focus on my studies.

I was extremely disappointed because this was the first time that anyone had seen me to such an extent. By that I mean in a long-term futuristic sense, identifying talent that could possibly take me to such high levels of success. I was bowled over by the idea of it. While it seemed surreal and impossible to me, the fact that somebody else, a coach of such high standing had such ideas for me was overwhelming but also extremely attractive and inviting. I tried to plead with my mother and talk her around and get her to follow his suggestion of giving it a fair trial period before making a final decision. She was having none of it. Her mind was made up and it didn't matter what I wanted; her decision was final. Once my mother's mind was made up neither God, love nor money would change it! I talked to my Da, my aunt, my granny, some of my mother's closest friends to see if they could persuade her to change her mind and just give it a try. But no! Her sights were set on that respectable, permanent, pensionable job at the end of the horizon and nothing, but nothing was going to stand in the way of that.

I was in a terrible state going into school after that and was dreading having to face the coach and Sister Isnard with the news. I knew like me they would be devastated and I didn't know how on earth I was going to tell them the bad news. They were very good however and made it easier for me because once they saw me, they could tell from my body language and my dejected face that I wasn't being allowed to pursue the offer. They were awfully kind and understanding, they knew it wasn't my decision, but they too were bitterly disappointed. They were so nice about it I began to cry and I cried like a baby for a long time. They too had tears in their eyes, the heartbreak of it was tough on the three of us. Sister Isnard decided, 'Hump this, I'm not giving up this easy.' She made an appointment to see my parents and she and the coach tried again to persuade my mother to have a rethink about the situation. But there was no budging my mother. She was like Mount Everest and she couldn't be moved.

Where to go from here was the next question. They put their heads together and decided that they would keep me on the programme and see how things went. The idea was, that if things turned out the way they thought it might, that my mother wouldn't be able to refuse any further. The risk would be taken out of the equation. She would be able to see that it was *real* and not a *notion* anymore. Then, maybe then, even she couldn't or wouldn't want to deny me the opportunity to become successful or famous as an athlete.

The outcome? Well, we followed the plan and the notion turned into a reality. But sadly, my mother remained steadfast and stubborn in her decision. She downright refused to relent despite the evidence in front of her nose, the persuasiveness of those around her, despite my wanting to go for it, despite everything and she denied me and them the golden opportunity of a lifetime. To say we were sickened to the pit of our stomachs doesn't remotely cover the depth of bitter, bitter disappointment and devastation that we felt. The cruelty of it felt unbearable. How could a secure, permanent, pensionable job equate to this once off golden opportunity of a lifetime. The coach said it was rare to see such talent in one as young. I think most parents would be proud and overjoyed if their child's ability and potential were seen and recognised like this and would jump at the prospect to support their child on such a rare quest. Talent and potential should be respected and nurtured, not annihilated. The shock I felt was palpable. It seemed unthinkable and unnatural! I was inconsolable. I shed many tears, had many outbursts of frustration and anger, pleaded, begged and plámás-ed – but alas to no avail. I felt I was living a nightmare – I was never going to fulfill my potential. I felt a profound sense of loss and hopelessness. Rightly or wrongly, I felt bad, I believed I was letting my coaches and the school down. Not only my dream, but my coach's dream for me was shattered. The psychological damage that my mother's narrow, closed and selfish mind caused was beyond belief. I felt dead inside. It was a shocking day, one of the saddest days of my life!

Approximately two months after the finality of my mother's decision sunk in, I was in the schoolyard one evening after school on my own, practising my basketball. Suddenly, out of the blue, my stomach felt a bit queasy. I just felt out of sorts and a little light-headed. I decided to sit down for a minute in the hope that the feeling would quickly pass. But then a strange thing happened. I felt my head was going to explode and a strong sensation surged from my head running through my body, down the soles of my feet, to the tips of my toes. My toes started to tingle. The sensation grew stronger, much stronger and gathered momentum. It feverishly started swirling and rushed back up my legs, up through my stomach and my chest. At this point I became frightened because I felt like a tornado and desperately tried to push it back down to stop it from getting worse. I felt the sensation in my head and further down my body merging in my throat. I couldn't stop it. I remember it soaring up the rest of the centre of my body, up my arms, along my shoulders until it came up my throat, to the edge of my mouth. It forced my mouth open and an unmerciful noise; a huge scream came out. The noise was so great that it filled the whole of the empty schoolyard that surrounded me. I couldn't hear the noise clearly myself, but I knew by its vibration it was huge. That scream seemed to have a whole story behind it to tell. After it escaped, my whole body started to shake and shake and shake, like nothing I had ever felt or seen before. Strangely enough, it felt comfortable, it felt ok. The shaking went on for quite a while and eventually, when it was ready, spun itself out in a natural way. It just went quiet and calm.

Just as I was beginning to come back to myself again, another sensation emerged. This one was completely different. It began running up and down my body, furiously gathering speed and momentum. There was no controlling this one. It took over entirely and I realised I felt rage coursing through me. I began to shout and scream with rage. The rage was so raw that once again my body was shaking. This feeling wanted to kill, to rip the world and everyone apart. A sense of injustice was fuelling it. The litany of injustices, in relation to my deafness, came galloping in, not being loved by my parents, being neglected, cast aside and the most recent injustice, not being allowed to have a fair chance to run competitively. My life was consumed with injustices. The innocence of a child, who feels hard done by and is vehemently saying to her parents, '*I HATE YOU; I HATE YOU; I HATE YOU.*' I realised, at that moment, that I was feeling an intense, irredeemable hatred for my mother. When the rage subsided, I began crying and wailing, an uncontrollable, continuous sobbing, sobbing that was wracked with deep, deep intense pain, heartbreak and agony. This agony I had always hidden behind a happy face, but it was bursting out of me and I couldn't stop it. I sat there, tears were rolling down my face and flowing like a river that had no end to it. My façade and barriers had crumbled around me to an unrecognisable pile of rubble. My sobs and tears were being fuelled by the reality of my mother's refusal to allow me to run. The facts were there before me! Her hatred for me and my hatred for her. The desolation and the pain of this raw truth felt unbearable to my eleven-year-old self.

My sobs and tears eventually subsided and stopped. I sat there alone, allowing everything to settle down, heartbroken beyond heartbroken. I felt stuck to the tarmac and couldn't move. My whole being and soul felt crushed. My breathing returned to normal as I sat quietly. How on earth was I going to be able to come to terms with and accept this truth that had dawned on me, like a penny dropping? Eleven years of pretending and acting gone down the drain. The secret that I had suppressed for many, many years wasn't just a secret I had kept from the whole world, it was a secret I had kept even from myself. Instinctively, I knew it wouldn't be wise to divulge this secret. Not only would it kill my mother, but her reaction to it would also rebound back on to me and make her hate me even more. No, she must never know! Like a thunderbolt, another realisation hit me. My mother and I were two sides of the same coin. I was the child who desperately wanted to be loved by her mother and desperately wanted her mother to be proud of her. My mother was the mother who equally wanted to be loved by her husband and children and who wanted her children to do exactly what she wanted them to do in order to be proud of them. I was trapped in my own inner, deaf, silent world, suppressing my hidden secrets, feelings and emotions. My mother too, was trapped in her own inner world of torture, whatever that was, also suppressing her hidden secrets, feelings and emotions. It was at that moment that I completely understood the hopelessness and pointlessness of chasing my mother's love and affection.

What now? Where, from here? How could I possibly deal with this? It was terrifying ... It actually felt as if I had a gun pointing at my head.

... There I was, sitting on my own, at the end of the basketball court, with the basketball between my legs and straight in front of me ...
... the empty court ...
… I felt alone, like a bereft little girl… so terribly alone…
… Exhausted from the upset and crying, the little girl decided to remain for a while longer and have a little rest before returning home. She moved closer to the wall behind the basket and used her school bag as a pillow as it was nice and soft. Picking the basketball up, she tucked her legs underneath herself, covered herself with her coat, firmly held on to the basketball between her two hands, close to her chest. Her basketball was her comfort blanket. She snuggled down into her cosy lying down position. She felt comfortable and at ease because she was in her favourite place. What could be better? A little doze would do her the world of good. Allowing her body and her mind to completely relax, she soon began to nod off. In her slumber she drifted into a dream-like state. She felt like she was dreaming and

yet she knew it wasn't quite like a dream. She felt like she was between two worlds, her real-life world and her dream world. It was an unusual sensation, but she liked the dreamy feel to it, it felt nice. After a short while her mind conjured up a lion that appeared in front of her. He looked her up and down and spoke to her.

'Well little girl what a mess you are in!'

'Yes,' she replied, 'one big, huge mess!'

'What are you going to do now?' said the lion.

She looked at him and shrugged her shoulders.

'Have you any ideas?' she asked.

The lion lifted his right paw and scratched his head, put his paw down again and remained still, thinking. After a while he looked at her.

'You must let go of the international runner idea, look to the future and don't let your mother kill your spirit.'

Her head sunk. She didn't know how she would be able to do that.

'I understand, that must sound extremely difficult, but you must do it. Anything else will be futile.'

'Thank you,' she said, looking back up into his eyes. 'I'll do my best to follow your advice.'

'Let's summon the elephant and see what the elephant has to say,' said the lion.

With that the lion let out an unmerciful roar and next, thump, thump, thump came the elephant's footsteps.

'You called,' said the elephant.

'I did,' said the lion. 'This little girl needs some advice and I thought you might be able to help.'

The lion filled the elephant in on the story and, like the lion, the elephant looked her up and down before he spoke.

'You're very small little girl,' he said.

'I am,' she answered.

'Those were very big ideas for a little girl.'

'They were, but now they're gone and I'm just back to being little me,' she said.

The elephant pawed the ground five times with his front foot, swung his trunk around and around, let out a little bellow and walked around on the spot three times.

'You might be small, but you need to think big,' said the elephant. 'Don't give up, all is not lost. Think big, dream big. Do you hear me? Think big, dream big.' 'Thank you, dear elephant,' she said. 'I will do my best to follow your advice.' The lion let another roar out of him and the little girl realised he was calling another animal. This time an owl appeared and sat on top of the lion's head. 'You called,' said the owl.

'I did,' said the lion.

'This little girl needs some advice and I thought you might be able to help.'

The lion filled the owl in on the story.

'Now dear wise one, any ideas?'

'Mmmm,' said the owl, 'interesting situation. I just have five important words for you. Trust yourself. Follow your heart.'

'Oh dear, Mr. Owl' she said, 'That is so hard for me to do. You wouldn't believe how hard that is for me.'

'Mmmm,' said the owl, 'I know! But you can do this. You must do it.'

'O.K. I'll try my best.'

The three animals looked at each other, looked at the little girl, looked at each other again and spoke in unison.

'Good luck with your decisions little girl.'

She didn't quite understand what they meant by that but thanked them very much for their advice and for helping her.

To the little girl's horror, the lion summoned her mother to appear. The lion spoke.

'Your little daughter needs some space away from you.'

In a flash, he gobbled her up there and then spat her bones out onto the ground and with his paw shoved them into the middle of the clearing where they were sitting. He let another roar out of him and animals of every kind, shape and size, came thundering into the clearing and surrounded her mother's bones. They formed a circle and did a dance around her, whooping and stamping. They cheered and shouted.

'The witch is dead; the witch is dead. Yippee!!! Woohoo!!!'

The girl was transfixed. She couldn't believe her eyes! They invited her to join in and she danced and cheered with them. When the cheering subsided, an amazing silence descended on the clearing! Everyone and everything went quiet. Only the hush of nature's elements could be heard, an eerie hush that transformed in to a peaceful, calm, still quietness. The animals turned and looked at the little girl. They bowed to her with their paws together. She responded with the same gesture and blew them a gentle kiss from the palm of her hand. Slowly, one by one, they turned and walked away until there was only the lion, the elephant and the owl left.

They stood, staring straight into her eyes and she could feel the strength of their stare coming right at her and penetrating her body. She didn't feel frightened, but instead felt powerful and confident. She knew they had given her important messages to hold on to. They nodded their heads and she nodded back, again blowing them a kiss from the palm of her hand. They turned, treading the ground gently, waving goodbye until they were gone out of sight.

She had tears in her eyes as she felt moved by the whole encounter and knew that something was changing inside her.

She remained seated with her back against the wall for a while longer to let everything settle inside. She knew that she had to write down everything that they had said to her, to make sure she wouldn't forget it. When she felt ready, she opened her eyes and took some paper from one of her copy books and slowly wrote down the messages and advice that had been given to her. She folded the paper up carefully and hid it in her bag and knew that she had to find a safe hiding place for it when she got home. Now, it was definitely time to go home.

CHAPTER 12
The Aftermath

I was quite distracted within myself for the next few weeks after the events that took place in the schoolyard. I didn't know what to think of the whole thing. I spent many hours trying to figure everything out. One thing was for sure however, something inside me had irrevocably changed. I felt much lighter in my body and in myself in general. I felt as if a ton weight had been lifted off my shoulders. I no longer felt depressed. My mood had lightened.

That day definitely broke something in me and made the space for something new to happen and to take over. Facing reality and expressing and releasing the emotions freed up the resentment, anger, frustration and bitterness that had been festering inside me for a long time. If I could only have the courage to take the necessary action to find a solution to help me to move forward and 'Look to the future.' At the time, I sensed that this could be a significant turning point in my life. I had a lot to think about. Something was egging me on to do the *Right* thing, whatever that was. At that stage I had no clue. I needed to understand, to make sense of everything and make use of the messages and good advice. I knew that was the key, but I knew also that it was going to take time and I had no clue what the possible implications would be.

I definitely needed time to figure out the answers to these questions and to come up with some sort of plan. I felt lonely and isolated. There was nobody that I could talk to who would understand my plight. It was my firm belief that nobody would. I was on my own and it had to stay that way. That made it harder for me. I would have loved to have somebody to help me to unravel these mysteries and questions and more importantly to give me the answers. How do I not let my mother kill my spirit? I felt she had succeeded in doing that already. How do I think big? My mother was trying to keep me thinking small. How do I not give up with the hopelessness that I was feeling? How do I trust myself and follow my heart? My mother had just taught me a big lesson regarding that one. The big question remaining was, what were the important decisions I had to make?

I slowed everything down because I didn't know what to do other than keep my mind on the advice that the animals had given me. I felt worried and overwhelmed by it all. I let everything settle down and take its own course. In effect, 'I slept on it' and brought my attention back to basketball. That was the beginning of where it started. 'Don't give up, all is not lost.' I had lost my running, but I still had my basketball. I had to keep playing irrespective of the outcome. That wasn't going to be hard because I loved it anyway. It was my passion. The words 'Don't let your mother break your spirit' kept running around in my head. That was it! If I kept playing, that would be a way of doing that, maybe? But I had to protect it, I had to make sure she didn't get her hands on it. How to do that? I had to figure that out and come up with a plan, a good plan!

I threw my heart and soul into basketball after that. I practised every morning for forty-five to fifty minutes before school started, practised again in the breaks and at lunchtime and stayed back every evening after school to practise for two hours before going home. At the weekends I went down to St. Clare's Primary School to practise on the court there for as many hours as I could, somewhere between four and eight each day. Most of my spare time went on practising basketball. Even though I had increased my practise time a lot, I kept it under the radar from my mother as much as I could. I told her as little as possible, always thinking up excuses in preparation for her questioning. She was a divil for asking questions. It wasn't easy to squirm out of answering her or to placate her. My mother had an extremely suspicious mind. I kept thinking of the promises I had made to myself and I most certainly did my best. Most of the time I spent alone practising because the other girls couldn't be bothered. 'It was too much', they said. However, while I always preferred to have company because it was more fun, I didn't mind being on my own and I got used to it. I used to imagine other people there and I invented loads of special drills which were game related, always imagining the people as the players on the opposing team to me. It wasn't long before my game started to improve quite dramatically. My hard work and practise was certainly paying off. I became the best shooter on the school team, the best defender and my dribbling and passing skills also improved enormously. Because I practised regularly, my consistency developed and it wasn't long before I became the player that everyone looked up to and depended on. My fellow players truly admired my tenacity, my devotion and my willingness and enthusiasm to train hard. They were able to recognise that it was the extra work that I constantly put in that separated them from me in terms of ability. They weren't jealous or envious of me which was great as it kept our good relations with each other well intact. In fact, they were always grateful to me and acknowledged me whenever we won medals or trophies as they realised that without my input, they may not have won them. The team loved winning and increasing their collection of medals and trophies. I became known as

The Basketball Fanatic. I didn't see it that way. I just wanted to be the best player I could possibly be and every time I saw an improvement in my play that just spurred me on even more.

While I was excelling in sport I was severely struggling academically. If I hadn't had my sport to de-stress me, I would have had a nervous breakdown. The transition from primary to secondary school felt like a big jump for many reasons. Having had Miss O'Flynn for eight years, who understood my struggles and cared for me and who had a maternal nature, the variety of teachers in the secondary school seemed colder and more impersonal. The grief of losing Miss O'Flynn and my primary school classmates who I felt so secure with, hit me like a ton of bricks. I missed them terribly and the stability and reassurance they used to give me. I felt intimidated and lost by my new surroundings. The secondary school environment was completely different to that of the primary school. The pace was much faster, more intense and businesslike. Having been pampered and minded by Miss O'Flynn, the problems my deafness created in relation to learning were more magnified by these changes. Due to the forty-minute class period and the different teachers for each subject, there simply was no scope for the teachers to accommodate my deafness. I kept picking up everything wrong due to my hearing problems. I just couldn't understand anything. Nothing made sense to me. I was constantly in a total state of confusion. This was quite daunting for eleven-year-old me. As an adult I realised that if free second level education had not been introduced into Ireland in 1966, my mother would have insisted on me going out to work, in that case I wouldn't have had any education or basketball. I was lucky to make it into the education system by the skin of my teeth.

In the classroom I was put sitting in the front row yet again. I became close friends with Marge who sat beside me. She used to let me copy her notes and homework as a way of helping me out of my distress. She was a very kind girl and she couldn't bear to see me constantly upset and always struggling. She always tried hard to help me to understand the lessons we were being taught and I too desperately tried to accept her help. At night-time at home doing my homework I would spend hours pondering over what she told me, desperately trying to figure it out and make sense of it. Most nights I never stopped studying after my dinner until twelve or one o'clock in the morning. I was always knackered by the time I went to bed and used to conk out accordingly. Every day was the same, a repeat of the previous day. No let-up, struggle, struggle, struggle.

My classmates were a lovely bunch of girls luckily for me and we got on famously. Even the swatsos and brainboxes weren't despised by the rest of us. They too were included in the pranks, divilment and fun times. I remember one of the girls went to the circus and she met one of the circus performers after the show and fell head over heels in love with him. This awakened in her an interest to become a performer herself. In the class, whenever we were waiting for the teacher to come in, she would go up to the top of the classroom and practise her circus acts. She needed a volunteer to help her and of course, because I was the tiniest one, I was the obvious choice. Muggins here, had to climb up onto her shoulders or stand on her head, alternating these two positions, while she tried to walk and balance herself making sure that she wouldn't drop me. The girls were *Oohing* and *Aahing* as she tottered along, wobbling around the place with me hanging on for dear life, trying not to fall off. Sometimes we got so carried away and everyone was engrossed in what was going on we didn't notice the teacher coming in. The teacher of course, was horrified to see girls carrying on like that, a rather unexpected sight to behold and would announce herself by saying loudly, 'Girls, what is going on here? Get back to your seats immediately. What unruly behaviour. Oh, my goodness, I can't believe my eyes. What are you trying to do? Kill yourselves? Most unladylike!' There was pandemonium, everyone scrambling back to their seats, trying to look innocent and saintly – too late of course – both of us usually falling over and crashing to the ground with the fright of it. The entire class got to go to the circus for our troubles and efforts because she got us free tickets from her boyfriend and that made it more than worthwhile. I loved the circus especially daredevil acts. Her boyfriend was a brilliant performer, a trapeze artist and an acrobat and with her dedication to practise with me in the classroom she began to get good herself. This trick acting went on for a long time until eventually their relationship broke up and she was so broken-hearted that she didn't want to do it anymore. I became redundant.

Our next bit of tomfoolery was playing the game Jacks. It became the fashion and everyone wanted to play it. There was fierce competition for it altogether and for some reason it brought out the competitive streak in everyone – even the swatsos. The jacks were plastic pieces made in a funny shape and there was ten of them plus a small rubber ball in the pack. You had to throw them out and start by throwing the ball into the air, picking one up at a time and catching the ball before it bounced a second time. When you successfully completed round one, you had to pick up two at a time, then three and so on until you picked up the ten in one go. Then you had to go back down from ten to one. There was a knack in throwing the jacks out and in selecting the right groups to pick up. My friend Marge and I were the champions in our class and eventually I became the jacks champion in the school. At one stage, I can't remember how, I broke my wrist on my right hand and couldn't play because I was right-handed. I couldn't stand not playing and having to watch, this prompted me to try and do it with my left hand. It took me a long time, but I eventually succeeded in becoming just as good with my left hand as I was with my right hand. When my right wrist healed, I used to alternate playing with both hands to keep my skill level up just in case anything like that ever happened to me again. I remember we had a history teacher who was extremely boring and rather than fall asleep in her class, my friend and I used to play jacks on the desk. Remarkably the teacher never noticed or caught us!!!

The other divilment we got up to was mitching. We were terribly silly about it because we didn't leave school, we used to mitch in a press that was at the bottom of the classroom. There was fierce giggling and sniggering going on whenever anyone was in the press and the teacher was doing the roll call checking everyone in. Talk about silly billys! Strangely enough though and as silly as it seemed, people got a kick out of doing it and felt it was an adventure. All in all, we had good craic in our class over the years there and for me especially it was a distraction from my academic torture.

I had regained my hearing between my Inter Cert. and Leaving Cert. years. Now you would assume that having regained my hearing my learning difficulties would disappear; however, this simply was not the case. I continued to struggle as I had fallen so far behind and it was simply impossible to catch up. My senses were overloaded by what seemed like just loud noise which was in stark contrast to my quiet silent world.

At about the age of nine or ten, I began to hear noise, although I couldn't understand what the noise was. Between the ages of ten and fourteen I was still seeing Dr. Johnson every month when he would work at reeducating me in how to differentiate the different sounds. For instance, he would go over words I had misheard and help me to correct the sound and see the difference between the misheard sound and the real word. This taught me to understand how my imperfect hearing was interpreting the kinds of sounds I couldn't hear properly. He would retrain me to use my mouth and my tongue differently to create the correct word. He did lots of different things of course, concentrating on making sounds and recognising the subtle differences, for example between two hands clapping together or a hand banging on the table or different notes made by bells or chimes. When I look back now, I can appreciate how astonishing Dr. Johnson's work was. The whole meticulous process of going from a series of regular operations on my ears, to learning how to understand and adjust the sounds my brain heard and subsequently learning how to recreate these new sounds. While the process was lengthy and difficult it was amazing to be able to hear again properly. Dr. Johnson's initial diagnosis and recovery time frame proved to be correct in every way.

It was only when my exams were over and the pressure of the academic deficit was lifted, that I could begin to relate properly to the impact being able to hear fully was having on me. Now with the exams over, I had more time to concentrate in a more focused way and pay more attention to Dr. Johnson's interventions and input for the final phase of the recovery programme. We worked awfully hard and it was only when I had adjusted and integrated fully into society and the hearing world, that I could truly appreciate and value to a larger extent the benefits of having my hearing fully restored. This adjustment took a long time, longer than I anticipated and I could see and feel the difference between being deaf and being able to hear properly. The latter opened up a whole new world of curiosity, interesting challenges and adventure for me that prior to that I had missed out on. It opened up possibilities of entering into diverse relationships that I had been previously excluded from. The choice to emerge from my introverted silent world out into an extroverted more proactive world was also presented to me. Previously closed doors were now there to be opened if I had the courage to truly step into this new world of hearing and dared to venture in to opening them. The prospect of coming out from behind my reclusive hiding place where I had developed coping strategies and sophisticated defence mechanisms as tools to deal with my disability, was daunting and terrifying. It had taken ten long years to not only develop but to implement these strategies and defence mechanisms. I had developed them to an extremely high level of proficiency and I had become the master of my own development. The daunting question now was, would I have to dispose of those precious mechanisms and recreate new ones as tools to deal with the challenges of my new hearing world? My deaf world was now in danger of being deconstructed. How was that going to sit with me? After all, the divil you know is better than the divil you don't know!

If it wasn't for my friend Marge, I don't think I would have passed my exams especially my Inter Cert. and Leaving Cert. The only subjects I was any good at was Irish and Music (General Musicianship). You had to pass five subjects to get an overall pass in both of them and you had to pass Irish or you failed the whole exam. This put terrible pressure on everyone and I think turned a lot of people off the Irish language. Most people seemed to struggle learning Irish. I honestly don't know how I managed to pass my Inter Cert. and Leaving Cert., but I just scraped through both by the skin of my teeth.

I was a nervous wreck over the summer waiting on my results to come out because I was sure I was going to fail and my mother would kill me. When the results did come out eventually and I passed, I was pleasantly surprised and delighted not to have to repeat the exams.

There were great celebrations. After the Leaving Cert. it was time to say goodbye to everyone and we were feeling sad at leaving our nice secondary school. Great friendships had been made and it was difficult to see how the friendships could be kept up because everyone was choosing what to do next and where to go to. Everyone was on a different path it seemed. College was not an option in those days like it is now. Most people went on to do secretarial courses to work in office jobs, banking and the Civil Service. Nursing and teaching were the other popular choices. Families were poor and parents were depending on their children to go out and work and earn money to keep the family afloat. I had started working when I was eleven years old in a grocery shop around the corner from where I lived. I used to work in the evenings sometimes and at the weekends during the summer holidays and other school holidays during the year. I liked working in the shop, but I didn't like having to hand up my entire wages to my mother.

The next big excitement after the exam results was the Debs Ball night out. Everyone was toing and froing deciding who they were going to ask to take them to the Debs. There was great chitter chatter between us girls, everyone throwing in their tuppence ha'penny worth of suggestions and advice to each other. We had an insurance man who was a friend of my aunt (my godmother) and I asked his son because I knew him a little from meeting him when I was down in my aunt's house. Thank heavens he accepted the invitation otherwise I don't know what I would have done. I was very sheltered in that regard as my brother and I weren't allowed to go out to discos or anything like that. Therefore, I was quite nervous as I wanted it to go smoothly. He was a nice lad and he was an ideal partner for the night. Of course, the next discussions were about the dresses and what kind of dresses was everyone going to wear. What style, what colour, long or short, fitted or flowing etc. etc. I was very lucky my aunt made my dress for me. It was a beautiful long white dress, with lovely long bell sleeves in chiffon, figured in at the waist and opened out into a lovely ripple shape at the end. I was thrilled with it and felt chuffed with myself. Of course, the girls looked beautiful on the night and we felt so grown up! A great night was had by all. It was especially meaningful for me as at this point, I had fully regained my hearing and for the first time I could hear the glorious music. Abba had just won the Eurovision that year with 'Waterloo.' The Debs brought a close to our five years in Eccles Street and it was a lovely closing. There were speeches made by the nuns and teachers and some interesting insights shared to help us on our way. There were many tears shed as we said our final goodbyes, five years is a long time to spend as classmates. I was very worried I would lose my best friend Marge because we lived a long way from each other, she lived on the north side and I lived on the south side. Because Eccles Street was on the north side of the city the majority of the girls lived on the north side, there wasn't many of us from the south side. It was sad saying goodbye to Sr. Isnard and the basketball and athletic coaches. They wished me well in my future life and encouraged me to keep up my sports. The final farewells over, we went our separate ways.

CHAPTER 13
H. Williams The Supermarket
And Brendan The Big Surprise

For me it felt extremely strange, suddenly not having the discipline and routine of going to school anymore. I felt like a fish out of water. I had enrolled into Sion Hill College to do the Froebel Teacher Training Course. Froebel teaching is named after the 19th century German educator and founder of Kindergarten, Friedrich Froebel (1782-1852). He advocated reverence for the child, learning through activity, exploration of the environment, enjoyment of beauty in its many manifestations and acceptance of the gifts of each individual. The college couldn't accept me as I was too young. They told me I would have to wait one year. Understandably, I was bitterly disappointed about this as I was looking forward to going there. What was I going to do now? I certainly didn't want to be at home around my mother. That would be intolerable. I couldn't hack that! My mother equally didn't want that situation as she had her secret routine that she didn't want anyone to find out about. She used to say she had spent the day cleaning the house but by the state of it she clearly hadn't or she'd tell us she had been to visit my nana's grave, but that was a common story she told us, that we knew was never true. I don't know what she used to get up to with her day. Therefore, I was ushered off to find a job to keep me occupied until it was time to go to Sion Hill.

Luckily enough, I quickly found a job in H. Williams supermarket. H. Williams was the first supermarket chain in Ireland opening its first store on Dublin's Henry Street in 1959. I was based in Terenure which was an ideal location for me. It couldn't have been better because I could walk from my house in twenty minutes or so and the 16 bus also went from the bottom of my avenue and stopped across the road, right opposite the supermarket. Because I had worked in the grocery shop around the corner from me, the experience of that stood me in good stead. I transitioned easily into the supermarket routine and I quickly settled in and loved working there. The manager, Mr. Reynolds, was a lovely man to work for. The supermarket had a bright cozy atmosphere and everyone got on great with each other. We had plenty of fun and laughter throughout the day and there were plenty of customers to keep us busy. One of my jobs was stacking the shelves and we each had our own special area that we were responsible for. We had to go to the storeroom to collect our boxes and put the products onto the shelves. At the end of every week, we had to stocktake our area and put in orders for items that were running out. I just loved stacking my shelves and keeping them tidy and in order. My Girl Guide days and memories came flooding back to me as I took great pride in doing my job properly.

My love of perfection also came shining through and my adoration for neatly stacked rows of items as in my father's shed, were the order of the day. When the shelves were completely full, right out to their edges, they were a perfect sight for my eyes to behold. I used to stand back and admire them and feel great pride and satisfaction in a job well done. I used to marvel at how beautiful they looked. Just like the other things I have described earlier I loved the variety of colours of the different items and when I stood back from the shelves the splash of colour was aesthetic and attractive indeed. Of course, childishly, I didn't want anyone to disturb them and woe betide anyone who dared to upset my perfect spectacle. Needless to say, it didn't stay long that way because people were naturally buying the items they wanted and had no qualms whatsoever disturbing my prided work of art. I used to silently wail inside myself when someone disturbed my lovely shelves and I would immediately run and pull the products in a line forward to make it look perfect again. These gaping holes didn't appeal to me at all, at all. It took me a long time to get used to this reality but eventually I had no choice and had to adapt accordingly, which I did.

After a few months I was trained in on the cash register and handling the money with the customer's purchases. This was a giant step-up for me in terms of responsibility and I felt somewhat anxious and nervous at the beginning because I didn't want to make any mistakes. At the end of every day, we had to balance our tills and I used to be a nervous wreck until I would know for sure that everything was ok and the till balanced. We were allowed a small amount of leeway in relation to the margin of error, generally pence but not pounds. Usually, I was good on the tills and there was only once that there was pandemonium over a large error. Another girl and myself were sharing a till but thankfully it got sorted quickly. The manager was astute and on top of things and was able to handle the situation quickly. I was hysterical at the time as I couldn't bear the thoughts of being accused of stealing because that was something I wouldn't dream of doing. I got into a terrible state about it and was very worried I would lose my job but thank heavens it didn't come to that; the problem was resolved to everyone's satisfaction.

My days and months in H. Williams rolled along nicely and there were two lads, Brendan and John, working in the storeroom who I became friendly with. We had great fun, chatter and laughter whenever I was coming and going, taking out my stock and bringing back the empty boxes. Being the innocent naïve gobdaw that I was, I never copped on that one of the guys, Brendan, fancied me. I was quite happy tipping along having the fun and craic with them, enjoying the slagging between us. Until this point, I didn't have any interest in boys or having a boyfriend because basketball was the love of my life. I hadn't had much exposure or opportunity to meet any boys. When Brendan finally plucked up the courage to ask me out (it took him a long time) I just couldn't believe it! I was totally gobsmacked and speechless! What the heck! I didn't know what to say to him and became totally tongue-tied. I must have looked like a goldfish with my mouth flapping and no words coming out. The poor fella! To say I was embarrassed is putting it mildly and I'm sure he must have felt embarrassed, patiently standing there waiting for a reply that wasn't forthcoming.

Eventually, with a quivering voice and what seemed like quite a lapse in time I accepted his invitation to go out. My face was a hundred shades of red and the sweat was pumping off me like I don't know what. I hadn't thought of him in this light before and I hadn't particularly noticed him in terms of being attractive or anything like that. But in hindsight he was a cute looking fella and had an exceptionally nice personality. He had a lovely smile and twinkly eyes which are two things I find attractive in a man. I became overjoyed and excited when the shock eventually wore off and couldn't believe that a boy actually found me attractive and wanted to go out with me. I was both mortified and excited at the idea of it. My heart was pounding and I felt on fire inside.

I began to panic like mad. Oh my God! It hit me that I hadn't a clue how to behave on a date. I hadn't been out on a date before (except for the Debs night but that was different, that didn't count). A wave of terror washed over me. Between the excitement, the joy and the terror I didn't know which end of me was up. I was totally mixed up. Everything was tingling and mingling inside of me. I felt chuffed however at the boost to my ego and I was flattered to be considered worthy of being asked out on a date. It was some rollercoaster of emotions I can tell you.

I couldn't wait to get home and tell my parents. I was sure they would be delighted for me. I was hopeful that they would remember their first date when my Da asked my mother out and they would be able to help me and give me some advice. After work I dashed home and burst into the house full of excitement dying to share my news. My mother was out. My Da saw me first and looked up from behind his newspaper to see what the commotion was about. I spluttered out my news to him in one go speaking at speed like a runaway train. He put his hand up and said, 'Whoa whoa missey moo, slow down and tell me that again, I didn't catch it.' I explained I was too excited to slow down but I would try. Second time around he said, 'O.K. now I understand why you're so excited. What's this boy like?' I described him as best I could and told him I had no clue that he fancied me, that the two lads and myself in work just got on famously and we had great craic every day. It was innocent and carefree. My father grinned and said, 'That's men for you, you never know what's going on in their heads.' I asked him for some advice as I was extremely nervous at the prospect of the date and he told me not to worry, that was normal everyone is nervous on any date but especially on their first date. He remembered being as nervous as hell on every date he ever went on. He also assured me that the boy too would be nervous and that I wasn't on my own, there would be a pair of us in it. He wished me luck with it and told me that the most important thing to do was to make sure and enjoy myself and enjoy the lad's company for the night, he sounded like a nice lad. My father's words helped to settle me a bit and it was good to know that the way I was feeling was quite normal.

Sometime later my mother arrived home. She seemed to be in good humour after her night out and I thought 'Good, this is a good time to tell her my exciting news.' I gave her time to take her coat off and made her a nice cup of tea. I relayed my news to her and before I had even finished, she interrupted me and said, 'You're not going out on that date, I'm not allowing it. You can't go out with a boy you work with, that's not a good idea.'

My father lifted his head from behind his newspaper and said, 'Why is that not a good idea, I'd like to know?' 'Because if it doesn't work out it could make things too awkward and she could end up losing her job,' she said. 'Nonsense my dear,' my father replied, 'Nothing of the sort would happen, she would have to carry on and get over it the same way many other people have had to do in these situations. She won't be the first and she won't be the last to have a romance with somebody from work. People are having them all the time. That is one of the ways people meet each other. It's normal and natural, there's nothing wrong with it. It will be good for her; she needs to go out and have a bit of fun. Don't forget we did it when we were her age.' 'We did not,' my mother replied, 'She's not going and that's that.' I nearly had a hissy fit; I couldn't believe my ears. I never for one moment thought my mother would stop me from going on the date. 'I've accepted his invitation,' I said, 'I have to go, it would be rude and bad mannered to not turn up, I can't do that.' 'You just go in to work tomorrow and tell him you made a mistake; you shouldn't have agreed to go out with him and that you've changed your mind. You can't go out with somebody you work with. It's a woman's prerogative to change her mind. My decision is made.'

As you can imagine, I pleaded with her and even my father to my surprise, tried to persuade her to let me go. But just like the running proposal, she wasn't having any of it, I wasn't going and that was that. I was deeply upset about it and stormed off to bed crying bitterly. My father followed me up to my room to console me. He genuinely felt sorry for me. He was obviously able to relate to my excitement and could clearly remember himself at that age in that same situation. After my father left, I was consumed with the thought of how I was going to do that? Go in to work and tell that nice lad I had changed my mind. I was mortified at the thoughts of it. I couldn't tell a lie like that and if I ratted on her and said she wouldn't let me go what would he think of that? Would he think I was a right little baby at my age not being able to stand up for myself against my mother? He probably would find it hard to believe that my mother would be that mean and horrible to make me do a thing like that. I was in a terrible quandary. I just didn't know what to do. I was angry and I was upset. I so, so desperately wanted to rat on her and expose her for the mean and horrible person that she was. Maybe he would understand and feel sorry for me having a mother like that. But he might also try and make me stand up to her or go behind her back and do it anyway. That was unthinkable! Jesus that would cause murder. All hell would break loose. She would come up to the supermarket and make a big scene and would make a show of me and him in front of everyone. I couldn't bear the thoughts or the embarrassment of that. If that happened, I would never be able to show my face in the shop again. I would spend the rest of my days cringing over it. My bubble was well and truly burst. I cried myself to sleep.

The next morning, I tried to stay in bed saying I felt sick – which was genuinely true – I did actually feel sick. My stomach was churning and queasy. My mother dragged me out of the bed saying I couldn't fool her, she knew exactly what was going on with me, I was pretending to be sick so that I wouldn't have to face the boy and tell him I wasn't going out with him. Well, she wasn't having that. The sooner I told him the better. She literally pushed me out the door and warned me not to come back home without having told him or I would be in big trouble.

I avoided going in to the shop for as long as I could, hoping that the ground would open up and swallow me. I was hoping for a miracle, any kind of miracle, something that would come to my rescue and save me from this horrible, sickening task. I looked a sight, a frightful sight. My eyes were swollen and red from the constant crying. The boy would most certainly not find me attractive now. I spent the entire day in the shop down in the dumps, agonising over and over in my head the words I was going to say to him. I didn't want to do it. I waited until the last minute, praying for a miracle to happen. But there was no miracle and I eventually had to face the music.

I was terrified out of my wits to go home to my mother not having done the awful deed. I hated myself for being so afraid of her and it brought back the memories of the running and that day in the basketball court in the schoolyard. Why did my mother hate me so much? Why? Why? Why? I just couldn't understand it. After the shop closed, I waited for Brendan to come out of the storeroom by the back entrance. His face lit up when he saw me and that immediately made me feel worse.

When he got closer to me however he could sense that something was wrong and he asked me if I was ok? I told him I wasn't ok and yes that I had been crying and that I was truly sorry for what I had to say next. I spun him my mother's yarn as best I could and he was quite taken aback. He tried to reason with me of course and explained how he felt about that as he had given it thought and consideration before he asked me out. He was satisfied within himself that he would be able to manage that situation if it should occur. He also pointed out that working in the supermarket was only a stopgap for both of us and therefore we would only be in the shop for a short while which meant it didn't matter what happened. I didn't have a good reply to that, how could I? It was a perfectly logical conclusion and a valid one at that.

This made it more awkward for me to stick to my mother's guns on the matter. I tried to counter his argument, but I knew it was a weak one. He was bitterly disappointed as I was and I tried to reassure him that I felt the same way as he did. I think he eventually smelt a rat and became suspicious that there was more to my refusal than met the eye. I think it dawned on him that if I truly meant what I said I wouldn't be as upset as I was. He took my face in his hands and looked deeply into my red and swollen eyes. I think that the hurt he could see there was deeper than the words being uttered. He held my face like that for a few moments more and took me into his arms and hugged me firmly, yet tenderly and compassionately. I needed that hug so badly it was unbelievable. I think he sensed my inner torture and somehow knew that I wasn't rejecting him – something else was at play. His kindness and tenderness caused me to cry again even though I was desperately fighting the tears off. I think that clinched his suspicions and he gently thanked me for having the decency to tell him face to face rather than standing him up on the night. I told him I felt bad about it nevertheless and apologised once more. We talked about work and how were we going to manage that. He said it looked like we would be both upset for a while and that was to be expected but in time we would return to the way things were before he asked me out. I nodded even though at that moment I didn't think that was possible. We said goodbye and he tried to reassure me one more time not to worry, everything would be fine. I realised on the way home what a nice person Brendan was and what I would be missing out on. For a young boy he was a gentleman no doubt about it.

I couldn't face going home. I dawdled along after our goodbyes were over feeling terribly upset and relieved in another way. I did it, it was over. Despite what he said I didn't know how I was going to face him in work after that. How could I look him straight in the eye again knowing that I had lied to him and him equally knowing I had lied to him? Truthfully, I felt awful about it and despised myself for being such a coward. The minute I rang the doorbell when I got home (I wasn't allowed to have the key to the door until I was twenty-one) my mother was waiting for me and immediately pounced on me to check if I had spoken to him and told him what she had told me to tell him. I told her yes that I did but she kept interrogating me because she didn't believe me and wanted to make sure I was telling the truth. The cruel irony and hypocrisy of that! I went straight up to my bedroom to get away from her and she sent my father up to me to check it out. Once again, my father tried to console me as I cried with him and tried to explain how bad I was feeling about myself. He put his arm around me and told me not to worry that in time I would get over it and that there were plenty more fish in the sea. He thought it was a shame as this boy sounded like he was indeed a nice boy. What a pity! He finished by saying, 'You never know, you won't understand now but maybe it's for the best. Things generally happen for a reason.' He brought me up a cup of tea and like a child tucked me into bed, kissed me on the forehead, turned the light off and wished me goodnight.

I was dreading the next day in work and dreading meeting Brendan, but when I saw him, he was true to his word, he tried to hide his disappointment and was pleasant and friendly in his behaviour towards me. That first breaking of the ice was difficult for us both. The other guy John in the storeroom was not only sensitive to the situation but acted as a buffer between us in a genuine and helpful way. His presence and his interactions with us helped to alleviate the disappointment we were both feeling. Two lovely guys!

CHAPTER 14
Sion Hill No More

Shortly after this, as if things weren't bad enough, I was dealt another big disappointment. I received a letter from Sion Hill College to say that they were closing the college down and would not be taking in any more new students. This decision was to take immediate effect and they were sorry to inform me that I wouldn't be accepted into the college as previously indicated. I was stunned! I just couldn't believe it and I read the letter over and over again. How could something that drastic happen so suddenly? I was all set and looking forward to going there. There was no hint whatsoever when I did the interview that this was on the cards. Talk about out of the blue. What a letdown! My mother was furious at the news and ranted and raved about it for weeks. Her permanent and pensionable job for me had just flown out the window. She too couldn't believe it. What now? Where did that leave me in relation to becoming a primary school teacher?

Openings for teacher training college were hard to come by. My mother rang the head nun in Eccles Street to see if she could give us any advice. She said she would make enquiries and get back to us. This she did but unfortunately there were none available and no other teaching opportunities that I could qualify for. My mother was like a raving lunatic and went on the rampage checking out other permanent pensionable jobs I could apply for. Somebody informed her about the Civil Service exams that were coming up and she entered me for those. I did poorly in those exams and was placed well over three thousand positions down the list. They were only calling between fifty and one hundred people immediately from that list so that was the end of that. My mother was furious with me. I didn't mind however because I didn't want to work in the Civil Service. It was common knowledge it was a dull and boring job. I much preferred working in the supermarket. I was lucky to have my job there. The manager was sorry for me about the college closing down but was also more than happy and glad to keep me on.

It took me a long time to get over my disappointment about Sion Hill College. It was such a shame about the whole thing. But in time I had to come to an acceptance around it. I did this by throwing myself more wholeheartedly into my job and in my spare time into my basketball. Many more months passed and I became even happier in my job and grew to love working there even more.

Ten months after my Leaving Cert. and working in H. Williams I received an official looking letter in the post one day. One of those letters with a harp on it. I was afraid to open it because I had no idea what it could be about. I was wracking my brain to see if I had done something wrong that I could be in trouble for. But I couldn't think of anything. Eventually, I gingerly opened it peering inside to see what it could be about. To my shock and horror, it was a letter from the Civil Service offering me a job. I couldn't believe it! It stated that they had reached my place on the list and they were offering me a job as a Clerical Assistant. I didn't want to take the job because I loved H. Williams so much as I felt happy and at home there. I wrote a letter turning it down, but my mother caught me unfortunately and nearly had a banana boat fit when she saw my declining letter. No way was I turning down a permanent and pensionable job for a more menial job as a shop assistant. As usual, she wouldn't hear tell of it and stood over me while she made me write a new letter accepting the offer. I kept telling her I wasn't leaving H. Williams. I didn't care what she said, I loved my job and I was staying there and that was that. There was absolute murder in the house and a lot of screaming and shouting and argument after argument which went on for days. My mother went ahead and posted the re-written letter despite my protests.

I went in to work in a terrible state and my boss, Mr. Reynolds, when he saw me, asked me what was up. I started crying and told him what happened. He was stuck for words which was unusual for him and I begged him to help me as I didn't want to leave the shop. Unfortunately, the fact that I was underage was a big problem. At that time twenty-one was the official and legal age before you were considered to be an adult and your parents were still responsible for making the decisions on your behalf until that age. Therefore, there was nothing he could do only write a letter to my mother, which he did, explaining how good I was at my job and tell her how much he didn't want to lose me. Of course, this had no effect on my mother whatsoever and she barrelled on ahead, the bit between her teeth like a horse, to pursue the offer. Another letter arrived soon after that informing me that I had to go for a medical check-up before I would be finally accepted into the job. Again, I didn't want to go for this, but my mother literally physically dragged me by the scruff of the neck and the arse of the knickers up to the Civil Service doctor for the medical examination.

I was praying and hoping that they would find something wrong with me so that I would fail the examination. It didn't dawn on me such was my desperation, that because I was super fit and healthy from my sports that it would be unlikely that I could fail it. When I was young however, I did have heart problems and was diagnosed with an inactive murmur on my heart. I made sure to tell the doctor this even though my mother was kicking me under the table not to mention it. It's a pity she was there because she reassured the doctor it was nothing to worry about. I tried to tell him otherwise. This caused an argy-bargy between us in front of the doctor. The doctor examined me more thoroughly and was able to identify the murmur. My mother was raging! I knew she was going to kill me when I got home. At that moment, my desperation ran the show and I threw caution to the wind. I didn't care. I didn't want this job. The doctor finished the examination and said that apart from the murmur I was extremely fit and healthy. He would have to check with the Civil Service Chief Medical Officer about the murmur and we would hear from the Civil Service in due course.

There was murder between my mother and I on the way home. She was like a demon. It was some time before we heard back from the Civil Service. During this whole waiting time I was delighted thinking my dicky heart was going to be a deal breaker and hoping beyond hope that I was going to be turned down. My mother reverted to not speaking to me and making our lives miserable in the house creating a terrible atmosphere. I was just as glad she wasn't speaking to me. I was sick and tired listening to the drivel that was constantly coming out of her mouth. It was a welcome break. We were both on tenterhooks for both our different reasons. Those weeks of waiting were pure torture!

One day when I came home from work, she greeted me in the hall with a smile from ear to ear on her face. She had her hands behind her back and as soon as I stepped into the hallway, she couldn't wait to take one hand from behind her back and wave the letter frantically at me. She had opened the letter even though it was addressed to me. I knew immediately by her reaction that she had won and I had lost. I was disgusted beyond disgusted and sickened by the contents that they were glad to inform me that I had passed the medical examination and they could now formally offer me the job. The letter stated that I was being appointed to the Personnel Branch of the Department of Social Welfare, Áras Mhic Dhiarmada, Store Street, Dublin 1. The starting date was the 18th of March, the day after St. Patrick's Day which is another reason that I will never forget the date as long as I live.

I can't describe or explain how I felt. Words wouldn't do it justice. I can however, remember thinking that there was definitely no God up there. I had prayed and prayed like mad over those weeks to God to make them turn me down. My rationale was, if God had loved me, he would have done that, sure doesn't he answer your prayers and gives you what you want. That's what we had been taught in school and at mass every Sunday. I came to the definite conclusion on that day that there was no God. It was a barefaced lie and if he was up there, he certainly didn't like me, never mind love me. I can honestly say as a result of the accumulation of the relentless traumas and situations with my mother to that point, it was the icing on the cake and the day I turned against God and the Catholic religion. I wished I was twenty-one and could make my own decision and wasn't answerable to my mother. She clearly didn't have my best interests at heart. She was just being selfish, looking after her own needs. It didn't matter to her what I wanted. She was quite happy to ruin and destroy my happiness in a heartbeat. My father challenged her which was extremely rare, pointing out to her that my happiness was more important than anything else. Wasn't it bad enough that I didn't get to pursue my first choice in the teaching without having another disappointment that was unfair and unnecessary? She fought with him and fell out with him over it as well as with me and the tension and aggro in the house was unbearable.

This didn't stop her however and once again she dragged me up to H. Williams and told them I was leaving even though I was resisting her like mad. The poor manager and the staff in the shop and Brendan and John felt really sorry for me. They couldn't believe it! They felt helpless and powerless. I think Brendan now fully understood why I couldn't go out with him. He witnessed her behaviour with his own eyes and acknowledged to me the tyrant that she was when saying his final goodbye to me. I was chronically upset, devastated and distraught by the time it was over. Some of the staff were crying and everyone told me how much they would miss me. I was the life and soul of the shop and they didn't know what they were going to do without me. While this was comforting to hear it was somewhat lost in the middle of all the angst. They gave me a lovely card and a present and tried to console me by saying I was welcome back anytime in the future if my situation changed or I changed my mind. Everyone hugged me dearly like they didn't want to let me go and I didn't want to let them go either. My mother however wasn't in any humour for any sentimentality and dragged me out in the same way she had dragged me in. My incredibly happy days in H. Williams were over and I knew with certainty that my mother as long as she lived would *never* allow me to return there ever again.

On the 18th of March, my mother was up like the lark – an extremely rare occurrence – to drag me off into the Civil Service. She didn't trust me to go in by myself as

I was still creating havoc at home over everything. I was dreading going in and she dressed me up in a pretty little outfit that she had bought me for the occasion, a matching top and skirt suit. My first day was awful, I hated being there as it was completely different to H. Williams. It was a big, huge office block and the various sections as they called them were separated off from each other. Everyone had their desk, but the desks were on top of each other even though it was a spacious place. I was put sitting beside a lady named Vivienne who I was going to be working with and who was going to train me. She was a lovely lady and the poor thing went out of her way to make me feel welcome and reassure me that in time I would get to know and like the job. With everything that had happened in the recent weeks, I had become apathetic, introverted and sullen. I tried to pretend I was ok and tried to force a smile but unfortunately, I just couldn't because I was gutted beyond gutted. Vivienne misread the signs as me being shy and nervous and put it down to me being young and new to the job. She copped on that I was naïve and innocent in terms of office work and was more than kind and patient with me in those early initial days. The boss of the section was a lovely man and Vivienne guaranteed me that he was a pure and utter gentleman and I had nothing to worry about in relation to him. Vivienne introduced me to everyone and told them I was the new girl joining the section. While thanks to Vivienne, I settled in better than I thought I would, I missed my friends and my job in H. Williams. I pined for them for months and months after leaving them. I lost a lot of weight because I was distressed and I couldn't eat properly. It got so bad that eventually I sneaked up to see them one Saturday when I was off, behind my mother's back. I got my Da to cover for me at home. I just had to see them; my heart was breaking I was missing them so much. It was Vivienne who gave me the idea when she realised what was truly going on for me. She was concerned because she noticed I had lost a lot of weight and she asked me if there was something wrong. I kept denying it at first but when I got to know her better, I eventually confided in her. She kept at me and at me to go and see them and it was thanks to her encouragement that I plucked up the courage to visit them. Needless to say, they were delighted to see me and there was great excitement at my appearance. They dropped everything they were doing and came running over to hug me. They gave me a huge welcome indeed. The customers had to wait but ironically enough they didn't seem to mind they too were enjoying the celebrations. Most of them knew me anyway and they too joined in the welcoming ceremony.

Someone ran out to get Brendan and John to complete the welcoming party. Brendan and John spoke to me before I left and expressed their worry in seeing how thin I had become because I was already thin when I was working there. They showed their concern for me by questioning me and giving out to me in a kind and caring way. They gave me a good ol' lecture and told me in no uncertain terms that I was to get my act together and start eating properly again. Mr. Reynolds gave them an hour off and gave them the money to bring me to a local café to feed me up. I couldn't resist this expression of kindness and concern; I did as I was told and went with them to the café. We had a nice bit of grub, a good chat and catch up on every scrap of news and it felt like the good ol' days again. I went back to the shop and thanked Mr. Reynolds for his generosity and he told me to come back again soon and not to leave it as long the next time.

The visit did me the world of good and I had to report everything back to Vivienne. She could see the difference in me after the visit and was delighted that her suggestion had worked out so well. This was one of the early incidents that brought me closer to Vivienne. Poor Vivienne, due to my upbringing and my background, it took a lot of work on her part to breakdown my barriers and resistance to prove to me that I could trust her. We got on extremely well, we were a good team work wise and as time went on, I was able to open up to her slowly bit by bit. It got to the point after many years working side by side that she became my number one confidante. We told each other everything and advised and supported one another in every aspect of our lives. There are many things that I am forever grateful to her for, far too many to mention, but she helped me through oodles of difficult times and we stuck together through thick and thin. She shared in the successful and big moments of my sporting career while relishing my achievements. Vivienne was not a sports person in active terms herself. In the early stages of our friendship she thought I was mad in my fanaticism. However, she is an avid lover of the G.A.A., no matter the weather, rain, hail or snow supporting the Dubs, her favourite team. I think I might have influenced her a little bit in that regard along with her dad who was the primary instigator of introducing her to the G.A.A. They used to watch the matches on the television and until the day he died he wouldn't miss a match for love nor money. Over the years, Vivienne became an extremely important person in my life and we are still the best of friends to this day.

Everything in life has its advantages and disadvantages. One of the advantages to working in the Civil Service was, I could focus on my basketball training a lot more because the working hours were 9.15am to 5.30pm, Monday to Friday. In H. Williams the hours were longer and more irregular and I also had to work weekends. We had a one and a quarter hour break for lunch in the Civil Service every day which gave me the scope to train at lunchtime for my basketball. I was able to develop a consistent routine for training and Vivienne supported me in this by covering up for me whenever necessary. She always had my best interests at heart and her motto was, once the work was done, she was happy to support me. Of course, the work never suffered, it was always done as I was a flyer at the work as much as I was a flyer in my sport. There were never any problems on that front. Vivienne used to marvel at my discipline, commitment, dedication and organisational methods both in my work and my sport. She said she had never seen anything like it. She was fascinated by it and greatly admired it. She was always praising me and couldn't speak highly enough about me to everyone including my boss. Vivienne herself, like me, was a perfectionist in her work, we were well-matched. Our love for perfection was a common bond.

Slowly but surely, I began to settle into the office routine although I still missed and yearned for my job in H. Williams. Vivienne was the key person in that process and I know for sure if it wasn't for her, I never would have taken to that job. I decided to use the positive elements and advantages it offered me for my sport and to focus on these a lot more. Between adopting this attitude and developing my relationship with Vivienne I was able to overcome a lack of enthusiasm for sitting behind a desk day after day. In H. Williams I loved the movement and action and constant activity. Unbelievably, the Civil Service was its polar opposite. The jobs were like chalk and cheese. H.

Williams was always alive, a hive of activity, a constant buzz. I loved the hustle and bustle. The Civil Service on the other hand was dull, dead, monotonous and boring!!!

CHAPTER 15
Haroldites And Sean 'The Animal'

After a few months of working in the Civil Service I was down in St. Clare's one Saturday practising my basketball. As usual I was on my own and Sr. Patricia spied me through her window and came out to have a chat with me. She told me that her sister Eileen was playing basketball on a club team and that she had been in to visit her. Eileen told Sr. Patricia that her team were looking for new players and asked her if she knew anyone who would be interested in joining the team. Sr. Patricia thought for a moment and immediately thought of me and that maybe one or two of the house girls would be interested. She told Eileen she would check around and get back to her if she could convince any of us to join. Of course, Sr. Patricia thought this was a great idea and without hesitation approached us and encouraged us to go for it. When she explained what was involved, I felt a bit shy and concerned I would be out of my depth playing with these ladies who were a lot older than me. Sr. Patricia pooh-poohed my fears and reassured me that they were a lovely bunch of ladies who would be only too delighted to have us on the team. Young blood is always a good thing and mixed with older and experienced players everyone gains she told me. According to Sr. Patricia I couldn't lose out, it was positive and progressive. She pointed out that playing at a higher standard would be the challenge that I now needed and was ready for and it would make me a better player. Naturally, I was chuffed at being asked and that Sr. Patricia thought me worthwhile to approach in the first place. I was feeling nervous and anxious about it and decided to run it by Vivienne.

When I went in to work on Monday, I couldn't wait to tell her and see what she thought. Immediately and without batting an eyelid Vivienne told me in no uncertain terms that of course I had to go for it. This was a golden opportunity that I couldn't turn down she said, I would be mad in the head not to go for it and at least try it out. She thought that if Sr. Patricia thought I was good enough that I should trust her and Vivienne felt that Sr. Patricia wouldn't lead me astray. She would have my best interests at heart. Vivienne promptly ushered me off in Sr. Patricia's direction to inform her I would be interested in joining the team and giving it a try.

This I did and by the time I saw Sr. Patricia she had convinced one of the house girls to join the team. Her name was also Eileen and she said she would only join if I joined (we had both gone to Eccles Street and knew each other quite well). Sr. Patricia was over the moon about it. She passed on the news to her sister and arranged for her sister to collect myself and Eileen to bring us to our first training session. The name of the team was Haroldites. This name originated from the village of Harold's Cross as the team members had started playing there. Basketball had primarily been an outdoor sport up to this time. However, it had begun developing into an indoor sport. Indoor gyms were few and far between but Haroldites were lucky enough to find an indoor gym in Wesley College in Ballinteer. Wesley College had a beautiful large full-sized indoor basketball court with a fabulously sprung wooden floor. Wooden floors were exceptionally rare in gyms and didn't exist in general. It also had amazing changing facilities and showers. Another unheard-of luxury!!! This first introduction was extremely seductive to Eileen and myself. We were used to changing in the freezing cold outdoors and going home either wet like drowned rats from the rain or sweaty and sticky if the weather was reasonable. Our little seventeen-year-old heads were turned and we were impressed beyond impressed.

Eileen Senior (Sr. Patricia's sister) introduced us to the team members and they were indeed nice friendly ladies. They genuinely seemed delighted to meet and welcome us on to their team. Eileen and I stuck together like glue. We were like Siamese twins that you couldn't separate. We were as nervous as hell. We could see straight away that the set-up was completely different to what we were used to. We were overawed by it initially, so better to stick together was our motto. This we did. Eileen Senior introduced us to the coach Sean, an ex-army man. While he too was equally welcoming to us, he did however frighten the daylights out of us. He was commanding and authoritative and he had a fine booming voice that could fill this entirely amazing huge hall. It seemed like his voice bounced off the walls and echoed right back at us. It would remind you of the acoustics in a high calibre concert hall.

Introductions over and out of the way, Sean insisted that we join in the training session. In one way we were glad to do this but the thoughts of those sharp army eyes watching and assessing us was quite daunting. By Jove did that man not miss a trick or what! He had razor sharp eyes and the speed of the movement didn't deter his observation one little bit, he was able to keep track of everything that was going on. The training session was well organised on his part. There were drills to beat the band and tons and tons of running and of course loads of army exercises for strengthening and conditioning. It was a two hour extremely intensive training session. Eileen and I had never experienced anything like it. Our school training, which was excellent, was blown out of the water altogether. However, we managed to do ourselves proud and to keep up with the pace. Eileen was struggling more than me but I kept dragging her along and wouldn't let her give up. Overall, we did very well especially for our first time. The ladies were delighted with us and gave us great praise altogether afterwards. They were used to Sean's training sessions and methods. It didn't knock a fonk out of them, apart from the fact that they were tired after it. I thoroughly enjoyed the training session. The intensity of it was right up my alley. I couldn't wait to tell Sr. Patricia and Vivienne about it. Sr. Patricia wasn't that surprised because Eileen Senior would have told her a bit about it from time to time when she would visit her. Vivienne on the other hand was hilarious. She nearly had a heart attack when I described it to her. She said she was exhausted just listening to the details and couldn't imagine anyone being able to train that hard – she certainly wouldn't be able for it. The sound of Sean frightened her too as Vivienne is a quiet genteel person and her father likewise was a genteel male, unlike Sean with his army disposition. Vivienne's face was hilarious to watch. Her facial expressions were comical when reacting to the descriptions I was giving her. She got worried that she could lose me if his training method killed me. I laughed my head off at her response and guaranteed her there was no need to worry I was well able for it. But poor Vivienne she could only say, 'But you're only a little slip of a thing Mary, he will kill you, oh my goodness'!

That was the start of the relationship between me and Sean. He was delighted to have such a fit gutsy player on his team and he was not afraid of taking advantage of that in the training sessions and the matches. He was a tough old trainer and a hard chaw if you ever saw one. He himself was as fit as a fiddle, took great pride in keeping his figure nice and trim and was, as we termed him, a *Vain Man*. He was a glutton for punishment training wise, known as an *Animal* for training. We got the benefit of this and he turned us into a tough, aggressive, competitive team who played with vigour, zest and zeal. We didn't have many skills between us but by golly we would drop dead to win a match. We used to batter teams off the court – and I use the word batter in a good way – such was our drive, grit, determination, commitment, dedication, passion and desire to win. One of the things I learned with Haroldites was that the team who wanted to win the most was the team who did indeed win. Haroldites under Sean's direction were the toughest, gutsiest team you could ever come across. The opposing teams *hated* playing against us. We terrorised our opponents. We won matches we should never have won and knocked the daylights out of the skillful teams who should have on paper beaten us. Our brute force and defensive play were second to none. Sean concentrated on our defensive play a lot to compensate for our lack of skill and this paid huge dividends. We were by far the fittest and toughest team in the league. Nobody beat us without earning their win over us. We made it difficult for them by pushing them to and beyond their limits. The game was never over until the final whistle blew with Haroldites. With Sean at the helm, Haroldites won leagues, tournaments and other competitions year after year. Many is the trophy and the medal I won with them. I played with them for many years and my play improved immensely through Sean's fitness and training programmes.

During this period Sean was a P.E. teacher in Emmet Road Vocational School and he invited me up there to train with him at lunchtime. Emmet Road had a tiny little gym with a wooden floor and bars hanging on the wall. Sean devised a circuit training programme for us to partake in together. I used to cycle three miles from Store Street on my little

Triumph 20 up to Emmet Road in Inchicore every day at lunchtime, five days a week, to train with *The Animal*, after which I cycled back the three miles to Store Street from there. Sean and I would always manage to fit in three circuits every day. As Sean got older, he truly treasured the training sessions with me because he couldn't find a male counterpart to push him and challenge him the way I could. We were well-matched, equally competitive, egging and driving each other on no end. Sean actually gloated at our training sessions and just loved being pushed to the pin of his collar. We broke through limitation after limitation and became the best of training buddies you could ever meet. There was no whinging, whining or moaning between us – there was no time for that – only pure intensive, hardworking training consumed with grit and determination to constantly challenge our bodies, minds and spirits in that tiny little gym. Expelling blood, sweat and more sweat was the order of each session, hanging off the bars, sprinting up and down like two lunatics, jumping up and down off benches and chairs amongst many other exercises. When I look back on it now, I honestly don't know how the hell we did it, but we certainly *did*.

Then Sean got the brainwave of bringing Haroldites up to Emmet Road one evening a week and introducing them to our training circuits. This meant that one day a week I was doing this circuit twice in one day. The girls nearly died on the first night. Despite their already extremely high level of fitness this was a completely different type of fitness. Nobody could walk the next day after that first training, they were in such agony from the accumulation of lactic acid. Every muscle, bone and joint in their bodies ached like nobody's business and if we had had a camera to photograph the pain and agony on everyone's face, we would have had a right lot of incredibly funny pictures of faces distorted beyond recognition. They looked like a right motley crew! We would have won first prize in a horror photography competition, no doubt about it! Of course, I felt sorry for them. That was the way I felt when I embarked on my circuit training with Sean, but now I was so used to training with him that my lactic acid tolerance had improved considerably. Those awful days were over for me, thank heavens. This pain and torture made the girls respect me even more because, while they knew I had been doing extra training with Sean, they had no idea of the intensity and difficulty it entailed. Their admiration for me climbed a good few notches higher.

There was one girl on the team who just couldn't stick this training and she used to find any excuse she could to dodge out of doing the exercises. Sean however wasn't having any of it and kept an eagle eye on her to make sure she stopped cheating. There was no cheating in Sean's class I can tell you!!! You could put on the most mournful face and it would just glide over his head. In the gym in Emmet Road, he used to make everyone wear their full tracksuits. No tops and shorts. 'Now ladies,' with his smug face he'd say, 'I don't want any embarrassing moments please, full tracksuits only.' In those days the material of the tracksuits were much heavier than todays. There were four big huge blow heaters, one in each corner of the gym and he would turn them on early in the day. By the time we came in the gym was boiling, hotter than any sauna. Within two minutes everyone was roasting, with the sweat dripping off them. As if the training session wasn't bad enough without the added extra burden of having the equivalent of the equator to deal with. Sean spent his time grinning and sniggering to himself upon observing the torturous reactions people were having. It turned out surprisingly enough that my teammates didn't like Sean's brainwave – ha ha! I was torn between feeling sorry for them and enjoying what Sean was enjoying. When you were able to step back from the scene and observe it from a more neutral perspective, it was rather funny watching the facial and emotional reactions of everyone.

There was no such thing as missing training on Sean's team. Even if you were injured you had to turn up and observe. He maintained that observing was as equally important in order to learn the offensive plays and defensive strategies he was teaching us. He expected everyone to be able to step onto the court in full knowledge of our game plan. No weak links were allowed on the team. Therefore, when it came to the training in Emmet Road, he always had substitute circuits prepared for anyone who was injured. Nobody was allowed off the hook. I liked this rule because it strengthened the cohesiveness on the team. No dodgers or mitchers were permitted on the team. There was no messing – this was serious and proper training. If you missed training, you weren't allowed to play in the next match. This rule was also good for increasing the competitiveness between players. A family death was the only acceptable excuse for missing training. This may sound extreme, but it taught us as individuals the importance of commitment and upholding an agreement. It also taught us the importance of every cog in the wheel. Every player had an important role to play whether sitting on the bench or out on the playing court. The interconnections and the sum of all the parts is what results in a unified team. The fine balance of individual and the collective input by everyone on our team led to our success. Through this teamwork the spirit and character of our team developed.

Sean was a great believer in the fact that effective and accurate communication amongst players is a key factor in determining positive outcomes in any team game. Failure to communicate in an accurate and timely manner will have negative consequences for the team, is what he continuously told us. He taught us that in team sports teamwork is an essential component to creating a cohesive, motivated, passionate and driven squad of players. He used to always say that the whole is greater than the sum of its parts. We learned that cooperation and the building of team spirit is of vital importance in creating synergy and unity amongst players. Sean operated on the basis that successful teams are seamlessly integrated despite each team having a star player. He was a stickler on the point that the entire team must work as one to win and to achieve their goals which is to ensure that collectively they would strive for perfection. Sean would quote Michael Jordan to us 'There is no 'i' in team but there is in win.' In our training sessions and whenever we played matches Sean used to make us talk and shout instructions at each other regardless of whether we were playing offence or defence. Failure to communicate effectively resulted in suicide runs or being benched. It didn't take us long to get over our shy and meek inhibitions and follow his instructions. We also had to be physical as well as verbal in our communication, especially in defence. This would involve literally pushing or shoving a teammate into a particular position if they weren't in the right place at the right time. According to George Bernard Shaw, 'The single biggest problem in communication is the illusion that it has taken place.' I can tell you by the time Sean was finished with us there was no such thing as illusion in the communication in the Haroldites camp. The word illusion wasn't in Sean's vocabulary.

Along with coaching us Sean was a FIBA referee – International Amateur Basketball Referee. He refereed matches across Dublin and Ireland during the week and at the weekends. He had to travel abroad representing Ireland as a referee and he refereed many games in Europe over the years. Whenever he was abroad, he would sit in on the coaching sessions of the participating teams and he picked up a lot of complicated and competitive drills which we got the benefit of as he passed them on to us when he got back. He never told us when he was going away, but eventually we got to know because a new drill would be introduced to us in training and we wouldn't have a clue what was going on. He used to love teasing us and driving us mad with his unusually complicated and unorthodox newly found drills. Talk about wreck the head jobs! We would be in total chaos trying to learn and implement them the way he wanted us to. Of course, eventually we did manage to get them because he wouldn't stop until we did and there would be great cheering, celebrations and jumping up and down with delight when we finally succeeded in mastering what we thought was the impossible. This was another thing that enhanced us as a team. The benefit of learning these complex drills gave us a big advantage over other teams because it developed our game tactics and skills. We were the only team who were lucky enough to have training of this calibre. It also increased our competitive edge as the standard of coaching in Ireland wasn't as high as that of Europe where basketball was played, coached and refereed at a much higher level with a huge amount of professional input, sponsorship and advertisement. Each of these factors raised the standard of the game in Europe and poor Ireland always had their work cut out for them trying to compete at international level. When I was growing up there were no opportunities for excellent players to progress to play at international level the way there is nowadays. I would have loved to have had the opportunities that the young people of today have.

Sean was a master at not only training us physically but mentally as well, preparing us for *Battle*. The torture in his training sessions toughened us both physically and mentally allowing our skills and confidence to flourish. One example of this is the pyramid sessions we used to do. There are four lines on a basketball court. We had to sprint from the first line to the second line, stop and do twenty press-ups there, sprint back to the first line, stop and do twenty sit-ups there. Next we had to sprint from the first line to the third line, repeat the press-ups and sit-ups procedure and sprint back again. Then sprint from the first to the fourth, the first to the third, the first to the second and back to first, doing the press-ups and sit-ups at every line. A tough and demanding drill physically but even tougher mentally. When you went up the pyramid and had to come back down again the mental aspect was challenged the whole way up. You had to fight the physical tiredness and the mental anguish of your body screaming to give up. Your body is telling you it simply cannot continue, it cannot give you what you want, it cannot go another step, it is crying out for more oxygen, every breath is laboured, every intake of breath is pure agony. You really have to dig deep, grit your teeth and draw on your own inner metal, that iron will, using the distant voice of Sean, roaring in the background like a sergeant major, using the fact that you desperately did not want to let your teammates down, using your personal pride to get you to the top of that pyramid. Having psyched yourself up to override the conviction of your body telling you it can't continue; you now have to tackle the downward slope of the pyramid with that same metal that got you there in the first place, as you still have a long way to go. A glimmer of relief descends upon you as you smell the finishing line and the realisation that each sprint is reducing and becoming shorter. Every step is a step closer to the end of the torture. Every cell in your body is hypervigilant, willing you to the end, willing you to finish, spurring you on, in spite of the oxygen debt, pushing you over the line. Having collapsed in utter exhaustion, the recovery time is a welcome reprieve... until it begins all over again.

The *Suicides* were a mental challenge we had to run whenever we did anything wrong. A Suicide was similar to the pyramid in that you had to run the four lines without the sit-ups and press-ups, but you had to complete it in a certain time between thirty to thirty-three seconds. If you didn't make the time you had to keep repeating it until you succeeded. The mental application to force yourself to do it the first time and the absolute not wanting to have to do it more than once, developed and strengthened our doggedness, our determination, our refusal to give up. We learned that we could always do more than we thought we could and we came to genuinely believe this. As Sean frequently said, 'There's always more in the tank, girls!'

Because the emphasis was on the physical and mental training, we never saw the Suicides as punishments for doing something wrong. We realised that they were specific training techniques to improve fitness, mental strength and application and were specially designed to develop our capacity to perform under pressure, especially when fatigue was setting in. We learned that if you don't train under pressure, you most certainly cannot perform under pressure when the competition requires it. This is one of the qualities that separates the good from the very good, excellent and outstanding players from each other. Sean was adamant on teaching and highlighting the importance of having this quality as a player.

Another mental torture of Sean's was, in turn we would one by one, have to dribble from basket to basket at full speed up and down the court and score a lay-up at each end. We had to score twenty without missing. Every time you missed one you had to do a Suicide and begin again from zero. Woe betide the person who missed on number nineteen. But it often happened because you would be quaking and shaking so much from the pressure that people often missed this vital shot. The cursing and frustration that was expressed in those moments was most unladylike!!! It took a lot of steel and nerve to score that 20th lay-up shot. A lot of the time the other girls would rig it that I would be the person who had to score it, because I was the most reliable and was deemed as having those nerves of steel required for the job!!! Sometimes if they weren't clever enough Sean copped on to this and would do something ingenious to scutter their plans. There were no flies on him! He was a great man for setting the cat among the pigeons. It was one of his fortes!

These intensive, gruelling and torturous training sessions had an important significance to them. In basketball and athletics (although it applies in fact to any sport) these hours and hours of training add up. They accumulate to such an extent that they are considered as *miles in the tank* or *money in the bank*. In other words, it is when the pressure is well and truly on in competition and you are at the pin of your collar to perform, that you draw on these sessions like the pyramids for example. The memory of your achievement, despite the agony, is what gets you through this critical moment. In that split second of experiencing defeatism, you quickly recall the visual images in your mind of that occasion when you felt you just couldn't go another step. Then you draw on the knowledge that you *did* without a doubt break through that perceived impossible barrier and you can apply the same principle to the current situation you find yourself in. It is the miles in the tank that add to the development of mental strength and application. Therefore, no training session, no matter how small, is a waste of time. Every training session counts. Every mile in the tank is valuable. Even *bad* training sessions or *off* days add miles to the tank. Just as with your money in the bank, you gain interest from your miles in the tank. It can be in that crucial moment, that defining split second of a game or competition, where this very concept separates the Olympic or world-class athletes from their fellow competitors. The ability to recognise, understand and implement this is a skill that comes from years of behind-the-scenes practise, countless training sessions and continuous repetition. The final fanfare of a winning ceremony belies the phenomenal sacrifice that athletes make. Some spectators may not be aware of this sacrifice.

In order to develop my potential further because I was small in height, Sean brought in a basketball player, a big, tall guy that he himself coached and trusted to train one-on-one with me. In basketball being small is considered a disadvantage as basketball is primarily a game for tall players. This guy was incredibly competitive and fitted Sean's ideas to improve my play perfectly. In our one-on-one games he used to beat the daylights out of me as his defensive skills were top notch. One-on-one in basketball is a vitally important part of the game. Outside the individual skills this is the most important skill. It has the same pressure and importance attached to it as scoring a lay-up shot. The game tactics in basketball are designed to leave players with one-on-one opportunities, as this is regarded as the easiest scoring opportunity a player can get. Two against one and three against one of course are much harder to score against. Sean's thinking was, if I could develop my one-on-one skills in order to beat his guy, I would be able to beat any tall female opponent. The tallest females were about 5'11" (1.80m). The battle was on! I was trying to beat Sean's guy and he had no intention of letting me. The fact that I was a girl didn't deter him. This was a good thing because it meant he treated me more like a guy, which essentially was the purpose of the exercise in order to toughen me up. He pushed me and challenged me day after day, unrelentingly. Sean used to stand with his arms folded, one hand on his chin grinning like a Cheshire cat and enjoying the battle between us. One day I got downright frustrated. I turned to Sean and asked him to help me, give me some sort of clue or guidance as to how I could beat this tough cookie. He just gave me that arrogant vain look and said, 'You will eventually figure it out. Keep trying!' A fat lot of help that was to me. I was raging!!! I could have killed him in that moment. He hadn't even the decency to take the smirk off his face. On I went facing this daunting challenge until one day many months later I succeeded in beating him. I couldn't believe it! But he wasn't happy and upped the ante to stop me. It took me a long time to get to the point where I became consistent in matching his impressive skills which put us on a more equal footing allowing me now to beat him more regularly. I was ecstatic! My perseverance paid off but the torture of it I will never forget as long as I live.

This was a major breakthrough for me as now I had the strength and capability to beat the *Big* girls. This enhanced me no end as a player. It was a major turning point in teaching me not to be afraid anymore of the tall girls. Now the whole field of players, small, medium and tall were within my grasp. Sean's guy and I became good friends off the court but on the court was something else altogether! We had a mutual respect and I think secretly he admired me for not giving up although he would never have admitted that.

My next escapade with Sean was when he invited me to go to a week-long basketball camp which was on in Dungarvan in County Waterford in the summer. He was one of the refereeing tutors for the referees' introductory course and he wanted me to partake in the players training camp which was specially designed to improve your skills. I couldn't believe it, a whole week of basketball. I didn't know such a thing existed. Sean didn't have to twist my arm on that one I can tell you. The thoughts of a whole week of training and playing basketball all day every day, sounded like heaven to me. Off I went and I had a brilliant time and learned loads of things which would help me to improve as a player. Sean being Sean, dragged the poor referees out of bed at 6.45am every morning to bring them running as part of their fitness training programme for referees. Referees had to be fit and be able to run as fast as the players according to Sean. He got me to join in with them which meant that he could work them even harder. That was the beginning of another regime of training between Sean and I. Running was now added to our circuit training every day. Sean being as fit as he was meant he could run extremely well and as happened in the circuit training, we pushed and challenged each other past our limitations yet again. Having done the little bit of running that I had done in school helped me enormously in our new quest.

Running with Sean brought back the memories of my past running experiences in Eccles Street. It was nice however, to have a running partner because even though it was still tough, it made it easier at the same time. It is understood and accepted that running is one of the hardest sports, for the simple reason, that it is such a lonesome journey and you are totally dependent on your own body in every way despite training alongside others. In a team situation like basketball the emphasis is on developing the team, albeit the individual contribution is of vital importance. In running however, it is the opposite. It is you versus the clock even more than you versus your opponent. Athletes are always working towards achieving personal bests (PB). This PB is time related, how fast you can run the distance whatever that distance is. The faster you can run and the more you beat the clock, the more likely you are to beat your opponents. Beating your opponent of course comes into the equation but that is more from a tactical perspective than anything else and is also something that must be developed in combination with learning how to use your opponent in order to help you to run faster. While Sean knew I was good at running from his observations of me on the basketball court, he was also surprised and taken aback at just how good I was at it, when we started running. I told him my story of what had happened in Eccles Street with the athletics coach and he commiserated with me saying, 'That was a shame, an awful shame. I'd love to see what you would be like now if you had followed that programme because you are a real flyer now.' He rubbed his chin, had a real serious pensive look on his face and continued by saying, 'Well you never know, maybe in some sort of way you can get some enjoyment at least out of our running together and you never know what might arise in the future.'

Little did I know at that time that Sean's words would come to fruition. A few years later I started running competitively in a meet and train group called Sportsworld. The group was being run by the former Irish Olympic boxer Mick Dowling and former International runner Emily Hopkins. Mick held 9 National Titles, won European Medals

179

and represented Ireland at 1968 Mexico and 1972 Munich Olympics. Emily was best known for her win in the second Dublin City Marathon in 1981. She also represented Ireland in numerous international competitions and was the winner of many Irish titles. The club used to meet three times a week, Tuesday and Thursday evenings and Sunday mornings, for official sessions. As people began to get to know each other, they would also meet up on other days of the week. With Emily's background in athletics and Mick's background in boxing, as a pair they were a good combination of expertise in training the individuals and the teams. They were brilliant at devising intensive training sessions. I always looked forward to their training sessions as they were extremely challenging. The club grew so much that they had many teams to enter in the cross-country, road and track competitions. They had a particular talent and instinct for blending teams together for the competitions to maximise each team's competitive advantage. They were great fun to be around despite their intensive competitiveness. Both had charming personalities and happy-go-lucky natures. I learned an awful lot from them and undoubtedly, would still be running in the club only for my car crashes, which I'll get back to later.

I was still playing basketball of course, running with Sean when I joined this running club. Emily put me on to a team and entered the team into a league. That became my first racing experience since secondary school. At this time, I had started training with lads from the Civil Service. We used to go running for an hour every day at lunchtime. I was the only female. They were extremely good runners, much faster than me and I struggled severely to keep pace with them. While they were running comfortably chatting as they ran, I was gasping for breath, panting like I don't know what and couldn't speak if you gave me the winning sweepstakes. Of course, they would try to include me in the conversation, but no way could I answer them, I was that out of breath just trying to keep up with them. At the end of the run, I would collapse over the wall feeling dead as a dodo while they seemed fresh as daisies. This used to drive me mad and I hated them in those moments that were like death for me. They would toddle off leaving me in a heap and I mean a heap. Vivienne always used to have to resuscitate me on those occasions. Poor Vivienne! She was so worried, 'Oh my God, these lads will kill you one of these days.' I had to agree with her. Even I thought they would.

One of the lads, Fintan, who was the fastest of the bunch took me under his wing and started telling me it wouldn't be long before I won one of the meet-and-train races. I thought he was crackers and told him so. But he persisted in filling my head with this idea and even though I didn't believe him for one minute, I think unconsciously, somewhere in my head, his words and belief in me were having a positive effect. To my astonishment, I did go on to win not only one meet and train race but the whole series of them. This was followed by me winning road races, cross-country and track in the Business Houses Athletics Association (BHAA) competitions. The BHAA was an association that organised races both individual and team for the various businesses in the country. The Civil Service had numerous men's teams and one women's team in these competitions. We had a strong women's team and we won a lot of these competitions because we were lucky enough to have a girl who was a short distance runner in athletics who was extremely good. I was usually second to her, so our third runner just had to complete the race in a reasonable time. One time we won a race as a co-ed team, two men and two women, which qualified us for a trip to New York to compete in a big race over there.

Training with the men improved my running immensely and my times kept dropping. I got to the stage where I was able to run a reasonable 5 minutes 15 seconds mile and 11 minutes 12 seconds two mile. These times were good enough for me to win the races. As a result I was selected to run on the Dublin team in the Cross-Country Championships which was a major honour and achievement. Training with Fintan especially, as well as the other lads, got me to the point where racing was easier than my training sessions. A complete turnaround from where I had originally begun.

This running was having a positive effect on my basketball career. Everything was coming nicely together. My physical fitness, strength, agility and endurance were turning me into a tough all-round competitive player. I won a lot of MVP (Most Valuable Player) awards, top scorer awards which were the only awards recognised in those days. Unexpectedly I was approached by one of the men on the Corinthians Men's Team, Jim O'Kelly, known by basketballers as 'Jimo.' He was a superb ball handler with amazing and unique ball handling skills. He offered to give me one-on-one training sessions to teach me those skills that he himself had. He had heard a lot of stories about me from Sean. Sean never praised me to my face, he only praised me behind my back. The Corinthians lads used to train after Haroldites in Emmet Road on a Monday night and that's how we got to know them. They used to joke with me telling me how much they *hated* me because they were sick and tired of Sean pointing out to them how useless they were and comparing them to me and how consistently good I was. He bragged vehemently about me to them on a constant basis every week.

At first, I didn't believe them and I just laughed at them. I thought they were seriously exaggerating because I hadn't received as much as one ounce of praise from Sean, never mind this abundance of praise. Sean wasn't prone to giving praise to anyone and for the duration of my playing years playing with Haroldites I can honestly say he kept his praise to himself. We certainly never received it. This was quite a shock to me. Anyway, Jimo started coaching me and his skill specialisation attributes unequivocally transformed me as a player. Jimo taught me how to dribble the ball behind my back and between my legs. He taught me various spin dribbles and various speed dribbles. He taught me how to do hook shots and reverse hook shots of various kinds along with bringing the ball around my waist before shooting as a fancy way of bypassing an opponent. He taught me slide shots and underhand shots with one and two hands holding the ball and spinning lay-up shots. He taught me many things I did not know, which was amazing.

By the time he was finished with me, I thought I was a right little female version of Michael Jordan. No kidding! In fact, the next day, my phone rang and to my shock, horror and delight, it was Michael Jordan himself asking me to come over to play with him. I was so excited I rolled over, fell out of bed and cursed my dream. There were no females in Ireland doing that kind of stuff to such an extent. Jimo was impressed at how quickly I learned and picked up the skills he was teaching me, but I was practising them a lot on my own when I wasn't with him. That helped me to speed up the learning process. I was extremely chuffed to be learning Jimo's skills. It gave me an injection of excitement and enthusiasm and catapulted me into a new horizon of experimentation. The fact that these skills were classy and fancy added an extra dimension of appeal for me. It was a completely different feeling playing the game from this new perspective. I became a flashier and more spectacular player to watch because it forced me to delve deeper into my creative self in order to succeed in developing the ability to execute the skills to a high level of perfection. These skills were hugely demanding in their artistry that the line between execution and non-execution was extremely fine. There was no room for error. The control that was needed, the sharpness of judgment and the final placement of the ball to the exact spot was of critical importance. You had to be on serious alert, completely focused and concentrated, with your antennae hard-wired to its capacity to execute these skills to perfection. It took a massive amount of training, practise and intensified nerves of steel. It also took courage to risk trying out these skills in the matches. Doing it in training is one thing but exploring and experimenting in the middle of an important match is quite something else. Jimo however worked a lot on my confidence to enable me to take these risks. He believed it wasn't good enough being able to do it only in practise sessions – you had to be able to produce it where it really counted and mattered – in the competitive basketball match where the audience was watching. It did unnerve me at first because I didn't want to let Sean and the team down by making mistakes.

This new uncertain, unchartered territory was frightening for me as it was challenging and taking me out of my nicely settled and secure comfort zone. I had to put my head down and barrel on regardless otherwise I would never have done it. This I did with a mixture of reluctance and determination. The determination won out in the end. I ended up, thanks to Jimo's tuition, winning the MVP award two consecutive years running, as the best player in Dublin, in the Second Division League which I was playing in at the time. The competition was extremely tough as the best players from every team were nominated for it. It was unheard of for a small player of my height to be in the running for such an award never mind winning it. There were great celebrations and Sean and Haroldites were thrilled for me and extremely proud of me. After this I went on to be selected to play for the Dublin Team which was also a great honour and privilege.

I played with Haroldites for many consecutive years (I can't remember how many exactly) and played under different coaches when Sean finally gave up coaching. From here I progressed to playing at the highest possible level with a team called Meteors. They were one of the well known Dublin teams of the time. I started on the Division 2 team and was elevated to the Division 1 team after a relatively short time. I played Dublin League and National League Division 1 with Meteors for a few years. I was part of the team when they won the Dublin and the National League against exceptionally stiff opposition. Killester were Meteors main rivals, therefore beating Killester always left a sweet taste in the Meteors' mouths. Playing with Meteors was a completely different experience for me than Haroldites because playing with a team who consisted of exceptionally good players was wonderful, albeit challenging. Here I had to fight hard to earn my place on the court and my guaranteed first five position was now something I had to work for again. This was much tougher due to the calibre of the players. As always, I persevered and bided my time until it happened. However, my playing time with the Division 1 was unfortunately shortened. I had started refereeing and when I was twenty-eight, I qualified as a Grade 1 Referee. I had to revert to the second team again as I wasn't allowed to referee at the highest level if I was playing at that level. It was one of the strict rules at the time of the Referee's Association.

It saddened me and it was an awfully difficult choice for me to have to make as I loved playing so, so much and I was thoroughly enjoying my time with Meteors. In the end it wasn't a choice. In truth, I had no say in the matter. I was given an ultimatum by the Referee's Association, therefore, reverting down to Division 2 was a sacrifice I had to make if I wanted to progress to FIBA International level. I was seriously considering not reverting, but my refereeing colleagues wouldn't hear tell of me doing that after the hassle I had had on my refereeing path. What clinched it in the end was I didn't have to give up playing. I could still play at the second highest level which, in reality, was more competitive from the perspective that these games were much closer due to the even standard amongst teams. Whereas with Meteors there was a huge gap between the top three teams and the rest of the teams in Division 1. Meteors hockeyed all the teams below 3rd position and the competitive matches were only between the 2nd and 3rd placed teams in the Dublin League and the National League. It was some consolation for me in that regard. However, I also really enjoyed playing on the second team because, like the first team, they were eager, passionate and competitive and were also a winning team in their own right. I won many trophies and medals with them while I was there and have lovely memories to cherish and hold on to from these times. I still have one important friend in my life, who was someone I befriended while playing with Meteors. I consider myself lucky and privileged to have had a varied, interesting and successful career with the Meteors Club, Haroldites and a couple of other teams I played with along the way.

CHAPTER 16
The 2 MJ's - My Idols

'I've missed more than 9000 shots in my career. I've lost almost 300 games.
26 times, I've been trusted to take the game winning shot and missed.
I've failed over and over and over again in my life. And that is why I succeed'

Michael Jordan

Michael Jordan and Michael Johnson inspired me. They were my basketball and athletics idols. Both were superb role models from a training and performance perspective. They strove for perfection to become the most outstanding athletes of their respective fields, both iconic athletes at a global level. Michael Jordan was believed to be the greatest basketball player in history. He was ranked as the greatest North American athlete of the twentieth century by ESPN Sports Channel survey of journalists, athletes and other sports figures. President Barack Obama honoured Michael Jordan at the White House with the Presidential Medal of Freedom. Michael Jordan's achievements, accolades and accomplishments include awards such as: Most Valuable Player, Top Scorer, Top Assistor, Slam-Dunk Champion, Defensive Player of the Year Award and many, many more.

The six-million-dollar question has always been, 'What makes Michael Jordan the best?' The answer to the question is quite simple. It was his gruelling training sessions and the accumulation and focus on repetition in practise, on and off the court for years and years, that enabled him to become the iconic player that he became. Everyone thought I was mad, nuts in the head to be training at such a high level of intensity. They thought Sean's gruelling and torturous training sessions were seriously over the top. When you analyse Michael Jordan's training sessions it brings a great sense of comfort to know that to be the *Best* at any level requires exactly just that. The approach I took was utterly inspired by Sean and my desire to be the best I could be. Ironically and unbeknownst to myself, Sean had me mimicking much of Michael Jordan's approach to training. Michael Jordan's ability to implement the elementary aspects of the game consistently and coherently and repeatedly reproduce those skills at every level of performance, especially when he was under pressure at the highest level of competition were paramount to his success. His determination to improve and challenge himself to develop into a more versatile player both offensively and defensively by increasing his skill range, raising the difficulty level and increasing his risk-taking was also a key factor. From his opponent's perspective he became impossible to defend and this contributed to him being deemed unstoppable. Michael Jordan was extremely competitive. He had a distinctive work ethic. He was a resilient and durable player as he was considered by his opponents to be indestructible. During competition he was a creative player with an extraordinary ability to be innovative and instinctive and used improvisation on demand – a rare quality in a player. He was able to outsmart his opponents with his mental application, his ability to concentrate and to focus and his ability to maintain his composure under pressure. He was regarded as a tough opponent and a strong clutch performer (a game clincher). He was trusted by his teammates to take the final shot of the game to seal their victory. Throughout his career he clinched many games in the final moments with his courage and self-belief that he could do it. Michael Jordan's playing attributes consisted of aggressive driving to the basket, drawing fouls at a high rate from his opponents, scoring fade away jump shots, his athletic leaping, his ability to leap and prevent his opponents blocking his shots and scoring slam-dunk shots. He was also a good rebounder, a notably impressive shooting guard, a competent three point and free-throw shooter and despite being a clutch performer also managed a fair percentage of assists with his teammates.

As I have mentioned already Sean's focus for us as a team was training to be aggressive defensively. Michael Jordan was a prolific defensive player recording a total of 2514 steals, which honoured him with numerous defensive awards including the NBA's 1988 Defensive Player of the Year Award. When we compare Sr. Patricia and Sean's training to Michael Jordan's training, we can see many overlaps. The same attribution of importance to such things as being adept at implementing the elementary skills of the game, the importance of repetition and being able to perform under pressure, taking risks and competency in defensive and offensive play. Sean most definitely was high on the distinctive work ethic, mental application, concentration, dedication, resilience and durability. Like Michael Jordan, Sean seemed to have a good handle on knowing what to do to become the best. He also valued greatly the striving for perfection in performance. Michael Jordan was noted for identifying the importance of thinking positively, finding fuel in failure and always 'Trying.' Michael Jordan states, 'Any fear is an illusion…failure always made me try harder the next time…sometimes failure actually gets you closer to where you want.' Michael Jordan believed in going for what you wanted to achieve. He believed that aggression supercedes passivity and that you have to approach practise the same way you approach games. He said, 'You can't turn it on and off like a faucet.' I think Sean's and Michael Jordan's philosophies were quite similar. They both believed in taking action and making it happen. They both believed in playing to win whether during practise or in a real game. Both Sr. Patricia and Sean shared his belief that if you want to be the best you must win all the time, regardless of the circumstances and turn winning into a habit.

While I was a long way from being a Michael Jordan, it is great to know that I applied some of the same principles to my own training thanks to my coaches and mentors. I realise now how much this increased my ability to defy the odds when it came to my Grade 1 and FIBA refereeing challenges. There is a lovely poem, written by McKay K. Echols about himself that captures his love for playing basketball. Reading this poem makes me think of Michael Jordan in the same way.

MY COURT

The dribble of the basketball,
The swish of the net,
The squeaking of my shoes against
The wood floor,
The passion and determination that
I feel is indescribable,
As sweat drips down my temples.

The basketball court is my home.
It is where all my thoughts and emotions
Are erased from my mind and all
I can think about is the basketball and
The hoop.

The court is a place that I can focus,
A place where I can put all of my
Thoughts and feelings into the
Things that are important to me.

Basketball is my life and
The court is where my
Life lives.

© McKay K. Echols
Published: August 2016

I like to think that Michael Jordan and I shared the same love and fanaticism for the game of basketball. We were both passionate enough to spend most of our youth training like mad, to become the best we could become. Basketball was our life and the court was where we lived our lives. This was true for both of us.

'How could you be more stupid, than to be the guy accepting a bronze medal in gold shoes'

I love this Michael Johnson quote. For me this epitomises clearly his character. He ain't goin' for anything only gold! Michael Johnson famously known as 'The man with the golden shoes' made history in the 1996 Olympic Games in Atlanta, Georgia, U.S.A. He won the double in gold medals. Gold in the 400 metres and Gold in the 200 metres. He was the first man ever to win Olympic Gold in those two fundamentally different races. As he said himself, 'A decade! Ten years of my life leading to this achievement.' Imagine that! Ten years is an awfully long time to persevere and dedicate to achieve one's ultimate goal. This statement gives us an insight into the commitment involved and the sheer determination of not giving up.

As I have said already, athletics is an extremely difficult sport. Michael Johnson obviously had immense mental strength to hold firm to his desires and beliefs to overcome the loneliness of the sport. In athletics the 400-metre race is regarded as the hardest race of the track distances. Like Michael Jordan, he loved the idea of perfection and said, 'Perfection, in the end, I suppose that's why I run.' Michael Johnson's book 'Slaying The Dragon' portrays the significance of the positive side of perfection and also asks if it is possible to run a perfect race. His determination to achieve greater levels of perfection had him questioning himself, 'How much faster could I have gone without a stumble?' He had the misfortune in 1996, when he set the Olympic record, to stumble when he was coming out of the blocks. The stumble posed further questions firstly of himself, 'Can I always go faster' and secondly, 'Is it possible that we can always go further and higher?' In his book he describes the importance of discipline, commitment, dedication, goal setting, planning the step-by-step approach and includes many other tips and advice on how to achieve perfection. It gives an in-depth account of the value of failure and success.

Michael Johnson was considered to be an athlete of superb performance ability with an innate capacity to apply discipline, physical and mental, to enhance his competition performance, particularly when under extreme pressure. He was known for what he referred to as *The Zone*, the place where nothing exists only the job at hand. The Zone is the place where the culmination of the hard work, discipline, hours and hours of practise, come together. 'Mentally, I enter what I call the danger zone, a place inside of myself with an incredible pool of focus, where I become acutely aware of my opponents and the fact that they are trying to keep me from winning.... I am simply planning, going over some technical checklist: React, don't wait for the gun. Stay low. Get up around the corner. I imagine myself becoming leaner and more efficient. For that one moment, I am a machine, perfectly designed and programmed for the task ahead of me. Hard, cold steel.'

One of the things I can relate to with Michael Johnson as a result of my own experience of training with a variety of athletes over the years is his explanation of what the dragon in the title of his book represents. It is those negative aspects of ourselves which impede our progress, our doubts and fears and lack of confidence. In other words, the negative aspect of ourselves and the negative voices in our heads is our own worst enemy and is what ultimately holds us back from reaching our potential. I think I can safely say that in my experience I witnessed this happening with other athletes around me, who, for one reason or another, let their negativity rule the roost. Johnson goes on to say, 'After you have stared long enough into the dragon's eyes there's nothing left to do but slay the dragon.' This means that you have to slay those negative thoughts and beliefs that you are carrying and allowing to get in the way and impede you. Michael Johnson believes that once the dragon is slain a rich reward awaits us. He believes that it is only then that we can truly meet our core, our ambition and our joy, these deep vital parts of ourselves that are necessary to potentially achieve perfection in a race. He invites us to follow his lead 'To places I have gone. To within a whisper of your own personal perfection. To places that are sweeter because you worked so hard to arrive there. To places at the very edge of your dreams.'

I find this extremely motivating as he is saying that this attitude is not for the elitist athlete only, it applies to every one of us. We can all reach our potential in relative terms on whatever podium that is for each of us. It could be the school finals, club finals, local competitions, county, country or international competitions. There are no holds barred. It doesn't only apply to sports. In his book Johnson shares his secrets to success and the components required to be successful whether in sport, business or life in general. The skills learned are transferrable to everything one partakes in in life.

In the preface to Johnson's book, Mohammed Ali concretises these facts when he states, 'Hard work, perfect practise and dedication to the goal of becoming better at your 'Sport' are just a few of the steps it takes to become a Michael Johnson.' Mohammed Ali had applied Johnson's principles to himself in his boxing career, no better man to know what it takes. His respect and admiration for Michael Johnson are

clear. It must have been nice for a sports person of the calibre of Mohammed Ali to have sat back in his retirement
and observe the same precious qualities that he himself
possessed in someone else. When we are truly focused and
concentrated on achieving our goals we can both omit and
fail to acknowledge or give ourselves credit for possessing
these qualities within ourselves. It often takes someone else
to mirror back to us what we could have seen in our own
mirror.

If we compare Michael Jordan and Michael Johnson,
we can see more similarities than differences in their phil-
osophical approach and attitudes in their training regimes.
The most singular focal point for both was their striving for
perfection. This involved seeing and acting on the positive
side of perfection which included welcoming and learning
the importance of failure and understanding the correlation
between failure and success. Success is the result of many
things, but it incorporates failure as a constant companion
along the way. Failure in their terms is a friend not an enemy. This is probably one of the most important and powerful messages that they passed on to us. If only we could
embrace our failures just like them and have the intelligence
and understanding in applying this concept to our own lives
and ambitions and allow the same in our children. I know
that my desire for perfection was a distinct asset in allowing
my failures not to lower my self-belief or self-esteem but
instead allowed me to carry on trying until I eventually succeeded. In hindsight, I think my perseverance with the guy
Sean got to help me, where I was constantly failing to beat
him in our one-on-one sessions, is a good example of this.
Another example is the running sessions with Fintan where I
was failing to keep pace with him and found myself permanently struggling against him. While what I am describing

here are examples of failure, I didn't feel like a failure. I felt the intense battle of working extremely hard. I felt the battle of digging deep within myself to draw on the resources that I could draw on. Both these struggles strongly challenged me to squarely face and slay my own personal dragon. Coupling perseverance with that understanding, that these failures were eventually going to lead to success was crucial.

When I was playing basketball, we didn't have any awareness around the concept of failure in the same way that Michael Jordan and Michael Johnson had. While we knew we were failing if we lost a match for example or if we kept missing our lay-ups and our shots or made bad passes and had many turnovers which lost us a match, the word failure was never used. Failures were considered an integral and natural part of the learning process and were just included as part of the normal regime on the road to success. Failures were not highlighted as separate entities. They were worked on by the coaches in a constructive manner. A coach would point out the negative aspect of our play as individuals and as a team and go about reorganising and restructuring the training sessions to improve and overcome our mistakes. From a psychological perspective, we had absorbed a full understanding of their approach to failure. Our self-confidence and self-esteem were not lowered in any way. We inherently accepted the importance of failure. It had become instinctive to us.

Aiming to correct mistakes positively in our time and striving for perfection through this process, diminished the psychological damage that the present-day fear of failure seems to have on people. We were never afraid to try anything in case we might fail at it. We tried it anyway and just kept on trying in the knowledge that relentless practise would eventually make us succeed. I think that nowadays people are afraid to try in the first place. As Michael Jordan says, 'Never ever give up…I can accept failure, everyone fails at something. But I can't accept not trying…if you quit ONCE it becomes a habit. Never quit!!!' As I've already said, our team never ever gave up trying, no matter how many points we were being beaten by, no matter how badly we were playing, we would drop dead to win the match. The match was **never** over until the final whistle went. Even in the midst of our failures, we kept going, kept trying and always had the pride to keep the outcome as respectable as possible. Sometimes we kept trying with the hope that a miracle might happen and, amazingly enough, to our surprise miracles did in fact happen. There are many examples of teams having a huge lead in matches and they end up becoming complacent and losing the match. In basketball many games have been turned around and won on the buzzer, in extra time or by one single point. This is one of the things that make basketball such an exciting game to watch and partake in. Like the positive attitude to perfection, a positive aspect to failure was naturally instilled into us in an unobtrusive manner.

It's fascinating to see that these world-class athletes, Jordan, Johnson and Ali, were of the same mind. It would suggest that the desire to achieve success taps into an innate knowledge that is shared between these elite sports people, but maybe we each have the innate ability to succeed but too often we lose sight of it. None of these people knew each other personally, yet they shared the same philosophy, mentality and approach to training. At my own lesser level of competing, I too had this same philosophy and approach. I was further inspired by the same thinking through Sr. Patricia, my coaches in Eccles Street, Sean and successive coaches on my path. Therefore, the drive for perfection, the drive to be *The Best* is, I think, a natural human desire or human endeavour. We each possess a strong *will* which is a strong force within us. Drawing on our willpower and delving into our unconscious need to stay engaged and not give up when the going gets tough, is quietly sitting there in the background and in the recesses of our minds waiting to be called on when we need it.

These three athletes and many others who followed in their footsteps had the desire and capability to draw on these human resources as an integral part of the components required to render them successful. It is reassuring to know that we too have it in us to do this. It doesn't matter what level you are at. The common denominator is the same for everyone and it comes down to a matter of choice, no easy way, no magic formula. You must abide by the same training laws as everyone else. There are no exceptions to the rules. Even talented people must abide by these rules. As Tim Notke, Basketball coach says, 'Hard work beats talent when talent fails to work hard.' Michael Jordan and Michael Johnson were talented athletes who worked extremely hard. Those ten years of struggling for Michael Johnson for that one sweet moment in 1996. What a major feat.

Jordan and Johnson's dance between failure, perfection and success was a graceful dance of synchronization. They were able to balance all three beautifully. Upon observation of their performance, it looks to me that this dance brought their bodies, minds and spirits together in a unified way and transported them into amazing feats of athleticism. Perfection in their minds had no negative connotations. They saw perfection as a positive means to a positive end. Michael Jordan says, 'If you accept the expectation of others, especially negative ones, then you will never change the outcome.' He also said that, 'Obstacles don't have to stop you. If you run into a wall, don't turn around and give-up. Figure out how to climb it, go through it or walk around it.' Michael Johnson had a similar belief. He said, 'Protect your good image from the eyes of negative viewers, who may look at your appearance with an ugly fiendish eye and ruin your positive qualities with their chemical infested tongues.... Life is often compared to a marathon, but I think it is more like being a sprinter, long stretches of hard work punctuated by brief moments in which we are given the opportunity to perform at our best.' What a profound statement!

I was ever so lucky in my sporting life to have had positive inputs from coaches and trainers along the way, particularly when I was young, during important developmental stages. Of course, in my competitive situations I had many an *Ugly Fiendish Eye* passed upon me trying to put a stop to my gallop. For me, thanks to Sean's gruelling training especially, I just looked upon this as part of the game in the same way as Michael Johnson saw his fellow competitors trying to prevent him from winning the race. In general, this didn't apply amongst my teammates as they appreciated the extra work and training that I put in. This attitude and acceptance were the winning combination for our team as we went on to win many medals and trophies as a result of this.

For Michael Jordan this appeared to be the same. Because he was such an outstanding player of such high calibre, a spectacular player to watch and play with, I think it was impossible to be jealous or envious of him. It is one of those extremely rare situations where a player is so mighty that he obliterates the jealousy, envy and the ugly fiendish eye. In contrast the solo nature of athletics, attracts this attitude

199

much more because everything hinges on the one person. Michael Johnson probably had many ugly fiendish eyes on him during his long athletics career. The desire and determination to beat *Him* was more personal and personally attacking than the desire and determination to beat the *Team* that Michael Jordan was playing for. Michael Jordan had the buffer of his teammates. Michael Johnson did not. I think this is one of the things that prompted Michael Johnson to develop the Zone, his mental focus, in the way that he did. He needed that level of focus to ward off those countless negative eyes and tongues. He often explained this by saying, 'As strong as my legs are, it is my mind that has made me a champion.' I wholeheartedly agree with this statement, as it can be a constant uphill battle to dispel the negative voices not only from within oneself but also from others when trying to reach our potential to perform at our best.

My playing career was well developed by the time I could access Michael Johnson and Michael Jordan to a much larger extent through the technology of T.V., radio, video tapes, newspaper and magazines etc. But by the time I became an international referee these mediums were more widely available to me, which meant that the philosophies of these athletes had a greater impact and influence on me than would have been possible before. My ambition to strive to become the first female international referee in Ireland was greatly aided by them. I was able to integrate Michael Johnson's and Michael Jordan's teachings into my own understanding to expand my competitive approach to my newfound cause.

I particularly used to love watching Michael Johnson in the Olympics and World Championships and I studied intently his mental preparation of entering into the zone right before a race. It never failed to fascinate me how even when observing him, you could clearly see how everything around him was blocked out of his mind and vision, as he was totally absorbed in this pre-race preparation of psyching himself up. The intense look in his eyes and the depth of focus and concentration that emanated from those eyes used to transfix me. That cool, calculated, determined, mean look in those eyes that spelt out the message – I mean business here - don't mess with me pal - sent a shiver down my spine and a cold chill would run through my whole body. Sometimes I could even feel a slight trembling in my body on those extra important occasions when the *Look* on his face was even more intensified.

I often wondered did his opponents feel like I did. Were they too trembling? Did they feel intimidated by that invincible presence and air of determination? How off-putting was it for them? Did it make them feel insecure? To my eagle eye Michael Johnson always looked like a lean machine that was pristine, well-oiled, in perfect mechanical working order and fuelled to capacity ready to go, ready to take off and surge into its fastest speed. I would have felt freaked out. Just like a spanking new, shiny car that seduces people by its very presentation in the showroom, egging you on to buy it and test it out to show and prove to you how good it is, letting you know that every penny you spend on it will be worthwhile – expensive yes, but extremely worthwhile! You won't be disappointed. When an athlete such as Johnson stood beside you, competed against you, it must have been daunting. You know he will do exactly what he is meant to do. You know that advert for Ronseal paint and the guy advertising taps the tin and says, 'It does exactly what it says on the tin.' For extra effect he holds the tin out towards the camera. The tin is in your face – boom! Yes! Exactly Michael Johnson!

CHAPTER 17
Nadia Comaneci – My Female Idol

*'I don't run away from a challenge because I am afraid.
Instead, I run toward it because the only way to escape
fear is to trample it beneath your feet.'*

Nadia Comaneci

I was 19 years of age when Nadia Comaneci, the Romanian female gymnast, took part in the Montreal 1976 Olympic Games in Canada. At the age of 14 she changed the sport of women's gymnastics forever. For as long as I live, I will never forget Nadia Comaneci and those games. Her face will linger in my memory until the day I die. I was glued to the television set morning, noon and night. I became square-eyed and it was a pleasure to do so. I had just embarked on my own competitive basketball journey in a more serious way and had just joined Haroldites Basketball Club. Nadia Comaneci's style and athleticism transfixed me in those two weeks of intensely electrifying competition. I couldn't take my eyes off her and a JCB wouldn't have extracted me away from the television. I studied her intently and carefully over those two weeks with an eagle eye of curiosity and awe-struck wonder. I desperately wanted to learn from this amazing young and talented athlete. How could I draw inspiration from her to enhance my own competitive desires? We had things in common which aligned me to her from first glance. She was tiny, I was tiny. She loved what she was doing as I did, she took great pride in her sport, was clearly a lover of perfection and she made history – and she inspired me to make history in my own way! I later learned more about her commitment and dedication to training, which was also similar to mine.

Up until 1972 it was the feminine balletic style that dominated this sport. Olga Korbut from Russia was the main gymnast responsible for initiating a shift in style which paved the way for women's gymnastics to be reinvented in 1976. Fundamental changes both technically and stylistically were introduced by Nadia Comaneci as she did things in gymnastics that had never been done before. The most prolific change was that of the judging standards. She was the first gymnast ever to receive a perfect score of 10, not only once but 7 times during this Olympic competition. This was a remarkable achievement given that the technical elements in performance for gymnasts are extremely stringent, intricate and finely tuned. A score of 10 was considered impossible. That perfect 10 had my blood sizzling. I remember being on the edge of my seat quivering with nervousness and excitement watching her perform. I nearly died. I was holding my breath in trepid anticipation, totally lured into a feeling of security that was polarised with the opposite feeling of insecurity, both at once, the two feelings churning and flip-flopping within me with every move she executed, whether it was on the beam, the parallel bars or on the floor.

The screams and roars that went up when it became clear that she secured the first perfect score of **10** was deafening. I distinctly remember the scoreboard not catering for the number **10** leaving a suspended silence in the auditorium until it was realised that the **1.0** was in fact a **10** and not a **1**. The audience jumped up in their seats, their hands on their mouths in total disbelief. Many of them were shedding tears with the pure euphoria and emotional charge that this historic moment was generating. For me at home watching it on

T.V. it was one of the most memorable occasions of my life. I was so thrilled, delighted and ecstatic for her I couldn't contain myself or my excitement. To witness such a major feat is one of the greatest privileges I have ever experienced. By the time the two weeks were over, I was a nervous wreck on one hand and a bundle of joy and ecstasy on the other hand. I soaked up every performance, every perfect 10, all 7 of them, like a sponge and I listened intently to the documentaries discussing her training regimes, her attitudes, her approach, her ability to be creative and think outside the box and most of all her unwavering courage, self-discipline, self-confidence and consistency. I have to say I truly learned mountains from watching her.

The documentaries unveiled some secrets to her success. It transpired that this major feat was no great surprise, a culmination of hard work, hours upon hours of practise and performing and peaking at optimum level when it counted and mattered the most. Her achievement was also attributed to a variety of factors including her drastically raising the difficulty level, using a new consistent repetitive style of training, introducing acrobatic skills and introducing far higher levels of risk and skill. Her coaches were also interviewed and it was fascinating listening to them explain the intricate and delicate details of her technical skills and how she incorporated them in to her routines, new-found complicated acrobatic and stylistic skills. From what they described these innovative ideas just oozed out of her yielding spectacular results. They explained that Nadia's beam routine included six flight elements incorporating flic flacs (backhanded tumbling) and aerials (a cartwheel executed without touching hands to the beam). These were executed five times more than Olga Korbut's winning routine in the previous Olympics. However, it was on the uneven bars that

Comaneci's influence was most significant. She performed the first true *Release* move where she let go of the bar, somersaulted forward and re-caught the same bar with her hands and completed her routine with a highly complex dismount incorporating a handstand and half turn in to a back somersault, landing perfectly with no faltering of movement at the end of the dismount. It was lovely having these technicalities explained and demonstrated in the slow motion of the replay on the television as it gave me a greater understanding and appreciation of her achievements.

Comaneci's consistently flawless routines and her repeated perfect dismounts were deemed the pinnacle of the century. Solid as a rock, that's what they were. How the heck did she control that rock solid landing after the speed of the somersaults with those little legs and small body of hers? You don't realise while watching her, waiting for that perfect dismount that you're holding your breath in anticipation. Nadia has two gymnastics moves named after her, the Comaneci Salto and the Comaneci Dismount which are still being performed by gymnasts today. I wonder if people truly realise the skill involved and the difficulty of this manoeuvre. I can equate it to a shot in basketball that soars high into the air with just the perfect amount of height, curve and spin on it ensuring that the speed carries the ball the distance it needs. It has to be in the absolute perfect position to go swish through the net without touching the backboard or the ring. Nadia was doing the same thing, flying through the air, somersaulting and landing boom! It is the precision, timing and accuracy that brings about this spectacular result. Pure genius! I always watched this manoeuvre with bated breath – one hiccup, one flinch and it was over, over and out. It makes you realise how lucky Michael Johnson was to get away with that stumble coming out of the blocks in the 1996 Atlanta Olympics. The same stumble by Nadia would have been lights out for her. In Nadia's routines there were no margins for error. This made the competition extra pressurised. Another thing I had in common with Nadia – I approached my refereeing exams with that same 'no margin for error.'

Another of her greatest assets was that she provided the public with aesthetic beauty in her performance, the beauty of fine engineering resulting in pure technical perfection, a beauty that had the audience completely captivated and eating out of her hand. She became an icon and legend for the sport and goes down in sporting history as the only gymnast to have ever achieved this incredible score in an Olympics. This record has never been equalled or broken. The word *Perfect* is always used in describing Nadia's achievement.

Nadia for me was the cutest, most adorable, gorgeous thing you could ever set eyes on. I had the feeling of wanting to put her in my pocket and run away with her. A remarkable athlete of great integrity. Her level of maturity, poise and grace was outstanding for one so young. She was a superb role model and a truly inspiring legendary character. She inspired me enormously and I tried to develop in myself the characteristics in her that I greatly admired.

One of the characteristics that intrigued me the most in Nadia and really grabbed my attention was her absolute belief and confidence in herself when performing and more particularly when performing under pressure. She never appeared nervous. Her presence at the beginning of every routine exuded a quiet, unflappable surety, an absolute air of confidence – not arrogance – she knew she was aiming for perfection and she would achieve it. So steadfast and sure was she that she did exactly that. I could relate to this because I remember having that same feeling every time I stepped onto the basketball court, especially when I had to score that winning shot to win the game. It is hard to describe or explain. It most definitely is not the arrogance that some people would misinterpret it to be. It comes from hours and hours of training and repetition, followed by repetition and more repetition. It's like the body and mind unite to become one in a singlehanded way to produce the perfection that's needed to achieve the highest possible results. The practise and repetition causes it to happen in an organic way. It gently lands and settles into the body just like snow falling and landing on the ground. It remains there, spreading its beauty all around, enhancing the already beautiful scenery even more. This feeling of surety is not run by the ego, there is no ego present. It comes from something much deeper within. Every cell, muscle, ligament, tendon and bone in the body is aligning together to create this affect, just like the elements of nature align to create this beautiful snow. Like the snow it is a rare thing which only becomes possible when everything aligns and comes together after everything that has preceded it.

This characteristic of Nadia's was probably the characteristic I admired the most. It's the culmination of; practise, repetition, personality, goals, dreams and desires. She always struck me as knowing she was the best and that this status was deserved, as it was born out of many life sacrifices. There were many reasons and justifications behind it. She worked extremely hard to step out of her comfort zone to confront her fears and, as the quote illustrates, to trample the fear beneath her feet and that is no mean feat (excuse the pun)! It takes enormous courage to not only adopt this attitude but to implement it in a decisive and productive way.

What makes it more special is the fact that she was a mere 14 years of age demonstrating this. How inspiring! From my own perspective I felt I had it in me to develop this characteristic in myself. If I could focus and stay conscious of it, I too could use it to benefit me the way that she did. Of all that I learned from her in those two weeks this characteristic was the most important quality I wanted to develop in myself for the future.

Little did I know at that time that I too would go on to make history in my own right or that how she inspired me would have such an influence that it would be a key factor in my future success. I am truly grateful to Nadia and the outcome that it produced for me.

CHAPTER 18
Desperate Jim
The Man Who Wanted To Be Good At Something...
Anything!

Jim Ryun was the first American High School athlete to break the 4-minute barrier for the mile distance in athletics after Roger Bannister. Unfortunately, I didn't come across Jim Ryun's story until much later in my own life, which was an awful pity as his story could have definitely helped me and inspired me on my own ventures in both basketball and athletics.

Jim Ryun's success story was such an enthralling story that he is still remembered as one of the best middle-distance runners ever. In 2007 the American sports channel ESPN ranked Jim Ryun just ahead of Tiger Woods and LeBron James as the greatest American High School athlete in American history. Fancy that! As they say in Dublin, 'You're not dealing with muck here.' He was ranked ahead of two extremely prominent sports stars – a majorly inspiring achievement. It was being true to his dream, not giving up and when things didn't work for him, starting the process again that set him up for his final successes. By observing his running style, changing his distance, upping his training regime, exploring what he could do differently and trying out different ideas again and again, he developed a wholeness in his character and performance. He found the *Perfect* way back, the *Perfect* coach to inspire him and ended up with the *Perfect* outcome that he so badly desired and deserved. As my friend Eddie Byrne said, 'Perfection can be both a momentary and lasting state of achievement achieved through perseverance.'

Jim Ryun, as a boy, spent hours and hours in his imagination visualising himself as a star pitcher on the National Baseball Team. He dreamt of being a pitcher, a catcher, a third baseman. This extended to him dreaming of being anything, it didn't even have to be baseball. For as long as the boy could remember, he had dreamed of being an athlete of any kind and he would take what he could get. He desperately wanted to aspire to something, to be part of a team, any team. He tried everything, baseball, basketball, long jump, pole vault, 100 metres hurdles, 50-yard dash and 400 metres. At everything he not only failed but failed disastrously. To deal with his floundering self-esteem and bitter disappointment, he turned to cursing, fighting, stealing, smoking, eating junk food and was even expelled from school. However, in the back of his mind somewhere his dream kept niggling at him. One day he decided to return to the track and the 400 metres for one more try. In the first race of his comeback, he led the 400 metres for the first half of the race, blew up, finished last and failed to make the team. However, having led the race inspired him to set a goal of running 52/53 seconds for the distance. The coach motivated him despite his defeat and this led to a major turning point in his running career. He went from not making it on to any team to eventually making it on to the C team. From here he progressed to Junior Varsity and ended up leading his team to the Kansas State Championship. At this point he was now competing in the mile distance.

This was Ryun's first major test in his new development programme. Egged on by his coach, he ran a blistering 4 minutes 21 seconds mile time which resulted in him not only winning the race but defeating the Kansas State Champion, a well renowned athlete in the process. On this occasion he had to run a perfect race to become the champion and he did. This race was the turning point for him beginning to make friends with the perfection principle engaging in what I call the process of perfection – he may have realised that paying attention to detail was the underlying component of achieving success in his sport. Therefore, perfection was a more sophisticated concept than he would have previously imagined. If this was the case, this realisation perhaps excited him and could have encouraged him to explore the idea further from a new perspective. At this stage, his transition from complete and utter failure to a newfound realisation of the importance of transforming failure into success was beginning to dawn on him. With the help of his coach, he learned that adopting a determined positive approach by setting goals was of the utmost crucial importance. The idea of achieving perfection is a daunting task as it is considered by most as impossible and it was alien to Ryun as he was only familiar with failure. However, there was something about overcoming failure that kept niggling at him. Reflecting on his progress to date, he could now clearly see that paying attention to detail was one of the underlying components of him achieving those successes. From analysing his strategies, techniques and training regimes, it would appear that every step he took to overcome his failures was bringing him a step closer to the principle of perfection.

After becoming the new Kansas State Champion and running that spectacular time of 4 minutes 21 seconds for the mile, Ryun's coach, Bob Timmons, during their race postmortem discussion, commented to Ryun that he thought he could and would become the first High School runner to dip under 4 minutes for the mile (just as Roger Bannister had done). Ryun thought that his coach was crazy in the head but nevertheless the seed had been sown and firmly planted. Ryun contemplated his coach's crazy idea despite pooh-poohing it initially and began to wonder was it a crazy idea or was it truly possible. His coach wasn't a man to say something he didn't mean or believe in which posed the question, what did his coach see in him that he didn't see in himself? He didn't have talent but did work extremely hard and it had paid off. He could see that since he had started aiming for the top, he made even greater strides in his improvement. His coach had managed to get it into his head that he could aim higher at each stage. His failure barriers were now beginning to be outnumbered by his successes. Could he obliterate his failures altogether? Could he turn the wheel around?

He knew that he would have to meticulously apply himself to this goal. He set about training with more vehemence and it looks like he consciously concentrated on perfecting his training regime a little more, hoping it would yield him further successful results. Later that same year of winning the Kansas State Championship he competed in another prestigious Championship and reduced his mile time to 4 minutes and 8 seconds. If his time of 4.21 was a blistering time I don't know how to describe this one. He knocked an unfathomable 13 seconds off his original time. This is a monumental result, in such a short period of time of just a few months and over a short distance into the bargain.

With his coach's predictions slowly but surely coming true, (although not slowly in the literal sense as Ryun was steaming ahead at great speed), he recognised his motivation had begun to soar considerably. The following year he began to train like a professional. His determination to achieve the goal set by his coach became his number one priority. The light at the end of the tunnel was drawing closer. Jim Ryun began to work extra hard, pushing through 100 mile training weeks and drastically increasing the intensity of his workouts, adding 40 repetitions of hard intervals of 400 metres to his training sessions and living with his coach in the summertime. He duly refined his attitude to paying attention to detail as a central part of his training programme and incorporated it into every single training session. This spurred him on to an incredibly high level of performance. There was no stopping him. In his Junior Year, at the age of 17 and after only two seasons on the track he attained his goal and ran the mile in 3 minutes 59 seconds smashing 9 seconds off his previous best time. Later that same summer he went on to qualify for the 1964 U.S.A. Olympic Team. I think we can safely say that at this stage his failure barriers had indeed been obliterated and put to bed permanently. He had transferred himself securely into a space where he utterly believed in his ability to be successful. His coach's predictions once again proving right and coming to fruition. In my view, each time he achieved a new personal best time in his races, going from 4.21 to 4.08 to 3.59 he could see that each personal best was an attainment of perfection in its own right. On each occasion he had run a perfect race on the day in question in order to win.

Jim Ryun's success story continued and at the age of 19 in 1966 he ran the mile in a world record time of 3.51.3. Only one year later, in 1967, he went on to break his own world record by running .2 of a second faster, recording 3.51.1. This world record remained in place for a remarkable 8 years, equivalent to a time span of 3 Olympics, remarkable considering that many athletes' careers are more short-lived. Jim Ryun's perfect race on that historical day in 1967, in my opinion, surely was the highlight of his career considering it was not a transitory moment, it had the sweetness of an 8-year lifespan which is a long time in athletics.

What an amazing, truly gripping and inspiring story. His journey from failure to indisputable success illustrates Ryun's qualities and traits. These traits culminated in him not being afraid to challenge and push himself beyond his limits and comfort zones, to achieve greater success than he ever thought possible. Jim Ryun's story is not only informative, but it epitomises the essence of greatness.

While I was never of course an Olympic champion, I do see in myself many likenesses to Jim Ryun. His need and desperation to be good at something, anything, matched my own. For years as a child growing up, I too wanted to be good at something, anything and I wanted to be acknowledged for this by my parents. As a child my mother had always compared me to my brother who was younger than me. She instilled in me a sense of my lacking in every field in comparison to him. According to her, he was good at everything and I wasn't. Like Jim Ryun, I chose sport as my way in, my hope, my dream. I didn't know how to deal with my floundering self-esteem and bitter disappointment or how to turn them completely on their heads. As a child I did the opposite to Jim Ryun. I dealt with my floundering self-esteem and bitter disappointment by keeping everything inside and secretly planning my destiny by fantasising. I was too terrified of my mother to act out the way he did because she would have killed me and it genuinely felt like she would have killed me.

I, too, was someone who always trained extremely hard and put 100 per cent effort into my training sessions. My desperation, like his, drove me on to do whatever I had to do regardless of the pain to achieve my goal. We were both good at doing what we were told, putting our heads down and getting stuck in. He responded extraordinarily well to his coach's encouragement and belief in him. I did the same. Having become acquainted with his story, I found it fascinating to later discover that I had increased my 400 metre training repetitions to 20, as he had increased his to 40. What an interesting coincidence! Jim Ryun, like myself, didn't believe he had any talent. We both pushed ourselves beyond our limits and comfort zones to achieve greater success than either of us ever thought possible. It would seem that we both befriended the principle of perfection. We both transformed our low self-esteem and bitter disappointment into self-belief which led us to success and joy. I was chuffed with myself to discover these likenesses between us. Jim Ryun's story reinforces even more the importance of the core qualities it takes to become successful and verifies that the bottom line is the same for everyone. Not giving up! Hard work, more hard work and even more hard work!!!

CHAPTER 19
The Year Refereeing Burst Into My Life.

It began with my friend Eileen. She joined Haroldites with me and took up the role of club referee for the Haroldites Team. The Dublin Ladies Basketball Board were the committee who organised the Ladies Dublin League and scheduled the matches for the Ladies Leagues from Division 1 down to Division 6. They had a rule which required every team to provide one referee to offer their services to referee the Ladies Leagues. If a team didn't provide a referee, they couldn't play in the competitive league. Of course, nobody wanted to become a referee, everyone wanted to play – who wants to be a referee when all that happens is you get screamed and shouted at, nobody likes you and everyone feels they have the right to abuse you? Referees were giving up their own personal and precious time for this incessant abuse and lack of appreciation! Referees were not paid either in those days, being primarily a voluntary position. This added to the lack of enthusiasm naturally. Ferocious abuse and grief for a big fat nothing in return. The clubs had to try and bribe their members in any way they could to become a referee in order to be able to play in the leagues. But this was easier said than done. No bribe was big enough to entice the players to succumb to this horrible task.

On the Haroldite's team, we were lucky that Eileen agreed to take it on. I don't know why she did to be honest, but nobody queried her about it too much, they were just grateful to her for doing it and were glad it wasn't them. Eileen was a good referee and she seemed to rather enjoy doing it which was even better for us. It took the pressure off the team having to worry about the problem recurring in the future. Eileen also played as well as doing her duty as a referee. We carried on enjoying ourselves playing. At this time Eileen was working in a solicitor's firm which had German connections and she loved her job. The working hours were ideal for her (9am to 5pm) as they didn't interfere with her basketball responsibilities.

Eileen and I by this time were growing closer as friends. Our friendship had developed nicely as a result of going to Eccles Street and as a result of playing basketball with Sr. Patricia and Haroldites. We socialised a lot together. When Eileen became an adult, she left Saint Clare's Children's Home and moved in to live with an aunt of hers by the name of Bridget. Bridget lived around the corner from me which was handy for myself and Eileen as we could see each other often. I used to call for Eileen whenever we were going to training and matches and she too would call for me. After training every week Eileen would bring me back to her house where Bridget would insist on feeding us lovely sandwiches and giving us tea to drink. Bridget was a gas character, great craic and extremely lively for her age. She loved feeding us as she maintained we were far too skinny and needed some extra padding especially if we were playing that terribly rough and fast game of basketball. She couldn't understand our enthusiasm for the game and the colossal amount of training that we did. 'You're cracked in the head the pair of you,' she would cackle at us. Of course, we would just shrug our shoulders and laugh our heads off at her. But we did love those sandwiches! At first when I tasted them, I didn't know what it was that was burning my mouth and setting my chest on fire. Eileen was in hysterics laughing at me as she had grown used to Bridget's cooking and her sandwich making and had developed a taste for Bridget's type of food. It transpired that it was raw garlic in the middle of the chicken sandwich. Bridget let me know in no uncertain terms that raw garlic was very good for your health, especially your chest and heart and with that mad crazy running around I was doing I needed something of substance to sustain me. I wouldn't dare refuse to eat it but over time just like Eileen, I got used to it and eventually developed a taste for it, I even got to like it. Bridget put garlic into everything she cooked so we had no choice but to get used to it. She was a superb cook and it wasn't long before I grew to love her mouth-watering and tasty meals.

We were going along merrily for a long time playing basketball, visiting Bridget and having great fun and great times. One day Eileen came home from work and told us that her boss had offered her a post in Germany for one year. Bridget and I couldn't believe it. It came out of the blue. Poor old Eileen, she didn't know what to do. It was a shock to her too. Her boss told her it would be a good opportunity for her to increase her work skills and it would also be a benefit to her to learn the German language. He knew she had commitments and he gave her plenty of time to think about it. At first, she felt completely overwhelmed by the idea, as did Bridget and I. The thoughts of losing my buddy was distressing for me and while Bridget had lived on her own before Eileen moved in with her, she had become used to Eileen living there and having her company. Naturally, she too was upset at the idea of Eileen going off. In the end, after much consideration and thinking of the pros and cons, Eileen decided to go. Poor Bridget and I were broken-hearted, but we also wanted to support Eileen in what she thought was the best thing for her to do. She kept telling us it was only for a year and she would be back before we knew it. We didn't feel that though, we felt that a year was an interminable length of time not to see her. Unlike nowadays, there were no mobile phones, emails or skype to keep in touch. The only way was through writing letters which took a long time to be delivered.

On Eileen's departure there were many tears shed and promises to write loads of letters to keep in touch. It was my first major loss of a friend. It hit me quite hard and it hit poor Bridget quite hard too.

A quick shimmy to tell you about Bridget: After Eileen left, I decided to keep up my visits to Bridget as if Eileen was there because I knew she would be lonely and missing her. Bridget was grateful for this and it was through this process that Bridget and I became extremely close staunch friends. As the years rolled by, she became one of the most important and significant people in my life. She influenced me in a productive and positive way.

Bridget was light years ahead of my own mother in terms of her modernised view of life. She was highly intelligent, sharp minded, quick-witted and an amazing independent thinker. An amusing story I'll always remember is when the first divorce referendum in 1986 took place and Bridget went to mass one Sunday. Outside the church were two elderly ladies campaigning against divorce. They assumed Bridget at eighty-six would be one of them and handed her one of their leaflets. Bridget took the leaflet, scrunched it up and threw it back at them saying, 'I'll have you know, I'm voting for divorce.' She took great pleasure in relaying this story to me. Her giggle was full of divilment. She knocked many corners off me and opened up my own thinking processes, challenging me to expand my narrow and linear thinking. We always had great discussions about anything and everything.

Bridget was an avid reader, reading newspapers and books from the library to beat the band. It was a pity that there was no such thing as going to college in her day, as I would say she would have been an exceptional student and would have ended up in a highly intellectual, sophisticated career of some sort. Bridget worked in a health shop which was unusual for someone of her generation. She was brilliant at her job and knew everything upside down and inside out about the ganzy loads of products in the shop. Whenever I had anything wrong with me, Bridget always had a cure. It never failed. She was a great woman for the various potions, vitamin tablets and everything else that was going. She kept up to speed on the most recent updated material and was great at trying everything out herself which ensured that she knew more about it!! Her knowledge and memory were nothing less than admirable. Every single piece of information was on the tip of her tongue and she cured many people of their ailments. So good was she that the shop kept her on until she was seventy-five years of age. Quite remarkable and unheard of in those days! I knew Bridget for twenty-three years in total and not once in those twenty-three years did I see her with a cold, flu or sick stomach. She was eighty-seven when she had to go into hospital for the first time in her life. An advertisement for garlic, cider vinegar and the many bits and bobs she used to take if you ever saw one.

Bridget was eighty-nine when she died and her death was one of the most harrowing deaths of my life. She gave me great reprieve from my own family environment with my own mother. We had hours and hours of fun and laughter that I'll never forget as long as I live. We had a great social life going to the theatre, the concert hall, the cinema, musical society productions, restaurants and hotels for meals. We shared family gatherings and get-togethers and she knew my boyfriends along the way. Despite her thinking I was nuts, she supported me and was extremely proud of me when I achieved my Grade 1 and FIBA Refereeing awards. She taught me a huge amount in those twenty-three years and she contributed enormously to shaping me into the person I am today. I have so much to be grateful to her for that it's impossible to record it. I loved her dearly and she loved me dearly. We were a perfect match for each other. We brought a lot of richness into each other's lives, colour, humour and adventure. We challenged each other in many forms which deepened our relationship in trust and love. To this day I think of Bridget frequently and visit her grave whenever I can. I often wonder and ponder on what she would think about me now if she was alive. For sure she would still deem me as nuts but I know she would love me for it nonetheless. It is interesting that all these years later I am writing this book considering reading was one of her favourite pastimes. I have no doubt she would have loved reading this book and would be chuffed at being included in it. The book would definitely have the word nuts in its title if Bridget had anything to do with it!!!

Getting back to Eileen's departure and its effect on us. The next effect was on Haroldites and her being our club referee. Before she went, she discussed the situation with the team. A team meeting was called and of course nobody wanted to take her place. Eileen tried to reassure us that it wasn't as bad a job as we thought but we weren't having any of it. We couldn't be fooled. As I've said already, not one of us could understand how she liked it. The team was in the complete doldrums over it and it was unanimous that everyone would rather stop playing than referee even though we didn't want to do that either. The meeting ended with no takers on the job.

During the next week Eileen called in to me and asked me to take over the job. She didn't want to stop playing either, even though she was going to be away for a year and wanted to be able to play when she came back.

Mary: No way Jose! I am not doing it! I would be no good at it anyway. I would hate it.

I could see by her face she wasn't accepting what I was saying but I was determined not to get hooked.

Mary: It's definitely not my thing. I don't have the time between work and the training I'm doing. You know how much I train. I couldn't possibly fit it in, it's too time consuming. I have enough on my plate!

She had an annoying pleading look on her face and before she could speak, I suggested one of the other girls who was a person that had more time on her hands than I did and told Eileen to try her. She gave in for now. She spoke to the other girl but to no avail and of course she came back to me. I nearly flipped at the pressure she was putting on me. She tried every angle possible.

Eileen: Ah go on, you're my best friend, won't you do it as my friend. You're always telling me how much you care about me. It's only for one year. Don't be selfish. Think about the team. They need you to do it, otherwise the team won't be able to play in the League. You'll have to join another team who has a club ref.

Mary: Yeah sure, I'll be stuck with it and anyway what happens if you don't come back? What then?

I knew she had got to me. I was beginning to falter. She promised me faithfully that she most definitely would be back and she would take it over again.

Mary: But it's only for one year. After that I'm out whether you come back or not, but if you don't come back, I will kill you.

She clapped her hands and jumped for joy.

Eileen: Let's tell the team, they'll be over the moon.

Mary: Well, I am *NOT* over the moon.
I said grumpily and resentfully.

It goes without saying, the team were thrilled to bits and couldn't stop thanking me for saving the day. It didn't help me to be more gracious about it unfortunately as I was **SO** against it. When Sean heard the news, he put his usual grin and smirk on and of course Bridget told me I was nuts. She was the only one with any sense!

I was dreading my first match and was like a divil when going out onto the court. In those days there was no training, you just put the whistle in your mouth and off you went. Eileen had shared many stories with me about the abuse she got while refereeing. I was in such bad humour that I said to her:

Mary: Woe betide anyone that says anything to me or dares to look crooked at me. I'll put them straight off and they won't play the rest of the game!
She laughed and said:

Eileen: You can't do that!

Mary: You wanna bet? Just watch me! If they think that I'm giving up my personal precious time to be abused they have another thing coming to them!

So it was. You know what they say 'Start as you mean to go on.' Well, I did. My foul humour and my resentful face obviously spoke volumes – more than I realised myself – so much so, that in that first match nobody said boo to me. When I told Eileen, she couldn't believe it. Upon reflection now, my bad humour did me a favour and replaced any nervousness I otherwise would have been feeling. It gave out a strong message 'Don't mess with me or you'll be sorry.' While that's the way I truly felt inside, I was rightly pissed off at having to referee, I had no idea at how tyrannical I was coming across. The resentment was oozing out of me and was running the show. I was that pissed off I didn't even notice players shrinking away from me, nor did I care. I just wanted to get the match over and done with so that I could go off and do my own practise. The teams were *not* going to delay me unnecessarily I can tell you. I had no intention of mollycoddling them and wasting time trying to humour them. It was a case of 'Keep your mouth shut and concentrate on playing the game. You play and I'll ref. You can't do both, do the one you are supposed to be doing and leave me alone to do my job.' Eileen was shocked at my authoritarian attitude. She said, 'Jesus, I've never seen you being so dictatorial before.' I said, 'It might have something to do with the fact that I'm seriously pissed off and it's not a good idea for anyone to cross me when I'm this pissed off.'

My refereeing career started with a bang as a result of this but in hindsight it was a good thing. It gave me a great presence and was extra beneficial when refereeing boy's or men's matches. Strangely enough, it earned me a lot of respect and resulted in me having no trouble in my matches. The players knew I meant business and they mostly just got on with playing and focusing their attention on the game rather than my refereeing. Because I was small in height, having a strong presence was an extremely important attribute to have as a referee. You can just imagine 6' 4" (1.93m) men standing over me, looking down on me, querying a call I made. 6' 4" (1.93m) or more didn't bother me I can tell you when I was in that mood. It took quite a while for my resentment to subside and by the time it did, I had found my style as a referee and had my matches under control. The Dublin

Officials Association (D.O.A.) got wind of the new kid on the block and sent a representative to observe me. I didn't know anything about anything at that time. I was just fulfilling my duty in replacing Eileen. The representative was highly impressed by my refereeing ability and approached me to have a chat with me. I let him know that I was just doing Eileen and the team a favour and that I wouldn't be continuing once the year was over. He was shocked at how adamant I was and was sweeter than sweet towards me and tried to exert his persuasive skills on me. It was bad timing on his part because I was still stuck in my resentment and fury. We chatted a bit more and then he left.

I was telling Bridget about my encounter and her first response was, 'You must be very good, much better than you think you are.' I pooh-poohed her response, telling her I couldn't wait for the year to be over and for Eileen to come back. She laughed at me and said as usual, 'Well you're nuts. They never said that to Eileen. Eileen was good but you must be better.' 'Not at all,' said I. 'He was just trying to plamás me because they must be short of referees. Nobody wants to referee.' I never thought any more about it and just continued doing my duty until eventually the year was up. I was so delighted and excited that I was done and I would be seeing Eileen again soon.

Bridget and I couldn't wait to see her. Bridget cooked Eileen's favourite meal as a welcome home for her and made her favourite desert. I got candles and we dressed the table nicely to make her homecoming extra-special. We were highly excited. Eileen's sister was collecting her from the airport and bringing her straight to Bridget's house. We had welcome home banners to create a welcoming atmosphere for her. She got the shock of her life when she entered the house. She had never seen the house decorated like that before. Eileen was thrilled at the welcome we gave her and was touched by it. We sat down the four of us and had a beautiful meal. We couldn't wait to hear her news. Even though we had kept our promises in writing regularly there was an awful lot of news to tell that we hadn't heard before.

Eileen had a great time away and only missed us and her basketball. Apart from that she had settled in well in Germany, had started to learn the language a bit and thoroughly loved her job. She said she was glad she went; it was a great experience. Her boss was right. He had been good to her and had gone to extra trouble to help her to settle in as he appreciated she was on her own and that must have been quite daunting for her. He admired her courage as not many people, women especially, would have managed as well as she did. According to Eileen, he continually supported her and watched out for her for the whole year.

We spent hours and hours that first night chatting, laughing and catching up on each other's news. Believe it or not, we didn't even mention the refereeing once!! At the end of the night we were exhausted and collapsed into bed. We needed no rocking that night I can tell you. We conked out asleep. The next day Eileen came down to training with Haroldites and they gave her a tremendous welcome back. We played around at the end of training and Eileen thoroughly enjoyed it. Playing basketball again made her realise how much she had missed it. There were great celebrations and it was great for me to have my friend back. I had sorely missed her. We took up where we had left off, as if she had never been away and quickly before we knew it, it was like the good ol' days again. Everything was back to normal. I was in heaven and in good humour again. The team were extremely funny in relaying the stories to her about my bad humour and how much I missed her and they mimicked some of my antics to her. She fell around the place laughing. She thought it was hilarious. Not for one moment did she think that her leaving would have that effect on me or that I would miss her that much. They told her that this was another reason they were glad to have her back because now I could be the *old* me.

For fun they exaggerated the refereeing stories to her, telling her stories about me terrorising the players into silence and not allowing them to complain about my calls. They made up a couple of fibs just to wind her up. They concluded by saying that for sure the players would be delighted to have her back refereeing instead of me. I concurred with this of course. I couldn't wait to get the whistle out of my mouth.

The summer holidays were starting at this time. The leagues were finished but Sean used to keep us training over the summer. It took Eileen a while to get back into it again as she had lost her fitness and her skills levels had dropped as a result of being out of practise. She couldn't get over how much we had improved while she was away and the training was a shock to her system. We dragged her along and kept encouraging her through her pain. 'If you don't use it, you lose it' became extremely evident to her in that time. Sean always made it his business to make sure we didn't lose anything whenever there was a break. This was another reason why we beat teams we shouldn't have. We caught them on the hop after a break.

It was a great summer that year for me especially as I spent many happy hours with Eileen again both playing and practising basketball and renewing our social engagements. Unfortunately, the summer flew in and we were back in autumn with the basketball leagues and games resuming in September. Eileen went back refereeing again as she had promised. I had done my first refereeing exam at the insistence of the D.O.A. before the season had finished. Having done exceptionally well in the exam I jumped two levels from trainee up to Grade 3. While I was glad to pass the exam, it didn't mean anything else to me because I was giving up refereeing anyway. Once again, the D.O.A. tried to persuade me to continue, but I said no, Eileen was back and she was taking over again.

Everything continued as normal until Christmas came and went. In the New Year, Eileen's boss asked her if she would like to go to Germany again. Ah feck! They were looking for someone to go and she was the ideal choice as she had been there already. Once again Eileen was torn, she had just settled nicely back into her job in Ireland, was enjoying playing and refereeing basketball again and was taken aback at this unexpected offer. I was furious with her boss and what I said about him I couldn't possibly write down here. I just felt he had the knack of destroying our perfect friendship by separating us and making things difficult for us. I wanted to go into the office and bite his head off. Needless to say, Eileen wouldn't let me do that! This time Haroldites and I fought a much stronger battle with Eileen to dissuade her from going, after the extensive torture we had gone through with her being away the first time. We begged her not to go because maybe this time she wouldn't come back. There was no one year stipulation on this offer. We smelt danger in the air. She said that she could come back whenever she wanted to, her boss had made that clear to her. I tell you that man was my least favourite man on the planet! How could he not know the torture he was putting us through! Bridget too was dismayed as she was delighted having Eileen back in the house with her and having someone to fuss over again. Like me, she had missed her terribly that year and writing those volumes of letters just wasn't the same as physically having the person present with you.

Eileen told her boss she needed time to think about it, that while she enjoyed the year in Germany, she also had been homesick and she was now enjoying being back home again. It was only now she realised how much she too had missed Bridget, me and her basketball. It turned out that she had thrown herself into her work as a way of avoiding the homesickness that she had been feeling. Because she was on her own, she didn't have anyone that she could talk to about it. She had no choice but to bury it and avoid dealing with the emotions it was bringing up in her. But now she could feel the depth of these emotions, especially when we were displaying our emotions to her.

She thought about it for a long time and decided to stay for the time being. She felt she wasn't ready to go back at this moment in time but didn't want to shut it down completely either. She wanted to leave the door open. Of course, there may not be an opportunity in the future either, this offer might be the only one but nevertheless she wanted to leave the door open. It was too soon to go back. Her boss was accommodating and understanding apparently. Hump him anyway! So well he might be! The cheek of him spoiling our lives!!! Anyway, we were relieved and hoped that in time it would be forgotten about.

Of course, we should have known better. Life has a way of messing up your happiness. The offer came up again eventually and the next time Eileen took it. We were broken-hearted yet again. Action replay. Take two! That's when the shit really hit the fan. The first time was bad enough, but the second time was worse. The worst thing that could possibly happen, happened to me, I had to take her place as club referee again. This was the icing on the cake. If you thought I was bad the first time, *well!* the second time was even worse. The first time I was resentful. The second time I was furious beyond resentful. As a result, I became rebellious. That old familiar feeling of injustice that I had grown up with reared its ugly head once more. That man! I wanted to kill him the same way I wanted to kill my mother. I knew in my heart and soul that this was it. Eileen wouldn't be coming back. I could feel it in my bones. She didn't announce that of course, but I knew, I knew, I could feel it. I think she knew too but she couldn't admit it or bring herself to say it.

The second goodbyes were completely different to the first ones. There was a dismal air of dismay. Would we see each other again? We didn't know. She did come back to visit twice in the following year that I can remember. After that she never came back. Once Bridget died, I had no link to keep track of her. The letters faded out and I never saw her again.

CHAPTER 20
The Power Of The Whistle.

Eileen's second departure threw me into another emotional state of chassis. For ages I felt down and out about it. Poor Bridget and I cried on each other's shoulders for months and months. The prospect that Eileen wouldn't be coming back weighed heavily on us. At least the first time there was no doubt that she was coming back and that made it easier to bear the separation, but this time was totally different. We were grieving her loss just as if she had died. Everything had changed. The energy in the communication through the letters going back and forth between us were streets apart in comparison to the first time. The first time we were delighted and excited to hear her news. This time we were secretly hoping that she wouldn't be as happy and content as the first time and we were hoping that her homesickness would escalate to an unmanageable level forcing her to return. Her letters seemed bright and cheery. Our letters were full of grief and missing her. I was upset, frustrated and angry but tried to hide these feelings whenever I wrote to her. It was lucky I had my basketball and running to release the excess energy of these feelings that were tormenting me, otherwise I do not know what would have happened. Running off all that steam and stress at least took the edge off it. I threw myself into my training even more as my way of trying to deal with these feelings. I increased my visits to Bridget to help her through too. I missed Eileen so much. It felt as if I had a huge hole in my stomach that couldn't be filled. Nothing I did or tried worked. It remained a big hollow hole like an empty vessel, a complete void. Haroldites felt sorry for me, they could see the effect Eileen's departure was having on me. They were incredibly good at trying to comfort me and supported me as much as they could.

Then of course the inevitable 'Don't mention the war' issue raised its ugly head again. *I didn't, DID NOT* want to be our club referee. The thoughts of it were overwhelming with the state of grief I was in. I had sworn the first time that if Eileen didn't come back, I wasn't doing it again. Like the previous time no one wanted to do it. Of course, they kept trying to persuade me, just like Eileen had done the first time, telling me how good I was at it etc. etc. Once again, I wasn't biting. I was in such foul humour; they had a mammoth task ahead of them. Eventually they got the brainwave of asking Sean to persuade me to do it. But I bit the head off him as well. This didn't put him off naturally being the ex-army man that he was. He probably thought, great! There's a war about to start. He just read the signs and bided his time to approach me again when he felt he had a better chance of victory. At this time, I can tell you *I WAS NOT* an easy person to get through to. I was completely embedded in my own state of self-pity and this made me quite impenetrable.

Anyway, Sean being the strategic man that he was, chose his moment carefully. He waited until he got me during one of our extremely intensive training sessions. In fact, he raised the intensity deliberately so that I was so wrecked from the session that my defences were down. We were both exhausted after it, but he managed to just about find enough wind to raise the topic with me again. In hindsight, if you were a fly on the wall, it must have been amusing. Both of us breathless, sweat dripping everywhere, two big red faces and barely able to stand up, we had what can only be described as a breathless argument. I don't know if you ever saw one of those before! Unusual and different! Due to the breathlessness and exhaustion, it didn't last too long. I explained to Sean that I didn't want to ref for loads of reasons. The two main ones being I didn't want my playing to suffer and lose my place of first five, full game, on the team and secondly, that it would remind me of Eileen too much and would make me miss her more. Having reffed that year that Eileen was away, made me realise that not everybody can referee. It takes a special type of person to become a competent referee. Refereeing is an extremely tough job. It's a job that nobody willingly wants to undertake. Before you even put the whistle in your mouth you are 50 per cent wrong. Referees must have the skill set to control and hold the tension and balance of everything that is going on around them including the match itself, the players, substitutes, coaches, table officials, the emotional element, pressure and emotional reactions instigated by the audience and the ability to be able to gel with your partner. It is a lot to hold and contain. Referees sometimes experience feelings of being criticised. They sometimes have had fearful experiences of having to be escorted out of the gym, having been locked in the dressing room until everyone has left. An odd instance of being attacked in the car park after the match has, unfortunately, been known to happen. There have also been episodes of referees receiving threats before important matches. No wonder it's difficult to get people to referee!

Surprisingly, through the sweat, Sean was very understanding and he guaranteed me that I wouldn't lose my place on the team. He panted and wheezed that playing and refereeing are compatible especially if you have a talent for both. He pointed out that I wouldn't have to referee many matches and could confine it to once a week. He also said that it could enhance my playing and vice versa. Sean said he would help me if I needed it and to feel free to go to him anytime with any questions or problems I might have. He asked me to give it a try for a while and see what happens and he promised to review the situation again in a few weeks' time. He also pointed out that I would be doing the team a great favour. I asked him what they had used to bribe him? He laughed and said, 'Ten free pints!' But only on condition that he succeeded in nobbling me! I managed a weak smile and replied, 'Well you better bloody well seriously reward me for sacrificing myself like this.' That was the first time I saw the *soft* side of Sean. I was surprised that he could understand my concerns and grief much more than I expected. Being the hard chaw that he was this was a nice experience. It was lovely to see the other side of him, as like myself, this side of him was well hidden. This was one of the incidences that brought us closer to each other. Some years later Sean's wife divulged to me that when he told her I was taking up refereeing he said, 'If she's a quarter as good at refereeing as she is at playing, she'll be a great ref and if she's half as good she might even go all the way to the top.'

I took Sean's advice and just signed up for one match a week. This turned out to be good advice as it gave me the breathing space I needed to break myself in gently and to adjust to life without Eileen. I was missing her terribly. Life felt extremely hard at this time. The team were so thrilled that they bought Sean twenty pints! (Not in one go obviously). They couldn't believe that he managed to overcome my defiance and pure stubbornness. They questioned him on how he did it. He just laughed and said, 'I used my (military) charm.' They roared with laughter and bellowed at him, 'What charm? You don't have any charm!' He just laughed and bellowed back, 'What do you mean I don't have any charm? You would be surprised at how much charm I have!' They cracked up laughing and replied, 'Yes we would, very, very surprised!!!'

So off I went again with a whistle in my mouth. I renewed my former style of *terrorisation* as described by Haroldites and this time it was fuelled further by my grief and further resentment of now being well and truly stuck with this job that I didn't want. My attitude had the added dimension of *you guys* meaning the players and coaches, 'better not even think about abusing, screaming, shouting at me or questioning my calls, never mind do it, as I am suffering enough and you are *NOT* going to add to my suffering. You will pay the price and be sorry if you do!!!'

At this time, I was quite naïve about the powerful position I was in as a referee and the power of the whistle in my mouth never occurred to me. I was just consumed with rage, resentment and bitterness. Prior to this everyone regarded me as the quiet, shy, girl. I was demure, extremely obedient and wouldn't say *boo* to a goose. This was the first mask I presented to the world upon stepping out of my home when I started to work for the first time. It was only through playing basketball at such an intensive level that a small part of a *hidden* me was given permission to emerge and reveal itself through my aggressive style of play. My drive to be the best I could be, created an outlet for this powerful hidden force. Suddenly, I could exert the pent-up emotions I had been feeling for years and use them productively, rather than in a destructive way. Being an army man Sean was the ideal coach to facilitate this process. His gruelling training sessions transformed these quiet, shy, demure feelings into a more aggressive, powerful, man-like expression. It suited the tomboy part of me that had developed through protecting my brother, by fighting his fights for him during our childhood. Unbeknownst to either Sean or myself at the time, this hidden part of myself was being given permission to gradually emerge.

Well, emerge it did! Refereeing introduced me to a new way of expressing myself. Part of my taking no shit style of refereeing was adopted from Sean, but I added in my own ingredients to create a potent force. This force I had was a mixture of my anger, resentment and sense of injustice from my childhood, a scary mix you might say but it seems to have worked. I had been severely repressed as a child through my upbringing and being deaf. The whistle in my mouth gave me a real sense of power and of having the ability to take charge. As a child I was never in charge of anything. The hidden wild animal that was somewhere inside me suddenly found an outlet. I could put the whistle in my mouth and give freedom to the wildness safely as the rules still provided a container for this powerful energy that I felt. Being quiet, shy and demure wasn't an option amongst those 6' 4" (1.93m), 6' 6" (1.98m) giants, especially the arrogant ones who thought they were God's gift to basketball. I needed the power of the whistle to be able to stand up to them in order to hold my own in relation to my calls and decision making.

I quickly learned that the way you blow the whistle is of vital importance in terms of selling your calls, thereby selling yourself as a referee. You have to blow the whistle in a sharp, authoritative, confident manner indicating that you are positive that the call you are making is the correct call. There's no room for indecision or being meek and unsure. You have to be clinical, factual and have a strong air of authority in your presence. The way you blow that whistle is one of the secrets to gaining respect from the players and coaches. You would be surprised at how many introductory referees blow the whistle in a nondescript way, shrinking away from the players as they blow it. This is like throwing meat to the lions. It gives the signal to the players that you are easy meat and they can devour you accordingly.

Coaches and players are constantly on the look-out to behave in a manner that is going to gain them an advantage to put them in a winning position. Taking advantage of the referees is their number one priority as they think that the more they can sway the referee and get the referee on their side the better. This can work two ways, by intimidation or by plamásing. With me they knew immediately that intimidation wasn't the way to go, better to get me onside in a more placatory manner. Thankfully they didn't bring me flowers, I would have chewed up the whole bunch. Mind you in the beginning of my career I wasn't easy to placate either.

Being small was a severe disadvantage. You can imagine why! In basketball it is considered that the taller you are, either as a player or referee, the better it is. The women who were generally small in Ireland, felt they were on an even footing and could come right up into my face to give out to me. The men, who when you are only 5' 1" (1.55m) and they are much taller, thought they could intimidate me by standing over me and looking down on me. I looked like half the size of most of the men. This didn't bother me in the slightest as my terrorising demeanour was ideal in standing up to them. I ended up intimidating them instead of the other way around. All thanks to the power of that whistle in my mouth... and the wild animal in me.

As I had my Grade 3 award, I was appointed to matches of a much higher standard than previously when I was a trainee. The D.O.A. were delighted I was back refereeing. Shortly after I returned, I was approached to see if I would be interested in joining the National League panel of referees. This would mean travelling around the country refereeing matches with different people in different places. It would also mean I would be refereeing at an even higher level which would most definitely improve me further. While I felt shocked at being asked, I wasn't keen to do this as it would be too time consuming. I discussed it with Sean and he encouraged me to give it a try, he thought it would be good for me. It meant I was going to be the youngest and smallest referee on the panel, a panel of 99 per cent men. There was only one other woman on the panel. The fact that it was all men didn't bother me. By this time, I was well used to being in men's company, between Sean and the guys I was running with in work. So that part wasn't an issue for me.

The main issue was I didn't want this to interfere with my playing career. I still wanted to put that first as I was enjoying playing immensely. When I look back on it now, it's amazing what you can do when you're young. I was still only about twenty-three. I learned a lot from refereeing with different people. It's fascinating at how different people's styles are. They vary hugely. Over time I was able to explore and incorporate aspects of other people's styles in to my own. It was fun trying things out, holding on to what worked and letting go what didn't work.

The turning point at which I began to enjoy refereeing came after I was appointed to referee a match with Sean. This was the first time we were to officiate together. I was thrilled to be his co-official. I couldn't wait for the match to come around. While Sean was a superb referee, he was also a controversial character. At times he was a pantomime. This is one of the things that made him quite unique. With his vain and commanding personality and being an army man, he was a tough one and nothing phased him. Abusive comments rolled off him like water off a duck's back. He could give as good as he got. His superior presence, which irritated some people, gained him a lot of respect with others. In refereeing terms, he was a force to be reckoned with. He could maintain control of a game no matter what the circumstances. He knew how to administer the power of the whistle! He was considered a legend.

That first game with Sean I will never forget as long as I live. It is etched in my memory for life. It was an exciting game which was highly competitive and went to the wire. I wasn't nervous refereeing with Sean because I knew him so well from his coaching and training. In general, referees were nervous and got rattled reffing with him because more often than not, they were trying to impress him and gain his approval and praise. *BIG* mistake of course! I knew all about that! I wasn't caught up in this behaviour, I was just able to be myself. I was able to weave myself in to fit in with his style rather than go against him. This was greatly beneficial as it kept me out of trouble, me being the rookie in this exceptionally close match. I remained calm and confident and didn't do anything stupid. I let him take the lead and followed tentatively, always remaining in my own place and not crossing over into his territory. Each referee has their own area of responsibility depending on where the ball is located at any given time. There is only one small area where both referees have dual responsibility and even this area has its guidelines as to how it is divided between them. I stuck to my own areas and left Sean to his which was the correct thing to do. Sometimes referees can step out of their areas of responsibility as a way of trying to impress or show off. This most definitely would **not** work with Sean. He liked his grade and his vast experience to be respected.

I had no trouble doing this and I didn't get unnerved by any controversial situations that occurred. Because the match was extremely tight, the coaches and players were on a knife edge. There was a lot of action spilling out everywhere on the court. I remained cool and calm and took it in my stride. I tracked Sean every step of the way and let him guide me through the challenges we were both presented with. As the lead and more senior referee, it was Sean's responsibility to stay in control and stay on top of the challenging and difficult situations that arose in the game. At one stage in the first half, when the scores were level, two players started squaring up to each other and there was potential for a fight to break out. Sean, as quick as lightning stepped in between the two players, blowing the whistle loudly and fiercely and separated them before they could hit each other a box. He signalled to me to stay where I was and to watch the other players, the coaches and the benches intently. If anything extra happened, it was up to me to pass on the relevant information to him. If players from either team come off the bench and come onto the court to get involved and encourage the fight as opposed to helping to break it up, all those players would be disqualified. I kept an eye on the benches, did what I was told and by doing this it prevented the situation from escalating any further, which was good.

Soon after this, due to the high tension in the game, we had what's called in basketball a *Special* situation. This is where more than one thing happens at the same time and you have to figure out what the penalties are and in which order they have to be administered. Sean blew a technical foul on a player for dissent. The coach started screaming and shouting at him, telling him he was blind and other colourful sorts of things. Sean blew a technical foul on the coach. In the meantime, while this was happening, a player from the opposing team committed an intentional foul (nowadays called an unsportsmanlike foul) on his opponent which I had to call. We had to record each and every foul and between us decide the penalties and the order. This was the first time I had a special situation to deal with. I was delighted to be with someone who knew what they were doing, because it meant I learned the correct procedure which would be helpful to me in the future.

I was delighted that this was Sean. It was helpful for me at this early stage in my refereeing career as we knew how to work well as a pair. We respected each other but in this instance and for the first time we were equals.

A technical foul is a foul which carries heavier penalties which helps to control the game. In those days, the opposing teams were awarded two free-throws plus possession of the ball for such a foul. These fouls on players also counted towards the players five personal fouls that you are allowed. So, it was a deterrent against abuse. Things were hot and heavy for a while after this melee and the teams eventually settled down.

In the second-half of the game one of the players on the away team committed a basket interference violation. The ball was on the ring and the player grabbed the net which caused the ball to be knocked off the ring. This is illegal and the team are awarded the basket. In women's basketball this doesn't happen often, especially in Ireland. While I knew about the rule, I had never seen this happen in real life, luckily enough for me it was in Sean's area of responsibility and he called the violation. I'm sure due to my inexperience I would have missed it and all hell would have broken loose as the match was level at this time. Quietly inside I breathed a sigh of relief and thanked the Lord for Sean.

After this incident, the next nerve-wracking thing that happened was one of the spectators threw a glass bottle onto the court which I'm pretty sure was aimed at Sean and myself. Luckily, it missed us and didn't hit anyone else either. Sean stopped the game and instructed the organisers of the home team to have the person removed from the spectator's area. The spectator had no intention of leaving the gym and a bit of pandemonium broke out amongst the crowd. Sean told the home team that if they didn't remove the person, he would stop the game and award the game to the other team. This shifted the organisers into action pretty quickly and they succeeded in removing the spectator from the gym. The spectator was screaming and shouting at us, hurling abuse to beat the band as he was forced out of the gym. While most people would have balked at this incident the thrill-seeker part of me liked the excitement of it especially as Sean remained as cool as a cucumber throughout the whole incident, acting as if he was used to dealing with this kind of situation every day of the week. This kind of incident wasn't unique to Irish basketball by any manner of means. Sean told me afterwards that the spectators in Greece were ferociously notorious for throwing coins onto the courts and the match organisers had to confiscate their coins from them before entering the gymnasium.

Looking back on this match now, I realise it was not only an important learning experience with such drama, but also because it lifted me up into a different relationship with Sean. I thoroughly enjoyed the match and reffing with Sean and we got out of the venue alive which was the main thing. Sean never commented on my performance on the way home in the car of course. What's new? But I knew myself that I had reffed a good match and used my intelligence wisely. I had the feeling that he was proud of me even though he didn't say so.

I learned a lot from reffing with him. I particularly learned about the importance of teamwork and respecting your elders and respecting experience over inexperience. I learned the importance of staying calm and cool under pressure. These were valuable lessons which stood to me no end in my future career. Sean also taught me some lessons in relation to the power of the whistle. He was a master in this regard. He used the whistle succinctly, effectively and creatively, conveying warnings to players and coaches alike, holding the whistle, sometimes wagging it, without one single word being uttered. Instead of using the whistle in a bossy manner, when circumstances warranted it, he could use it in a more genial manner, his body language conveying the message, accompanied by a roguish glint in his eye. This was a good preventative technique which stopped players from receiving technical fouls against them. His use of the whistle had the players eating out of his hand and contentious players were put back in their boxes. The players knew not to cross the line and to respect the threshold. When the match was over, it was over. Time to shake hands and have a few pints.

The whistle is truly an extraordinary thing. It has dimensions to it that I never thought possible. I have witnessed men, who are small and who feel insecure and insignificant because of their lack of height, using the whistle as a means to make themselves feel taller, more secure and more significant. Small men who told me they were often slagged on a sexual basis because of the small sizes of their willies – yes, driving to and from matches in the car we'd talk about anything – reported feeling that the whistle and the air of dominance it gave them made them feel powerful and forget their inadequacy down below. They described it as making them feel more like a man, more manly, more equal to other larger men. I couldn't believe this! I was shocked! This is one of the things that happens when you're around men all the time, you have to listen to and put up with the male talk, which of course, more often than not, is peppered with sexual innuendos and sexual jokes. All I could think of was 'I have many problems but thank heavens I don't have that one.' It made me feel sorry for men and the terrible sexual pressure they are under just as a result of their mere physicality. Incidentally and strangely enough, irrespective of whether I had a boyfriend or not, for these sexual innuendos the men never tried to chat me up or make a sexual move on me. Perhaps they saw me in a more brotherly way or maybe because of my strong tomboy male energy they perceived me as one of *Them*.

Another time in the National League I was refereeing with another veteran referee who was of Sean's generation and era. During the match a player on one of the teams was giving him an awful time, constantly demanding him to call the fouls on his opponents who he maintained were continuously fouling him. My partner eventually got pissed off and after a few warnings the player continued to question and moan at him and didn't stop. The next time the player was defending, my partner called a phantom foul on him. I couldn't believe it and was thinking, that wasn't a foul, he didn't touch the attacking player. Luckily, however, I minded my own business and said nothing. The player went berserk naturally. During the immediate next play, when the player was defending again, he called another phantom foul on him. At this point I had copped on that there was a method to his madness, even though I couldn't quite see what it was at the time. Well! The player went berserk again screaming, 'I never touched him, I didn't touch him.' This time the player stormed over to me repeating himself, looking for me to agree with him. My partner looked at me and I looked at him! Quick decision needed here! Shit! So, I looked the guy straight in the eye, shrugged my shoulders and gestured with my hands a gesture that said, 'I don't know mate' and pointed him in the direction of my partner as only he could explain what was going on. The player tramped back to my partner, ranting and raving like a lunatic. My partner also looked him straight in the eye, lifted the whistle up to show him and said, 'I think it's about time you realised that I'm the man with the whistle. I can blow what I like.' The player was totally gobsmacked, to such an extent, that he couldn't reply or retort to that one! The power of the whistle hit home to me. In that instance it worked a treat and the player never uttered another word for the whole match. It made me grin and smirk to myself for the rest of the match. How clever! I hadn't seen that one before! You sure do learn something new every day.

Whenever I was partnered with anyone in the National League, I always took the opportunity to ask them why they liked or even enjoyed reffing. Many of them said that the whistle made them feel important, in control. Back in the car some of them described feeling hen-pecked by their wives and that the whistle gave them the opposite feeling. The whistle made them feel they were the dominant one... well at least for an hour and a half a week! They liked that I would ask, 'Why can't you use the whistle feeling with your wife then if it makes you feel that good and stop the hen-pecking?' They mostly said, 'Oh, I couldn't do that, my wife wouldn't like it. I would be afraid she would leave me if I did that.' To my young mind that didn't make sense although I understood it completely because that's what my Da did with my Ma. I would reply, 'Is your wife not afraid that if she over hen-pecks you, you might leave?' Of course, this idea didn't occur to the men. It was an interesting observation.

In those days men always came across as the dominant ones, the breadwinners, the master of the house and yet underneath all that, these men were disclosing different information to me about their private lives. Yet on the basketball court while reffing I could see the opposite, their male dominance. The power of the whistle increased male egos. The whistle made the men stand up and walk tall. It gave them a commanding air of authority and, like they said, a sense and feeling of importance. The whistle enabled them to mask their vulnerabilities.

In the army you can see the way the whistle is used for training purposes both physically and administratively. The whistle has a military association to it. The trainers used the whistle to gain the attention of the officers and to request and demand silence. The whistle by the nature of its shrillness, loudness and sharpness gains an immediate response. It's amazing the effect it has. In a room full to capacity of people, the sound of the whistle blowing brings the whole room to a sudden, abrupt standstill. Complete silence descends and everyone's attention is focused on what's about to happen. A feeling of suspense hangs in the air. The same thing happens in basketball, football or any sport where a whistle is involved. Once the referee blows the whistle, silence descends and everyone is anxiously waiting to see what the call is. Players are always waiting in anticipation, wishing that it's not them, not their team, please let the whistle be against the other team. In the army and in sports training the whistle is effectively used to enhance training sessions. The sound of the whistle instils order, sharpness and stimulates alertness and concentration. A quicker, sharper response to the drill at hand gets activated by the use of the whistle. It makes people run in to place instead of walking in to place or remain standing. The whistle can be used to practise and develop stop-start reactions. It evokes a physiological response in the body, an urgent response. It alters consciousness and increases eagerness.

In general, people have a natural positive response to the sound of a whistle. From a human perspective, the whistle gains an alert reaction in the same way that the animal sounds alert each other to danger or a calling to come together. In the film 'The Sound of Music' there's a funny scene where the captain is demonstrating his control over his children to the prospective nanny. He uses a whistle, in true military style, to call the children to attention. They each in turn, in true military style, have to step forward and back to announce their presence and their names. The nanny (Julie Andrews) is of course horrified and completely taken aback by his authoritative military style. From his perspective however, he's convinced that it works, which it does in fact appear to do. His whistle commands respect, although the nanny had her own way of commanding respect!

Do excuse me while I go off on a tangent about the mighty whistle. People with sensitive ears, well any ears at all, will jump out of their skin if a whistle is blown right beside them into their ear. It's a horrible experience. Piercing, deafening and painful. It leaves you with a ringing in your ears that stays for a long time afterwards. It causes people to hold their ears and it takes a while to be able to hear properly again. Likewise, when you're blowing the whistle, the sound vibrates around your mouth. Biting down too hard on the whistle can damage your teeth. These are the aspects of the whistle that referees must become accustomed to in order to use the whistle in a proper manner.

When you think about the size of a whistle it's amazing that such a small thing can be such a powerful tool. Whistles are extremely durable and last for years despite the fact they are made from plastic. They are no weight and are easy to carry around. Whistles are used extensively throughout the world by referees, the army and the police. Rescue Services such as Mountain Rescue and Marine Rescue rely on whistles to save lives. Lifejackets on-board airplanes have built-in whistles. The thinking is that in rescue situations if you can be heard you can be saved. It's a known fact that during a traumatic situation the body goes into fight-or-flight mode, the laryngeal reflex could prevent someone from screaming but they can still blow a whistle if they have it available. The fight-or-flight reaction (and even a panic attack) affects each of us differently depending on the degree of stress and how we handle it and blowing a whistle just might be enough to get out of a bad situation.

Like everything in life, whistles and whistling can be misused. If misused they can have a negative effect on society. The captain in the film believed that he was using his whistle in a positive manner, however, using the whistle in the way he did could equally have had a dehumanising effect on his children. In basketball, spectators have been known to whistle derogatorily to let their disagreement and discontentment be known at the referee's calls. This is meant to and often succeeds in intimidating the referee. It can shatter the referee's confidence and unnerve them for the remainder of a game. Some spectators in the crowd may even possess their own personal whistle. They use the whistle to confuse and disrupt the game in order to gain an advantage for the team they are supporting.

On a personal level, I have been lucky to have had an overall positive experience in relation to the whistle. For me, it was just part of the game in the same way that the actual basketball is part of the game. The game can't be played without it. As a child, when I was deaf, I never heard the sound of a whistle. When I began to hear again and was being reintegrated into the hearing world my tolerance and threshold for noise was understandably low. When I started playing basketball, I had to be careful to stay away from the whistle as my ears were still extremely sensitive. The loud shrill sound of the whistle in my ear caused me severe pain. By the time I became a referee, thankfully I was now able to tolerate that shrill piercing sound. Lucky enough, my hearing had come a long way from when I was a child, otherwise, I may not have been able to referee. My own sensitivity around the shrillness of the whistle gave me the awareness to be mindful of the same thing happening to the players on the court. I was conscious that the sound of the whistle for anyone, hearing or non-hearing, can be painful and disturbing.

There you are. I'm back off that tangent. Let's get back to basketball. By the time I decided to upgrade to Grade 2 level, I had learned to master the whistle in a cohesive, effective and authoritative way. This was a huge advantage and helped me enormously for that exam. After just one season of refereeing at Grade 3, I was able to apply to go forward for my Grade 2 exam. This was a quick progression because normally it took a few years at Grade 3 level before one would be ready to apply for Grade 2.

CHAPTER 21
Onwards And Upwards.

As I became more experienced, I became wiser in relation to improving my refereeing style and improving the way I used the whistle. I was able to read the game better and become more selective in choosing what was appropriate and what wasn't appropriate to call in certain games. I learned that different games required different application of the rules, the whistle, refereeing style, personality traits, communication and teamwork with co-officials. It was important to be versatile and flexible in my approach to games. I became aware that one size does not fit all. Game management and game control are two of the most vital aspects of refereeing. However, games can be managed and controlled in a variety of ways. The more options you can apply the better. These qualities are ones that separate the average referee from the excellent referee. There's always something new to learn and new challenges to master. It is good to keep an open mind and to be willing to be adventurous when endeavouring to become the best. Due to the speed of the game of basketball, things are constantly changing and never remain the same. This is one of the things that makes the game exciting to play and exciting to referee. It most certainly is not a game that becomes dull and boring.

When I applied to the D.O.A. to sit my Grade 2 exam they were open and receptive to me. I had to attend a Grade 2 refereeing course which went on for a long weekend, at the end of which you had to sit the written examination. Upon passing the written exam you went forward to the practical stage. You were then appointed to a high-level match which had to be Men's Division 1 standard. For this exam the person being examined had to be appointed as the lead referee. The criteria for passing the practical exam was strict. The examiners were assessing to see if you could step-up to taking the lead position, apply the refereeing mechanics properly and if something happened that meant you had to referee the game on your own would you be able to do this? They were also assessing your ability to manage and control the game, manage and control the players and coaches and manage and control any unforeseen situations that might unexpectedly arise in the game. One of the biggest requirements was your ability to watch off-the-ball incidents.

This was extremely different from the Grade 3 requirements. For Grade 3 you had to be able to blow the whistle, blow the fouls and violations accurately and be able to apply the rules at a basic level. The standard of the match just had to be good enough to make this assessment. The Grade 2 was much more challenging as, to begin with, the game had to be of a much higher standard. That raised the bar considerably from the get-go. I was lucky that the match I was appointed to was competitive and close. I referee much better under pressure and also find it much easier to keep my concentration when the match is tight. There's no room for my mind to wander. It's also easier to make the foul calls and violation calls because generally in a close match these can be more straightforward. It is, therefore, easier to be more decisive because everything is more clear-cut. In Men's Division 1 the players are extremely skillful and minor violations that happen in lower standard games don't occur. Skills such as screening on and off-the-ball are more commonly found in the higher division matches rather than the lower division matches. Screening on and off-the-ball tests your ability as a referee to focus on your area of responsibility, trust your co-official and apply the principle of preventative officiating. Screening is an offensive devise where the player blocks the defensive player to create an opening for the attack. Training oneself as the referee to watch off-the-ball is a mammoth task as the ball is like a magnet and it is extremely hard to take your eyes away and *NOT* watch the ball. It requires excellent peripheral vision and acute observation. When the action is hot and heavy, we referees would need eyes in the backs of our heads. However, it's extremely important because more often than not, it is the off-the-ball incidents that cause fighting situations to develop and occur. The players need to know that you **are** watching them closely because if they see that you are not, it is easy for them to take advantage of this and take risks which end up causing trouble.

This is one of the hardest skills of the game for referees to master. Some referees succeed and some actually don't succeed. If you don't master this skill, it is unlikely you will progress any higher than Grade 2 level. This was one of the areas I had been working on in my National League matches. Because I was reffing with higher graded and more experienced referees, I was able to truly practise this skill as I never had to worry about my partners not being good enough or capable enough of blowing the calls in their own areas of responsibility. They encouraged me to practise this skill and taught me it's importance. I used to ask them to point it out to me when I didn't do it to become more aware of it. This they did which helped me enormously. Sometimes we even had fun doing it because something funny might happen instead of something serious. One time I remember two players off-the-ball were behaving childishly, sticking their tongues out at each other and making horn signs with their fingers on their foreheads, singing, 'Nah nah ne nah nah you can't stop me!' Would you believe it? It was something you would only see in kindergarten but here they were, two grown men, behaving like babies. My co-official and myself had a good ol' laugh at it at the time, discreet sniggers and afterwards it ignited one of those driving home in the car discussions on the journey and our sniggers were less discreet.

Anyway, back to my Grade 2 exam, I passed with flying colours and was delighted with myself. I felt this was a big achievement and it increased my motivation to continue. For someone who was giving up refereeing forever, at that time when Eileen took over again, I had come a long way in one year. The advantage of having my Grade 2 meant that I could now be appointed to even higher standard games and be appointed to other games as lead referee. This put me in a position of extra responsibility which was great for my further development. By now I was enjoying refereeing much more than in the beginning. The fact that it didn't interfere with my playing career and that I was able to hold my position on my team assisted this process. Sean was right when he said playing and refereeing could enhance each other. Referees who have played basketball have an advantage over those who haven't. Their feel for the game is enhanced through playing. Referees who have a good feel for the game are more popular than referees who ref by the book only. What am I saying here? I was popular as a referee?

My playing also improved as I understood the rules better and was able to relate much more to the referees than before. Refereeing also helped me to observe and appreciate other players' skills which I was able to add to my own repertoire. It improved my judgement as a player and the fact I could now read the referees gave me an extra advantage in determining what I could and couldn't get away with in any given match. From the opposite perspective the fact that I was playing at such a high level improved my refereeing. It gave me a stronger feeling for the game as I could understand what the players and coaches were trying to do and achieve. These combined skills of refereeing and playing brought me to a new level of what I call perfection. The foundation of my love for perfection which originated in my childhood through my father's shed, my auntie's dressmaking and my experiences with the Girl Guides was growing and developing through these extra skills I was acquiring. I was then able to transfer them to all aspects of my sports.

In those early days of refereeing, I didn't realise exactly how uniquely my skill set was developing. Let me explain further. I mentioned previously the ball is like a magnet for the ten players for the duration of the game. For the referee, perhaps surprisingly, that's not the case. Their focus is the ten players on the court. When I was a player, I was 100 per cent a player, totally focused on the ball, winning the ball, winning the game. When I was reffing, I was 100 per cent the referee, focused on the 10 players, impartial, controlling and managing the game, tasked with providing a professional service. For me the boundaries between these two roles never became blurred. It was like there were two succinctly different brains in operation, player brain versus referee brain. Passion versus professionalism. My player brain operated within a pure passion for the game, while my referee brain was acquiring predominantly a purely professional approach to the game.

I continued on as a Grade 2, developing more and more as I began to take the lead referee role in matches. Various aspects of my style were also improving. My hand signals were becoming perfect, crisp, sharp, clear. There was no indecisiveness in them. Their perfection gave me a greater air of authority, made me look surer of myself and more in control. Some of my brashness disappeared and was replaced by a confidence that wasn't arrogant but self-assured. It communicated a sense of knowing, that I knew what I was doing, that I wasn't guessing or doing things just for the sake of doing something.

Referees sometimes can go quite a while in a match without making any calls. This can be unnerving, especially if it happens that your partner is making all the calls and you are not. Due to the different areas of responsibility this can happen. It's very important not to panic in this situation, to stay calm and wait for your turn to come. It *will* come. But often referees panic and make a call just for the sake of blowing something and as you can imagine this is not a good thing, it never works out. It generally results in the players becoming angry and frustrated and disturbs the balance of the game. In basketball it's extremely important to allow the game to flow and not to stop the game unnecessarily for incidental things that have no effect on the game. It comes under what is called the advantage/disadvantage principle of officiating, allowing play to continue if a foul doesn't impede the progress of the player. I was good at this which was another advantage I gained from playing that had enhanced my refereeing.

I was enjoying the extra responsibility that the Grade 2 award provided me with and I was settling into my new role nicely. Before I knew where I was, a year had passed by. I was 26 at the time. As I mentioned already there was only one other female referee, Rita, on the National League panel at this time. She decided to apply for the Grade 1 award. This was ultra-prestigious as there was no Grade 1 women, they were all men. Being the only other woman, of course I was one hundred per cent behind her hoping she would make it through. It would be a great day for women if she succeeded in breaking that male dominance and barrier. When it came to her practical exam, I went along to support her. I was fond of her anyway and I thought she was an incredibly good referee. I liked her style. She refereed what I thought was a good match with some mistakes but nothing of great importance. Unfortunately, I was wrong because she didn't pass and she was sorely disappointed afterwards as like me, she thought she had done enough to succeed. This meant if she wanted to do the exam again, she had to wait another year and return to the probationary stage. I felt sorry for her because it's awful to do well or think you've done well and find it's not good enough. I tried to reassure her as best I could that for sure she would pass the next time. By the time she repeated the exam I had completed my second year as a Grade 2. What a quick two years!

Rita decided after much ado to have another bash and take the Grade 1 exam one more time. She worked extremely hard during that time, trying to improve on the areas of her game that the examiners had given her critical feedback on. She felt she was ready and in good shape to give it another go. Once again, I went to support her and I could see the difference in her performance. There were fewer mistakes, she was much more dominant and confident and she most definitely stepped up to the challenge to a far greater degree than the first time. I was delighted for her and was totally sure that this time she couldn't fail, she most definitely was going to pass. As you can imagine there was huge tension and pressure on the game. This second time she was more prepared and was able to stand up to the pressure and handle it much better than the first time. I thought this was another plus in her favour for passing.

After the match was over, I waited for her with her husband. He too was a referee and knew about the significance and the importance of the finer details that would go towards the examiner's decisions. He too thought she had reffed a much better game than the first time. We were both quietly confident and hopeful that this time she had succeeded and would go down in the history books. It seemed like we were waiting for her for a long time to come out of the room where the examiners had taken her to discuss the match with her. I don't know if it was our nerves or what, the tension in the air, the unrelenting suspense that was gripping us, but we thought she would never come out. After what seemed like an eternity she appeared and we knew by the tears in her eyes that it was bad news. The three of us headed off as she wasn't able to speak to us immediately. We left the gym and went to a nearby pub to have a chat. When she regained her composure, she told us that she had failed again. She was bitterly, bitterly disappointed as she too thought she had upped her game considerably which she hadn't thought was possible after her first failure. This added to her disappointment naturally. After all that hard work and improvement and to do exceptionally well on the day under that pressure and to still fail was a bitter pill to swallow. It made her think and question what did she have to do to pass? If this wasn't good enough, what would it take?

Her husband was sympathetic and tender towards her. He too was bitterly disappointed for her and could relate to her devastation as he had supported and encouraged her and honestly felt she could do it. At the end of our chat he said to her, 'Third time lucky.' She replied, 'There won't be a third time. I can't see how I can improve to the level that they are looking for.' The examiners had given her positive feedback which left her questioning how could she have failed? They told her they were surprised and amazed at how much she had improved after the first exam and had very few negative pointers to point out to her. So why did she fail? Was it simply that they didn't want a woman to enter their all-male domain? If that was the case, why? What harm could a female do in a 99 per cent male-dominated arena? 99 to 1.... What was their problem?

Her husband and I advised her not to make any rash decisions right now. It wouldn't be the right time. Better to feel the disappointment and give herself time to recover from it. It would take a while to get over it and to feel strong enough to pick herself up and go for it again. I said I would keep in touch with her and would help her in any way I could. This I did, but unfortunately, she got such a sickener from the whole experience that she decided not to re-apply for the third time. She genuinely felt she couldn't hack a third fail. Two was enough for anyone. I tried to explain to her that it wasn't only herself she was fighting, it was the system and it would take a lot of guts and courage to break the system. She agreed but felt she didn't have it in her to take on this battle, this enormous battle, probably this futile battle. I pleaded with her to take more time before making a final decision. Maybe in a few weeks she would feel different. Herself and her husband continued reffing for another year, after which they moved to Donegal and both stopped refereeing altogether. It was an awful shame because they were a lovely couple and lovely people. I was sorry for Rita that her reffing career ended in this way. She never did get over the disappointment fully I think and I can totally understand why. It's one thing to see results for your hard work and commitment but it's another thing when you end up feeling that the hard work didn't pay off and not only that, but the hopelessness that nothing would be good enough no matter how hard you tried. I'm sure that has to be soul destroying.

That was the end of Rita and now I was the only female on the National League panel. Rita's parting words to me were, 'Maybe Mary you'll be the one to do it – you never know.' I could only think I had two chances to do that, slim and none! However, her words continued to tumble around in my head for months. In order to apply for Grade 1, you had to be a Grade 2 for two years. I honestly didn't think I could do it. I didn't think I was even at the same standard as she was never mind higher, which obviously I could see I would have to be. Nevertheless, I couldn't get her words out of my head. I tried to dismiss them numerous times, but they kept creeping back in. What to do now? Where do I go from here? This was a completely different ball game altogether.

I was convinced it wasn't just an exam I had to tackle; it was an exam plus an impenetrable system. Two challenges for the price of one!!! How could I possibly take that on? If she couldn't do it, what would I have to do to surpass that mega resistance? Up to this point I had been popular amongst my male refereeing colleagues, but my head went into a period of turmoil. Would my aiming for this goal threaten them to such an extent that I wouldn't be popular amongst them anymore? I couldn't bear the thought of that. Would it interfere with my newfound enjoyment of the job? Alarm bells were going off in my head and at the same time there was a little voice niggling at me, spurring me on to take Rita's throw away comment seriously. I was torn. As the words of Mary MacGregor's 1976 hit song says, 'Torn between two lovers, feeling like a fool, loving you both is breaking all the rules.'

There was no doubt about it that trying to beat the system would be breaking all the rules. Would I be a fool to even think I could try, never mind do it? The pulling at my heart strings and being torn about it was unpleasant. But there was still something tugging at me and it wouldn't let go, a bit like when you see young children holding on to the bottom of their mammies' skirt or legs. They are holding on for dear life and they won't let go. Rita had planted a seed in my head and it was slowly but surely filtering into my brain. I would have to give this careful consideration and time to grow or throw caution to the wind, take a good deep breath and just go for it. Being the impulsive person that I am, maybe the latter would be a better option. It would reduce the torture. Nevertheless, I was sensible and mature enough to know that I couldn't be reckless either. I would have to think about it wisely and develop a realistic and viable strategy. The most important elements of goal making are: the goal must be specific, realistic, achievable/attainable and challenging. This goal was most certainly specific and challenging, no doubt about that, but was it realistic and more importantly was it achievable/attainable? The last two had been blown out of the water by Rita's double failure.

Thinking back over this now, here, in the present day, it can be easy to overlook the fact that Ireland was quite a different society in the 1980s. Socially, there was an expectation on women that you finished school, got a nice little job, married in your early twenties, relinquished your job to devote your time to your husband, children and the kitchen sink. As I look back now it makes it easier for me to understand why that male dominance existed in the basketball refereeing world. Traipsing around the country refereeing matches wasn't the done thing for women. But I was not a woman to conform to such social norms. I wanted to achieve that elusive Grade 1.

While I've referenced already the enormity of the task of not only passing the exam itself, but also breaking the male-dominated refereeing system, I now see in fact there was a third element called for, a truly gargantuan task, of breaking down this social norm that had women in a position of inequality and tied to the kitchen sink. It has taken women forty years since those 1980s to be recognised and make a dent in the male-dominated world. Even now, heading into the 2020's, with the gap narrowing there's plenty of progress still to be made. At the time I wasn't conscious of this element, but looking back on it now, I realise I may have in some way been aware that I was also stepping in to *New Woman* territory, not just basketball territory. I was paving the way for future generations of women particularly women in sport to also enter into their own unchartered waters. At this time, women's participation in sports such as rugby, gaelic football and soccer were in their infancy, never mind refereeing. The task I was facing was more enormous than was apparent to me at the time.

I felt I would have to reflect on attempting for the Grade 1 Refereeing award, take some time to mull it around in my head and see what I could come up with. Having gone to support Rita on both occasions was helpful in making me see some of the obstacles that needed to be overcome. What things could I draw on that would inspire me and give me the edge I needed to proceed with this crazy idea? I didn't know. I felt a bit at sea. I also felt alone. I knew there was no way the men were going to help me! Sleep on it! That's always a good idea! See what Bridget has to say apart from, 'You're nuts in the head.' Vivienne might be a good person here. At one level she would think it's impossible but at another level she might think, knowing me the way that she did, that it was worth a try. I decided to sleep on it, discuss it with Bridget and Vivienne and take it from there. Rome wasn't built in a day. Taking the time to weigh up the pros and cons and see where I could take inspiration from was the best bet. Inspiration. I badly needed inspiration.

CHAPTER 22
Inspiration Lands On My Lap.

Well, true to form and exactly as I had anticipated Bridget's first words were, 'Yah, you're nuts in the head! What do you want to do that for?' However, Bridget being Bridget, was always up for a good ol' discussion. As per usual, we discussed my predicament in detail. By the end of our conversation, she changed her mind upon the realisation that this would be a *History Making* event. This really took her fancy. Bridget loved her history and loved reading about it because she had come through a long history herself in her own upbringing. Having been born in 1909, she lived through the Irish Easter Rising, World War I, The Irish Civil War, World War II, the electrification of Ireland and many more historical events. I distinctly remember her telling me that at the time of her engagement and wedding she couldn't get her rings as a result of the shortages after World War II. From a modernisation perspective, she went from listening to the wireless to the introduction of T.V.s, microwaves and showers. When it struck her that I would be in the history books if I succeeded, that's what clinched her saying, 'You're still nuts in the head, but I think you should go for it. Mind you though, you will need every one of those nuts to help you get there, ha ha ha! Your nuts are going to have to be able to crack all those other nuts that you will be up against.' We had a good hearty laugh about the whole thing which was great because it put a dent in the impossible-ness of it all and lightened up the tension it was presenting.

Vivienne was next and of course, just like Bridget, Vivienne was Vivienne. Her first reaction was one of, 'Oh my

God! That's very tough, oh I don't know, I wouldn't be able to do that, that's a huge undertaking. Heavens above, where would you even begin to do that?' We had a discussion about it and as I had anticipated, Vivienne came around to the idea that knowing me the way she did that it certainly would be possible. While the magnitude of the idea of it frightened the daylights out of her, she knew that it wouldn't have that same effect on me, I would be much calmer and able to take it in my stride. She knew how much I thrived on challenges and felt that perhaps the challenge would be stimulating for me. She advised me to go for it and felt I had nothing to lose and everything to gain. So why not? She offered to help me in any way she could. According to Bridget and Vivienne, I shouldn't waste any time, I should get down to it, get cracking and get the ball rolling. Where to start?

Rita, Rita, Rita! How the hell was I going to surpass her efforts and attempts? She had done her best, given it socks and it wasn't good enough. How could I possibly make my attempts good enough? How could I climb that same wall and make it over to the other side? Rita, yoo-hoo, wakey-wakey, I need some inspiration please....... Help!

Calling on Rita I knew I desperately needed some inspiration as I felt I hadn't a ghost of a chance in overcoming the unquantifiable amount of obstacles that were in front of me. She was the only person who could advise me having been through it herself. How was I going to turn her failure into success? Not an easy thing to do. As I sat pondering it, suddenly, bing, out of the blue, the word perfection dropped onto my lap. It was like Rita was giving me a message, a clue. Perfection.... hmmm. The penny dropped. Of course, perfection, that's it. Perfection was the key. Nothing else would do. Thank you Rita, thank you, thank you. This was the inspiration I desperately needed. I began to realise that I would need to adopt a determined, positive approach by setting goals that were perfection orientated. This would be the first thing to do and of the utmost crucial importance.

The idea of perfection was not alien to me. I loved striving for perfection. I enjoyed the challenge of it and I didn't find it scary or daunting. To help me in my quest I could draw on my childhood memories and recall examples of perfection that I experienced and loved. My Da's shed with his perfectly arranged tools, my aunt's dressmaking shop with the perfect rolls of fabric, the perfection in the beauty of the flowers in nature and the teaching in the Girl Guides on how to do things properly. I'd use them to spur me on.

These experiences helped me to develop my own ideas on perfection. I don't agree that perfection doesn't exist. It exists for those who want it to exist. I believe we have a choice to look at things from two perspectives, positive and negative. It's the glass half-full or half-empty concept. For me perfection is like this concept. We have the choice to look at something and that can be anything and either see the beauty and perfection in it or see only the flaws. But why do people continuously bang their heads off the walls striving for perfection if it's not attainable? Why bother? It doesn't make sense, because if that's what you believe, then no matter what you do it will never be good enough.

I believe it's better to approach life from the principle that, yes, there is always more, always more to achieve, always more to believe in, always more to explore. That makes it exciting and keeps the fire burning and alive, whereas the reverse idea just deflates one's hopes and dreams and creates a sense of hopelessness and despair. I find this way of thinking destructive. It drags you down, not up. Things are hard enough to achieve when you have a positive attitude towards them, adding in negativity will only make them impossible. If we take Jim Ryun for example, his first time of 4.21 *was good enough* at the time he achieved it. The fact that it was good enough is what spurred him on to his faster times. If he had a negative attitude towards that first time, he would never have gone on to realise his dream and fulfil his potential. When something proves to be good enough then *it IS*. It is perfect at that moment in time.

Perfection was the goal to strive for. It was the goal I needed to set myself. I liked the positive element in this thinking and I felt that positivity was most definitely what I needed to tackle my Grade 1 exam. In the meantime, I would have to think about what else I needed to adopt in order to crack this exam. The first place to start was to write down my critique on what I had learned from observing Rita and make a list of what I considered to be my own weaknesses.

When I started my critique on Rita, it made me realise the importance of learning from failures. I realised that failure was not a word that had been used in my sports career to date. There was no reference to it. It was simply the stepping stone to the next improvement. One such stepping stone was identifying and learning from the mistakes and trying not to repeat those same mistakes again. We should use the failure to help us to surge forward, so what could I learn from Rita's experience?

Rita had tried her best to do that and indeed had succeeded in improving her refereeing in leaps and bounds. I just had to do the same as her, plus raise my own standard even higher by going a few steps further than she did. One thing I had learned early in my training days was, that you always had to aim twice as high as you want to go in order to achieve the level you actually want. Aiming for the level itself is never good enough, because it leaves you open and vulnerable to dropping below the required level if you make a mistake. Aiming much higher, gives you more scope to make a mistake and drop, but still be above the required level. I knew this was a big focus point that I would have to keep to the forefront of my mind every single day until I did my exam.

What else did I need to prepare me to tackle my Grade 1 exam? I was aware from watching The Olympics over the years that the essence of greatness is what carries athletes to the top of their careers. I would need the same essence to carry me through this challenge. I would have to apply myself to my goal in the same way as the top athletes did and put in the same work physically, mentally and emotionally that they did. The next time I watched events like the Olympics, I would have to glean some tips from them as inspiration to propel me forward. In general, I had noticed that the athletes' qualities and traits culminated in them not being afraid to challenge and push themselves beyond their limits and comfort zones, to achieve greater success than they ever thought possible. I would have to do the same, just exactly that. I could take advantage of my need and desperation to be good at something to drive me forward.

Like with all champions, the feel-good factor which is exhilarating and has a euphoric feeling to it, was another key focal point that I would have to hold on to. Incidentally, I always got these feelings whenever I refereed a perfect match. This is something that had been relentlessly drummed into me by Sean particularly and that I had gained from other experiences in my own sporting journey. Always hang on to the feel-good feeling. It's a particularly motivating feeling and can yield unexpected results. I responded extremely well to Sean's encouragement and motivation. My desperation could be fuelled in a positive way by Sean's belief in me. I would have to stop doubting myself and my ability and allow Sean and others to be instrumental in helping me to address and overcome my lack of self-esteem. I had been lucky with my coaches to date. It can take an awfully long time, if someone else has the patience and the persistence to hold the belief on your behalf, until such time as you can take it over yourself. Fintan my running buddy, was a good example in the athletics for me. His continued belief and perseverance in telling me that I was going to win a race did in fact actually come true. Likewise, Jim Ryun's coach telling him he was going to break the four-minute mile barrier did come true. Sean on the other hand, didn't verbalise his belief in me but he communicated it strongly through his body language and his actions. I mustn't give up.

I was someone who had always worked and trained extremely hard and I never ever gave up. Drastically increasing the intensity of my workouts is something I would have to keep doing. At this time, I was doing hard intervals of 400 metres in my lunchtime training sessions. The men I trained with wouldn't dream of doing more than 10 or 12 repetitions of those. However, I decided to increase mine to 20, which was considered madness by the men.

The more I studied and copied the athletes in the Olympics and World Championship events, the more I could see how I was becoming more like them. I noticed myself becoming more single-minded, more focused and more determined. I started to have a lot in common with them as a result over time. It was indeed inspiring to develop these comparisons.

It gave me a quiet sense of hope that maybe, just maybe, I could do this impossible thing. It made me question further, could I, could I really do it? After all, look at what they did. If they could do it, could I? Maybe I could! Perhaps if I applied myself with the same ruthlessness, the same wanting, wanting it badly enough just like them, I could do it. At this point in time, I was feeling totally unsure and insecure about it. This would have to change drastically if I had any hope of achieving my goal. How to do that? They just went for it, threw caution to the wind and just did it. Could I do the same?

What about the other obstacles - breaking the male dominance and the social norms, for instance, what about them? The Olympians didn't have those to deal with. Lucky them. How do I overcome those obstacles? How can I use the Olympians' experiences to help me with those? More thinking to be done on that score! Lots to take in. Lots to consider. Despite their individual obstacles, they journeyed and rose to finishing in a place of indisputable success. If I was to take a leaf out of their books, could I end up with the perfect outcome that I so badly desired? Could I make use of my desperation in a positive way and could I apply myself physically, mentally and emotionally to achieve my goal? I would have to let my observations of these athletes seep into my brain for starters and slowly penetrate in to the rest of me so that I could, in an intelligent and cohesive way, use the inspiration that their competitiveness had impressed on me. I would have to start taking action and fully commit myself to the task at hand and, like them, begin by taking baby steps and progressing from there.

Thinking about the Olympics, World Championships and other competitions that I had watched over the years got me all fired up with enthusiasm and excitement. A nervous tension was running through my veins. It felt like I was doing my homework and it was paying off. It fired me up even more realising that I had indeed many characteristics in common with these athletes. My teammates had often described me as the gutsiest female they had ever known. I was genuinely beginning to feel that I should go for the Grade 1 exam and give it a bash. Vivienne's words were sinking in, I had nothing to lose and everything to gain.

I should pinpoint some of what I considered were the important qualities the athletes displayed that I had watched over the years. Along with the obvious characteristics, commitment, dedication, repetition and paying attention to detail, there were other elements such as superstitious behaviours and mannerisms which were incorporated into pre-competition mental preparations. Athletes psyched themselves up by going through a set routine. In basketball, teams had specific warm-up drills and players religiously stuck to wearing the same numbers on their shirts. Michael Jordan, for example, always wore the number 23. Footballers are notorious for laying out their football kit in a particular sequence before putting it on. They too have specific prematch warm-up drills. Individual athletes often wear jewellery of sentimental value and for luck which they cling to, for example kissing their necklaces or blessing themselves by making the sign of the cross before the event starts. These gestures are ways to psyche themselves up as a way of eliminating errors and aiming for perfection.

I made notes of everything that came into my mind. I now knew that the deciding factor in the outcome if I were to be successful would be that there would be no room for errors. No mistakes, no hiccups on the day. I could not give the examiners *anything* to find fault with, especially if they were hell-bent on not letting me through. This was an extremely daunting task, but I knew I was right. I would have to referee a *perfect* match. I was inspired by remembering that the Olympians and successful athletes had done that. They had achieved perfection in their performances. I had to believe that I could also do the same.

While I knew people who felt that they were on shaky ground when they started their quest for success, I can tell you in no uncertain terms, that I felt a hundred times shakier. I knew I was aiming for something that hadn't been done before. A shaky prospect. While I had to banish the shaky thoughts in order to concentrate on positivity, deep down in my heart and soul, the loneliness of the solo run that I knew I was on was always bubbling underneath. Nevertheless though, another lesson I had learned from Sean over the years was, that once someone aspires to something that is a major feat which was considered impossible, it means it is impossible no more. Sean had always taught us that we had a responsibility as athletes to respect and honour people who had aspired to seemingly impossible feats. He believed that we should follow in their footsteps and use their example and the inspiration they had provided us with to inspire ourselves in the same way. He always stated, 'Nothing is impossible anymore once it's been proven to be possible.' I decided to get cracking and get the ball rolling before I changed my mind.

While I had people in my camp who believed in me and were eager to help me, the bottom line was, I essentially had to do this on my own. It was me who was going to have to step-up to the challenge, me alone who was going to have to put the hard work in and get myself to the level I needed to, in order to achieve that unprecedented goal. It was me alone who was going to have to overcome my self-doubt, my lack of self-esteem and my nervousness. I was going to have to find greatness in myself!! It was going to be a long, lonely road, a road that was going to be purely down to me and nobody else.

CHAPTER 23
Cracking The Nut Commences.

I put in my application for the Grade 1 exam. Unexpectedly it was accepted without any resistance! At first this surprised me until I realised that it was probably a foregone conclusion on their part that I wouldn't succeed anyway so there was no harm in allowing me to proceed. I had to spend one year on what they call probation, at the end of which I would have to take a written exam and if I passed that I could proceed to the practical exam.

That year, 1987, was an immensely pressurising year as once again the matches I was appointed to were of the highest standard in both the local and national leagues. This elevation, while challenging, was extremely important to my further development. This was the standard of match I would be appointed to for my exam, I had better get used to it rapidly. The National League season only runs from October to March making it a short year. I knew I had so much hard work to do in that short year to raise myself to the required standard. I thought of Jim Ryun's huge improvement over a short period of time. It spurred me on.

The first thing I did was I made a list of the technical elements of the game that I needed to perfect. These included hand signals and other signals for illustrating the fouls, violations and information to the table officials. I spent hours and hours practising my signals in front of a mirror, which was the most proficient way to get them perfect and to see how I looked while administering them. I didn't want any marks deducted for technical elements as these are one of the few things you have full and definite control over in every game. Practising in front of the mirror allowed me to pay more attention to detail as I could see everything perfectly. I transferred this practise into my game refereeing to ensure that I would end up in a place where I did them naturally and perfectly until I didn't have to think about them anymore. I studied the rules consistently as this was important. If I didn't pass the written exam, I couldn't proceed to the practical exam. Of course, the fitness element was well looked after, I didn't have to worry about that I just had to maintain it. With the technical elements out of the way, I was able to focus my attention on improving my actual refereeing and my refereeing mechanics.

For Grade 1 the examiners are looking to see if you can referee under pressure, if you can apply the mechanics properly including watching off-the-ball and if you have a good feel for the game. They need to see you can apply the advantage/disadvantage principles and can read the game, which means understand what the players and coaches are trying to do. You need to be able to read and anticipate the set plays that teams are trying to operate and control the game by blowing the whistle less, based on these principles. This of course, is a totally different type of refereeing to anything I had been expected to do prior to that. Luckily for me however, as I had played at National League level, I had a distinct advantage and I was able to transfer the playing skills of the set plays into my refereeing. I found it easier to referee this type of game, both the top Men's and Ladies' Divisions and because of Sean's complicated practise drills, reading the game and anticipating what set plays the teams were trying to operate came easy to me. I was surprised and taken aback at how quickly I got to grips with this type of refereeing and how comfortable I felt in it.

Naturally, this was a good bonus for me as it lifted me up to this higher standard quite nicely. After this, I wrote down the critical feedback that had been given to Rita after her attempts and I started working on these elements next. I had seen how hard she had worked between her first and second exam and I had seen the improvements she had made. It became obvious to me that I had to crash train myself into those improvements and apply them to my own refereeing style. In that year I was quite lucky with the matches I was appointed to. I had some crackers which gave me good experience at reffing under pressure. As I've explained already, I loved, loved, loved refereeing under pressure. So that was right up my alley.

At this time, while I felt like the lone ranger, my confidence was growing. I was enjoying refereeing this higher standard of game and I kept Jim Ryun's story firmly planted to the forefront of my mind - keep working hard, perseverance, perseverance, do not give up, attention to detail, perfection – everything perfect, go, go, go! You can do it!!! Keep trucking! I like this Dublin saying. I did it. I kept trucking. Before I knew it the year was up and I had to take my written exam. I knew the rules inside out because thanks to one of the FIBA referees who helped me, I was extra competent in that regard. I passed the rules test comfortably. Hurdle number one crossed. Of course, now the biggest hurdle was still ahead of me – that practical exam.

I was appointed to the Men's Top of the League clash. I was delighted with this as I knew it would be a humdinger. The perfect match for me to ref. The next stroke of luck that I had was the partner I was appointed with. Roger, an established FIBA referee, was to be my partner. If I could have chosen someone myself it would have been Roger. I couldn't believe my luck. I knew Roger admired me and that he was on my side. He wanted me to pass, that in itself was the motivation I needed. I arrived early at the venue to meet Roger to mentally and psychologically prepare for the match. We had a prematch discussion, which incorporated the potential aspects of the game that we needed to be ready for and discussed our partnership and how everything would be handled and managed between us.

Roger pointed out the importance of maintaining consistency between us. He also pointed out the importance of me refereeing this match perfectly, 100 per cent perfect, no mistakes. This was crucial if I was to break this impenetrable barrier. I agreed with him, but I also pointed out to him, that he too, would have to referee 100 per cent perfectly with no mistakes so that the examiners couldn't use him as an excuse for dragging me down to a fail result. Roger was completely stunned and taken aback by my comment, as he was an international referee, one grade higher than I was aiming for and two grades higher than my current grade. 'Well, I'll be damned,' he said. 'You cheeky little thing! I've never been challenged or had anyone ever say anything like that to me.' I grinned and said, 'Well if you stop and think about it, cheeky as it may seem, I'm sure under the given circumstances you'll agree it's true.' He paused for a moment and thought before replying, 'To be honest, I never thought of that, but you're right.' Another pause, 'OK cheeky madam, you're on. We have to referee a perfect match together. Let's go for it. I wish you the best of luck. This is going to be the most important match of your life to date. Give it your all. Do your best and I'll be right there to support you all the way.' 'Thanks Roger,' I replied. 'I'm so glad it's you, I couldn't have asked for a better partner.' We shook hands and headed out onto the court.

The atmosphere was electric. There was a huge crowd of spectators because it was expected to be a great match. The examiners, three men, were sitting in their positions. There were many referees there, those who wanted me to pass and those who wanted me to fail. Sean wasn't there as he was away refereeing an international match. You could cut the tension with a knife. You could sense the frenzy of anticipation in the crowd. Everyone knew it was 'D-Day' for me. Roger gave me the ball to throw up, shook hands and winked at me, a wink that said, 'Let's go kiddo, this is it, it's now or never!!!' I took one big deep breath, composed myself, thought about Jim Ryun, the possible history in the making and entered into my *Perfection Zone* where I lingered for a moment. I tossed the ball up, a perfect throw, good start.

True to its expectations, the match was indeed a humdinger. It threw every possible situation at us from the rules of the game to every action on the court. Roger and I were in complete sync with each other for the whole first half. It had overtime written all over it. Basket for basket, up and down at breakneck speed, free-throw for free-throw. The defensive play by both teams was stupendous and challenged our off-the-ball skills. The defensive play was ferocious, tenacious and unrelenting. Neither team deserved to lose this match. It had the spectators constantly jumping up and down out of their seats, screaming and roaring like mad, desperately cheering their team on. At half-time Roger and I had a quick chat about how things were going. 'So far so good,' he said. 'But now this is where the fun really starts and the real test begins. This game I'm sure is going to go to the wire. Stay alert, stay concentrated, remember no mistakes.' I nodded. I was thinking, long way to go but we were half-way there and, in another way, we were on the home straight. Stay in the zone, don't budge from the zone. This is the pressure you thrive on make the most of it. *The zone, stay in the zone.*

I tossed the ball up for the start of the second-half. Another perfect throw. Good stuff! Another good start! Keep trucking! What a cliffhanger Roger and I were reffing. It was unbelievable. However, we remained steadfast as a team and never wavered in our calls. Up and down the court we ran, whistle after whistle we blew until eventually that final buzzer sounded to end the game. The scores were level and the team who had the ball got a shot away in the dying seconds of the match. The final buzzer sounded; the ball was in the air on its flight to the basket. Everyone in the gym held their breath, you could hear a pin drop and finally after what seemed an eternity, the ball thumped off the backboard, landed on the ring and rolled and rolled around the ring before finally entering the basket. There was dead silence for a moment while that ball was rolling around the ring. It took everybody a few seconds to realise the ball had entered the basket. The spectators went berserk, all hell broke loose as the supporters of the winning team charged onto the court to embrace their team and the man, the hero, who scored that clinching shot.

Roger and I heaved an enormous sigh of relief. No overtime thank heavens. Game over. Phew!!! Up to that point I have to say that match was the most enjoyable match of my life. The most electric, fastest, challenging match I had ever reffed. The perfect match for a Grade 1 exam. The perfect match for me and my style of refereeing. The perfect partner. It took Roger and myself a few minutes to gather ourselves as the customary post-match handshakes had to be made. Both teams, the losers included, congratulated me on a match superbly reffed. Likewise, the coaches and managerial staff of both teams. Unusually, nobody had a bad word to say to us.

Roger embraced me in a bear hug fashion shaking my shoulders with delight. 'You son of a gun, I can't believe it, you did it, you reffed the perfect match, no mistakes. They can't fail you now, they just can't.' I replied, 'WE reffed the perfect match, thank you very much.' He laughed and said, 'We sure did cheeky.' Despite being drained we were elated and most definitely on a high. The refs who wanted me to pass jumped on me in delight, singing my praises at the unbelievable accomplishment they considered I had made. They actually started giving me the bumps, throwing me up in the air and thankfully catching me on the way down. The examiners had left the gym and gone into a room to wait for us. Now it was time to face them.

I went into the room with Roger and we were met with staid faces. There was no air of the jubilation that we were feeling. I began to get a bad feeling. They weren't going to fail me surely. They couldn't! I put them in an awkward position yes, I knew that, but with that many people watching, that many witnesses to my impeccable performance, surely, they wouldn't compromise themselves by failing me. It was sometime before one of the three of them spoke. The waiting was agony. Roger had a quizzical look on his face. I could see he was wondering what the hell was going on here. The examiner that spoke first said he wanted to congratulate me on an exceptionally well refereed game, that unanimously among the examiners they were shocked at my performance. Unfortunately, while they couldn't fail me, they felt it was too good to be true and to prove that it wasn't a once off performance, they were appointing me to a second game in a fortnight's time at which they were going to reassess me.

Roger and myself were shocked, totally gobsmacked. Roger said to them, 'Do you think in all sincerity that that's fair? I've no doubt had that been a man you were giving that feedback to, he would have passed with flying colours. Why should Mary be any different?' Of course, they dismissed his comments and tried to make light of it. Roger wasn't having any of it, 'Well, if my input counts for anything' he said, 'that is the best match I myself have ever refereed. Mary's performance as my co-official, was the best performance of a co-official I have ever had accompanying me and that includes all my FIBA appointments to date. That was an exceptionally tough, competitive, high-class game and I was put to the pin of my collar and challenged beyond measure to maintain the high quality of refereeing that I did. I think it's unfair to suggest or imply that Mary's performance was a fluke which is what you are implying. My God, if she can referee like that under such pressure, I've no doubt she'll be wearing a FIBA badge in the future, never mind gaining a Grade 1 award. We have seen this girl's potential today in no uncertain terms. I'm woefully disappointed with this outcome. We should be celebrating her victory today not in two weeks' time.'

I was bowled over by Roger's reaction and I admired his guts in responding to them in the way that he did. It gave me the confidence to say, 'It's ok Roger we will be celebrating my victory in two weeks' time. I most definitely will repeat my performance of today. Today was no fluke. These examiners have no idea how hard I've worked for this exam and they don't realise or respect, that it's all the hard work I've put in that gained me the result I got today. The hard work has paid off and it will pay off again in two weeks' time.' The examiners said nothing, they just looked at the two of us, stood up to leave, indicating that the meeting was over.

When we came outside, I thought Roger was going to explode. He was equally upset and disappointed as I was. It was an outcome that neither of us had thought possible. It was a first. It had never happened to anyone else before. People either passed or failed. He couldn't believe it. As someone described the examiners afterwards, 'The crafty buggers.' Well hump them anyway! What a letdown! I was touched by the fact that Roger was perturbed, upset and disappointed by the outcome. It put a small spark in to my own disappointment. Roger was one of the senior referees I respected, liked and admired as he was a man of integrity. I had always found him to be a fair and honest man.

The referees were waiting outside for us, dying to hear the result. You must remember that this was the late 1980's (1987). Since that time, much progress has been made to redress that gender imbalance in sports. It may be difficult to appreciate that I was the sole female amongst all these men on that memorable night. There was pure and utter shock and disbelief at our news. At first, they thought we were joking, just having them on to wind them up before we broke the good news. The referees who wanted me to pass were raging at the injustice of it, especially after seeing the match with their own eyes. The referees who wanted me to fail were delighted and I could see some of them rubbing their hands in delight and cheering with their fists up. Believe it or not, I was so disgusted I made a mental note in the middle of my disappointment. Up yours, guys! You shitheads! You won't be rubbing your hands or waving your fists in two weeks' time, I'll make sure of that. Roger put his arm around me and said, 'Come on Mary, let's get out of here! Let's go for a short walk.'

Roger conveyed his disappointment to me once more and asked me how I was feeling. I told him I was shocked and it felt dreadfully unjust the whole thing. I told him it was hard to fathom but obviously they just weren't having their male domain broken. He reiterated to me how well I had done and that I unequivocally deserved to pass. He told me again that he was stunned at my performance and that he had underestimated me drastically. He said he didn't realise the good stuff I was made of. He said he didn't think I could step-up to that level, never mind in the comfortable way I appeared to do it. Furthermore, he told me he truly admired my guts and tenacity. 'You really want it,' he said. 'You will get it next time, no doubt about it and when you do, I'll be the first to celebrate your success.' I thanked him for everything, for being such a wonderful co-official and especially for sticking up for me the way that he did. I said to him that the good thing was they didn't fail me and at least I had another chance. It would be difficult to repeat that performance because it was unlikely I would have a match of that calibre again. Also, I would have a different co-official, the next match was going to be a different ball game. In light of Roger's belief, support and encouragement I just felt I owed it to him, not to let him down and also to myself, not to let myself down, after the relentless hard work I had done. While I was disappointed, yes bitterly disappointed, I had every intention of picking myself up again and not giving them the satisfaction of failing me. I was determined I was going to prove to them that my performance was not a fluke. The cheek of them even thinking that, never mind believing it. I would show them! Jim Ryun sprung to mind again and I would take a leaf out of his book. They weren't going to get the better of me.

Roger asked me to keep him informed about the next exam and he would meet me beforehand and help me to prepare and get psyched up for it. When Sean came back, I told him what happened and Sean, being Sean and true to form just said, 'Well now Miss Whelan, action replay take two, that's what you have to do in two weeks' time.' That was it! No commiserations, no 'There, there Mary,' just good ol' typical Sean.

The first few days of those two weeks dragged by while I was feeling my disappointment. I needed to get up and running again. I decided to focus on the positive things from the assessment. Roger pointed out the positive things to me: 1. That I had forced the examiners into a corner which was a brilliant thing. 2. Not for one moment did they believe that I was capable of passing but I proved them wrong on that one. 3. They couldn't keep putting me off now if I reffed a perfect match next time. 4. It was up to me to force them to succumb. The ball was in my court now, not theirs. 5. Action replay take two. I could easily do it. I just had to hang in there. 6. My hard work, desire and passion were going to pay off. I just had to believe in myself.

I decided to use my anger, my disappointment and infuriation at the injustice of it in a constructive way. I spent the rest of the time preparing like mad, revising everything and getting my head into the Perfection Zone once more. I seriously battened down the hatches and started to think about perfection again. A repeat performance, I had to referee another perfect match, no mistakes. I knew if I did it once, of course I could do it again. I just had to apply myself to the task at hand, pay attention to every single solitary detail just one more time. Every match I refereed in those two weeks I focused on perfection, reffing a perfect match as part of my preparation. I wanted to be psyched up for the exam. Each and every one of those begrudgers were going to suffer, I can tell you. That was my aim. I was no pushover. They weren't going to keep me down. I didn't train like an animal with the *animal* himself for all those years for nothing. The animal in me was going to show them.

I had to stay positive, no negativity. I also had to remember that despite everything, I hadn't failed. I was still one step closer than two weeks ago to achieving my goal. By match day I was in tip-top shape again. The match was expected to be a good one, but I knew straight away that it wouldn't be a patch on the other one. I had to be extremely careful and diligent. Roger, true to his word, had met me and given me some important good advice and tips. He knew the two teams and my co-official much better than I did and he told me the things I needed to watch out for. This time the crowd of supporters was smaller. The atmosphere was not electric like the previous game. It had more of an air of anticlimax to it. Therefore, I had to step-up in myself in a completely different and drastic way in order to adjust to the differences this game posed. I did exactly as I did for the first match. I took one big deep breath, repeated that same sequence, but this time adding in 'Right you begrudgers, here we go, I'm going to show you all what I'm made of.' I tossed the ball up, a perfect toss, a good start yet again and that was it, I knew I was on my way to my grade one. The match was neck and neck. Up to half-time it was basket for basket. Five minutes into the second-half there was an incident which involved my co-official calling an intentional foul on one of the players on the defensive team. The player was raging and fiercely started screaming and shouting at my co-official, disputing the call. My co-official gave him a warning to calm down and told him he would call a technical foul on him if he did not stop arguing the call. As my co-official went over to the table to report the foul the player gave him the *Two-Fingers* gesture behind his back and muttered under his breath, 'Fuck you, bastard.' I immediately blew my whistle and called a disqualifying foul on the player. The player looked at me gobsmacked! He couldn't believe it. He roared at me, 'Why are you disqualifying me? It should only be a technical foul!' I replied, 'Sorry buster, you have just stepped way over the line, you need to leave the gym now please.' He stood over me, glaring down at me, steam coming out of his ears. I calmly pointed to the exit door and told him he had one minute to leave. He was so disgusted that I actually thought he was going to spit on me, but the coach intervened and dragged him off the court and told him to leave. The coach naturally was dejected because this player was one of his best players and with the scores tied, he couldn't afford to lose him. However, he accepted my decision gallantly, as he knew I was absolutely right to take the action I did. I never looked back after this incident and I refereed another perfect match, no mistakes. Unfortunately, this incident changed the course of the game and gave the opposing team the opportunity to take advantage of this player's absence. After another five minutes, they opened up a lead, which left them comfortable winners in the end.

When the game was over and we had signed the scoresheet, it was time to face the examiners again. My co-official didn't say anything to me, other than, 'Well done.' I felt myself I had certainly put it up to them and there was no way they could fail me. However, after what happened the first time around, I wasn't sure if it was possible or not, for them to pull a second stunt. When we stepped into the room there was no air of good promise. Their faces were like stone and I found it difficult to decipher the outcome. They were giving nothing away. They questioned my co-official and myself on how we thought we had refereed the match. They questioned me about my disqualifying foul call. They wanted to know the reasons for it and why it wasn't just a technical foul. I explained everything to them and, of course, they hadn't heard the words the player had muttered under his breath to my co-official. They looked disappointed with my reply. They excused themselves and put their heads together for a quick tête-à-tête. One of them spoke and said, 'Well, in that case, that being your reasons, we have no option but to pass you and award you your Grade 1 qualification.' I looked at my partner and he looked back at me. We weren't sure if we had heard correctly or not. He checked with them, 'Mary has passed, she's a Grade 1 now, is that right?' The examiner replied, 'Yes, that's correct.' With a begrudging shake of the hand, he said, 'Well done Miss Whelan.' My partner grabbed me, hugged me and spun me around in delight. 'You did it, you did it,' he yelled, 'Whoo hoo!!! Let's go and celebrate.'

I think in all fairness the examiners would have been lynched if they didn't pass me this time. Whatever about me, my fans would have gone berserk if I had fulfilled the criteria a second time and not passed. This match in itself was an easier match to referee, as it didn't have the contentiousness of the previous match. I had refereed many matches like this one, I knew once I stayed in the zone, didn't get distracted and didn't make any mistakes I was on a winner.

Now, once the verification that I was, indeed, a winner was announced and clarified, it took a while for the penny to drop. Somewhat stunned, I left the room with my partner and it was he who shouted at everyone outside waiting for the verdict, 'She's passed, she's passed. We have Ireland's first female Grade 1 referee in our midst. C'mon everyone it's time to celebrate.' Of course, there were great cheers and claps on the back, words of congratulations, well done, super news etc., etc. and it felt a bit surreal. The anticlimax feeling of the match itself was now suddenly transformed into whoops of joy and delight, excitement and affirmation, with a buzz of such positive energy that it was invigorating and uplifting. I couldn't wait to tell Roger my news. I knew he would be delighted and over the moon.

The begrudgers weren't happy, needless to say. Some of them, reluctantly, as if it were sticking in their craw, congratulated me, while others stormed off in disgust. I didn't care. I was thrilled to bits that I had shown them what I was made of. In fact, I got great satisfaction from their reactions. Soon afterwards, Roger joined us. He lifted me up and swung me around, the way a parent takes a child by the two hands and swings them around. He couldn't believe it. He was worried and concerned that the disappointment of the first match might get to me and drag me down.

Victory it was and great celebrations all round. From my perspective, had the celebrations come after the first match it would have been more meaningful due to the excitement and electrifying atmosphere and in a strange way the first match performance felt more deserved than the second one because it was more intense, more difficult, more challenging and really put me to the test. This match and everything surrounding it felt like an anti-climax. However, despite that it still had to be refereed to the standard and criteria required. Therefore, it had its challenge in another way. The celebrations went on well into the middle of the night and we had a great time into the wee small hours of the morning.

Roger arranged to meet me again on his own, which turned out to be a great thing as he listened to the details of my performance on the second match and reminisced with me about the fabulous things in relation to our first match. He recreated the scene so well that by the time he was finished I felt as if it was the first match I had walked out of and not the second match. He brought alive again those wonderful memories of the two of us working in such sync and before long, he had me feeling as if I was floating on air. His 'Overjoyed-ness' was infectious and it lifted me up into the same space as himself. I was then, thanks to him, able to appreciate my achievement for what it truly was.

It took some time to sink in. The utter and absolute relief of my first feeling was indescribable when the pressure was over. A kind of numbness followed this initial feeling encompassed with shock and disbelief I suppose.

When the match ended I was being congratulated right, left and centre by those around me and I was in a state to some degree of disorientation. You know when everything is going on around you, there's a lot of high activity, but you are not connected to it fully because your mind is in a haze. It was a bit like that. It was only after I met Roger that I connected to everything properly and was able to let in the impact of achieving my goal. I completely forgot about the fact that I had made history and the implications that went with that in those initial moments. The emphasis was on the fact that I had passed the exam. The remaining consequences didn't enter my head. It didn't take long for the real celebrations to begin after that. The celebrations were many for days and weeks. Of course, Haroldites were delighted for me, as was Sean but Sean, to my face, just said, 'You did what I told you to do.' That was it, no congrats, no well done, no nothing. However, it was through the inimitable grapevine that I heard afterwards that he was super proud of me and singing my praises behind my back. I can tell you that was good enough for me. After all, Sean is Sean – some things never change!!!

I received many good wishes and congratulations cards over the following weeks and the Dublin Ladies Board presented me with a most beautiful vase which was engraved for the occasion. Being the Ladies Board and being the first woman to achieve Grade 1, they were incredibly proud of me, which was lovely to see. Unexpectedly, I was approached by reporters from the National newspapers, looking for my photograph and interviewing me about my achievement. I don't know how or where these emerged from. That was some experience I can tell you. Little ol' me splashed in the newspapers. I never, ever thought I'd see that day. I couldn't believe it when I saw my photo with a heading on the article 'Mary's got high hopes as a Ref!' I was tickled pink when I read the description 'Diminutive Mary Whelan has just been appointed Ireland's first female referee for Senior League basketball.'

As if that wasn't enough excitement, the next thing that happened was that I got a phone call from RTE asking me to do a radio interview with Des Cahill. I could not believe it, I was stunned. I went down to the studios and it was the weirdest thing being on the other side of the radio talking, when I was only used to listening to it in the kitchen. Des Cahill was so lovely to me, because naturally I was nervous as a kitten and I will never forget him for that. He made the interview easy for me and the fact that he was genuinely interested in my story made me relax and feel at home with him. Des was dumbfounded by the fact that 'A little scut of a thing' like me was blowing a whistle, controlling men who were six foot plus in height. He couldn't get over it. Of course, the fact that he could see me in the flesh made it more unbelievable because being tiny in size was more obvious when I was standing beside him. We got on well, had a good interview and he was in no hurry to let me go. We got each other laughing with the slagging back and forth about me being a titch and he thoroughly enjoyed some of the answers that I gave him to his questions. My nerves had disappeared completely, he made me feel thoroughly at ease with him and he wished me the best of luck in my future refereeing career and said he hoped he would be hearing more news about me in the future.

RTE gave me a copy of the recording and it was interesting to see the difference between that and the newspaper article. While I answered the journalist's questions, the actual printed version were my words but edited by the reporter. My photograph captured perfectly my *Diminutive* stature. The radio interview with Des Cahill was a pre-recorded interview, which flowed like a conversation between the two of us. When I listened back to the recording, after my initial shock of hearing the sound of my own voice, I was chuffed to realise that the interview hadn't been edited in any way whatsoever. Therefore, when it was broadcast over the airwaves to the nation, it was incredible and thrilling to hear how authentically live it sounded. A proud moment for me.

That was the icing on the cake of the celebrations and acknowledgements of my achievements and I will always hold Des dear in my heart and remember that wonderful day with him. It was a combination of the celebrations, newspaper reports and radio interview that eventually helped me to let the achievement well and truly sink in. The knock-on effect of it went on for ages and ages afterwards. People who had seen my photograph and newspaper write-ups and had heard me on the radio were stopping me everywhere I went, congratulating me and asking me questions. I even had to sign autographs! I couldn't believe the response the whole thing evoked. It was an extremely exciting time after the long hard harrowing road it had taken to get there. I would most definitely have to say it was all worth it in the end. Haroldites topped it off by slagging the daylights out of me, reminding me about my refusal and defiance in *never* wanting to be a referee. 'Look at you now' they said, 'it's a long way from there you are now. Can you believe it?'

Time to let everything sink in and let it settle. There's always more. What a perfect end to what was deemed to be impossible, to what up till then had in fact, been impossible and the examiners after the first match showed the level of resistance that they had to such change. Goal number 1 achieved. Onwards and upwards.

CHAPTER 24
FIBA – Here I Come

The next thing I had to do was to settle in to being a fully fledged Grade 1 referee and adapt to the extra responsibilities that the grade brings with it. The good thing now was that the grade qualified me to be appointed to the much tougher matches. I could also be included in the important competitions such as Cup Competitions, League Play-Offs, Top-Four Competitions and Invitational Tournaments. My begrudging colleagues weren't too happy about that, but that didn't bother me. I was looking forward to the challenge of it and the excitement it was going to bring. Of course, on this journey I made further history by being the first woman to be appointed to matches in the various competitions. I hadn't realised or thought about that until it was pointed out to me by one of my non-begrudging colleagues.

These extra tough matches and refereeing at the highest possible level helped me to grow in strength as a referee. I loved the challenges, l loved learning and I was an eager and enthusiastic student. I was making up for what I didn't do in school. I made sure to take the opportunity to develop, grow and expand as much as I could and to learn from my more experienced colleagues. It was rather interesting, as the more I developed the easier it became. I slotted into the job naturally, like it was made for me and the job fitted me like a glove. It seemed I had found my niche. It didn't take long for the players and the coaches, both men and women, to accept and respect me at this higher level. This was a nice experience. I felt at home amongst the male referees and the majority of them eventually accepted me also. As a woman

I had always got on well with men in all walks of life. I think that this, along with my personality, which men found comfortable, helped me enormously in achieving this. I always loved men, their male energy and their straightforward thinking, their logical minds. It suited my black and white pragmatic way of thinking at that time.

Once I became accepted and respected everything changed for the better. It became an important turning point in my development, more important than I realised at the time. It made it much easier for me to be appointed to the more prestigious matches such as Quarter-Finals, Semi-Finals and Finals. The people making the appointments were able to take risks by appointing me to these matches and of course, I never let them down which was an added bonus for them. Knowing that I had to sustain refereeing to perfection, continuously and unrelentingly on this progressive journey, was a focus I maintained consistently throughout this whole period of time. I was practising it so much that it became automatic and the more automatic it became, the more dependable and trustworthy I became in the eyes of the appointment officers. This set me up nicely for further progression.

The time ticked by, and before long it was appropriate for me to apply to do my examination for FIBA, the International Basketball Federation. I had fulfilled the criteria which was refereeing as a Grade 1 for three years. This exam was a completely different exam to the previous ones. It had to be undertaken abroad in Europe and the examiners were from the top ranks of the FIBA association. It would be an extremely gruelling exam composed of five parts: a fitness test, a rules test, a video test and two practical exams. There was also a social skills assessment done. The pass mark for each part was 90 per cent.

There was no training in Ireland to prepare referees for this exam. You had to go it alone. The only help I had was from Sean and Roger but things had changed from the time they had done it and they couldn't help me with these changes. However, the fact that they were still active was an advantage somewhat at least. The fact that Roger had reffed that cliffhanger game with me for my Grade 1 was an advantage in him being able to help me. He explained that I would have another huge step-up to make for the FIBA exam as the standard of the game in Europe was far higher than the standard of the top Irish games. He explained that the pace was faster, the action and reactions of the players much faster and the skill level naturally was exceptional. There being only five women in the world who were FIBA referees, it was again primarily a male-dominated arena, just like Ireland. I would be facing the same problem again, the difference being at a much higher level.

Roger and Sean explained that the FIBA set-up was an extremely professional set-up, again far higher than the Irish one. FIBA viewed everything from a professional perspective and their expectations were wildly demanding. There was no room for error, mistakes were unacceptable, out of the question. Once again, I would be looking for a perfect performance in the five areas of the exams. FIBA, according to Sean and Roger, were absolute sticklers on the fitness and mechanics aspects of refereeing. These were their *Babies* or their *Pet Hates* to word it differently. Every examiner had their baby element and pet hate element, apparently. The fitness would be good for me and the mechanics I was quite proficient in. Those two augured well for me which would give me a good incentive for the rest.

Sean and Roger also explained to me that on the international scene, when referees are being hosted by the home team, having flights and accommodation paid for, being brought to expensive restaurants for meals, refs must be mindful and hold their integrity not to be swayed by the home team's generosity while refereeing the match. Remaining impartial and being able to hold the boundaries of fair play are essential.

The Referee's Association had to put my name forward and nominate me to attend the next available clinic. They received a reply indicating that the next FIBA clinic would be in Dortmund in Germany the following April 1990. That was less than six months away. My nomination was accepted and another male referee who had also applied, had his nomination accepted too. I was delighted to have company; I can tell you. The whole situation was daunting and somewhat overwhelming. I thought it would be a bit easier with two of us travelling together. There was one downside. The spoken word was that it was expected that FIBA would choose the male over the female if they were looking to only pass one. Another barrier, another hurdle for me to jump. I decided to remain positive. It was super important, more so now than the last time, to dispel any negativity that might be lurking about.

I talked to Sean and Roger about their own exam experiences to enable me gain an insight into the core qualities required to tackle this exam in a realistic way. How could I give myself the best possible chance to have a real and genuine go at it? Roger's words to the examiners after my Grade 1 exam sprang to mind regarding the potential I had exhibited during that game. How could I hone my potential to the required 90 per cent pass mark? I gave these core questions serious thought as once again I had to venture on another preparation plan like I did for my Grade 1. This one seemed trickier as it was not tangible. I was beginning to realise that it would take many qualities, intrinsic core qualities and extrinsic motivational qualities to become a referee of international status. At least the last exam was in Ireland and I could familiarise myself with the standard of games, the standard of referees and the criteria required. The fact that this exam was abroad made everything more elusive. Games were not televised in those days to the same extent as nowadays and even if they were, they weren't available in Ireland. I felt totally in the dark despite Sean and Roger's efforts to help me. I found it hard to visualise the scenarios they were describing to me.

I had written down everything that Sean and Roger told me. I forensically examined every detail of what I had written down and had come up with some ideas as a result. The core elements I identified were: passion, work ethics, competitiveness, courage, creativity, fitness/body, perseverance, psychological strength. I reckoned that if I could explore these core elements in myself, identify and work on the weak areas and maintain and even build on the strong areas that I might be able to raise the bar to the level I needed. The lads had said that perfection was required for FIBA.

Passion most definitely wasn't something I was lacking in. My love for the game and the love that I eventually developed for refereeing were rooted in passion. I felt passionate about going for my FIBA exam and the motivation to be the first female FIBA referee in Ireland spurred this on even more. A common phrase in sports fits the bill here, I had the *fire in my belly* that I desperately needed. Fire exudes passion. It's a good image. The question was how could I portray my passion and love for refereeing to the examiners in Europe? It probably couldn't be spoken, given that German was the language I would be faced with. Although English is the international language for FIBA referees, in Dortmund, German was the main language I would hear on a daily basis. It became clearer that my passion would have to be portrayed in my body language and somehow through my actual refereeing. Perhaps the preparation week in Dortmund itself might provide some opportunity for me to show it. I would have to keep an open mind on that one and maybe that would require some ad-libbing when the time came. This element I would undoubtedly have to work on and develop in the next few months.

My work ethic while it was one of my strong points, would have to be considered carefully. I would have to adapt it if I wanted to make this 'Step-up' that Sean and Roger were talking about. How to do that when the standard I was working at in Ireland was way below the standard I had to aspire to? This was going to be a tricky one! I would have to be pragmatic and creative in my thinking to find a way to overcome this problem. Here I would be working blindly a lot because of the unchartered territory I would be stepping into.

Competitiveness is not something I was lacking in by any manner of means, but, again, on this front, the competition I would be up against would be far greater than anything I had experienced to date and what I experienced to date had been quite a minefield. The competitors, as in the other referees who would be taking the exam, would be of a much higher standard than any Irish referee I had come up against to that point. These referees were reffing in their own National Leagues where the basketball was at an extremely high level. Some of them would even be professional as in Europe there were many Professional Leagues in many different countries. I would be up against these ultra-experienced referees. The likelihood was that their level of competency would be far higher than anything I was used to. I would have to be able to step-up to that and not only match it but aim to exceed it in order to be considered equal to them, especially the men. I would need to shine and stand out. The men would undoubtedly feel and believe they were far superior to any woman never mind a 5' 1" (1.55m) squirt of a thing like me.

Courage. While I had courage in bucketfuls or should I say basketfuls, I would have to dig deeper in myself than I ever had to before. I would have to find extra courage in myself not to crumble under the severe pressure I would be under. I would have to have the courage to take risks in order to step-up and I would have to be on the ball regarding dealing with the unexpected that might present itself. Once again, I would have to take on the male domination aspect of the situation but this time it would be more intensive than the previous time. The examiners would be male, the participants more than likely would be mostly male and the German Federation would be a formidable bunch of men. For my Grade 1, it was me versus the examiners and the system. This time it would be me versus the examiners, my own colleague, the other participants, the German Federation, the level of competition and the system. A daunting combination!!! Courage – I could see there was no end to the courage I would need.

Fitness was my easiest core element. I just had to maintain my level and make sure I was running at the same speed as the men. I needed to hone my body into a super fit state of operation and develop some extra strength as a buffer against potential injury and as something extra to have in the tank as a back-up. That should see me through and not only on the physical level. There was an added dimension to operating at this level of fitness. A super fit body meant a super fit mind enhanced with my sense of utter confidence in what my body was capable of.

One of the requirements for FIBA was body composition, that is, you had to have the perfect figure for the job. FIBA expected you to *Look* the part, as well as *Play* the part of the job you were undertaking. Believe it or not they actually had what was called the *Fat* list. If you were overweight by as little as a quarter or half a stone or more, you were put on the fat list and they wouldn't appoint you to games until you lost that weight and got back to your normal size. Thank heavens this wasn't an issue for me, but it was for some of the men.

Perseverance was going to be a biggy. I would have to persevere not only at everything regarding my preparation in Ireland but equally during that whole exam week in Dortmund. My perseverance would have to incorporate dedication and commitment to a level I had never achieved before. A big step-up would be required in this department. It's easy to persevere when things are going smoothly but quite a different thing altogether when the going gets tough and you feel you want to quit.

The most important and difficult core quality I would have to work on was definitely going to be psychological strength. Back in the 1980s there was no such thing as sport's psychology the way there is today. You just had to find your own way of building and strengthening your own mental capacity. There were no courses or training to help you in

299

this area. We weren't blessed with such things as motivational speakers or spiritual directors to guide you through your anxiety, nervousness or lack of self-esteem. You had to muddle along by yourself not having a clue what to do. This was going to be a major challenge. The European referees would be psychologically more developed than me due to the pressure they were constantly under while refereeing much higher standard of games. On this front I would be up against it and I knew it.

Now that I had established the necessary criteria I would need, where was I going to begin? I had an awful lot of work to do. My strengths were many as were my weaknesses. How was I going to get my head around all this? I needed to get cracking; the clock was ticking! In situations like this I always turn to my one and only saviour, Cadbury's milk chocolate. A good ol' bar of my favourite chocolate would help me to clear my mind and get me up and running.

I decided to take a trip down to the local library in Rathmines… but they didn't sell chocolate! No, I went to see if I could find any inspirational books on my required topics. Again, however, in the 80's there were no books written on any of those subjects. Nowadays, you would have no shortage, in fact there would be too many to get through. I spent a good few hours poring through different types of books but to no avail unfortunately. I ended up coming back home none the wiser.

I didn't know what to do. Unlike today, there was no internet, no Mr. Google to give you the answers to your questions, no videos or DVDs to watch, no blogs and no Wikipedia. It took another bar of chocolate to help me to realise that the only option I had now, was to use my own imagination to visualise what I was up against and to practise hypothesising as best I could whatever materialised. At least now I felt I was doing something proactive at last and beginning to take steps towards my goal.

During this six-month period, I had the great fortune of being appointed to my first T.V. game. The National Cup Competition was being televised and I was chosen to referee one of the women's semi-finals. The game was televised live and it was a perfect opportunity for me to experience a new realm of pressure. Here was an example of the stepping-up that I needed. While I was extremely excited of course, I could also feel my nervousness. It was strange being hooked up to a microphone and having to run around with the attachment in your pocket. It felt totally weird. However, I had to forget about it once the match began because my attention had to be directed solely on the match. The semi-finals are in a way more important than finals because if you lose, you are out, whereas once you're in a final you have nothing to lose and everything to gain. It was a great match and, like me, the players were also nervous playing on T.V. For once the players and referees were on the same page. A pleasant change!

I heartily enjoyed this match and the hype of it all and luckily for me I refereed an excellent match. A friend taped the match for me and I watched it later in her house. It was awful at first seeing myself on T.V. I couldn't believe I looked the way I did. I don't know what I thought I looked like, but it obviously wasn't like this. It transpired to be extremely helpful though, because I could watch the game over and over again to get an insight into my behaviour and mannerisms. I was also able to observe my lead and trail mechanics, my signals, my foul calls and violations. This proved in the long term to be extremely helpful to me for my preparations.

The fact that I did so well inspired the appointments officer to keep giving me good games. My FIBA exam was drawing closer. I now had less than 3 months to prepare and finalise the things I had to work on. I couldn't believe it. I decided to increase my overall training regime and get stuck in, really get stuck into perfecting those aspects of my refereeing that needed to be perfected. I did visualisations every day imagining myself in the five categories of the exam and achieving 100 per cent as much as I could. I did my best to visualise and imagine this higher standard I would have to step-up to. As they say in the country, I gave it wellie! Before I knew where I was, I was in Dublin airport boarding the flight with my colleague Ian, heading to Dortmund.

CHAPTER 25
Dortmund

I had a pleasant time with Ian travelling to Dortmund in 1990. We chatted about anything and everything and of course about our nervousness of what lay ahead. We reckoned it was going to be an incredibly tough week. We had no idea what to expect. When we arrived, we were greeted by a member of the Dortmund Basketball Federation. Thank heavens he could speak English and he brought us to our residence and showed us around. There was a meeting organised for that evening to meet the candidates, the examiners and the relevant personnel. This was to be followed by everyone having dinner. Ian and I went to our rooms to unpack and settle in and arranged to meet and go for a walk to get a sense of our surroundings before the meeting.

The meeting started sharp on time – German time –much different to Irish time which is quite lackadaisical. The Germans, we were to quickly discover, were sharp as a button, never late and extremely efficient. So, lesson number one, do *not* dare to be late for anything! This set the tone of the atmosphere that this efficiency would create. A lot of the other candidates were able to speak English in some shape or form, some well, some not so well and some with broken English, but nonetheless, enough to converse and hold a conversation with each other. Only the German candidate could speak German, but he too could speak some English. It was a nice and relaxed social way to be introduced to the other candidates and it took away the competitiveness that otherwise would have been palpable if it had been left to meeting in the basketball setting only. This was a clever intervention by the Germans. There were sixteen candidates in total, fourteen men and two women, myself and one other lady. The candidates had their own personal mentors/tutors with them and Ian and I were the only two candidates who didn't have anybody. This put us at a huge disadvantage immediately as the mentors attended regular meetings to receive information and remain updated on the exam requirements. After the meeting and the dinner, we went to bed. There would be a meeting early the next morning to outline the requirements of the exam and discuss the daily itinerary for the week ahead. We went to bed exhausted little bunnies from our first day of travelling and our first social gathering. There was no doubt in my mind that while this was an enjoyable evening that the next day would see the tension mounting. A good night's sleep was going to be important.

Next morning it was time to rise and shine and head down for breakfast at 8am. Breakfast was continental style, no cornflakes, weetabix or porridge for me and Ian. We had to manage and make the best of what was available. We would have to get used to it for the rest of the week. The meeting started at 9.30am sharp and the head person of the German Federation introduced us to the FIBA committee and the examiners. A new man by the name of Nar Zanolin had recently been drafted on to the FIBA committee and he was responsible for coordinating the fitness sessions for the entire week. It turned out that he was another version of Sean. That was cool for me, not for everyone else though! Then we were introduced to the remainder of the committee and the head man who was Mr. Schaffer. He would be the man with the greatest influence as he was extremely experienced and was a long serving member on the FIBA committee. I liked him on first impression. While you could see immediately that he was a sharp cookie with no flies on him, he also came across as a proper gentleman. Nar Zanolin on the other hand had a strong outgoing personality, knew his stuff on the training front and wouldn't take any prisoners on board with him. He also had a good sense of humour but was extremely serious when he had to be. A tall man, with an athletic figure, not an ounce of fat on him.

With the introductions out of the way, it was straight down to business. One of the men went through the timetable for the week and the extra-curricular activities on the itinerary. The days were going to be, as we expected, ultra-long and ultra-hard. There would be no time for relaxing or lounging around. It would be all go! The only time we would sit down would be at mealtimes. Every day there was going to be theory sessions and physical fitness sessions. There was going to be a lot of preparation work for the exam itself. We were given a quick tour of the areas that were being used for the various sessions, the last being the basketball gymnasium. It was a beautiful hall and to our little Irish eyes, looked absolutely gigantic. Our biggest gym in Ireland would have fitted in to one corner of it! Boy was I glad that we saw it in advance or it would have been a massive shock to enter it on the first night of a first match.

The morning flew by and we were sent to lunch and after lunch we had to report to the gym kitted out in our training gear for our first training session with Nar Zanolin. We had a gorgeous lunch. However, I held back a little bit because I never ate directly before a training session, I generally ate 3 – 4 hours beforehand. Well, lucky I did! What a blessing! The first training session was tough out, well on a par with any of Sean's. I felt lucky that here I could shine and not only did I shine, but I stood out drastically in comparison to the others. I was shocked at the low level of fitness of some of the men. I thought I would be struggling to keep up with them, I certainly did not expect to be ahead of them. They equally were shocked at me, equally expecting me not to be able to keep up with them. Nar did a seriously tough fitness exercise which left a lot of them puking up that gorgeous lunch. He was standing in front of us and he called out various instructions which we had to follow, for example, he would say, forward and we had to sprint forward until he changed the instruction. Then he would say, 6 front, 20 back. This would mean 6 press-ups and 20 sit-ups. If he said backwards, we had to sprint backwards. We had to do this for 10 minutes non-stop on the first day and every day afterwards it would increase by 5 or 10 minutes which meant that by the end of the week we would be up to 1 hour non-stop. Each day he would add in another instruction. Personally, I loved the exercise, it was no problem for me. The most important thing about it was you had to give 100 per cent from the beginning and continue giving 100 per cent throughout the whole time. You weren't allowed to pace yourself. The sprinting forwards and backwards and up and down had to be done at full speed. When you were the first finished after the instruction you had to jump and keep jumping until everyone was finished and they were up and jumping. This was good for testing the frustration of having to wait on others – the slow ones. There could be killings over that one.

On the first day, I was one of the few people who didn't get sick and throw up. After that I can tell you, people drastically reduced their lunch intake. However, there was a couple of them who still got sick due their lack of fitness. Boy was I glad I wasn't one of them. Nar Zanolin was taken aback with my level of fitness especially taking into consideration the fact that I was a woman. I was always first finished and first up jumping waiting on everyone else. I was in my element. My years of training with the *animal* were finally paying off. Nar did lots of other fitness drills including Suicides which I was also brilliant at and first to complete every time. The Suicides for the fitness test had to be run in under 35 seconds and there was going to be 3 Suicides with 1 short and 1 shorter break between them. By the end of that first training session everyone, except me, were on their knees wrecked and exhausted. At this point I was wondering how the hell were these people going to pass their fitness test. To me it was a given that the candidates would be well up to scratch for it. I was totally taken aback to see them struggling and on top of that, some of them *not* in shape at all. There was one candidate, the son of the top international referee, who was ranked No. 1 at that time. It was expected that on the back of his father's reputation he would fly through the exam. Shockingly, he was one of the candidates that was completely out of shape and his fitness level was awful. The idea of the training was to bring people up to the level they needed to pass by the end of the week. I doubted that this lad would make it, he was that far behind on that first day. Anyway, time would tell.

That was our first introduction to Nar Zanolin and his training regime. I seemed to be the only one who enjoyed it and was looking forward to the next one. The lads mostly were cringing and sickened at the thoughts of the next day. The times were going to be increased and they felt how the hell, if they couldn't even do the short time, were they going to double this? More puking ahead!!! The heads went down and I tried to encourage them by saying that although it would be tougher, they would get used to it in time. But of course, one week is a short time and a big ask under these kinds of circumstances. Fitness doesn't come in a week. It takes tons of training and a phenomenal amount of hard work. A tough week ahead for sure. The next session after the fitness training was a rules session. This brought us up to date on the most recent rule changes. There were a few changes but not too many, thank heavens. After that the leader of the German Federation informed us that he had an important announcement to make. Everyone was all ears. The lads who were in the doldrums after the fitness training were sighing, wondering what next? Well, it was a huge shock! Nobody could believe it! The gross unfairness of it! The leader informed us that FIBA had brought in major changes to the refereeing mechanics. They had been working on this for quite a while and were now ready to introduce and implement these new mechanics with immediate effect. This meant that over the course of the week we would be taught them and implementing them would be part of our exam.

Understandably, there was major uproar at this announcement. We had spent three years practising the original mechanics. How were we supposed to learn and implement new ones in just one week and not only that but already under the existing pressure of the exam itself? I can tell you in no uncertain terms, there was an absolute bedlam reaction. To say that the whole room was up in arms, candidates and mentors/tutors alike, is putting it mildly. I thought a few people were going to have heart attacks they were so seething and red in the face with rage. Obviously, it goes without saying, that Ian and myself were not happy campers either. We had no tutors with us, we had no one to fight on our behalf. We felt doomed! We would be depending on the others to bail us out as well.

After the session was over the mentors/tutors decided to meet to have a conflab about this latest development. It was unanimously decided that this expectation was a grossly unfair one. They went through the reasons and made a written list of their complaints and decided to approach the FIBA committee as one group to present their complaints and their viewpoints. They felt that the fact that they were in total agreement with each other would be in their favour. They knew however, that the FIBA committee would be no pushover either. They took their time to make sure their arguments were credible and would be listened to. Without further delay they approached the FIBA committee. There was no time to waste. The meeting with FIBA went on a long time and we were, in the meantime, biting our nails in dreaded anticipation of what the outcome would be. The candidates felt, that surely once the mentors protested so vehemently, we had a good chance of the decision being reverted to its original status.

While we waited patiently you could see everyone's nerves were frayed and the worried expression on people's faces were transparent. There were no long nails left after all that waiting I can tell you. Eventually and at last, the mentors returned to their candidates telling them what had taken place at the meeting and the outcome. Ian and I had no clue what was happening. We were completely in the dark. I decided to approach one of the mentors to find out what was going on. I chose Andy, the Swedish mentor as I had noticed that he spoke fluent English. He was also a nice man, friendly and outgoing. He told me that FIBA had listened to their complaints and arguments and both sides of the table had argued backwards and forwards quite fiercely. It finished up with FIBA saying they would discuss it further amongst themselves and think about it overnight and come up with a decision by the next morning. I said to him we would have another few hours of agony ahead of us. He laughed and replied yes, we would have to suffer for a while longer. He told me that in all the years he had been mentoring candidates at FIBA clinics that something this drastic had never happened before. He said that if FIBA did decide to go ahead with it, we would be most unfortunate and decidedly unlucky. I asked him from his experience of knowing FIBA what he thought they would do. He thought for a moment and said that normally they wouldn't do that but because of the new additions to the committee he wasn't sure. He didn't know these new people himself. He felt on first impression that Nar Zanolin, having seen him in action with the fitness training, would be an extremely competitive man and would demand everyone else to aspire to his level. If that was the case, he thought they would stick to their original announcement. He didn't know how much influence Nar Zanolin would have on the committee, that also would be a deciding factor. He told us not to worry, that he would keep us informed as we were at a distinct disadvantage not having our own mentor representing us. I thanked him for his help. His parting words to me were, 'What will be, will be, no point in worrying about it, at least everyone will be in the same boat.'

By the time we went to bed that night, the majority of the candidates were agitated as hell about the whole thing and it transpired that they didn't sleep well. I, on the other hand, decided to take the Swedish mentor's advice and not worry about it. I realised he was right. FIBA had the control and once the mentors had protested it was out of their hands too. They had done their best and couldn't do any more than that. A good night's sleep would be important especially if the decision went against us. We would need to be alert and mentally fit to tackle the problems that might lie ahead. Being tired and frazzled wasn't going to benefit any of us. I hit the hay feeling more relaxed and fell into a deep sound sleep. Next morning, we were up at the crack of dawn. Today was the day that the real work was going to begin. The schedule was jam packed. We were going to be tired out bunnies at the end of this day. After breakfast we went straight to the rules session where the FIBA decision was going to be announced. We sat with bated breath with fingers and toes crossed, waiting to hear the decision. FIBA announced, after much discussion and giving the situation much consideration, they had decided that they were going ahead with their original announcement. They felt that while it would add to the pressure of the exam of course, that it was fair as everyone was in the same boat, it was new to everyone, both candidates and mentors. They reasoned that it would be a good test of character as well as a good test for evaluating referees. After all, the basis of refereeing is that referees must be prepared and able to deal with the unexpected in every game. This challenge would be of a similar nature. It would test people's ability to be flexible, which is also another important quality for referees to have. It would challenge our alertness of mind, our focus and our ability to adapt, which are vital components of refereeing.

They made it sound like they were doing us a favour by the time they finished justifying sticking to their decision. Of course, while the points they presented were indeed valid, it didn't take away from the fact that it felt like three years of intensive training down the drain for us. To say we were sickened by the news doesn't cover it. The amount of moans and groans from the room was deafening. Some people put their faces in their hands and mumbled heaven knows what into their hands. It sounded like a lot of cursing by the tone of it. FIBA informed us that it would be prudent to get cracking now on learning the new mechanics and that they wanted to start the tuition immediately after a short tea break. The tea break was a good idea because it gave people the opportunity to vent their reactions and let off steam. The tea could be used as a calming potion and a calming potion was badly needed!!! Back into the room we went and the real work began. The tuition was excellent and the plan was to introduce the mechanics on a gradual basis every day. Each day they would revise what they taught the day before and then add in another phase each day. They decided this was the fairest and most productive way of doing it to yield good results.

The whole morning was spent on the rules and the mechanics. The first major change was in relation to the movement of the lead referee (the ref who stands behind the endline under the basket). Normally the lead would stay on the left side all the time, but now FIBA wanted the lead to move across to the other side of the basket whenever there were four or more players on that side. When most of the players are on one side, in basketball terms, it's known as the strong side. This required viewing the game from a different angle which took quite a lot of getting used to. I could understand the logic and reasoning behind it, but it meant you had to be extra diligent using your peripheral vision. It also made it more difficult for the trail referee to switch on to watching off-the-ball. The trail referee is so called because s/he trails the play.

In the afternoon we had the fitness training with Nar. He upped the training a lot this day and I guess part of the reason was to give everyone an outlet for their frustration and anger. Once again, I was the first to finish the exercises despite the increase in intensity. Nar was watching everyone like a hawk, noting everyone's participation. Again, some of the lads were puking and I don't know if it was the fitness only or part of the fact that they were feeling sick from the shock of the changes. I decided I was taking a pragmatic approach to the whole thing. My emotions needed to be dealt with succinctly, so that I could move on and focus on the daunting task at hand. It was going to take an enormous amount of hard work, blood, sweat and tears, to get through the remainder of the programme. Every training session, whether practical or theoretical, was going to be tough out and would need the highest level of focus and concentration possible.

During the lunch break on this day the Swedish mentor approached Ian and I with a proposition. He offered to help mentor us on the understanding that he had to give precedence to his own candidate first. As he only had one candidate, he felt he was in a position to help us providing it wasn't at his expense. He explained that if his candidate was to come up against Ian or I in the practical exam he would have to mentor him against us. If we were willing to accept these conditions and take the risk, he would be willing to help us. We thanked him profusely and said we would be delighted to take him up on his offer. He arranged a time and place to meet us after the last session of the day as the mentors had a meeting with FIBA regarding the exam. After this meeting we would have a better idea of what was expected. I turned up at the appointed time but there was no sign of Ian. I couldn't find him anywhere. The Swedish mentor arrived as planned and was surprised Ian was missing. However, he went ahead with me on his own and brought me up to date on the information he had received. He went through the morning's mechanics session with me again and gave me specific exercises to do that would bring me up to speed on them. He told me that I would have to practise them every spare moment I had and he suggested doing the exercises not only in front of the mirror, but *every* time I was walking from one place to another, if I didn't mind looking stupid that is. I realised I had no choice but didn't mind of course. His candidate whose name was Mikael, and myself, started doing what he told us to do and it wasn't as bad when you had someone to share looking stupid with!!! The two of us got on well and became good buddies. I was dearly hoping that we wouldn't come up against each other in the practical exam.

Some of the other candidates thought we were nuts and were slagging the daylights out of us, but we didn't care, we just slagged them back saying, 'You won't be saying that when we pass the exam.' Now it was a case of not only attending the FIBA sessions, but we also had to practise every minute of our spare time. It was a tough and demanding schedule, utterly exhausting. One of the exercises the Swedish mentor gave us to do, was to get the cutlery in the dining room and play a game arranging the cutlery in the formation of the new mechanics. One of us had to lay it out in the wrong order and the other had to rearrange it in the correct order according to the new mechanics. Mikael and I enjoyed the game and we had great fun playing it. I think this is what helped us to get a good handle on the new stuff and helped us to remember it better. Of course, the dining room staff thought we were mad!!! They had never seen anyone doing that before. It was a clever idea and worked wonders for us both. I found the exercises helpful in terms of raising my confidence and becoming more familiar with the new mechanics. The visual imagery appealed to my learning style. It helped me to absorb and retain the information. One time I was walking down one of the corridors practising my signals. I was in a world of my own, totally absorbed in my practise with the world around me completely blocked out when I bumped straight into Andy. I didn't see him coming. He gave me an unmerciful slagging saying, 'What kind of referee are you going to make when you can't see someone straight in front of you'?! There you are. You can't win. However, the truth was, he was delighted to see me practising with such intensity.

After that despite his slagging, I began to feel a bit more confident in relation to the new changes. I was hopeful I could master this challenge by the time I had to. From a basketball perspective, I had always been quick to adapt, learn and pick things up. Sean's training sessions had helped enormously with this. Once I got stuck into it, I became determined and didn't feel as overwhelmed as some of the others did. This made me feel good and gave me a sense of hope.

Another day had passed. I had survived and was even beginning to feel good. Things were seriously beginning to hot up now. Andy told us that only six referees out of the sixteen were going to be given a FIBA award. He pointed out how hard it was going to be for Mikael and myself to make the cut. They would eliminate four straight away which would leave twelve. From this twelve they would eliminate six more. Every mark we could get in everything was going to count. The first exam we had to undertake was the written exam which was scheduled for the next day. I was hoping to do well in that as I had been doing well in the theory sessions in the classroom part of the teaching. Naturally, everyone was nervous. This was the first part of the test and it was an important one. After the exam was over Andy went over the questions and the answers with Mikael and myself and I got 100 per cent which I was delighted with. It brought back memories of my Grade 1 exam in Ireland. A good start! It was great also to have made a dent into the exam. It felt like one monkey was gone off my back. It's hard to referee a match with monkeys on your back!

Matches were also starting that day in the evening time and four people would be taking the first half of their practical exam. We had to ref twice each. Everyone was hoping it would be them, because the first four people had a huge advantage, as they would only have the first phase of the mechanics to implement. As each day went by the next people were going to have more to implement which would be tougher of course. Ian, myself and Mikael were not in that first four unfortunately. Whether we were reffing or not it was compulsory to attend the matches. I was glad of this and would have done it anyway because it was the only chance we were going to get to see what everyone was like and the standard of the game also.

In the meantime of course, we had our fitness training with Nar and even though people had matches that evening, there was no let-up in his training sessions. He was still forging ahead like there was no tomorrow. At this point, I was still maintaining my first place in the exercises even though Nar was increasing the intensity. I was thrilled with my efforts and this just spurred me on even more to maintain my standard as much as possible. I kept expecting the others to catch up with me, but they didn't. Inside myself my confidence was growing slowly but surely and I was secretly hopeful that if I could maintain what I was doing, I could come out close to the top, if not top, by the time the fitness test came around. Just a few more days to go, to keep holding my position. My perseverance was helping me to grow in my determination to commit myself to this task. Courage – I had to remember my resolve from my preparations in Ireland regarding courage and to keep applying it from day to day.

In another way it was good not to be refereeing in those matches. It gave me an opportunity to observe the standard of the game and see what I was up against. The teams were excellent and the standard, just like Sean and Roger had said, was way higher than the Irish standard. I enjoyed watching the games however and felt if I could feel the same while refereeing that would be a good thing. I thought it would be better to approach the game mentally from this perspective, rather than a negative perspective of feeling overwhelmed. I enjoyed watching my colleagues refereeing and I learned a lot from watching them. They were exactly as I had expected them to be, very proficient indeed and, while they were a bit shaky, they did ok with the new mechanics. They made a couple of minor mistakes but nothing too major and all in all, they were happy with their performances. It was a good start for them and they were relieved to have their first match out of the way.

Of course, while this was good for them, it increased the pressure because they had set a remarkably high standard for everyone else to compete against. It wasn't going to be easy to raise the bar on them. I didn't think about this too much or let it get to me, I knew I just had to stick to my game plan and stay extremely focused on my goal. It was no shock; this was exactly what I had spent the last six months visualising in Ireland. I knew I had to step-up and match them as I had practised in my visualisations. The good thing however was, I realised I had done a great job with my imagination and those visualisations were very, very close to what the standard turned out to be. This, when it dawned on me, increased my self-belief and my motivation. I had to remain positive at all costs and acknowledge that, so far, so good, I was doing well. I was shining in the fitness training and had achieved my 100 per cent in the rules test. I just had to keep the ship steady now and stick to my game plan. I had to reinforce my perfection principle and apply it to the remaining parts of the test and keep doing what Andy was telling me to do and that was it. Throughout my life, it never ceases to amaze me how people refuse point-blank, in general, to do what they are told to do, when someone is trying to help them. Instead of responding positively they get up in arms and rebel against it. I think it's a common trait in Irish people. Mikael wasn't like that and I certainly wasn't either. We were delighted to be receiving the help and deeply appreciated Andy's expertise and influence on us.

During the course of Andy's proposal, I had a chat with him about the video test and my concerns about it, as it was something I couldn't practise or work on in Ireland because this facility wasn't available. He spent time with me every day showing me loads of basketball clips and explaining how the test worked. Back then there was no DVDs never mind You-Tube, it was only VHS cassette tapes. There was a little knack to it that he showed me which was hugely helpful. After a good few clips, I began to the get the hang of it and get my eye in on it too. He had hundreds of clips; I couldn't believe it. It made me realise that we were way behind in Ireland.

The next day the programme was much the same as the previous day. More people were appointed to the evening games and Mikael and Ian were in that bunch. I was delighted not to be up against Mikael. It also meant I could go and cheer him and Ian on, which I did.

Mikael was happy with the game he was appointed to and delighted with the co-official he was matched up with. He knew him and had reffed with him before and from what Mikael said they had always been a good team. Ian on the other hand, of course like myself, didn't know anyone and didn't know his co-official, it was merely potluck for him.

By this stage there were several additional changes to the mechanics which we had learned, one of them being in relation to teams playing a full court press in defence. A full court press is when the defending players, after they have scored, pressurise the attacking team immediately from the end line, rather than crossing the halfway line to set up their defence. The idea of this is for the defensive team to steal the ball or cause the attacking team to make a mistake. The new mechanics required the trail ref to follow the ball the whole way across the court to the far sideline and the other ref had to watch from a different angle the off-the-ball play. Once the players crossed the halfway line both refs had to revert to the regular positioning. This change in the visual angles made boxing in the play between both refs more difficult. Mikael's match was first and he was thrilled about that, as having to wait would make him more nervous. He knew that this was one of the new mechanics changes that he would have to implement in his match as one of the teams was notorious for playing a pressing defence. He and his partner reffed extremely well and I was delighted for him. It was Ian's turn next. The second game was a completely different game to the first game. It wasn't a smooth game and required a lot more decision making. Ian's partner was a strict, sharp off the whistle ref and was getting stuck in from the get-go. It looked like Ian was caught off the hop a bit with that and it took him a little while to settle into the game. Once he settled, he did well enough.

It looked like my game was going to be the next evening. I was going to have a lot of the new mechanics to implement by that stage. One such change was when reporting a foul to the table we now had to run out instead of walking out,

319

come to a complete stop in a space away from the players, report the foul in a particular sequence order, i.e., show the number of the player who fouled and indicate the type of foul, for example say pushing foul, indicate the penalty, i.e., 2 free-throws or sideline. This was good because it made it clearer and easier for the table officials and the spectators to know what was happening. I was matched up with a guy that Mikael also knew and Mikael told me he was lovely to ref with and he thought I should be able to get on well with him. This was a relief to hear. It turned out that Mikael was right, he was indeed a lovely guy and he made it his business to meet me beforehand and go through everything that he expected we would need to be prepared for. We were both well psyched up for the game and I was glad to be getting it over and done with. Andy also gave me a pep talk and of course Mikael and Ian were there to cheer me on. The game was a cracker which was lucky for me because I referee better in those games and it tested us both and presented an opportunity for me to show what I was made of. I gelled with my partner and I made no mistakes. My partner kept reassuring me during the game that I was doing extremely well and to keep it up. I guess while he was genuine, he didn't want me to bring him down either. I was hugely relieved when the game was over and my partner was thrilled with my performance. Mikael was delighted for me too and told me upfront that I was a much better referee than he had expected me to be, given the standard of the game in Ireland. He was joking with me saying, he had better watch out and watch his back, that I could be the one to knock him off his perch. Andy also reported the same to me and commended me especially on my application of the new mechanics. He said my performance was going to set the cat among the pigeons. I didn't understand what he meant by that, but he was grinning when he was saying it.

Another hurdle crossed. I was holding my position. The next day we had the video exam and I got 100 per cent in that to my immense surprise. I was hoping to scrape the 90 per cent pass mark and if I got a bit more it would be a bonus. For me it felt that the worst exam was over. Needless to say, this boosted my morale no end and my confidence took another leap. I was heading in the right direction no doubt about that, but there was still a long way to go.

At this point the pressure was mounting. Everyone was competing superbly. It looked as if it was going to go to the wire and it would go until the last match and the fitness test. We had one match each left to ref and the remainder of the mechanics to learn and implement. The fitness test was the last exam. Everything now was going to hinge on these last two. The fitness test I wasn't worried about, I was still ahead in the training for that and only the German referee was catching up on me. My second match was going to be the crunch.

I don't know how FIBA chose the order for the candidates to ref in, but I wasn't in the first two groups again. I was at the end. You could certainly feel the tension mounting now and at this stage everyone had to implement all the new mechanics. They had finished teaching them to us before the final round of practical exams began. People were becoming slightly irritated as a result of their nervous tension and a bit short tempered and snappy. I remained as cool as an Irish cucumber though, I did not want to ignite any unnecessary anxiety. I kept using my mantra, 'Stay positive, perfection, perfection, no mistakes, in the zone, stay in the zone, concentrate, focus, stay focused on the goal. Remember so far so good, you're doing well, you've got to maintain it now, no slip-ups.' These were the words I was repeatedly saying to myself every spare moment I had and particularly when I saw the others becoming nervous.

The next round of games was of a higher standard than the first round. Another step-up was required here. I watched the others refereeing and made sure to learn from their mistakes. Andy was prepping Mikael and myself like mad, tracking everything that was happening with the others and giving us the necessary advice to avoid making the same mistakes. Ian had the misfortune of having a grave mistake in relation to the rules in his match. It was his partner who made the mistake, not Ian. Ian however, made no visible attempt to correct the mistake, which would have shown that he knew the correct application of the rule. It made him look at fault as well as his partner. Ian took the viewpoint that once it wasn't him who actually made it, he would be ok. According to Andy this wasn't the case. During his interview after the match, Ian was grilled on this issue by the examiners. He insisted that he knew the rule, but they wanted to know why he didn't step-in and correct it and help his partner out. The examiner's viewpoint was that it would have been better to have applied the correct decision rather than letting the mistake take precedence. Poor Ian was in a bit of a state afterwards. I felt sorry for him. It's an awful thing when a mistake is made and it isn't you who makes it. But this is where the teamwork comes in and we are supposed to work as a team in every match.

Anyway, I can say that I benefitted from this mistake and learned a valuable lesson for my own exam. That was one of the advantages of being last, you could learn from others if you had your wits about you. During the second round Ian and his partner were not the only ones to make a mistake. A few people crumbled under the pressure. Mikael refereed another powerful game, he was quite happy with himself. Between the others and Mikael it spurred me on to really give it a Go! Get stuck in! Go for it! Throw everything at it! Give it my all!

I was partnered with the other lady for my final exam which was an enormous shock. FIBA had never ever put two women reffing with each other and especially two women on a men's match. Andy said that in his whole career this had never happened before. He reckoned that this was their way of scrutinising our abilities and putting us to the test. They probably doubted that two women would be good enough to control a men's game. Andy warned me in no uncertain terms what I had to do. He talked me through it step by step. He told me to take the game by the scruff of the neck and not to wait for my partner or depend on her. Andy based his advice on having seen her referee in her first match. If she was nervous, which she undoubtedly was going to be, she could freeze and that would leave me in the lurch. I listened carefully to Andy's instructions. I knew I had to get my head in to the right frame of mind and psyche myself up considerably. Under no circumstances was I going to let her drag me down and cause me to fail. Andy reckoned that she would freeze at the beginning and depending on how she reacted to me being in control of the game, would either stay in the freeze or come out of it at some point. The crunch factor would be determined by how badly she wanted to pass the exam.

I met her before the game to have a chat and prepare ourselves. She was shaking like a leaf. She was horrified that we had been partnered for this match and this rattled her. Andy had sized her up correctly. I tried to encourage her and lift her up, but her nerves got the better of her. That was it, I knew what I had to do. Effectively, I would be reffing on my own for the beginning of the match, no doubt about that. I reminded myself that I had reffed many matches on my own over the years and I was well able to do it. I just had to do it now and do a good job of it into the bargain. That was what the examiners were looking for to see if we could control the match, control the men, not lose our nerve and maintain control over ourselves under pressure. This was an even bigger step-up than I had ever imagined. It was a daunting prospect, but I was totally determined to do it. I was not going to give up. I thought of all the years preceding my Grade 1 and that enormous battle and the last three years preparing for this exam. No way Jose, no way was I going down, over my dead body would I crumble.

Everyone was there watching us because this was history in the making, two women reffing together. I had to throw up the ball, which had to be perfect to set me up for a good game. I repeated the same technique that I had used for my Grade 1 and my last thought was, you did it once, you can do it again. So, I did. A perfect toss was the result. I did exactly what Andy told me to do, I was quick, sharp, decisive and took no guff from any of the players. I took complete control of the match while she was in her freeze and I was firing on all cylinders. The fire in my belly was igniting me. There was no stopping me. I was like the cowboys in the film 'Gunfight at the O.K. Corral' when they were gun fighting. The bullets were flying everywhere. Well, that was me. I didn't miss anything, I just kept going and completely focused my mind on the task at hand. Boom, boom, boom. Foul after foul, violation after violation, I was just forging ahead, no let-up, no drama, just doing my job. There wasn't a beep out of the players, they got the message clearly, don't mess with me or you'll be sorry. They just concentrated on playing and left us alone.

During the first time-out I glanced over at Andy and he gave me the thumbs-up. That was precisely what I needed and I continued in the same manner for the remainder of the game. My partner eventually came on board and came out of her freeze which was a good thing in the end. By the time she did I had shown my worth and now just had to maintain that until the end of the game.

Mikael greeted me with a major slap on the back of congratulations after the match was over. He was genuinely delighted for me that I had put up such a good show. He was shocked and couldn't believe it. He was slagging me saying I was a right little dark horse. 'Where did you pull that out of?' he asked me. I said, 'The depths of my being, way, way down there somewhere,' pointing to my gut. He laughed and said, 'Well I would never have guessed you had that in you, you're a mighty big warrior for such a half-pint.' I laughed again; I was relieved to have the nightmare over. Nar Zanolin passed by and while he didn't say anything, reminiscent of Sean, he gave me an approving look. Andy was also extremely taken aback and obviously delighted. He said, 'I have never seen anyone doing what they were told to do to that extent before. Well done, I take my hat off to you.'

My post-match interview had also gone very well and I was able to answer the questions put to me. The examiners were nice, extremely professional in their approach and questioning and were good at giving nothing away! They didn't give the faintest inkling as to how they viewed our performances. The interviewer was professional, pragmatic, down to earth and straight to the point. This of course suited me and my personality. I like things to be clear, black and white, no ambiguity.

It took me some time to settle down and go asleep that night. My adrenaline was still pumping and mentally I was wound up. Reflecting on the match I was delighted with my performance; everything had gone to plan. I had repeated what I had done in my Grade 1 exam, reffed a perfect match, no mistakes and I did the new mechanics extremely well, which was an added bonus. So many things to think about and operate at the same time. It's not as easy as it looks, I can tell you. I settled down eventually and fell asleep. The next day was a big day according to the organisers and the following day would be the fitness test. One more training session left with Nar Zanolin. I would miss his training sessions when they would be over as I loved them and got great enjoyment from them. I couldn't wait to get home and tell Sean all about them. He would be super interested in them and no doubt would adopt them for himself to add to his already gruelling repertoire with great pleasure and satisfaction.

The next day we spent some of the day in the classroom covering a lot of the remaining theory. Now that the mechanics were finished, we had more time to spend on the basketball court revising them and correcting the mistakes that had been made during the practical exams. This was more helpful especially now that the practical exams were over and everyone was more relaxed and able to absorb it better. We also had to tog out and play a match and everyone rotated in order to have a chance at refereeing. This was great fun, I really enjoyed it and the lads couldn't believe how good I was at playing the game. They were joking with me saying I was too small to be that good. The accuracy of my shooting stunned them. When the training was over, we stayed back to play a game called Knockout and I won it despite their best efforts to knock me out. It was great craic because each time I knocked one of them out they were cracking up. Half-Pint winning the game was inconceivable to them. Their poor ol' machoism got a right ol' battering – the poor things – I did genuinely feel sorry for them but nevertheless was chuffed at being the winner. Those hours and hours of shooting practise was showing its worth.

That night everyone went to bed early. With the fitness test looming the next day, everyone wanted to get a good sleep to be well rested, fit and ready to go for the test. The test was in the afternoon replacing our fitness training with Nar. You could feel the tension in the gym. Everyone was as nervous as hell, especially those lads who were in a bad way at the beginning of the week. The three suicides were first and because the hall was big and wide, we were able to fit comfortably in one straight line and do the test altogether. This was good because it was much easier with everyone working as a unit. Having people beside you can help to pull you along. The whistle went and we were off on our first suicide. I ran like the clappers and came in first and everyone else managed to squeeze in in the time allowed. 45 seconds break and we had to go again on our second suicide. I don't know what happened, as in how it happened, but I fell in the middle of it and hit the ground with an almighty bang. The lads kept running, no one came to my aid and as quickly as I hit the ground, I jumped up again, galloped after them like mad and I ended up finishing joint first with the first lad. Andy happened to be standing right there, looked at me grinning and said, 'It's much easier Mary if you stay on your feet.' Ha ha, very funny, I thought. But with the break being reduced to 30 seconds this time, I didn't have time to respond to him. Off we went again and being the last one, I gave it everything and came in first again. A few of the lads didn't make the time. The famous ref's son was one of them, he was struggling badly coming in last.

After a short break we had to get ready for the bleep test. This was the crunch test. The lines are 20 metres apart and your task is to run up and back and touch the lines at each end with your feet only. It starts at a slow pace and builds up to fast, faster and faster as each minute goes by. If you miss a line or don't touch it on the bleep, you get one chance to catch up and if you don't catch up, you're out. The toughest aspects of the test are the turns and the fact that as you tire you have to run faster. From a physical and psychological perspective this is extremely difficult. It puts enormous stress and pressure on your lungs and heart. Your breathing increases and keeps increasing with the speed. By the fifth minute your lungs are beginning to heave and by the end they are truly bursting. Cardiovascular and anaerobic fitness, speed endurance and high lung capacity are vital components of fitness for this test. Once you miss a line, it's downright impossible to catch up because at that point your body and mind is beginning to disintegrate and psychologically it's a big ask to apply the mind over body principle. Everything at this point is caving in. Your legs are turning into jelly! You might even begin to see stars! These are the reasons why Nar Zanolin's fitness sessions were extremely tough and demanding. The bleep test is an indisputably demanding test. It also requires discipline and pacing, especially in the early stages and when it gets extremely fast, you just have to run like billio! There's no time for hanging around. The requirement to pass the test was 10 minutes which is 86 lengths in total, quite a fair amount even for fit people. The speed of the bleep test was also a faster pace at that time. This was the inaugural trial of the bleep test in FIBA! Nowadays they have reduced the speed to make it easier for people to pass.

Having done so well in the suicides, I was feeling confident and well warmed up for the bleep. The whistle went and we began simultaneously, keeping the pace beautifully and staying in line. It was when the tape hit that lethal 5 minutes that some people became uncomfortable and began to struggle. The straight line began to waver and as the speed increased some people began to drop off the pace. The surrounding people did their utmost to encourage them to stay with it and hang in there. This helped some of them, but others just couldn't respond. As a result, a few of them did not make it and failed. I kept going and the remaining bunch kept egging each other on not to give up. When the tape hit the end of the 10 minutes everyone stopped, some of them literally collapsing over the line except the German guy and myself. We kept going apace up and down and up and down we went. We were at the end of Level 16 when the organisers decided to turn off the tape because it looked like we weren't going to stop (we thought they were hungry and wanted to go for dinner!). We were both raging because we wanted to see how far we could get. The organisers informed us that it was a record and had no chance of being beaten. The level we reached was the equivalent of what an international track athlete would achieve if they were to run it. That soothed our annoyance a little bit. We slowly calmed down.

The German ref gave me a hug and congratulated me on such fine running. He said he most definitely would have given up much sooner only for me and thanked me for carrying him along. He had the graciousness to say that I would have eventually outrun him if we had gone on because at the point we stopped he was feeling under severe pressure. I thanked him too because he had also spurred me on and joked that I had just started to warm up. It just so happened that our running styles were suited to each other, which was ideal for both of us.

Now that the Fitness test was out of the way and knowing I had passed with such distinction, I felt happier and lighter in myself. Nar congratulated the two of us and Andy told me he was ever so proud of me. This was sweet and felt like the icing on the cake. Mikael and I had a kind of post-mortem talk with Andy after that to see where he thought we ended up in the rankings. Andy thought, while we had both done extremely well overall, it was difficult to say what the outcome would be. It would totally depend on the examiners and what impressed them most. He thought we were perhaps in the top 8, but whether we would make the top 6 or not was another thing. If it was a close battle, which it was going to be, it would depend on what the examiners believed was most important. Would they have to go with a political agenda or could they stay neutral and rank on true merit. We would have to wait and see. From my perspective of being a female in a largely male-dominated set-up, he felt that, as he had already said, I most certainly had set the cat amongst the pigeons and disturbed their equilibrium. Having received 100 per cent in the written and video exams, done well in the practical's and excelled in the fitness test, I most definitely had put it up to them, no doubt about it. He said we would have to keep our fingers crossed and hope for the best. There was no way of knowing what the final outcome would be. After our discussion I was happy enough that Andy felt we might be in the upper half of the group. This gave me hope. The problem now was, we were going to have to wait for two whole long agonising weeks before we would know. FIBA would meet and discuss the candidate's results and what had transpired throughout the week and base their decision on these factors. They would then inform each Federation of their decision.

I can tell you; those two weeks were the longest two weeks of my life. In the meantime, with the exams completed, we had our final farewell dinner. The food was gorgeous and we made up for the reduced lunches we had suffered by getting stuck in and gobbling everything in sight. It was great to be free again and not to have to worry about the trivialities of the test. We were sad saying goodbye to each other. Considering the competitive environment we had been in for the week, we got on extremely well and gelled unexpectedly well with each other. The majority of the men had taken a great shine to me and of course Mikael and I had become good friends. We exchanged addresses and phone numbers and promised to keep in touch. I had an emotional goodbye with Andy and thanked him profusely for all his help and taking such an interest in me. I thanked him for his generosity, his sense of fun and for sharing his immense knowledge and wisdom with me. I told him words couldn't explain how much I valued and appreciated his input, how blessed and privileged I felt and how lucky I was that I met him. We also exchanged addresses and phone numbers. In those days there were no mobile phones, computers or fax machines. The only way of keeping contact was by handwriting letters and using your house phone or work phone to ring someone.

This was our last night together. After the delicious dinner we went into the lounge and some of the men couldn't wait to have a drink. No alcohol had been consumed during the whole training week. Some of them had what the Irish call 'A thirst on them.' It was nice to be able to sit down, relax and have a chat and have a beer as some of them did. I don't drink, I was happy with my good ol' Seven-Up. We had a great time sharing stories, laughing, telling jokes and we even ended up on a nice little singsong. We stayed up later than we had been all week, but eventually, even with that, it was time to go to bed.

We decided to say our goodbyes before going to bed as we might not see each other the next morning. There were two people who had to leave before breakfast. It was sad saying goodbye as we didn't know if any of us would see each other again. It would depend firstly on whether or not we passed the exam and secondly, if we did pass, whether we would ever be appointed to the same matches or not. Between everything it was more unlikely than likely that we would meet each other again. Although I would have welcomed it, the odds were stacked against it. Therefore, an emotional goodbye with lots of hugging and goodbye happy wishes for each other was the order of the night. We went to bed eventually, emotionally drained and physically exhausted.

Everyone was leaving the next day starting in the morning before and after breakfast. People were leaving at different times during the day. The German Federation were going to be kept busy, chauffeuring everyone to the different bus, train and airport connections. Once the first two people were gone it changed the atmosphere considerably and we could feel the closure of the week setting in. We hung around until gradually, one by one, people were drifting off. Ian and I were nearly the last to leave as we had a late flight back home. By the time we left we realised it was over and our tough week was now history. We said goodbye to Mr. Schaffer, Nar Zanolin and anyone who was left from FIBA. We thanked the German Federation for their help and organisation and for bringing us to the airport. Mikael and Andy travelled together as Andy had driven them both from Sweden to Germany. They now had to face the long, lonely journey back but at least they had each other. It was strange being down to two people again, Ian and myself, back to where we had started a week ago but what felt like a lifetime ago. We had come full circle. Ian was staying in my house overnight as it would be too late for him to get a train home. My parents didn't have a car, which meant we had to get the bus from the airport home to my house. It felt strange being home again. Our week away had felt like we were on a different planet. Now we were back to reality. Good ol' reality! We would have to put our feet on the ground again and get back to daily ordinary living. The next morning Ian got a taxi to the train station and we said our goodbyes. I felt sorry for him having to complete his journey on his own. Although I wasn't happy to be home at least I was at home. He didn't seem to mind too much though and promised to ring me when he got home to let me know that he was safe. This he did and that was it, the end of our FIBA experience.

CHAPTER 26
The Wait

As I've said already, the next two weeks were the long-est two weeks of my life. The waiting was pure torture. My parents had already questioned Ian and I on how we got on and how we thought we did. Ian was much more confident in his reply to them than I was. When I went into work for my first day back Vivienne was all over me like a rash, dy-ing to hear the gory details and dying to know how I got on. Of course, Vivienne, when she heard the finer details, was panic-stricken at the thoughts of the harrowing pressure we were under. She couldn't understand how I could possibly cope with it and said that if it was her, she most definitely would have crumbled under that immense pressure on the first day, never mind by the end of the week. Her poor little eyes were popping out of her head and she made me laugh with her expressions, facial and otherwise, as she listened intently to my story.

I was quite distracted in myself as you can probably im-agine. My mind kept wandering to the exam. I kept wonder-ing if I would pass, would I be lucky enough to pass, did I do enough to pass? I knew I was in with a chance. Mikael, Andy and some of the other refs had given me extremely positive feedback and felt there was a strong possibility that I was in the running. Of course, with something of this na-ture you never know, stranger things have happened. Nar Zanolin when saying goodbye to me, while he didn't give anything away, had been very positive in his comments re-garding the fitness training and encouraged me to keep it up.

Vivienne, bless her, was just as nervous and anxious as I was which was lovely. You would think she had undertaken the exam herself. Vivienne was always a great listener. She absorbed the information like a sponge and she could visualise it clearly, it was like she was actually there herself. She decided to bring me to Bewley's for a cup of tea to help me to pass the torturous time away. We were sitting quietly at the table and my eyes kept wandering off into the distance, causing me to lose touch with what was going on around me. I was stirring my tea distractedly, but not actually drinking it. Suddenly Vivienne said, 'I'll give you a penny for them.' This jolted me back into reality and I said, 'Oh, you can guess what my thoughts are about, that flippin exam!' This was only my first day, what was I going to be like with thirteen more days of waiting. At this point I began to feel that the exam was easier than all this waiting! It was unbearable.

My mother had me demented! I couldn't understand why she was in such a tizzy about it. It wasn't in her nature to have my interests at heart. It wasn't until my Da told me that I understood. She wanted to be able to brag to her friends about it and in her usual way take the credit and glory for it. She would make them think that if it wasn't for her and her input (which by the way, from my side, was nothing), I wouldn't have done as well as I did. As usual, it was all about her and not about me. My Da was highly amused by it. He was tickled pink because he knew that I had done it by myself. He had, in fact, felt bad about the fact that they weren't able to help me. They hadn't even contributed any financial support, never mind emotional support.

The next twenty-four hours felt like forty-eight hours and each day after that felt like the hours were trebling and quadrupling. At long last one week had passed. Just one more week of agony left. That week however felt like an eternity. I tried to keep myself busy to take my mind off it but realistically how was that possible? I had to get Vivienne to keep nudging me at work to bring me back to what I was doing. Poor Vivienne, she was the closest person to me and the one who shared my torture the most. As usual she was extremely kind and understanding about it and supported me every inch of the way. I promised her that she would be the first to know the result. This kept her happy, poor thing!

We had a diary in work and Vivienne kept striking off the days as each one passed. There were more visits to Bewley's, we had no nails left, Vivienne had no hair left (she was always pulling at her hair when she was nervous or anxious), there was a lot more staring into space, little or no productivity, I learnt about automatic pilot and we were out of our minds by the end of the two weeks.

CHAPTER 27
The Fated Phone Call

Finally, it came, that fated phone call. I had given my work number to the Irish Basketball Association as I did not want my mother to be the first one to get the phone call. As requested, the call came into work. I was in the toilet at the time. There had been a lot more visits to the toilet too! Isn't it always the place where one is when something important happens or someone is looking for you? Vivienne luckily enough happened to be the one who picked up the phone when it rang. She asked who was speaking and when they said it was the Irish Basketball Association, she told them to hang on and wait a minute, dropped the phone like a hot potato and came belting out into the toilet, screaming at me to come in quickly.

I didn't cop on at first because she didn't say it was them, she just kept telling me to come on, hurry up, hurry up. On the way in she told me. I was planking. Oh shit, ahhh, oh no! And now when it seemed the torture was finally over, I was afraid to take the call. I said to Vivienne, 'You take it, you take it.' She was shaking her head frantically, 'No,' she said, 'They won't tell me, they will only tell you.' Of course, I realised that she was right. She picked up the phone and thrust it into my hand and made me hold on to it. I was shaking like a leaf. I needed to go to the toilet again. My nerves were activating my wee! Vivienne put the phone up to my ear. By this stage, everyone in the office had gathered around my desk and the word was spreading through the building like wildfire. More and more people were gathering around me. I nearly fainted. Vivienne gave me a poke in the back to say

337

hello. My voice sounded peculiar; I didn't recognise it. A shaky hello was eventually tweeted out and the voice on the other end of the phone was quite officious. 'I would like to inform you that the FIBA Federation have been on to us to inform you that you have passed your FIBA examination. Congratulations Miss Whelan.' I was shocked. I couldn't believe it. 'What?' I said, 'I passed, is that what you said?' 'Yes,' the voice replied. 'Have a nice day Miss Whelan' and she hung up.

There was an almighty roar from everyone when they were sure I had passed. I dropped the phone out of my hand and slunk down into my chair. The nervous tension of the interminable waiting had utterly drained me. I was feeling the effects of it now. It looked like the whole building was in our office, they were like sardines in a can. Vivienne, who was normally quite reserved, went mad with delight. Everyone started hugging me and slapping me on the back, congratulating me. The excitement was electric. I will never forget it as long as I live. A few of the men picked me up and gave me the bumps. The rest were counting at the top of their voices, '1, 2, 3, 4, 5, 6, 7, 8, 9, 10. Woohoo! She did it, she passed.' They started singing 'Congratulations,' Cliff Richard's song. Our A.P. (Assistant Principal) who was in his office came in to see what the commotion was about. They yelled at him, 'She passed, she passed, she's the first woman in Ireland to get the FIBA International Refereeing award. She just got the news.' 'Oh, I see,' he said, 'No wonder you're all so excited. This is a great day for Ireland. Congratulations Mary, the drinks are on me.' The hip, hip, hoorays followed and she's a jolly good fellow. I was thrilled to bits but still dumbfounded. 'Speech, speech,' someone roared. I indicated to Vivienne to say something as I was actually speechless. This was the day Vivienne became my Public Relations Officer (P.R.O.)!! No better woman! She gave a grand rendition of all my hard work and how much I deserved it and nobody knew it better than her, she had been with me every step of the way. Our A.P. said, 'O.K. everyone, close shop and straight down to the pub. This is a day for celebration. I'm afraid the public will have to wait. This is a once in a lifetime achievement and we are going to celebrate it in style. Let's go.'

Off we went down to the pub. I have never seen people to move that fast. I was literally carried down. The pub was right next door to the office, which was handy because we didn't have far to go. The pub owners knew us from going in and out to the pub regularly. They were wondering what the hullaba- loo was all about. Someone told them and they gave us the first round of drinks on the house as a token of their respect in relation to my 'Outstanding Achievement.' I was bowled over by both my boss's gesture and the pub's gesture.

A great afternoon and evening was had by all, and, when things died down a bit, I rang Sean, Roger, Bridget and my parents to tell them my news. I was glad it was my Da who answered the phone at home as my mother would have been raging if she realised I was in the pub. My Da didn't even notice he was that happy for me. Sean, Roger and Bridget were absolutely thrilled for me, Roger in particular was dy- ing to hear the gory details. Bridget was her usual self, say- ing, 'You're nuts already. I suppose this is going to make you more nuts. You'll be traipsing the length and breadth of Europe now! Heaven's above, what next?' But she was ex- tremely proud of me nevertheless and she insisted on bring- ing me out for a celebration and a show. Sean, of course, was his cool non-committal self, saying, 'Well Miss Whelan, you must have done what you were told,' but behind my back it was different though. He was singing my praises.

It took some time for the news to spread that I had passed my FIBA exam. Unlike the Grade 1, it was more incognito this time. I think, as I've said already, because the exam was outside the country it was nearly like it was being undertaken in secret even though this wasn't the case of course. It's not hard to imagine why the news took a long time to spread. It was primarily by word of mouth. Back in 1990 there was no such thing as email or social media and certainly no smartphones which we have in abundance today. One of the National evening newspapers contacted me for an interview. The article drew a lot of attention and highlighted my achievement. It was a newsworthy item that Ireland, after 8 Male International Referees, now had its First Female International Referee to join that elite squad. The reporter was a pleasant man who was bowled over at the fact that I was barely over the five-foot mark and able to stand up to these giants of basketball players. The title he gave his article was 'Mary walks tall.'

Following the article there was great excitement and as people found out, they were organising little surprise get-togethers and parties of congratulations for me. The celebrations this time were quite different to those of the Grade 1. These were exceptionally nice and genuinely thoughtful and I thoroughly enjoyed them. There were many of them. I couldn't believe it. The FIBA celebrations went on a lot longer that the Grade 1 did. It was quite intriguing the difference in both, yet they were meaningful and special in their own unique way. I would now have different and lovely memories to cherish again this time around.

Naturally, it took quite a while for it to sink in that I had passed. That torturous two weeks of waiting had me numbed out to some extent. After the intensity of the week away and its gruelling schedule, it took time to get back to a sense of normality. It was strange now being a FIBA referee, being at the top of the ladder with nowhere else to go. While I felt truly chuffed about that and chuffed with myself, it had a level of surrealness about it. Now I was up there with the best of them in Ireland and Europe as well. It took me some time to get my head around that one, I can tell you. I soon found out that Ian hadn't passed the exam, but that Mikael did. I was sorry for Ian and of course delighted for my buddy Mikael. Andy of course being Andy, knew I had passed before I did. News obviously travelled faster in FIBA than in Ireland would you believe! I rang Ian to commiserate with him and he was extremely disappointed. While he congratulated me, I knew he was feeling pretty miserable about the whole thing. I bought a congratulations card for Mikael and a thank you card for Andy, wrote two letters, put them in with the cards and sent them off immediately. Roger met me afterwards and boy! was he eager to hear the ins and outs of the week! He couldn't believe the number of changes that FIBA had incorporated into the test in comparison to when he did it. He was totally and utterly shocked at the mechanics changes and how we had to learn them at the clinic and put them into operation as part of our exam. He thought it was extremely unfair. He thought I did brilliantly not to crumble under this pressure and to be able to adapt the way that I did.

I thought it was funny when he declared that now I was the only FIBA referee in Ireland who was up to date with the new changes, rules, mechanics, fitness test etc. that I would have to teach it to the Irish FIBA's to bring them up to date. I said, 'What?! You can't be serious!' He laughed and confirmed that yes indeed I would have to do that. I was mortified at the idea of it. There I was, just in nappies as a FIBA referee and he was putting me into a situation that was completely unexpected ground for me. Talk about going from the frying pan into the fire and being thrown to the wolves. He broke his heart laughing at my reaction, 'Now Miss Cheeky young lady, that's part of your job now as a FIBA referee. You'll have to educate others!' Well, I'll be damned I thought, I don't even get a chance to settle into my new grade, it's all guns blazing. I felt like I was back in Dortmund!!!

Anyway, I had no choice, I had to do what he said as it was a short while before the FIBA material arrived in the Irish Basketball Association office outlining the most recent updated changes. I did my best with it and everyone seemed happy enough with my presentation.

CHAPTER 28
The Ineluctable Next Step

I was given my first FIBA nomination shortly after giving the course to the other FIBA referees. I was thrilled to bits to get one that quickly as I wasn't expecting that to happen. I was appointed to the World Student Games in Sheffield in England and it was a two-week trip as there were a lot of games. The next best part was that Roger was also nominated to the same tournament. Roger and I had come full circle again. What a coincidence. I was delighted beyond delighted, *delira and excira* as they say in the good ol' Dublin accent. It was 99 per cent certain that we wouldn't be appointed to the same matches but we would be able to hang around a bit and dine with each other at least.

I was a bit nervous naturally going in to my first FIBA tournament. Roger was well used to it and he just reassured me I would be fine. He told me that the exam was the hardest part and this would be chicken feed in comparison. I was hoping he was right and at the same time dying to get stuck into the reffing. It was a huge affair, exactly like the Olympics. The ceremonies were a direct replica of the Olympics. I was bowled over by it, the fireworks, the music, dancing, the razzamatazz. We had to march with the Irish team behind the Irish flag in the opening parade ceremony. The atmosphere was electric. There were a lot of teams, delegates and people from countries all over the world. You name it they were there. I hadn't realised that this was going to be such a prestigious event. There were thousands of spectators watching, clapping and cheering on their countries. It was a spectacular opening. I was so excited and I felt extremely proud to be representing my country and FIBA of course. We looked well marching in our green, white and orange. It was superbly magical the whole thing and truly uplifting. I felt privileged to be not just a part of it, but to have an active part in it.

The next day the matches started and they were being played in a few venues due to the large number of competitors. The venues were beautiful and of equal standard and each one was able to hold huge numbers of spectators. My first game was Russia Vs Greece. I was told that on paper it should be a good match. I was delighted to hear this. There were assessors from FIBA present at every match observing and marking the referees. The marking system was out of a score of 10, 1 being the lowest and 10 being the highest. We were informed it was not possible to achieve a 10 and that 8's and 9's would be considered extremely high and good scores, but they too would be difficult to achieve. I had reminiscences of Nadia Comaneci at her Olympics where she scored her first 10. I couldn't believe that I was now in a similar position.

Over the course of the days, I made friends with one of the organisers who was in on the act with the assessors and he gave me my daily scores once I promised him faithfully that I wouldn't divulge them to anyone. This I did of course because I was seriously grateful to know how I was doing and I didn't want to get him into trouble. My first match was a tough one as expected, but I reffed extremely well and scored an 8. He explained to me afterwards that this was, for the match in question, an extremely high score as my partner scored less. I was thrilled to hear this and it spurred me on to do as well and if possible, better in my next match. I had no idea how Roger was doing because he was always on a different court and sometimes our games clashed with each other.

Every game was extremely competitive, even if teams lost by a clear margin. Mostly however, the games were close in scores and there was an extremely high standard of play. I thoroughly enjoyed my first game and because it was a tough one it set me up for the rest of them. Later in the week I had another extremely tight game, China Vs Spain. It was an absolute humdinger and it went to overtime. The game was won by 1 point by China in the end. China had a girl who was uncharacteristically and unbelievably tall, just under 7 foot at 6 foot 8 inches (2.03 metres). She was extremely difficult to mark, as Spain's tallest player was 1 foot (0.30 metres) smaller in height. She had a lot of jumping to do to mark her and a lot of physicality to exert to prevent her from scoring. They had a royal battle between them and it provided great entertainment for the spectators. You couldn't hear your ears for the screaming and shouting. The spectators were roaring their heads off for the whole match. The spectator area was completely full and people were lining the walls all around the gym. The atmosphere was indescribable.

I was more than happy with my performance after the match as I knew I had reffed a good decent game. I was completely on the ball and never faltered once. The crowd inspired me as opposed to intimidating me and this made me raise my standard of reffing to a much higher level. I had never experienced such a crowd before, never mind such a volatile, noisy crowd. But I was in my element and it carried me to greater heights in myself to reach my optimum performance. My friend told me afterwards that the assessors were extremely impressed by my performance and were arguing over the marks as some of them wanted to give me a 10 and felt I deserved a 10. While the others, according to my friend, were not in disagreement with the 10, they were adamant they didn't want to set a precedent. After much arguing and debating they settled on 9.5 as a way of keeping everyone happy. While it would have been amazing to get a 10, I was delighted with the overall result. My friend reckoned it would be verbalised back to FIBA anyway, who were sure to query the 9.5 result. I was happy with that and the knowing that they felt it was a 10 performance. I so nearly joined Nadia in the history books!

The rest of the tournament went extremely well for me and I received a lot of 9's over the course of the fortnight. My lowest score was 8 and my highest score 9.5. I got great pleasure and enjoyment reffing my matches and felt I had a lucky and charmed start to my FIBA career. My friend, the organiser, told me I couldn't have had a better start and he said it would most definitely set me up for more matches in the future. I felt greatly enthused by this. Of course, unfortunately I couldn't break my promise and tell any of this to Roger or anyone else. I just had to keep telling Roger that I had reffed well. One of the assets of this was my consistency in the marking. That stood me in good stead and put me in an advantageous position, especially with the standard of matches being exceedingly close and fiercely competitive. I thanked my friend profusely for his help and came home an incredibly happy FIBA referee.

It turned out my friend was right. My next appointment from FIBA followed quickly on the heels of the first one. Again, I couldn't believe it. I was delighted. I was appointed to a European Cup match in Sweden. When I was nominated to the match, I didn't know that this appointment was an extra-special one. It transpired that I was making history again. I was about to become the first woman to referee a Cup match in Sweden. It was only when I got there that I found this out. I was wondering what the hullabaloo was about when I arrived at my hotel. There were reporters and camera men waiting on my arrival. When I saw them, at first I thought there was something special going on in the hotel. I looked around behind me but there was no one there of importance. I suddenly realised they were there for me! I played it cool (or was I just in shock?) and checked in at the reception desk but they were hanging around the foyer waiting for me to finish my business at the desk. They started following me up to my room. Luckily enough there was a representative from the club with me making sure everything was in order and making arrangements with me regarding the pickup time to bring me and my co-official to the match. He explained to me eventually what was going on. I nearly died. What the heck I thought, I'm famous and I don't even know it! That's a bloody good one alright!

Anyway, the club representative decided not to leave me, he thought it was better to stay and act as my bodyguard. I was glad for him to be there because there was quite a commotion going on between the photographers and the reporters vying against each other to get the news. They started yelling questions at me, right, left and centre and my head was spinning trying to look from one to the other as the questions were coming fast and furious. I felt as if I was watching a Wimbledon tennis match. I copped on finally and tried to slow things down a bit. This helped enormously as it became a bit more civilised. They asked me questions like, 'Are you nervous? Will you be able to referee such a tough match? Have you ever refereed a match this pressurising? Do you feel the pressure? What will happen if you fail? Do you feel the pressure, do you feel the pressure? You must feel the pressure!' This seemed to be their favourite question, 'Are you afraid?' I remained cool, calm and collected and answered that no I didn't feel the pressure. I explained that I was an extremely competent referee and that I had nothing to fear, nothing to be afraid of. FIBA don't award this grade unless you're good enough and they don't give you nominations unless they know you are up to the required standard. I told them that I was actually looking forward to the match and was excited to be reffing it. They looked at me in disbelief as if I had 10 heads. They obviously were not expecting an answer like that. Believe it or not, my answers rendered them speechless. Quite a rare thing for reporters! The club representative was impressed with my coolness and said that the answer I gave was a particularly good answer. The reporters informed me that they would be at the match to witness the outcome for themselves. 'Good,' I said, 'I hope you enjoy the match.'

Sure as eggs, they were true to their word and they were there. Heaven knows what they were thinking, probably something in the vein of how could a 5' 1" (1.55m) titch be any good at refereeing. My co-official and myself had to get really psyched up for the match. I knew I couldn't go down after all that bravado on my part! I had to give them something good to write about. I didn't want to give them the ammunition or the satisfaction of being able to annihilate me.

It was a super match, nail biting and well fought by both teams. Just like Sheffield, the gym was thronged with spectators making the atmosphere electric. Of course, the home team had the advantage of having the most spectators which was extremely uplifting for them. My co-official was a lovely guy and we got on famously. Like myself, he wasn't ruffled by the whole scenario and was actually great fun while at the same time being utterly professional. He helped me to relax and was amazingly encouraging towards me. We reffed a superb match together. We were clever, smart, astute and remained on the same wavelength throughout. We really gelled together and were in control of everything. Nothing escaped us. We were on top of our game to such an extent that it was impossible for there to be any complaints against us. Naturally, this was a good thing and augured well for the future.

It was an exhilarating match and we were on a high afterwards. Having showered and changed after the match the reporters were waiting for us in the lobby. It was hard to know what they thought. The club representative said that they were probably disappointed because they were looking forward to slating me and having a big juicy story to write on how bad I was and how many mistakes I made. As this wasn't the case and they couldn't write complete barefaced lies, he said that what they usually do in the situation is write something short without going into any great detail. Alternatively, he said, you would be splashed all over the headlines if you messed up and that would be the end of your FIBA career.

He congratulated me on a fantastic match and told me that from a FIBA perspective I had undoubtedly passed the test they had set me. He grinned and said, 'You did exactly what you told the reporters you were capable of doing.' He brought the commissioner, my co-official and myself to a fabulous restaurant for a meal. We had a lovely evening and it was late when we got back to the hotel as the match didn't finish until 10pm.

The next day he collected me from the hotel to bring me to the airport. I had said goodbye to my partner and we had promised to keep in touch. The club representative presented me with a newspaper and laughed as he handed it to me. 'I was right,' he said, 'here, take a look for yourself.' Of course, it was in Swedish and I couldn't understand a single word of it. He translated it for me, it was exactly as he said it was going to be. Short and sweet like a bellyache. The poor reporters didn't get the drama they were looking for. Anyway, from my perspective with FIBA, it was the best result. They don't like their referees hitting the headlines for the wrong reasons. A perfect outcome all told!!!

It was hard to believe that after only two FIBA nominations I had twelve matches under my belt with the eleven I had done in Sheffield! A remarkable start to my FIBA career. These two nominations set me up nicely for my future. Because I had done supremely well and stepped up to the challenges I was presented with, these ensured further nominations in the future. The fact that the level of these games were of high quality and standard and had to be refereed, as in really refereed, was also a key factor in determining my future. Being able to gel with my various partners and earning the respect I earned from the players and coaches was another thing that stood to me. Handling the pressure in a cool, calm way and thriving on that pressure rather than disintegrating under it, also gained me a lot of respect. Because I was assessed by the FIBA assessors right from the beginning of my career, for my first 12 games, it gained me the recognition I needed, to be considered competent enough by FIBA to be awarded nominations on a regular basis in accordance with my availability. A charmed start as I've said already and a lucky one too, especially considering I was a woman in the middle of these men who were dominating the sport. I never looked back after that and I just had to maintain my standard of refereeing and keep learning from these wonderful experiences. The more I could improve as I went along, the better. The most important thing that I had to remember and respect was the golden rule 'You're only as good as your last match.' This is every referee's mantra and it is the sword that you live by and you die by. One bad match and you are out. Finito – you may hang up your boots and your whistle! The level of professionalism and demand for perfection at international level does not allow for anything less.

After my match in Sweden, I had cup and league matches and tournaments in many other European countries over the next number of years. I sustained my high standard of refereeing and improved further as I picked up some useful tips from assessors and my refereeing colleagues. At one of our FIBA tuition courses, which was part of a week-long tournament, one of the speakers gave us some worthwhile advice. He said to develop our styles of refereeing we should imagine a huge spread of a buffet with many, many varieties of foods to taste. You taste the different foods and only eat what you like. In refereeing terms this meant that if you like what you saw other people doing, try it out and if it doesn't fit discard it and only keep what fits and what suits your personality. I always remember his words, for some reason they always stuck in my head. I think it was because in that actual clinic the speaker had a practical session with us where we had to try this out. People amazingly were quite shy and feeling inhibited about doing it. That didn't stop him though, he barrelled on and we had to do it whether we wanted to or not. Nobody got to shirk out of it.

First, we each had a turn to do something and everyone else had to try it out. Some of the things were hilarious and when it didn't fit in with your own style and personality, we felt like right gobshites altogether. It turned out to be great fun once everyone got over their inhibitions. Some people became extremely creative with their ideas and on the whole that was a hoot. One guy who was quite timid in an overall sense, tried something boisterous and dramatic that was presented to us. Well! The poor fella, not only did he frighten us, but he also frightened himself! Poor thing! He had to drop it like a hot potato because it was just **not** him. We and he himself, had a good laugh about it afterwards and there was plenty of slagging that went on for the whole week of our tournament. There were others of course quite similar, he wasn't the only one. It really added to the enjoyment of our week.

It was an interesting process. It helped us to discover a lot about ourselves. It is amazing how we think we know ourselves and instead it turns out that you don't know yourself in the way that you think you do. Even being shy and feeling inhibited was a surprise to most people. One that caught me out was something that would suit my bossy nature. This guy who was a lot taller than me had a particular body stance that he used quite naturally. I can't explain it properly, but he did something peculiar with his lower body which made his bum stick out at the back but gave him a bossy stance in front. When I tried to do it, it made me look like a complete nerd as it didn't fit in with my small height.

I did this for many years and it never tired of being great fun, trying out the various things that other people did. It was good advice which I was able to pass on to others.

The things that I was able to keep definitely enhanced my refereeing style. The more I practised them, the more comfortable I became doing them and over time, they came to look like a natural part of myself. This was only one of the amazing and interesting things I learned at my FIBA clinics. I used to look forward to our teaching sessions as FIBA, as an overall body, were fantastic in their teaching and incredibly progressive in their thinking. They were also highly creative and open to trying out ideas by other innovative speakers just like the speaker I've talked about. FIBA had the ability to see, no matter what it was or how strange something might seem, how it could be applied to the refereeing situation. They were masters in adaptability.

As their core ethos was based on perfection in professionalism, they were always striving and looking for new ideas to copper-fasten their professional approach. I think this is one of the main reasons that their professionalism never wavered and was never compromised in all the years I refereed with them. They never took anything for granted, they were always learning themselves and raising the bar for both themselves and their officials. This was one of the aspects of FIBA that I loved and admired the most. Nothing ever became static, dull or boring. It was forever moving forward and progressing. This kept people who were refereeing a long time interested and motivated to maintain their high standard of officiating. FIBA's referees never became stale or burnt out. Their referees also maintained their enthusiasm for reffing as a result and it benefitted everyone in the game.

CHAPTER 29
The Big Bang

Having had a wonderful start to my FIBA career everything went along nicely for the next seven years. I was extremely happy with my progress. I was refereeing in Europe (France, Germany, Italy, Spain, Portugal, Madeira and Israel just to name a few) thoroughly enjoying my matches and enjoying gaining this wonderful experience. It was an adventurous time. I met some amazing and fantastic people along the way, befriended many and had a lovely time refereeing with my male counterparts. I was tremendously lucky to have partnered as many nice men as I did. During the in-between parts we always had great fun and wonderful, interesting conversations. It was lovely getting to know them at a more personal level.

We always held the boundaries and never crossed the line from a sexual perspective. For me I felt what I was doing was professional and I was representing my country. Therefore, it wasn't an option, no matter how much I liked the men, to cross those boundaries. The men were also respectful in that regard and felt the same way as I did. This made it easier for us to uphold a firmly platonic relationship.

Only on one occasion in my whole FIBA career did one man try to cross the boundary line with me. I didn't engage with it, so nothing untoward happened. When you are both refereeing at such a high level and under such immense pressure and you are working as a team, a certain intimacy develops between you. Both are working hard to gel with each other, supporting and assisting one another while maintaining their own independence and style. It's a tough combination. Therefore, it can leave a vulnerability that, through misinterpretation, could expose people to stepping over the line. I consider myself exceptionally lucky to have escaped this possibility for the extent of my whole career. It made my whole FIBA experience much more enjoyable. I found men to be great companions when there was no threat involved and I could relax and chill out and have a great time with them which was super. During my conversations with men, I could be my true self. I found a freedom of expression through the conversations, which suited my curious mind, as they were stimulating and varied in their content. It also provided me with a space for my competitiveness to be appreciated, understood and accepted. My ferocious competitive nature couldn't be understood, in general, by the women in my life. To them it was alien. They thought I was nuts and mad in the head. Whereas, with the men, they totally understood. Men are different to women. It was invaluable gaining an understanding of what makes men tick and how and why they are different to women. It was a worthwhile education that has stood to me throughout my life when dealing with men in different situations.

I continued and progressed further and got to the stage where in some of the tournaments I was appointed to Quarter-Finals, Semi-Finals and Finals. This was a great achievement. Overall, my life was going supremely well. I had a genuinely nice boyfriend who was an athlete and we spent lots of time running together and competing in races. I was running exceptionally well, was winning races on the road, in cross-country and on the track. I had been picked to run on the Dublin team and ran an extremely good race, along with the other team members, to earn a place on the National team. My times were getting faster and faster and my training was paying off.

In basketball my international refereeing was going better than I could have hoped for and my playing career was booming. I had won several MVP (Most Valuable Player) awards, Top Scorer awards and had won the Best Player award for two consecutive years as the Best Player in Division 2. The last one specifically, was a major feat as it was unheard of for someone of my height to be nominated for such an award, never mind winning it. These years were the best years of my life, having picked myself up from the earlier disappointments I had experienced. It was all going fantastically well. I was on the crest of a wave.

Then splash, in 1997, out of the blue, it happened – the big bang! My life was turned upside down in one fell swoop, one click of the fingers and my life came tumbling down around me. It started with my boyfriend of two years, Gerry, having a serious accident while he was on a mountaineering climb in the Himalayas in preparation to climb Mount Everest. He fell into a crater, was abandoned by his friend, got frostbite and ended up losing 9 fingers and one leg from below the knee. It was horrific. I was devastated and he was gutted. I just could not take it in and neither could he. I remember being intensely angry with his friend who I knew and eating the head off him, giving him a serious piece of my mind. It turned out that when they got to one mile from the top of the mountain, the stoves at this camp weren't working to melt the snow for them to drink. They should have stopped and gone back down. They foolishly insisted on continuing their ascent. My boyfriend became dehydrated in the high altitude, and as a result, became disorientated and fell into the crater. It did not bear thinking about, the whole scenario.

As if that was not bad enough, I had my own personal big bang. I was doing a good deed for a friend of mine, taking her out to the pictures, having lost her thirteen-year-old son to cancer. She desperately needed a break and I offered to drive her. We were sitting in the car at the traffic lights which were red, completely stopped. Suddenly out of the blue there was an unmerciful bang, which was followed by two more bangs, one after the other. We were stunned by the impacts. We did not know what had happened. It all happened so fast and without warning. My friend started screaming like mad and jumped over from the passenger seat on top of me. I had no idea what was happening. I was just trying to hold on to her as she became more and more hysterical.

Eventually there were people gathered around the car, trying to see if we were dead or alive and trying to get us out in case the car went on fire and blew up. There was such a commotion, with many people screaming and shouting everywhere, people dashing forwards and backwards, people rushing around trying to knock on the houses to get someone to call an ambulance. In the end I managed to get out of the car with the assistance of someone and to my shock and horror realised it was a horrendous car crash. There were five cars piled up and smashed into each other. There was one car behind me with a husband, wife and child. Everyone was in a terrible state. The man who had caused the accident had run into the car behind me, spun around as a result and hit me a second time on the passenger side. I got hit three times, back, side and front. The impact was colossal and I was pushed into the car in front. The sirens started blaring and the people from the five cars were put in the ambulances and brought to the hospital.

At this stage, I had no idea what my injuries were or how bad I was because I was wildly concerned about my friend. I couldn't stop to think about myself. I was completely numb and dumbstruck. The only immediate feeling I had being one of guilt. I felt so guilty about my friend. Here she was, already in a terrible state having just lost her son and now this had happened to make things worse for her. How could this happen? The whole thing was completely unfathomable. I remember when I got out of the car, the person who helped me out brought me over to the van of the driver who had run into everybody. The driver was pallatic drunk and his van was full of bottles and bottles of whiskey. He feigned shock and demanded to be brought to the hospital immediately, as a new law had just been passed to allow a doctor to test for drink at the scene of a crash. He dodged the doctor and when he got to the hospital, did a runner to a pub nearby and slugged a load of pints. When the Guards came to the hospital, he told them that his nerves were gone and that he had to have a few drinks. They couldn't test him for drink-driving as there was no way of knowing what he had drank before the crash and in that time in the pub.

My friend's husband came to the hospital to collect us and bring us home. I was grossly concerned for my friend; she was in bits. I could not sleep that night with the worry and the guilt. I will never forget that night for as long as I live. The cars had been towed away and the next day the man from the garage who had my car rang me. He told me he could not believe I was alive, that judging by the state of the car, I should have been killed outright. He said we had been hit at 80 miles (128kms) an hour speed and the car was mangled, a complete and utter write-off. He encouraged me to go down to him and he would show me the car. It was supposed to be important to do this according to him. I dragged myself down and what a horrendous sight. You know the saying, 'Seeing is believing' well that was it. I could never have imagined it like it was if I had tried and hadn't gone to see it. While it was appalling to see it, I was glad afterwards that I did go. The man was extremely nice and understanding and told me what I had to do next. I dragged myself back home again and at this point was completely disconnected from my own injuries. I just could not feel anything I was so numb and distraught over my friend. My Da was worried sick about me as he had never in his life, seen me like that before. I had no recollection of what had happened at the hospital in relation to myself or what they had said. I didn't get myself checked out properly because I was busy looking after my friend and completely dismissed myself. It was only as the days passed that gradually, bit by bit, it became clear how severely injured I was myself. It took quite a while for the extent of the injuries to be uncovered. I kept wanting to believe I was fine and the only thing I wanted was to go back to work and pretend the whole thing hadn't happened.

I went to the doctor to get checked out and a whole course of investigations into my injuries began. The usual things x-rays, orthopaedic specialist and physiotherapy. I was in severe pain everywhere in my body and the doctor prescribed painkillers and anti-inflammatory tablets to reduce the swelling which was quite extensive. How I hadn't broken every bone in my body was a miracle. The physio explained to me that it was my extreme high level of fitness and the immense physical strength in my muscles, ligaments and tendons that saved me. Not only should I be dead, but I should be dead with a lot of broken bones and other injuries. One fecked up corpse!

Despite having my seat belt on, I had been propelled forwards and backwards in my seat in the car with my head violently ricocheting with force off the windscreen. This happened several times. The force of the ricocheting caused my head and neck to violently rebound off the headrest. Through the forward and backward motion, the front of my head and the back of my head and neck had been severely damaged. Because I am small and have short legs, I have to sit right on top of the steering wheel in order to be able to reach the pedals. Therefore, my sternum and the front of my body, from my chest down to my thighs, got mangled with the force of the steering wheel crushing into me as I was being thrown forwards and backwards. The impact of the collision at that high speed made the whole situation worse. I don't know how on heaven's earth we survived.

The final diagnosis was an acutely injured back which had a bulging disc (in the L5 S1 lumbar spine), severe whiplash and a huge amount of scar tissue injury both in the back and the front of my body. To me at the time, the gravity of the injuries didn't impact or get through to me in those waking months of medical investigations. The fact that I hadn't broken anything and I was still able to stand up camouflaged the critical aspects of the underlying effect that this was going to have on my body. I had no idea what it meant in real terms. As my threshold and tolerance for pain, stemming from the trauma in my childhood was extremely high (described later by one of the specialists as dangerously off the Richter scale) it made it impossible for me to get a true understanding of the level and seriousness of the whole situation. I was also used to recovering from my sports injuries in double quick time. In those early stages I thought that yes, I've been badly injured but sure I'll be grand in a short time once I get enough physiotherapy and do what I'm told regarding doing the exercises and rehabilitation programme. Looking back on it now, I can see it was an innocent and naïve outlook rather than an arrogant one. I was so used to my body operating like a 'Well-oiled and well refined machine' that I innocently thought my body was going to be fixed just like you would mechanically fix a broken-down car.

Little did I know then, at the age of 39, that I would be plagued by this event for the rest of my life. Also, the fact that doctors and specialists, in general, dismiss whiplash and back injuries to the extent that they do, added to my own ignorance and outlook. The treatment and intervention that I had received from the specialist who was recommended to me by my doctor, made my injuries much worse and set me back considerably. An unfortunate start to my recovery programme and bad luck to add to the bad luck of having the car crash in the first place.

I was extremely anxious to get back to work and to regain some semblance of normal living and of course to get back to my running and my refereeing. I was lucky that I had my father (both my mother and her sister had died five years previously) as he was able to help me with my treatments, exercises, rubbing creams in and using ice packs etc., etc. After two weeks I went back to work despite not being in good shape and was at a huge loss not having Vivienne's emotional support, understanding and care. By now I was working in a different department to Vivienne. My new boss was completely unsympathetic to my condition and because I couldn't work to full capacity, felt I was of no use to her.

Poor Bridget was inconsolable, she couldn't get over what had happened. The fact that I had been stopped at traffic lights, somewhere in her opinion that you would imagine you would be totally safe, wrecked her head altogether. But good ol' Bridget of course got down to business immediately and started giving me many different kinds of medicines and potions from the health shop to speed up my recovery. I took and did everything she gave me to do as I was desperate to recover as soon as possible.

During this time, my father was an absolute brick. He came up trumps and pulled out all the stops to help me. He had to take over the complete running of the house which we had previously shared 50-50 as well as attend to my injuries. He was more than happy to do that. Since my mother had died my relationship with my father had improved on many fronts as she was no longer there getting in between us and trying to cause a rift. We had become a lot closer. For both my father and I, living on our own was absolute heaven. As we were two of a kind in many ways, we were extremely compatible. Our lives had changed for the better.

This unfortunate accident totally disturbed our equilibrium. My father, who was much more easy-going and relaxed now since my mother died, became worried and agitated about my condition. I kept trying to reassure him that I would be ok in time, that everything he was doing was helping me and in no time at all I would be back to my normal happy self. My father however, shook his head in disagreement with me. Being the wise man that he was, he could see clearly what I couldn't see because I was caught up in the whole thing. On one particular day he said it to me, 'This is different Mero. This is not the same as the other injuries you've had in the past. This is not going to get fully ok.' His words shocked me and stunned me into silence. After a pause I pooh-poohed him and said, 'Of course I will Da. You're right it is different, but I will get on top of it eventually, it's just going to take more time than I thought it would.' Another shake of the head, 'I'm sorry Mero, it's not. This is different, very different. I can see the difference in your body and this is your whole body, not just one part like it used to be in the past.'

Again, his words and adamancy stunned me. They also frightened me, but of course I wasn't emotionally connected to my fear at this time. My physical condition required 24 hours around the clock attention. It was a full-time job in these early stages. There was no room or time for an emotional connection. I have always been a wise person from a very young age and I think it was from my Da that I inherited some of this wisdom. He was the only person who could truly see the reality of the situation. The doctor and the orthopaedic specialist most certainly did not see it. The physiotherapist to some degree saw it but not fully either and as for me myself, I was in complete denial or should I say, to be more accurate, I was doing my damndest to stay in denial and not face reality. As there was a lot at stake and a lot to lose, my father's words penetrated my brain, bypassed my emotions and hit the pragmatic part of me that does indeed face reality. Deep, deep down in that wise part of myself I knew he was right. He was seeing something that I could feel and his words and shaking of the head turned the spotlight right on to the factual evidence that I was battling with inside of myself.

He did me a big favour by being as honest as he was with me. While I didn't like the reality of it, as we all know the truth hurts, but at least it gave me the incentive and motivation to tackle the problem in a more determined and conscious way. I could also hear his concern in his words as he was being unusually terribly serious. There was no messing, slagging, joking or making light of it. It was this fact that made the penny really drop for me.

From that moment onwards I attacked my rehabilitation programme in a more fervent, determined way. I had no idea at the time how brave and courageous I was being. I was on a mission. I started putting my head down and bulldozing my way through the impenetrable wall caused by my injuries towards the path of recovery. I was lucky that the refereeing season had just finished both in Ireland and abroad and there was a break for a few months which gave me time to pull myself together to some extent at least. My first goal was to try and get better so that I could ref in my international tournament which was scheduled for late in the summer.

I set about working tremendously hard to achieve my goal and get myself back in shape. Pain became my constant companion and I had to make friends with it rather than keep fighting it which I was trying to do at the start. Focusing on my mobility, coordination and flexibility became my first priority. A wise decision. The physio treatments and the physiotherapist were exceptionally helpful to me and Sean helped me with a training programme. At this time, I had no understanding of my diagnosed condition. There was no internet or Doctor Google to explain in detail the finer points of the underlying issues and giving advice as to how to help it. I just had to tune in to my body and figure out what worked and what didn't work. From the get-go it became crystal clear that exercise, movement and lying down helped my condition whereas sitting down aggravated it immensely. I had to move and stand as much as I could and avoid sitting altogether. In work it was difficult to do this as my job was a sitting job. I tried to rearrange my work as much as I could to move and stand rather than sit but this wasn't possible at that stage and in fact sitting at work set me back. It was slowing down my progress, undoing the benefits I was getting from physio. When I went out with my friends I did the same and this was dreadfully awkward and embarrassing. It caused people to stare at me and those who had the nerve would ask me outright why I was standing instead of sitting down. This went on for quite some time and slowly but surely, I began to make progress. This spurred me on.

Throughout this suffering my hatred and rage for the drunken driver who caused this nightmare would spring to the surface. The fact that he was never prosecuted added to my rage. If I could have gotten my hands on him, I would have killed him with my bare hands for sure. As I unfortunately could not do that, I decided in my wisdom to use my hatred and anger constructively to help me to get better rather than give in and give up and which, I have to be honest and say, I felt like doing many a time during this period. It was my goal that kept saving me.

I also decided to draw on my childhood experiences of being deaf and throw them into the pot to help to keep me motivated. The excruciating pain that I had endured with my ears kept reminding me that the current pain I was in could also be tolerated in the same way as that one had. At another time I had had an unbelievably bad ankle injury and I had to have an operation to have it stretched and manipulated under anaesthetic. The surgeon had told me that I would never run or play basketball again. Well! He had told the wrong person that! I wasn't having any of it! The mere thought of that was unbearable. Me not run or play basketball. No way Jose! I was determined to prove him wrong, which I'm delighted to say I did as I am still running to this day. Anyway, I also used that as another motivator to drive me on to recovery.

While this may sound all well and good, I am skipping over some of the emotional parts. Coming and going throughout this whole phase were a mixture of emotions. I was deeply upset, devastated on many levels and at times thought I was losing my mind. I was angry, frustrated and totally pissed off by the sheer and cruel injustice of it. Here it was again that pervasive injustice that kept following me everywhere in my life. There was no let-up. Every time I thought things were going well for a change, bang! The injustice would knife me in the back again. I was infuriated by it.

While I could clearly feel the magnitude of these emotions, I could not express them. I was not permitted to cry – I had been taught that one in my childhood from an early age by my mother. The more I cried the harder she hit me, so that was the end of that! The tomboy part of me had the added stipulation that applies to men – men are not allowed to cry. Little girls are not allowed to be angry, it's unladylike and don't you dare make a show of me by throwing a tantrum or I'll kill you.

These intense emotions that I could feel had to be kept pent-up inside of me. There was no freedom to express them. The only thing I could do to stop myself going mad was to channel them into my sport and therefore into my recovery. Probably not the best idea in the world in hindsight, but better than diving into a depression and never coming out of it. It also stopped me from turning to alcohol and drugs and prevented me from committing suicide. I had often entertained the idea of all three and in fact friends often suggested alcohol as a way of numbing the pain! All in all, a worthwhile decision and probably fair to say the second-best decision that was available to me.

I called in to my friend to see how she was doing and like myself she was severely struggling. She had many of the symptoms that I had and was having the exact same problems as me. While I was upset at this it was nonetheless consoling because at least I felt I wasn't going mad altogether and imagining things. She couldn't sleep, I couldn't sleep. We had both lost our appetites, we were in permanent pain and surviving daily was a major challenge. She had been given the same advice as me in relation to exercising, reducing sitting and taking medication. I think like me her emotions became stunted. Her grief became somewhat suspended because the physical was taking over and had to be attended to and put first. Her husband insisted on her going to a solicitor to make a claim, but I did not want to do that. I just wanted to focus my full attention on getting better. I didn't want to go down the legal road and start playing games in relation to compensation and suing. I had no intention of entering into pretending I was worse than I was. I just wanted my life as it was before the car crash to return and I was grateful I hadn't been killed and was at least somewhat in one piece. That was enough for me. No amount of money was going to make up for the trauma I had to endure and no amount of money was going to improve the life altering damage that had been done to my body. I believed that your health was your wealth and that was the thing that mattered most in life. My thinking at the time in relation to wealth was, that the stories I had heard and the people I knew who were wealthy were unhappy people, constantly dissatisfied and always seeking more. Nothing was ever good enough. Their materialistic greed was the ruination of them. I didn't like that. I just wanted a simple, natural, normal, healthy life.

Alongside this, my poor boyfriend was struggling with his own injuries. We were a right motley pair. We became completely incompatible. The things he could do, I couldn't do and vice versa. I couldn't go out for a meal and sit down and he couldn't use a knife, fork or spoon anymore. I could go for walks and light runs but because of his leg he couldn't. Eventually he had to get a prosthesis for his leg which was uncomfortable and cumbersome. I couldn't look after him and he couldn't look after me. It was a terrible, terrible time for us both. The physical side of the relationship deteriorated drastically as we couldn't touch each other due to the high levels of pain, internal bruising and swelling that we both had. It was a pure nightmare. Being a man, he shut down his emotions in order to survive! We were both on the same page for that one. Because he was an athlete, he too had a determined and positive approach to taking on his recovery. He even had hopes of maybe running again to a lesser extent obviously. His competing in races was over, that was definite. He had to learn a new way of using his hands minus his fingers and this was quite daunting and tricky. He couldn't hold things properly anymore, couldn't lift things, couldn't tie shoelaces or fasten belts and buttons anymore. There are so many little things you take for granted every day and don't even think about.

We both became shocked and surprised by the effects our various injuries had on us. Everyday there was a new discovery as in a negative discovery. We began to wonder how the relationship was going to survive the drastic changes and incompatibilities that had developed between us. How were we going to manage it? Was it possible to sustain the relationship? The relationship was under immense strain, trying to cope and adapt to our new physical limitations. We talked about it as much as we could and decided to give it our best shot, take one day at a time and see what happens in the future. It was early days yet and we felt that a lot can happen in a few months. We would keep our fingers crossed (well I would, not him) and we would wait and see.

We trundled on as best we could over the next few months and I managed to referee in my international tournament. To be honest, I don't know how I did it. It was down to pure grit and determination. I got through it ok which was incredible in itself but of course I was a long way off being the 'Old Me.' As I am a master at putting the good side out and hiding whatever it is I want to hide, I was able to cover up a lot of what was truly going on underneath. This served me well and boosted my morale and confidence which was a positive for going forward. I had successfully crossed my first hurdle, achieved my first goal and that was satisfying and encouraging. It made the suffering, hard work and effort worthwhile. I felt that at last, at long last, I was making inroads into my recovery. It lifted my spirits and egged me on to continue my programme. I resumed my refereeing at the start of the new season and got back running incrementally. There was a steadiness beginning to develop into my training and refereeing as I desperately worked hard to get back on track. I threw everything I had at it and into the pot. There was no holding back. I felt it was paying dividends, my physio and my training. I just had to continue now and not let anything stop me.

Before I knew where I was it was Christmas. My Da and I had a good Christmas under the circumstances. We both loved Christmas and since my mother died Christmas was much more enjoyable because we approached it differently. We organised and planned everything and took our time buying the presents and writing the Christmas cards. We had fun putting up the decorations in the house, although that particular year I couldn't do as much as I used to. I had to cut back and only do the things that didn't aggravate my condition. I didn't want to set back the progress I was making. My Da had no problem with that of course as he fully understood and equally didn't want me to have any setbacks.

It was my Da's birthday on the 1st of January and as this was going to be a significant one, his 70th birthday, I had to arrange something special. I had a small surprise party for him and he chose other things that he wanted to do himself. It was a lovely memorable occasion and he was delighted and chuffed with the various celebrations. He had a new girlfriend at the time who he had being going out with for about a year and she too made a great fuss over him and organised a nice night out for them both. My boyfriend, my brother, Da's sister and several of his good friends came to the surprise party. Of course, Bridget was there, cackling and laughing having a great old time as only Bridget could. My Da loved Bridget and thought she was great craic. Vivienne was also there as Da also loved Vivienne and had great time for her. He was surrounded by all the women in his life. What more could a man ask for? What could be better than that?! We had a great time and it was a lovely start to the New Year.

I was, for once, looking forward to the New Year. I'm not usually a fan of New Year. I would be delighted the old year was out. 1997 was such a horrific year. I was going to approach this New Year with optimism. I honestly felt things could only get better, they most certainly could not get worse. Boy was I wrong!!!

CHAPTER 30
Bridget & Da

Just a few days into the New Year, 1998 and after my Da's 70th birthday celebrations, Bridget took sick suddenly and unexpectedly. She ended up in hospital for only the second time in her whole life. It didn't seem serious, there was no definitive diagnosis and I thought she was going to be ok and recover the way she had the previous time. Out of the blue, she started slipping and I became fearful. I talked away to her to keep her alert and conscious and she was eyeballing me but not talking back. Because I knew her as well as I did, it felt like I could understand what she was trying to communicate to me. At one point I felt she was saying goodbye, her facial expression and her body language was emphatically strong and clear. I suddenly realised this was much more serious than I thought and I got really upset. I had my little goodbye chat with her and told her all the things I wanted to tell her and the most important thing being how much I loved her and I was going to miss her terribly. It was too much to take in and everything seemed to be moving at lightning speed. I had to leave to go and referee a match as I couldn't find a replacement at such short notice. There was no time to organise anything as it happened in the blink of an eye. I said goodbye to her and told her I would be back the minute the match was over. She nodded to me and at this stage seemed to be fairly ok. I did not want to leave her. I had a chat with one of the nurses who checked her for me before I left and she too thought she was grand and would definitely be alive when I came back. That reassured me a little. I charged off and charged back only to find she had died shortly before I arrived. I was in a terrible state, dreadfully upset and the nurse told me that she had given her a drink of water, went off to dispose of the glass and when she turned around, she was dead. The nurse could not believe it herself how quietly and quickly she slipped away. This was the 10th of January 1998 and it was a Saturday afternoon. She was 89. One I will never forget.

Her niece arrived in and she too had missed her going and it transpired that I was the last person, apart from the nurse obviously, to see her alive. I was both glad and relieved I had gone in to see her and spent the whole morning with her and had said my goodbyes to her, although I dearly would have loved to be there holding her hand when she slipped away. I always think it must be awful to die alone, but probably in Bridget's case because she was well used to being on her own and being independent, it most likely was fitting for her to die that way. I never feel fully convinced by that though and always regret not having been there with her.

Her niece told me she would contact me later with the funeral arrangements. I went back down later in the evening to the hospital to sit with the coffin after she had been laid out and I spent the rest of the night there. We were totally alone. It was just her and me but now completely different to the way we were when she was alive. It was quiet and eerie; the silence was deafening. Everything was cold, there was no warmth even though I was well wrapped up. Bridget's silence was the strangest thing I ever experienced because she was so full of life, never short of something to say and her cackle of laughter was loud and contagious. I loved her vivaciousness which I was inherently accustomed to, but now the polar opposite I was experiencing just didn't fit at all, at all. This silence felt awfully weird and strange. You don't realise the effect someone is having on you until you don't have it anymore. I remember sitting there with her, deeply, deeply upset and it was hitting me like a ton of bricks that this silence was going to be what I would be left with of Bridget. The idea of it was insufferable. Losing Bridget out of my life was going to be the biggest blow I ever received or so I thought at this moment in time. How was I going to cope with it on top of my boyfriend's problems and my own problems from the car crash? It did not bear thinking about. I just felt that my life was being turned upside down and I couldn't understand why. One thing, two things, now three things and not minor little things, but major, major, major things.

My Da was upset too because he loved Bridget. He and she had great craic and interesting chats about current affairs and a range of other topics. Like Bridget, my Da used to read the newspaper from cover to cover which meant they were both well versed in the topical matters. Many a hot and heavy discussion they used to have whenever they met up. Like she did with me, Bridget used to challenge my Da's tunnel vision and limited thinking and I believe he genuinely respected her for that as it made their conversations extremely stimulating.

Bridget's niece rang me with the funeral arrangements. Bridget was being brought to the church on Monday evening with the burial after 11am mass on Tuesday morning. I made arrangements with my Da and my Aunt Philo (his sister) to pick them up. I had asked if I could get off work early because I wanted to attend both the removal and the funeral mass. There was no problem as everyone in work knew how close I was to Bridget. It was the equivalent of losing one's mother. I got everything ready on Sunday and spent my last hours sitting with her. I said my final goodbye to her because I knew the coffin would be closed by the time I got to the hospital the next day. I was late getting home and went straight to bed.

The next morning, I got up and went over the arrangements with my Da again while we had breakfast. I said goodbye to him, gave him his usual kiss and hug and headed into work. At lunchtime my friend Mono from Wexford rang me to say that she had rung my Da to get my work phone number from him because she had mislaid it and couldn't find it and she wanted to ring me. She said she was worried about him because he wasn't his usual friendly upbeat self, that in fact he had told her he was sick, too sick to get it for her. Knowing my Da as well as she did, alarm bells went off in her head and she did not like the sound of it, thought it most unusual and out of character and had a sick feeling in her stomach. She went out of her way to find the number as something was prompting her, a sixth sense, that there was something seriously wrong here. It wasn't what it seemed like on the surface.

I nearly dropped the phone with fright because immediately like her, I sensed there was something wrong. I rang the house to talk to my Da and my brother answered the phone. He said Da was fine, he just had a stomach bug and was going to stay in bed. He wasn't well enough to go to the removal. That was it! I knew then this was extremely serious. My brother was his usual casual self. I told him to ring the doctor immediately, that this was not a stomach bug. He pooh-poohed me saying that I was just panicking now and that it was because of Bridget's death and I was over-anxious. He tried to reassure me again that everything was alright, that Da would be fine once he got a good sleep. I became quite hysterical at this point and screamed down the phone at him again to get the bloody doctor. Everyone in the office was wondering what was up and of course gathered immediately that there was something seriously wrong.

I belted home and called in to Philo on the way to tell her that Da was sick and there was something serious the matter and I would have to get the doctor. I told her to go on ahead of me to the removal and I would meet her there once I got Da sorted out. When I got home Da was in bed, was white as a ghost and looking anything but well. It was obvious to me there was something more wrong with him than a stomach bug. I had phoned the doctor before I left work, but he said he would not be able to make a house call until a few hours later and that by the sound of it I should bring my Da straight down to his surgery. He agreed to wait for me even though it was near closing time. I asked Da what he wanted to do, wait or go now. When he said, 'I'll go now as the sooner the doctor gives me something to take the pain away the better, I won't be able to stick this for a few more hours.' That was it for me, alarm bells were going off in my head, I felt a cold wave of fear sweeping through me. I felt the game was up and that he must be feeling like he was on the way out for him to agree to that. My Da hated going to the doctor. I said to him, 'Come on, leave your pajamas on he's closing soon, we'd better hurry.' But no way would he go in his PJs, he insisted on getting dressed.

I drove as fast as I could to get him there. The minute we walked into the surgery the doctor took one look at him said, 'Good God Bill, what's happened to you?' This freaked me out into an even more hysterical state, although I kept it hidden because I didn't want to frighten my Da any more than he was already. He examined my Da very quickly, asked him several questions and said, 'Right, ambulance straight away, you have to go to the hospital immediately.' My Da looked at him in shock and horror and said, 'Hospital, no way am I going to hospital. I don't do hospitals. I haven't been in hospital in my life, I'm not going now.' The doctor was ringing the ambulance and replied, 'Sorry Bill, not only are you going to hospital but you're going to have an operation.' 'What?' my Da replied, 'No way, not on your life am I doing that.' The doctor replied, 'You've no choice Bill, you've got to go now, pronto, it's urgent.' He tried to reassure my Da when he saw how frightened he was, that it was just a small operation and he would be fine. With that, my Da fainted right there on the spot. 'Jesus,' I screamed 'What the heck?' The doctor tried to bring him around while we were waiting for the ambulance. I asked the doctor what was wrong and he said that somehow, he thought my Da was losing blood, maybe bleeding internally, but he said it was difficult to diagnose because my Da's answers to his questions were throwing him off and were confusing.

He got my Da to come around. My Da started to puke and there was blood in it. The doctor roared, 'Shit Bill, you told me there was no blood when you vomited at home.' With that the doctor wrote a letter for the ambulance men. As soon as the ambulance arrived, there was no hanging around, he was whipped off immediately. I shot the doctor one final glance and one final question as I was running out the door, 'Is he going to die?' The doctor didn't respond and I knew by the way he looked at me that it seemed likely. I screamed at the doctor again, 'Is he going to die, tell me, I want to know?' The doctor this time said, 'No maybe not, but it is serious, go on now, get out of here and follow that ambulance as fast as you can.'

My head was reeling. I drove like a mad woman after the ambulance doing everything that ambulances do, breaking all the traffic lights, driving on the other side of the road, up and down off paths until I got to the hospital. I literally abandoned the car somewhere outside the gates and ran like the clappers after the ambulance up the driveway to the Accident & Emergency. He was brought to St. Vincent's on the Merrion Road. As I arrived, they were just taking him out of the ambulance on the stretcher. I grabbed hold of the side of the stretcher and my Da's hand as they whizzed him and I mean whizzed him, in that door.

He didn't have to queue or wait; he was immediately brought into a small cubicle where they got a scissors and literally ran it up the whole length of his body to rip his clothes open. I remember being shocked and stunned. We had often discussed different scenarios in work about being caught in certain situations and about being conscious of having clean and respectable underwear on you in case of emergency. Well, I can tell you that one got knocked on the head fairly rapidly when I saw what they did to my Da. The urgency ensured that nothing was seen, it was all go, all hands on deck. Everyone was working at a ferocious speed. It was hard to keep up with it.

My Da was conscious at this point and to say he looked like a frightened rabbit does not cover it. The look of terror on his face will be etched in my mind until the day I die. I had to keep holding his hand, stroking him and reassuring him that he was going to be ok. It comforted him to know I was there as he was terrified and his eyes were popping out of his head with the fear. I kept talking to him to take his mind off it, although this was difficult with the scurrying around they were doing. I had often watched E.R. on T.V. and used to be flabbergasted at the high drama. Well, I tell you, I thought we were making an episode for that

E.R. series. When you watch something like that on T.V. it seems surreal and you can't imagine it happening in real life. Well, here we were, Da and myself, in the middle of the exact same thing. I couldn't believe it and he most certainly couldn't believe it either. The minute they were finished doing their assessments, which it turned out afterwards were based on the doctor's diagnosis and recommendations, he was whipped off to theatre for surgery. The intensity and urgency of the whole thing was extremely frightening. As he was being wheeled off the surgeon came over to me and told me that if I had anything to say to my dad, I had better say it now because he may not come off the table alive. What a nightmare. My ears were buzzing. 'What?' I said. He repeated it again and I am not joking you, I nearly fainted. How I didn't I will never know. Somewhere inside of me, I must have known I had to keep it together for my Da's sake and not frighten him any more than he already was. But of course, he heard every word of this and just looked at me in total disbelief. I told him that I loved him and that if he wanted to survive the operation and stay alive that he would find it in himself to do it. I told him I wouldn't be going anywhere; I would wait for him and that I would be there when he woke up. I told him that it was his choice and it was up to him, he had to do whatever was right for him. His last words to me were, 'What about Bridget?' and, 'I love you too Mero.' I stayed as close to him as I could while we went up in the lift to the operating theatre and squeezed his hand and kissed and hugged him goodbye. I wished him the best of luck.

These minutes passed in the blink of an eye. Suddenly, in a flash he was whisked away into the theatre and I was left wondering was he gone temporarily or gone forever. I didn't know which. The surgeon told me it would be a long operation, at least five hours. I was distressed and in a panic. What should I do now? I had to stop and think. I needed to find a phone box and start contacting people. I rang Philo first and told her what was going on. I told her to go to the funeral and tell them what had happened, that I couldn't leave the hospital and when the funeral was finished to hurry out to the hospital as fast as she could. Next, I rang my brother and asked him to hurry up and to come out as quickly as he could. I was a nervous wreck waiting on him. It was three hours later before he showed up. Those three hours were the loneliest hours of my life. I will never forget them as long as I live. The waiting! It was like my FIBA exam all over again, only this time it was much worse, a matter of life or death!

To keep myself occupied and to make the time pass, I kept making phone calls until my money ran out. I had a friend Lizzy at the time who was a nurse and I rang her to get her help and advice. She was great and knew my Da very well. Lizzy never pulled any punches and was always straight as a die and I loved her for that. I knew I could depend on her to tell me the real state of play and keep me updated on the medical side of things.

Those five hours crawled by and another friend of mine, Dick, who had gone to the funeral, knew immediately that something serious must have happened to my Da when I didn't show up at Bridget's funeral. They were there waiting and waiting on me until Philo eventually arrived and gave them the news. Poor Bridget, no Mary! Dick knew there could only be one reason that I would miss Bridget's funeral, he knew how close I was to her and how much I loved her. When the funeral was over, he kindly came out to the hospital with his wife Alison and they brought us lovely homemade sandwiches. They reckoned we would have had nothing to eat with the unfolding crisis. I wasn't feeling hungry. I was in such a turmoil and my stomach was doing somersaults with the anxiety of waiting and missing Bridget's funeral.

But Dick and Alison persuaded me to eat them anyway, that I needed to keep my strength up for the days ahead. Of course, once I opened them and smelt them, I tucked into them and enjoyed them a lot more than I thought I would. I hadn't eaten since breakfast time with the shenanigans that were going on and I was hungrier than I realised. I was truly grateful to them for their kindness and thoughtfulness.

I could visualise Bridget if she had been there with me, giving Da a good ol' hearty slap, laughing at him and popping some garlic and brandy into his gob to help him through the operation. Heaven knows what she would have said to him, something in the vein of, 'Come on Bill, show us what you're made of. You will fly through the operation, don't worry you'll be grand, the brandy will settle your nerves.'

The five hours turned into six hours and the six hours turned into seven hours. I felt this was a bad omen. Finally, another half an hour later, the surgeon came out to us to tell us that Da was still alive. He had made it through the operation. My brother and I yelped and jumped for joy; we could not believe it. The surgeon told us that there had been complications, but, nevertheless, he was alive. He was going to be transferred to I.C.U. and we could see him briefly in a short while, after they got him set up and comfortable. He told us there was a long way to go yet and that we were incredibly lucky because the majority of people, who undergo that surgery, die on the operating table. It transpired that he had an aneurism in the aorta of the stomach which had burst and was at high risk of bleeding to death. They had to give him 52 pints of blood during the operation. They said that he would not be here only for the doctor's diagnosis. It was the accuracy of the diagnosis that saved his life. According to the surgeon, it was a remarkable diagnosis, given the fact that he was bleeding profusely. Aneurisms, he explained, once they burst, are impossible to diagnose. The surgeon was extremely impressed with the doctor and did not know how he did it. It was due to him, that they could act so promptly which was the critical factor in saving his life, a few more minutes and it would have been too late.

We were so, so relieved. At least he was alive after all that waiting and the waiting now felt worthwhile. When we got in to see Da he was awake and gave us a weak smile. I told him the worst was over now and that slowly, bit by bit, he would start to recover and get better. He definitely seemed relieved to be alive and he was delighted to see us. He spoke to us a tiny bit, but we told him to save his energy and he could talk to us more the next morning after he got a good night's sleep. We kissed him goodnight and told him we were staying in the hospital. He seemed content and happy with that. He wanted us to be close by. Of course, the surgeon's words were hauntingly unnerving. We did realise that Da was not out of the woods yet. He had told us that the next 48 hours were critical. We had to stay in the hospital, there was no other way around it. We tried to get some sleep, sleeping on the floor of the waiting room. But sleep was not viable with the constant noise, lights, sirens blaring and doctors and nurses coming and going.

The next morning, we checked in on Da again and he seemed to be ok. According to the nurse on duty he had had a stable night. That was good news. She told us to go and get some breakfast. It was important we kept our strength up as it was going to be a long, long day and night again. We didn't feel that hungry, but we headed off anyway. We didn't stay away long and by the time we came back, nothing had changed. Another day passed and the 48 hours were up and we thought things were looking good. The complications however, which had developed during the surgery, began to have repercussions on the third day. The only time we left the I.C.U was to go to the toilet or grab something quick to eat. But on this day, every time we left, we got an emergency call over the intercom system to come back immediately. The first thing that happened was Da's kidneys failed and they had to put him on a kidney machine. This obviously was not good, but the surgeon said it was expected and not to worry too much. This wasn't the worst thing that could happen. The second time we were called back his temperature had dropped and they had to wrap him up in tin foil. I had never seen this before. Lizzy told me they often have to do that with people and hearing this helped me not to worry too much. He looked strangely peculiar covered in tin foil. He looked like a chicken ready to be put into the oven, a rather large chicken, in an enormous oven.

This turn of events started a downward spiral for our Da and he went from one crisis to another. It left us reluctant to leave the waiting room. Lizzy came in and because she was able to read the machines, she was able to give me an accurate account of the impact these developments were having on him. She told me out straight that she didn't think Da was going to make it, his condition was very poorly. While I was appreciative of her honesty, it was hard to take the reality of it in. Everything had been sudden and intensely dramatic. The pragmatic part of me however, heard her message loud and clear and I set about organising visitors to come and spend their last time with him if they wanted to. Lots of people had been enquiring if they could come and see him. Things remained hectic after that. To our shock and horror, the surgeon approached us to tell us they wanted to amputate our Da's leg. Well! We nearly had a coronary. Da was a dancer and had been out dancing the night before the aneurism had burst. To amputate his leg would have been his worst nightmare. My brother and I were horrified and when our Da's girlfriend heard about it, she collapsed and passed out in the I.C.U. I discussed it with Lizzy. She recommended saying to the surgeon that unless he could guarantee a 100 per cent recovery for our Da, that we would not give permission for that. If Da was going to die anyway, what was the point of doing that? My brother and I both knew that if our Da woke up to find his leg gone, that in itself would kill him. He would not be able for the shock of it. The thoughts of not being able to dance and end up in a wheelchair would most definitely kill him. Put simply, he would have died outright with a heart attack if he awoke to that. My Da had always made his dying wishes known to me, what to do and what not to do, if he ended up in a situation like this. One good thing was, at least my brother and I were on the same page for that one. We had one more conversation with Lizzy, just to make sure we were making the right decision.

The surgeon could not of course guarantee that doing the amputation was going to save our father. He knew well that his condition was critically serious and it was going to take a miracle to save him. Soon after that Da had to be put on a life support machine and that was the last straw. The beginning of the end for him. The last time Da had spoken to us was only once, the night after he came out of the operation. After that, we had no verbal communication from him anymore.

The time eventually came when we had to decide to turn the machine off and let him go. It was both the hardest and, at the same time, easiest decision we had to make. There was a part of us that absolutely knew it was time and most definitely the right thing to do. But of course, there was the child part of us that did not want to lose their daddy. The child part wanted to keep hoping for a miracle to happen. As children have the ability to live in hope forever, obviously the adult part had to take over and make the decision. It became evidently clear the extent to which, it was the machine that was keeping Da alive and not his own body. Lizzy was, once again, a great help to us. She explained everything in detail which made the decision easier. She was better than the surgeon and the doctors at explaining everything and putting us right. We made the decision and the surgeon told us that he would only last about 23 minutes after the machine was switched off. The positive side of that was, it gave us time to gather the family to be there with him. We had had his favourite music playing in the background for a long time before this as it was a comfort to him. His girlfriend and my boyfriend were there as well. When everyone arrived, we were gathered around the bed and they switched the machine off. I was extremely relieved to be at his side as this was one of the anxieties that I had carried from the beginning. I had wanted to be there at the end. I was always afraid to leave in case I missed this moment, as had happened with Bridget.

As the surgeon had predicted, Da died exactly 23 minutes after the machine was switched off. He went very peacefully and we were all holding on to some part of him. I was holding one of his hands and stroking his head. We talked to him until the end as the hearing is the last sense to go and we kept his favourite music playing in the background. It was a sad, sad day and we were all broken-hearted. The hospital staff were incredibly good to us throughout his whole time there and it was the same during his death. He died in the afternoon on the 5th of February 1998, four weeks after he had been admitted.

When Da had been admitted to hospital, my brother had gone home to his own house after the first few days and had gone back to work as we didn't know what way things were going to develop. I however, didn't do that. I decided to stay in the hospital for the full four weeks, as I didn't want him to be on his own and especially when it came to the end. Also, I wanted to spend as much time with him as possible in case it proved to be our last days together. I was in some state as you can imagine, practically no sleep, not eating or drinking properly and the whole emotional drain of the drama and crises. I had no time to think about my back and injuries despite the fact I was in agony as I had to let go of my physio and my exercises during this time. Putting myself on hold was becoming a habit. My friend Dick, who had given me a blow for blow account of Bridget's funeral, couldn't believe the situation I was in. The two closest people in my life, dying at the same time, back-to-back. He didn't know how I was going to cope and survive this, especially on top of the injuries. I didn't know either. As I've said already, my Da was a topper and a great support to me after my car crash. That was only one of the many things I was going to miss him for.

We had to make the funeral arrangements and I had to go back to my own house. This was difficult as being in the hospital for four full weeks was like being on a different planet. Strange as it may seem, there was a security for me being surrounded by everyone in the hospital and at least Da was still alive and it was possible to feel and touch him and to talk to him there. The raw reality of the empty house without him, never to have breakfast with him again, I knew was going to be horrendous. Philo came with me and offered to stay with me, which I was grateful for. The thoughts of staying on my own in our empty house, now that Da was dead and after the buzz and noise of the hospital was unbearable. When we arrived at my house, my neighbours John and Eily were waiting for us and Eily brought us into their house and cooked us a gorgeous Irish breakfast. I never forgot that breakfast or that kindness. They were close staunch friends of our family and John and Da were as thick as thieves, they had had a thriving friendship. Poor John was awfully upset and just could not get over how Da had been perfectly healthy today and gone tomorrow. He only expressed exactly what we were all feeling. John always said afterwards, that for him, Da died the day he left the house to go to the doctor. That was the date he always relayed to me as Da's anniversary every year after that.

The next while was a complete blur. Once the funeral was over the loneliness hit me like a ton of bricks. No Bridget to call in to anymore. No Da at home anymore. I couldn't go back to work for a few weeks as the exhaustion and ill feeling from lack of eating and drinking had me quite weak. I was in no shape to work. I was in tatters actually and didn't know which end of me was up. I had much to contend with, much to get my head around while at the same time a large part of me, physically and emotionally had shut down in an endeavour to get through the whole catastrophe in one piece. I didn't know where to turn or what to do next.

These initial weeks after Bridget's and Da's deaths were the next most torturous weeks of my life. The bottom had fallen out of my world completely. Everything as it was before the car crash was no more. I desperately wanted to turn the clock back, but I knew I couldn't. My boyfriend. The car crash. Bridget. My Da. The realisation was pure and utter agony. I felt so sorry for myself and awfully hard done by. How can your life be turned upside down like that in just one fell swoop? How, how, how? The injustice of it all! Was I such a bad person that I deserved this level of punishment? For what? What had I done that was so terrible that I deserved this incessant torture? I couldn't make sense of it and I most certainly couldn't answer any of these questions.

The time crawled by. I was feeling a hundred per cent battered and bruised, both physically and emotionally. It seemed impossible to pick myself up. I felt as if I had been steam rolled into the concrete, so much so, that I was now a part of the concrete and could not get up. The physiotherapist contacted me to check in on me as I had left a message for her when I had to cancel my appointment due to my Da's crisis. She strongly encouraged me to make an appointment. I no more felt like doing that than the cat. She kept at me until she managed to persuade me. She was shocked and taken aback when she saw me. I had no idea how awful I looked. I was just struggling to get through one minute at a time never mind one day at a time. Of course, inevitably, my condition had worsened considerably from the lack of treatment and exercise regime and I had a major setback as a result of the whole situation. While she was extremely sympathetic with me, she also took complete control of the situation and put her foot down with me in relation to getting back on track. She pointed out the importance of getting back to where I was before this had happened. I told her I couldn't care less. I didn't give two fiddlers about anything now. Everything had changed, drastically changed and there was no way I could even think about that, never mind doing it. I was too low in myself, too down and I had no energy. I was completely drained. My battery was flat as a pancake. She tried to cajole me a bit, but that didn't even work.

Luckily enough, she persisted and didn't let any of that put her off. She gave me a treatment and didn't give me any exercises to do, as she knew and could clearly see there was no point. I was grateful for that because no way could I have done them, even if I had wanted to. It was she who started to get me in to a routine again and that eventually led me to going back to work. I was dreading going in to work and having to face my boss, knowing how she had felt about me before this had happened. I knew she wouldn't be impressed.

However, the most senior boss John, took me under his wing and brought me in to work in his office. He was a lovely, exceedingly kind and understanding gentleman, who fully understood grief and depression because he had experienced them himself. He made sure that my office boss didn't give me too much to do and he eased me back in gently which was extremely helpful to me. He also insisted that I took the time to do my physio exercises and he even helped me with some of them. This however, also upset me no end because he was reminding me of my Da and it was bringing up the grief around him. He understood this too which was great because he gave me some space to express my grief. Another great thing was, he didn't rush me and told me I could stay with him for as long as I needed to, until I felt I was ready to go back into my own office.

John probably had no idea of how helpful he was being to me, but I felt it deeply despite the awful state I was in.

He was so kind, caring and patient that it was not plausible for me not to feel it. It was through feeling it that I began to thaw out somewhat and the armour I had built around myself during those weeks in the hospital began to soften. Gradually, after a period of weeks, my grief became manageable enough to return to my own office. He had given instructions to the girls and my boss there, that they were to go extremely easy on me and be gentle with me as I had been through a horrendously traumatic time. John totally understood the gravity, enormity and extent of my losses and was well aware that any one of them on their own would be traumatic enough to deal with, never mind as many as four. He also had a good grasp on the massiveness of having the four in quick succession of each other.

I was tremendously lucky that he was a learned and insightful man. It was his soft, gentle, compassionate caring nature that started me on the road to feeling human again. He was such a dote that I learned a lot from him in that time I spent with him. He had the unique gift of being able to double role as a boss and a friend and I was later to learn that this is an invaluable skill to have in life. It is a rare quality for anyone to have and I was privileged to be exposed to it. I didn't know at the time that I already had started to develop this skill myself through my various basketball roles and it was John who helped me to develop this further through my learning from him. In years to come, it was going to be one of my greatest strengths in my personal and professional life.

Once I got settled back into my regular physio treatments, the physiotherapist suggested that I should go for bereavement counselling. I tried the hospice in Harold's Cross which was conveniently down the road from where I lived and would be handy for me. They were able to take me on since my mother had had home care service from them during her cancer and subsequent death. I was assigned a lovely elderly woman, Virginia who was extremely experienced. She was as overwhelmed by my story as I was but was absolutely brilliant. According to her, my grief was what was termed as *Complicated Grief* as a result of the nature of the incidents, the volume of them and the depth of the relationships involved. She recommended psychotherapy as a more suitable type of counselling, given the multiple losses and the fact that they were in short succession of each other. She said that while she most certainly could be of help, she wouldn't be qualified enough to deal with the level of trauma arising from the complications I had to contend with. I told my boyfriend what she advised and, interestingly, he had had a previous girlfriend who had attended counselling due to a major trauma that had occurred in her life. I wasn't too fussed about this as at the time there was a huge stigma attached to counselling, not like nowadays. Counselling was pretty unheard of in those days. I didn't want to be viewed as Whacko Jacko or mad in the head by my family and peers.

My boyfriend made the necessary enquiries for me and had to take me, as we say in Dublin, by the scruff of the neck and the arse of the knickers and bring me there himself. I would never have gone on my own. The woman that had dealt with his previous girlfriend had moved on and they recommended another woman to me. She was unbelievably different to Virginia and she took a lot of getting used to. She was based near where I lived which helped a lot. I kept going to Virginia while I was also seeing the new person, until she felt I was ready to finish with her and just continue with the new counsellor. After a long time, she too felt she could take me no further and passed me on to another therapist.

This woman Ann, I really clicked with and she was indeed the perfect person to take over. She was a loving, caring, motherly type of person with endless patience, was easy-going and laid-back while at the same time extremely challenging. She had her work cut out for her trying to deal with me and my problems. Extremely intelligent with a broad outlook, highly knowledgeable on all matters and with a great understanding on how the psyche works and how and why defence mechanisms are securely entrenched in people.

Taking this step, which was majorly daunting and frightening for me, was a vital turning point in my life. At this point in time, I had no idea as to how it was going to save my life in the future. I began to slowly and gradually place my trust in her. Over time we were able to unearth the root causes of my underlying problems that were paralleling my current problems. It was a tough and agonising process, but exceptionally worthwhile in the end.

It was coming up to Bridget's and my Da's first anniversary and I was beginning to make a small breakthrough in my grief process. Ann suggested that I do a special ritual with her and a group of people to help me to deal with the fact that I had missed Bridget's funeral ceremonies. She thought Bridget's anniversary would be a good time to do this. She guided me as to how to approach it, which included a lot of creative ideas. I put a lot of effort in to preparing for it and it was an amazing experience. I had never had an emotional experience like it in my life before. It proved to be greatly beneficial and worthwhile. The dam of tears and immense pain that had been suppressed at the time, due to being put on hold as a result of Da's crises, burst open and got released. I couldn't believe the amount of tears that got shed and the intense wailing of pain that accompanied them. The regret and anger that also had been suppressed surged out and there was no stopping them or the tears. Releasing these pent-up emotions was incredibly healing, especially considering I wasn't able to cry due to my childhood upbringing where crying was forbidden. It gave me the opportunity as the saying goes 'To kill two birds with the one stone,' unleash the present and unleash some of the past at the same time.

While the anniversary was tough going, the ritual empowered me because of course, it also tapped into my grief around my Da. Because both deaths were intertwined, it was impossible for Da not be included a lot as well. Ann's facilitation of the ritual, which was tender and full of care gave me great comfort. She was a loving and tactile person. Her physical contact with me and her holding and hugs benefitted me enormously. She gave healing to the isolated part of me that had been alone and lonely during those many, many hours I had spent in solitude during both crises. It was a comfort and solace that I unknowingly had been craving for.

The benefits and effects of the ritual stayed with me for a long time afterwards and I was able to use it as a building block in developing my trust and relationship with Ann. The seeds and the foundation had been sown for therapeutic progress in the future.

CHAPTER 31
Grieving

Extracts from
"A Grief Observed" by C.S. Lewis and
"The Lessons of Love" by Melody Beattie

"Grieving is inherently and mysteriously connected to loving deeply."
Melody Beattie

"And grief still feels like fear. Perhaps more strictly like suspense. Or like waiting; just hanging about waiting for something to happen. It gives life a permanently provisional feeling."
C.S. Lewis

"I not only live each endless day in grief, but I live each day thinking about living each day in grief."
C.S. Lewis

"Grief is like a bomber circling round and dropping its bombs each time the circle brings it overhead."
CS Lewis

"Looming ahead were endless days of pain and missing them. The simplest acts required an inordinate amount of effort and triggered a volume of feeling."
Melody Beattie

"My life had slowed almost to a stop."
Melody Beattie

"I had been flung into a
dark black sea of grief
and despair as vast as
the ocean that crested
and receded below me."
Melody Beattie

"The part of me that squared my shoulders,
bounced back,
got up, and kept going
no matter what; had disappeared.
My warrior spirit was gone
and I didn't know how to get it back."
Melody Beattie

"Nothing made me care
about life again."
Melody Beattie

"How many times,
how many days in a row
can you answer the question,
"How are you?"
with
"Not good."
Melody Beattie

"I hated the greyness of my life,
the lack of passion for anything."
Melody Beattie

"My world had shattered
and I couldn't put the
pieces back together.
I was shattered too,
broken in a way
I had never been before."
Melody Beattie

'How often – will it be for always? – How often will the vast emptiness astonish me like a complete novelty and make me say 'I never realised my loss until this moment' the same leg is cut off time after time. The first plunge of the knife into the flesh is felt again and again'

C.S. Lewis

By now I was beginning to pick myself up a bit and get back to a somewhat normal way of living. Of course, I was missing Bridget and Da terribly. That was never going to go away. I knew that the hole in myself and in my life that their deaths caused could never be filled. Melody Beattie describes perfectly how I felt in her book 'Lessons of Love' when she says, '…. you're so close and love each other so much that it matters a lot when they're gone. You have a big hole in your heart, an empty spot that doesn't go away.' One good thing was that despite my injuries I was somehow managing to get back on track with my reffing and running. My steel determination was producing results. The emotional release of the gut-wrenching pain as a result of the floodgates being opened by the ritual had continued and it freed up a lot of tension and holding in my body, which in turn helped me to improve on the physical front. My body became freer in other places, separate to my injuries.

Getting my sports back on track gave me renewed hope which put a dent in the overwhelming darkness that had enveloped me. While I still had a long way to go, I felt that at least there was some light in the tunnel. I could not see the end of the tunnel but that didn't matter. I was happy and content that there was a shift occurring.

When someone very close to you dies that first year is a torturous year. (Joan Didion describes it brilliantly in 'The

Year of Magical Thinking'). The grieving process is a long lonely one. People tend to drift away after the initial stages and those birthdays, Christmases, anniversaries, Easters etc., are tremendously painful when you are minus your loved ones. Even close friends, who are more aware of what's going on for you, can find it difficult to be around you when you are grieving. C.S. Lewis describes it aptly, 'An odd by product of my loss is that I am aware of becoming an embarrassment to everyone I meet. At work, at the club, in the street, I see people, as they approach me, trying to make up their minds whether they will say something about it or not. I hate if they do and if they don't. Perhaps the bereaved ought to be isolated in special settlements like lepers.'

I decided to abide by the old Irish custom of wearing black for the year to explore and see if it would help me with my grief process. I found it helped me a lot and it was beneficial in keeping myself connected to the grief and not running away from it.

Ann encouraged me to do this although my friends were horrified at the idea of it. They thought it was morbid and dull and couldn't understand my thinking. One of the things it showed me was, that the previous generations were much better at supporting people in grief than the present generation. It would appear that that's because they processed their grief better by adhering to the customs and this made it easier for them to support others. The modern generation avoid grief now and once the funeral is over, you are supposed to pull yourself together, snap out of your loss and get back to work as soon as you can and forget it ever happened. This attitude of course forces people to hide their grief to prevent them upsetting others which in many cases causes people to bury their grief. This isolates people in their grief and leaves them with the feeling that, as Melody Beattie says, 'Your fight is just beginning. Sometimes no one will want to hear what you're going through. You are going to have to learn to carry a great burden and most of your learning will be done alone.'

The grief process is a normal and natural one if we allow it. Under the old customs, people were given permission to grieve for one whole year. The neighbours, along with family and friends, were extremely good at supporting the grieving person. They took turns at calling in every night to encourage the person grieving, to talk and talk and talk about their lost loved one and to cry and express their anger. It was generally understood that the grieving process is such a difficult one, that attending parties, weddings or any other celebrations was too much. The custom of not sending Christmas cards was also born out of that understanding. It was recognised and acknowledged widely that the grief process on its own was enough for the person to contend with.

I found that by wearing black it caused people to question me which gave me an opportunity to talk about Bridget and Da, which I desperately needed to do. I wanted to talk especially to the people who knew Bridget and Da as these people could engage better because they knew them. Nowadays, people avoid talking to the grieving person, the excuse being that they don't want to upset them by reminding them about the loss, but this is the complete opposite to what the grief process is about. The more the person becomes upset the better because this gives them the opportunity to cry and shed the tears they need to shed. This was particularly important for me, especially as I am a person who finds it extremely difficult to cry. Many people unfortunately however, tried to stop me crying and did me a huge disfavour because that only suppressed my grief. For someone like me, who finds it hard to cry, doing this made it even harder for me to cry the next time I felt upset.

I remember feeling violently angry when people did this to me. I could not understand what the big deal was with them not being able to sit with me when I wanted to cry. Ann explained to me about the old customs, the relevance and importance of them and that because people weren't following the old customs anymore, it meant they weren't getting the benefit of that themselves and therefore couldn't do it for anyone else. She explained that it's only people who have done their own grief work properly, that are truly able to sit with others and support them through their grief. While it was helpful to understand this, it still made me angry, as I realised we had lost a precious custom and I was now suffering because of that. It was lucky I had the hospice counselling and Ann or, like everyone else, I would not have gone through my grief process in any sort of a way, never mind properly. I later discovered that unresolved grief can not only cause misery but can cause serious illness such as cancer for example. When people get stuck in their grief it puts their life on hold. They also become stuck in not being able to move on in their lives.

I also discovered that while the first year is extremely difficult for the reasons I've said, the second year was even tougher. The reason being that you are so busy the first year, firefighting the many Firsts that you don't exactly feel the loss at the deep level it hits you. I knew in my head that Bridget and Da were dead. Despite this however, while the pain had diminished by only the most imperceptible amount, it still felt as it did the day I walked into the hospital to see Bridget and into the Emergency Room to see Da. I could clearly still remember, like it was only yesterday, how the nurse and doctor had looked at me in that stricken way. The feeling, that someone had held a shotgun to my chest and blown a hole through my heart was that deeply imprinted in my body and in my mind, I knew it would stay with me forever. In that first year, while I was in the height of my pain, it was simply unimaginable to me how the world and time could possibly move on while my world felt it had come to a complete standstill. I was still at the stage where I was expecting, longing and waiting for them both to walk in the door at any minute. It was only in the second year that I truly realised and came to understand that they weren't coming back, that they were dead and gone forever. With the activity of the first year out of the way and the dreaded first anniversary, a space seemed to open up to allow room for the deeper impact to set in.

> If you simply
> cannot understand
> why someone is
> grieving so much,
> for so long, then
> consider yourself
> fortunate that
> you do not
> understand.
>
> *- Unknown -*

FOR GRIEF

When you lose someone you love,
Your life becomes strange,
The ground beneath you gets fragile,
Your thoughts make your eyes unsure;
And some dead echo drags your voice down
Where words have no confidence.

Your heart has grown heavy with loss;
And though this loss has wounded others too,
No one knows what has been taken from you
When the silence of absence deepens.
Flickers of guilt kindle regret
For all that was left unsaid or undone.
There are days when you wake up happy;
Again inside the fullness of life,
Until the moment breaks
And you are thrown back
Onto the black tide of loss.
Days when you have your heart back,
You are able to function well
Until in the middle of work or encounter,
Suddenly with no warning,
You are ambushed by grief.
It becomes hard to trust yourself.
All you can depend on now is that
Sorrow will remain faithful to itself.

More than you, it knows its way
And will find the right time
To pull and pull the rope of grief
Until that coiled hill of tears
Has reduced to its last drop.

Gradually, you will learn acquaintance
With the invisible form of your departed;
And, when the work of grief is done,
The wound of loss will heal
And you will have learned
To wean your eyes
From that gap in the air
And be able to enter the hearth
In your soul where your loved one
Has awaited your return
All the time.

'For Grief' by John O'Donohue, from *To Bless the Space Between Us: A Book of Blessings* (Doubleday, 2008).

CHAPTER 32
Big Bang No. 2

It was during the same year of Bridget and Da's death in 1998, when I was truly in the throes of my grief, that I had my second bang. I was driving over to A.L.S.A.A., (Aer Lingus Social and Athletic Association) near the airport, to meet my friend Dick to go training with him. I was stopped at traffic lights on Upper Drumcondra Road, outside the Skylon Hotel. I was thinking about what type of training session would be the best one for us to do. I heard an unmerciful screech of brakes which caused me to look into my mirror to see what was going on. I couldn't decipher immediately what it was, but something was completely taking over my whole mirror. Then bang! A huge bang!

Before I knew where I was, I found myself and the car catapulted forward through the traffic lights into the middle of the junction. The car was shaking and reverberating like mad and I was holding on to the steering wheel for dear life. The same thing that had happened to me in my first car crash happened again and I smashed my head off the windscreen and my neck off the headrest. This time, thank heavens, I was on my own in the car. I was absolutely rigid with shock and disbelief. What was happening? No! It couldn't be! It couldn't be what I think it was! It just couldn't! The disbelief had me completely immobilised. If you gave me a million pounds I could not have moved. I was rooted and I mean rooted, to the spot. My head was spinning.

Eventually someone came up to the driver's door to see if I was dead or alive and seemed surprised that I was alive. It was a man and he kept asking me questions. I couldn't speak or answer him with the shock. My throat felt constricted and I couldn't open my mouth. It was like my lips were stuck together and my voice was completely gone. At one point my eyes were rolling around in my head. I was sure I was a gonner! The man had difficulty opening the driver's door and when he did, he asked me if I was able to move. I couldn't answer him and I certainly couldn't move. By this time people were gathering around the car and someone had rung the Guards. The Garda Station was literally 3 minutes up the road.

The man tried to check me over to see if it was safe to take me out of the car. I had to be lifted out, I couldn't walk. I couldn't feel anything. I was numb all over. A lady had come out of her house and told the men to carry me into her house which they did. They put me on the sofa and she got loads of blankets and wrapped me up in them. I was shaking from head to toe and still could not speak. I cannot imagine what I must have looked like. It transpired that a forty foot articulated lorry had crashed into the back of me. I was lucky that there was no car crossing the junction when I got catapulted through the red lights. He was going too fast and even though he tried to brake and stop, he couldn't because he was carrying a full load and the weight of the load wouldn't allow him to stop. I was out of it at this stage because I was consumed and paralysed with the shock that this horror was happening to me yet again. Not only that, but the fact was, here I was obeying the rules of the road, stopped on the red light, supposedly a mundane situation where we should feel safe. The feeling of being in this horrific position, a position that was beyond my control, it is a wonder that I didn't have an out of body experience. I had no concept how serious the whole thing was until I looked out the lady's window. When

I saw the size of the lorry and the length of it – it was huge - it was completely taking up the whole of the lady's window – I nearly fainted. The lady gave me a cup of tea and some smelling salts to try and keep me conscious. I couldn't see my car. I could only see this monstrosity of a lorry. It had mangled my car, especially at the back obviously. The lady was concerned about me and tried to keep me warm, kept talking to me and encouraged me to drink the tea. At this point I simply was not capable of anything, not even drinking her tea and when an Irish person can't drink a cup of tea, things are bad.

The Guards arrived quickly. They examined the car, spoke to the lorry driver and came into the house to check on me. When they saw I was alive and in one piece, so to speak, they asked me some questions. I still couldn't speak, I couldn't answer them and I was still shaking like a leaf. They advised me to drive the car home if I could, that they had checked it over and it was drivable from the front. The lady nearly had a hissy fit at this suggestion. She said there was no way she was letting me get into the car in the condition I was in. They were quite insistent however and said if I wanted to drive in the future this would be the best thing to do. The lady thought they were mad in the head and told them this quite bluntly. I was so dazed and shocked I just did what they told me to do. In fact, what I actually did was I continued on out to A.L.S.A.A. as in my shocked state I was more worried about Dick, waiting for me and not knowing why I didn't turn up than I was for myself. Just like Bridget's funeral, when I didn't show up on time, he knew that something serious must have happened. This prompted him to wait rather than go home. When I eventually arrived, he could not believe his eyes when he saw the state of the car. The back of the car was like a melodeon and the back seats were up on top of the two front seats, where they had been forced forward by the weight and speed of the impact from the articulated lorry. Dick didn't know what to say or do, he too was shocked when he saw the state of the car and the state of me, still in shock and unable to speak. Because he wasn't caught up in the drama of the accident, he could clearly see the wreckage that I not only stepped out of, but somehow had managed to drive. This hadn't registered with me; I was still immersed in the shock. As Dick had been waiting for me for a long time, I was quite anxious for him to get home as I knew his wife and family would be worried about him. There were no mobile phones to ring people in these types of circumstances. While Dick was reluctant to let me head off on my own, I reassured him I would be fine, sure hadn't I made it out to A.L.S.A.A., of course I'd make it home. He made me promise to ring him the minute I got home to let him know I was safe. We said our goodbyes and we left.

When I arrived home, I knocked up my neighbour John. The thoughts of going into the empty house, by myself, especially after the shock of the accident and the state I was in, knowing that Da was not going to be there to look after me like the previous time was unbearable to me. I parked the car in the driveway. John and Eily were in an awful state when they saw both me and the car. They could not believe what had happened. They thought I should ring one of my friends to see if they could come over and stay with me overnight. They could see I was in no state to be able to do anything for myself.

Strange as it may seem, at no point had anyone suggested either calling an ambulance or going to the hospital. This was quite staggering when I think about it.

In hindsight now, perhaps it was because there was no blood and guts flying, that I appeared to be in a better state than I was actually in. Despite the shaking and not being able to speak, I must have been giving off vibes that I was doing ok, though in reality these vibes were extremely misleading. Or could it have been that everyone was in their own state of shock, something like mine. I wonder perhaps, did the fact that I was dressed in my running gear, looking fit, healthy and brown from being out in the air, did that create an illusion that I was in better shape than I was in truth.

I was convinced I was never going to be able to speak again. Another couple who were friends of mine, came over to stay and look after me for the night. They boarded up the back of the car and the windows where the glass had shattered in smithereens. My friends gave me a cup of tea, but I couldn't drink it. I couldn't eat anything either as I still couldn't open my mouth. They wet my lips with the tea to try and hydrate me a little bit at least. I had started shaking again but this time much more violently than the first time. They changed me into my pyjamas and put me into bed, hoping that if I could sleep it would help to calm my system down. I couldn't sleep for ages and eventually, many hours later I dozed off for a little while. The next morning my friends reluctantly had to leave to go to work. They got John and Eily to come in to me before they left to make sure I wouldn't be on my own.

John and Eily were worried about me and they called the doctor to come and see me. When I look back at this, I am amazed that it was only the next day that I saw a doctor and, at that, a G.P.! Like everyone else he could not believe what had happened. He checked me over and said I didn't seem to have anything broken but undoubtedly this was going to aggravate my previous injuries and set me back considerably. When he saw the car he said I was lucky to be alive and how I did not have any broken bones was beyond him. He said I must be made of steel. He explained to John and Eily that it was the shock that had rendered me speechless and probably the psychological shock that went with that as a result of having had the first car crash. He was hoping that in a few days, when the shock subsided a bit, I should be able to talk again.

He told them to keep me warm and not leave me on my own. Eily said that was no problem she could stay with me. The next few days were like a whirlwind from an emotional and physical perspective. They dragged by at a snail's pace. Eily rang work for me to tell them what happened and my boss John called in to see me on his way home from work. He was chronically upset for me. He couldn't believe it. He thought I was the most unfortunate person on the planet for this to have happened to. Just as I was beginning to come around and get back on my feet again after all that had happened. When Eily let him out to go home, he told her he was very concerned about me. He thought it was not possible for me to recover from this. He said this was the icing on the cake, one too many to recover from. He told them that no one, no matter how strong and determined they are, can sustain taking that many knocks. Everyone, in his opinion, had their limits and boy did I need this like a headache! Enough was enough! Boy, was this enough!

He left terribly upset, asked them to keep him informed and said he would keep in touch as well. I appreciated him calling in and his concern for me, even though I was not able to tell him that. It was approximately a week before I could talk again. When I began talking my voice was weak. I had to be careful not to talk too much initially, to give my voice a chance to recover. I rang Ann to see if she could see me and she was speechless herself when I told her my news. She too was concerned like John about my psychological wellbeing. Nobody knew better than her what I had physically and psychologically gone through after my first car crash and that was excluding all the other traumas. She was shocked at the state I was in when she saw me, as was the physiotherapist when I eventually went back to see her. That time was a bad black period of doom and gloom.

John told me not to attempt to even think about going back to work. I would need to take a lot of time off work if I were to have any chance of making a recovery. Obviously, everyone except me, could see how bad I was. I was disillusioned and shocked beyond shocked to see or care how bad I was or how bad I looked to everyone else. I was obviously in a much more fragile state than I realised. I didn't dare to look into a mirror. From everyone else's reaction, that would have finished me off altogether and put the final nail in my coffin. As I never liked looking at myself in the mirror anyway, this was easy to do.

You can imagine how much I was missing Bridget and Da during this phase and especially Da, as he had looked after me superbly well after my first car crash. Not only was I in bits from this car crash, but it was also triggering my grief again around Bridget and Da. I spent days upon days bawling crying with Ann during this time. My tears could have started a second River Liffey in Dublin. Poor Ann! She had her work cut out for her trying to help me and take me through this awful time. I can honestly say I would never have made it without her. She was exceptional in every way and was there for me 100 per cent consistently throughout this living nightmare. I would have been lost without her, my boss John, my neighbours John and Eily and my friends.

CHAPTER 33
The Trauma Begins To Sink In

Another series of investigations began and the orthopaedic surgeon was strangely, anything but sympathetic to my plight, as if he could not be bothered dealing with this second car crash. It was an inconvenient nuisance to him and he was not impressed by it. This was the last thing I needed in my condition and I was shocked at his attitude. In my opinion, he was the most arrogant, ignorant man I ever met or had the misfortune to deal with. He was rude, aggressive and bullying both to his staff and to me. I stood up to him as best I could and he did not like that. Who was I to question him? According to reports he was a big noise in his field and people were intimidated by him. Subsequently, I met two people afterwards who both had equally bad experiences with the same surgeon. It's a pity I didn't meet them beforehand, I would have avoided attending him. Hindsight is a great thing.

This was a disastrous turn of events for me. It made my recovery more difficult and feel like it was not far off impossible. Ann, however, stepped in strongly and point-blank would not let him get to me. She knew this was the last thing I needed and that it could be detrimental for me and that the result could be irreversible. She herself at this point was extremely worried about me. She helped me to combat his total and utter negativity and gave me the sympathy and understanding that he refused to give me, as a way of contradicting my awful experience with him. Ann was ultra-dogged and determined in her approach with me and it helped me a lot to counteract my experiences with him. It was unnecessary hard work for both of us, as if we didn't have enough to contend with.

I was in constant horrendous pain all day every day. My muscles were continuously spasming badly with the result that my body completely seized up as if I were paralysed. Something similar to locked-in syndrome. These seizures could last anything from one hour to seven hours. This was terribly, terribly frightening as there were times when I thought I was not going to come out of them and that I would end up in a wheelchair. I continued with my physio treatment and Lizzy my friend the nurse, found me an acupuncturist who lived close by, as an additional form of treatment to see if it would speed up my recovery. It transpired that he was not only an experienced acupuncturist, but he was a herbalist as well. His name was Michael. His knowledge of the musculoskeletal system was second to none. I never met anyone in my life who knew it as well as he did. He had many other bodywork techniques and a vast knowledge and understanding of Chinese philosophy. As a result, he was able to treat not only the symptoms that were surfacing, but the underlying issues using a holistic approach. Unlike the orthopaedic surgeon, he had extensive knowledge of the interrelationship of the bones, muscles, ligaments and tendons and an in-depth knowledge of the tissue, fascia, myofascia and sacro-cranial fluids in the body. He was ultra-proficient in understanding the knock-on effect that each problem had on the next and the ingenuity of the body's compensatory system and how it worked in relation to my multiple injuries. Again, unlike the orthopaedic surgeon, he had a major insight in to the physical, emotional and psychological protective defence mechanism that my body had no choice but to adapt to, as a result of the multiple traumas caused by the two car crashes.

He explained to me in layman's language how the tissue in these situations gets stuck together like chewing gum and how difficult it is at the physiological level for the tissue to let go and stay unstuck. From the mental and physiological level, he explained that my body would also be tensing up, waiting for the next car crash to happen. The body had its own way of preparing for the next trauma and protecting itself in anticipation. Fear was a key element running the show. I could totally relate to this explanation because that's exactly how I felt. Believe it or not, I genuinely could feel the chewing gum effect and the resistance to the treatment to letting go. He went on to explain that unfortunately because the body's response was in relation to true reality, i.e., I did actually have two car crashes, the fear that emanated was in fact, a rational fear as opposed to an irrational fear. This also was going to make it more difficult to get the stuck tissue to release.

Michael explained further that it would take a humungous amount of work to convince the body to cooperate with any kind of treatment, not just his kind of treatment. The only way forward was to find ways to trick the tissue into releasing and try and use reverse psychology. Given the fact that tissue damage is an extremely painful condition, that too would interfere with the process of making progress, never mind rapid progress. There was also the problem of the scar tissue that had developed at the stage of the orthopaedic surgeon's interventions which was another serious problem. He explained it was going to be a long, slow process. Another element to the slowness was the fact that my body was not physically fully recovered from the first crash when I had the second. Therefore, we were dealing with a situation of injury on top of another injury. It does not take a genius to figure that one out. This was going to complicate matters further.

There were many other factors that Michael went on to explain to me, too many to go into here, but at least I had a much better understanding of what I had to contend with and what I was facing into in terms of treatment and effect. The whole scenario was depressing to say the least of it and it seemed insurmountable.

The only positive thing that came out of it was that movement, constant movement, was critical because movement increases blood flow, which in turn helps the tissue to release, thereby giving temporary relief from the pain. Sitting down was out of the question altogether now and I had to be extremely stringent in developing a constantly moving programme as much as I could.

At first, I felt slightly heartened by that until it occurred to me that my job was a sitting down job. While I was an extremely active person and it would appear to others that I was always on the move and always exercising, the cold hard facts of reality were, I was sitting for a minimum of seven hours a day. This meant I was not going to be able to go back to work for a long time – heaven knows how long. Michael couldn't put a time frame on it due to the complications that were grossly evident. The physiotherapist had already told me that it could take between three and five years to make a full recovery, providing a full recovery was possible. Between her and Michael it became clear as day that my condition was far more serious than I could ever have imagined it to be.

The thoughts of being out of work long-term was inconceivable to me. I had started working part-time at 11 years of age in a shop around the corner from where I lived. From a financial perspective, I felt that it was not possible for me to financially survive without proper earnings. How was I going to afford to pay for the treatments and pay for Ann? It wasn't viable. I was worried sick about the whole thing and my anxiety levels escalated up through the roof. Naturally, this was not going to help my condition, it was only going to increase the tension in my body which was the opposite of what needed to be done. My family had always been a poor family and while I had a steady income, I was still in the lower-class bracket in society. A total and utter sense of doom and gloom descended on me. I felt so alone with this trauma beginning to sink in on me. Ann being the cool, calm and collected person she was, told me not to worry. Her exact words were, 'Don't worry Mary. Worrying is a futile exercise, it does not solve anything. It's a waste of time and energy.' Of course, I went ballistic and lost the head with her replying, 'It's all right for you to say that you're not the one in my shoes. You don't know what it's like to be broke.'

This predicament started a long string of ding-dong battles between Ann and myself. She was ferociously challenging me and I was in full-blown hysteria. I desperately, desperately wanted and needed to go back to work, but she would not hear tell of it. I felt angry as hell with her and severely miffed at the fact that she was agreeing with Michael and the physiotherapist and not me. 'You're supposed to be on my side, not theirs,' I yelled at her one day out of total frustration and panic. The more she tried to get me to calm down and not worry, the more irate I became. Although I could not see it at the time, she was perfectly right of course, worrying and getting hysterical wasn't going to do anything in the remotest to solve my problem. I was stuck with the reality of it whether I liked it or not and of course I *so* did not like it! If I had had the good fortune to run into those shitheads who crashed into me, I tell you I would have summoned up every ounce of strength in my body that I could and murdered them both with the greatest of pleasure. I couldn't begin to tell you the amount of venomous rage I felt towards them during this time. I was spitting fire like a dragon, a frenzied fire that was blazing and rampant and no amount of water would have put it out. With their sirens blaring, the fire brigades in the whole of Ireland, had they arrived on the scene and tried to, wouldn't have extinguished one flame never mind the whole fire.

Poor Ann was on the receiving end of my fury and I remember feeling highly embarrassed afterwards when my fury eventually subsided. Ann being Ann of course, had no problem with me expressing the ferocity of these pent-up emotions and in fact was only too happy to egg me on to release them. Once I let go of control and let rip, I was like a volcano erupting. The hatred I felt for the irresponsibility of these two men could not be quantified during this time. Unexpected feelings that I had suppressed came tumbling out and I had no idea that the pain I had been enduring and the limitations I had been suffering were fuelling my rage and hatred the way they were towards those two men. I'm telling you; they were two lucky men that Ann stopped me from going after them. I was incensed, seething and that wired to the moon I could have killed them with a look and would not have had to physically touch them. It would be like touching an electric fence and getting electrocuted. When I was in the throes of experiencing these emotions, I was deeply connected to my feelings and I had no clue of how loud I was or how volatile my expressions were and that the room was practically vibrating with the force of it. Someone knocked on Ann's door because the noise was obviously disturbing them. Let me give you an example of what I said and I apologise for the bad language:

'Fuck off with yourself
and don't dare tell me to keep quiet or I'll kill you too.
The fucking cheek of you, who do you think you are telling me to shut up.
You can shove it up your arse.
I've been shut up all my life.
Well guess what, sorry mister, not anymore.
If I want to shout and scream, I will
and no one, no one, is going to stop me
and that includes you. Get it?
Well, you had better get it because NO MORE. I'm done.
I've had enough of people shutting me up.
And, anyway, I have bloody good reason to be shouting.
If you had my problems, you'd be shouting too.
So, fuck off with yourself asshole.'

And with that I fired one of Ann's bean bags s at the door.

When I finally, one hour later, got all that out of my system also having beaten the shit out of two bean bags, one for each driver, I felt a lot better. I could not believe how a small little body like mine could possibly hold so many trapped emotions. I was impressed at its storage capacity. My body as a container seemed like an endless pit. An endless pit of feelings of frustration and hatred with an intense desire to savage and rip apart those who had unforgivably wounded me. I didn't want revenge, I just wanted to tear them to pieces and eradicate them so that they couldn't do damage to anyone else. I felt if I did that, I would be doing the world a big favour.

Of course, one session didn't cure these pent-up feelings. It took many sessions to get to the root of these feelings and to release and clear them out completely. There were many more vibrant and colourful sessions to follow that one. These men were the butt of my therapy sessions for quite a while. Ann was a gem throughout the entire process. It didn't knock a fonk out of her. With her level of expertise and experience she was able to therapeutically hold me during the whole time. It was no problem to her. I felt safe in her hands and knew I could trust her completely. It was an incredible experience to be able to express myself at such a deep level. It was an experience I was extra grateful to her for as there were not many therapists out there who could have taken someone into, through and out the other side of such deep-rooted feelings and sensations. It was also an amazing experience to learn that there was no need to be afraid of expressing such deep and volatile emotions. The philosophy of better out than in springs to mind. I had always been afraid to express emotions and in particular strong emotions such as anger and rage in case I went out of control to the extent that I could be *Locked Up*. But I also learned that with proper facilitation and support that that's not likely to happen. As the body has its own way of regulating itself, it will only express what's necessary and it knows when to stop. It is just like children asking questions. When they are satisfied with the information you give them, they toddle off happy with themselves and don't ask any more questions. They know when to stop and exactly how much information is enough for them. Ann always taught me during this period that emotions are transient. They come and they go. There is no need to be afraid of them. The more you can roll with them the better.

It transpired that Michael and the physiotherapist were absolutely right – bang on in fact. I kept thinking that soon in a few months I would be able to go back to work, but each few months kept extending to the next few months. Six months passed, one year passed and no sign of being

417

able to go back. It was because the job was a sitting down job involving computers. The sitting was bad for my back and the computers were bad for my neck. It was not a job I could do lying down. Michael and the physiotherapist were strongly encouraging me to ease back in to my reffing and running again. They felt that at least from a physiological level that would help my physical condition especially and it would also help me mentally and emotionally. Ann supported them in their advice as she too felt it would break the desolation and isolation I was desperately feeling. While people thought I was mad when I was in such pain to go running and reffing and that surely, I could injure myself more, the reality was that the opposite was what was true. The movement in running and reffing would hugely increase the blood flow which would give me relief from the recurring spasms and would improve my mobility and increase my flexibility. All these improvements were desperately needed.

Believe it or not I hadn't the slightest interest in going back running or reffing. I was feeling down; depressed, sorry for myself and hard done by. I couldn't have cared less if I never ran or reffed again. This worried everybody as it was totally against my personality and my love for both. It is amazing how everything can go out the window when you're in a total state of depression and disheartenment. There is no doubt I was at the lowest I had ever been in my life. The three of them kept at me, prodding me, bribing me, doing anything they could do to get me started. I was throwing major tantrums with the three of them. Were they blind? Could they not see and understand the state I was in? I could hardly stand up, never mind run or ref. How was I supposed to run and ref when I was in such high levels of pain? Did they think I was Superwoman? I was raging with them.

When I got the tantrums and poor me feelings out of my body, I felt a bit more rational. Ann encouraged me to start by just going for a short run around the block and to build it up slowly again. Eventually I did this and it was a positive move for lots of reasons. Of course, once I put my training gear on and actually went outside it was like riding a bike, you never forget and I began easing back in to it much easier than I thought I would. While I was in severe pain, the movement most definitely helped to take the edge off it. It's obviously not nice running while in pain but it broke the mode of staying at home moping around, not being able to do anything and feeling useless. Taking this step had a positive effect on me physically but it activated my emotional responses even further against the men who caused the accidents, against the world in general and against that fucker God – another man incidentally. How ironic is that? I was having a bad run with men. The two drivers, the orthopaedic surgeon and now the main man himself!

CHAPTER 34
The Rant
Hell Hath No Fury Like The Wrath Of A Woman Scorned

I have mentioned already that I lost my faith in God when I was deaf as a young child and in relation to the horrible cards life had dealt me. After my second car crash there were people offering to pray to God for me and advising me to pray to St. Jude for hopeless cases. Another man. How does that grab you? Well, it didn't grab me. All I could think of was that fucker God and another fucking godly like saint of a fucking man. I had my bellyful of men at that moment in time, especially that God do-gooder gobshite. That fucking God, how I detested that man with every bone and drop of blood in my body. My feelings of rage, hatred and contempt for God and the men who damaged me so atrociously were all consuming. The feelings were pulsating and coursing through my veins. My body was vibrating like a vortex of energy you see in a tornado. I was the tornado. The feelings of injustice were fuelling this vortex even further. I felt as if it would take an exorcism to rid myself of these feelings.

Then the rant began.

'If there was such a person as you, God, an 'all loving, all caring' God, how could you possibly put me through all this mega torture? How could you take away all the people I loved most in my life? How could you damage my boyfriend so diabolically? How could you leave me with no job, no money? How could you take my job away forever? How could you inflict me with such physical unbearable pain? How could you traumatise me so badly emotionally? How could you, all caring God, mentally annihilate me? How could you smash my spirit into smithereens? How could you take away my sport, what I loved the most in my life and what I was good at? How could you leave me to cope with all this on my own? I bet you fucking couldn't cope if it was the other way around. Like all men you would be useless at suffering pain! Everyone knows that! All loving, my arse! Well fuck you! How dare you inflict all this pain and suffering on me! What did I ever do to deserve this and for you to hate me so much, you bastard? How about changing places, see if you like it? Not only one but two, not only two but three, not only three but four, not only four but five, if you were real how could you inflict five major traumas on me in short succession. You masochistic, sadistic, misogynistic, cruel creepo of a man. Only someone who is psychotic and a psychopath would do all that to someone. You must hate me. Well in case you didn't know it I hate you too. I hate you more than you hate me if that's possible. Unfortunately that's probably not possible because I'm much more of a softy than you are. You are a hypocrite of the highest order and I HATE HYPOCRITES. You are more evil than the devil, even the devil wouldn't dream of doing that I'm sure. The devil would have been kinder to me and would have made sure I died in the first car crash which I should have done incidentally. Had I died I wouldn't have had to go through any further torture. The torture would have been over and done with in one go. But no, not you! You wanted to twist the knife in my back, didn't you? Twist it as many times as you could. Just like my mother. Well, you and my mother would go well together wouldn't you? Now that I come to think about it I realise that's another shitty thing you inflicted me with, my mother!!! She hated me as much as you do! You big fat bollocks of a prick of a shit head!

The ranting, the cursing, the swearing that came out of me was unreal. My bad language was in full flow. It took on a complete life of its own. Words were rolling off my tongue like nobody's business. Words I did not even know I knew existed, never mind know the meaning of! Oh boy! There was no stopping me. What I did not call those fuckers or say about them was not worth saying. I do not know how Ann's poor ears didn't fall off with all the venom that was spewing out of me. It's lucky she wasn't a religious person. She might have been deeply offended if she was!

Did I care? No, not me. Not during this storm of emotions, I can tell you. Ranting and raving like a lunatic was the order of the day. At that time, I didn't know Stephen Fry, but I can tell you if I did, he would have been a man after my own heart. He and I would have had a lot in common and got on famously, no doubt about it. In fact, we would have had the perfect thinking partnership. Whenever I hear him having his spiel nowadays, I laugh to myself as it brings back the memories of this particular time in my life.

When Irish broadcaster Gay Byrne died recently, they showed a clip of him interviewing Stephen Fry, a well known British comedian on the RTE series 'The Meaning of Life.' I found it hilarious, both listening to Stephen Fry and watching Gay Byrne's facial reactions. When Gay Byrne said to him, 'I don't think you're going to get inside the Pearly White Gates if you give that answer,' I nearly wet myself laughing. Stephen Fry would no more be interested in getting inside those Pearly White Gates than I would. It would be a case of 'Shove the Gates up your arse, Mister.'

You may have guessed by now that I love the F-word. In fact, it's my favourite word in the dictionary which states that Fuck is used to express anger or annoyance, the reason being that you can get your teeth firmly stuck into the F bit and your whole body gets behind it which gives it extra credence. The ck part of it allows you to linger, as a way of expressing the venom behind the anger and annoyance and in my case my frustration and rage. Without its sexual connotation the F-word is an expression of a feeling rather than a doing. I never think of the sexual side when I'm using it, it's purely a word to get your teeth stuck into and to release in an energised way those feelings of anger, annoyance, frustration and rage.

CHAPTER 35
The Final Loss And
The Magnitude Of The Overwhelm

There were many more rants like that one in the coming weeks which had to be expressed and expelled out of my body. One of my rants was in relation to my mother. I went through a totally irrational belief that my mother was inflicting this on to me from the grave. She had sent the car crashes on purpose to get at me and to hurt me as much as she could. I could not dispel the belief; it was so real and lifelike. Poor Ann had an awful job with that one I can tell you. There was no shifting me out of it.

As each day was passing, the magnitude of what I was dealing with was sinking in more and more. It's like everything in life, it's only when you are experiencing the reality of something that you truly connect to its cause and effect. The more I tried to get back to normal living after the second car crash, the more its effect and the increased limitations it was inflicting on me became clearer. Everything was in my face much more now than after the first one.

I ended up not being able to go back to work. Sitting down jobs were out of the question. But of course, most jobs are sitting down jobs. Again, you don't realise how much sitting down we do. Sitting down at a desk. Sitting in the car. Sitting on the saddle of a bike. Sitting down at home to eat your meals. Sitting down to watch T.V. Sitting in the pictures when watching a film. Sitting down when eating out in restaurants. Sitting on buses, trains and airplanes. Sitting in pubs. Sitting at a concert, play, musical or show. Sitting in church at mass, weddings or funerals. Sitting on the toilet. Sitting when attending courses or meetings. Sitting at the cash register at the supermarket. Sitting down chatting and listening to a friend. Sitting down because you are tired. Sitting down daydreaming, watching the world go by. Sitting with children, playing, colouring or reading them a story. Sitting down with your pets. Sitting down to put your make-up on. Sitting, sitting, sitting. We do an awful lot more of it than we realise.

Once I couldn't sit any more, these realisations around sitting were looming in front of me on a daily basis. I couldn't believe it. They became quite overwhelming for me. I had to start lying on a mattress when I went to see Ann (her idea of course). I had to stand when visiting friends or when they visited me or when out socialising. They told me it made them feel extremely uncomfortable. They didn't like it. For the above list of sitting situations, I had to either stand or lie down. In the early stages I couldn't sustain standing for long either. Sitting and standing were both painful for me and increased my spasm attacks.

It wasn't long before I stopped socialising and going out altogether. It just wasn't worth it, the embarrassment, the feelings of being constantly uncomfortable, the spotlight being shone on me, drawing unnecessary and unwanted attention to myself. The extra pain and suffering I would have to endure when I came home afterwards, as it was exacerbating my injuries was not worth it either. The frustration of people not being able to understand my condition was infuriating. Therefore, there was only one solution. Withdraw into myself, become a hermit and stop trying to socialise. Making the effort just was not paying off and was not worth it. It was making everything worse and adding more problems to my already problematic existence at this stage. In a sense it was akin to being deaf all over again, the isolation and the loneliness were overwhelming.

Then I had loss number 6. My boyfriend Gerry and I had already been struggling, severely struggling since his accident. My bunch of traumas added a huge amount of pressure to our lives. My intense grief for Bridget and Da were having a huge impact on our relationship. He was emotionally inept at handling my grief. Our injuries were incompatible as I said already and now the second car crash and the setback it caused in relation to my injuries heightened this even more.

During the year following the second crash we both realised we hadn't a hope in hell of continuing our relationship. There were too many obstacles on both sides and now more than ever on my side than his, for both of us to overcome. We did not want to end up fighting and hating each other. We wanted to end the relationship on a mutual and amicable understanding and not end up badly, that at least we could end up as friends rather than enemies.

It was an extremely difficult decision for us to make as we both knew that if we could return to normal, to the way things were before both our accidents that everything would be fine between us. But neither of us could envisage that happening. We couldn't see it happening even in the long-term never mind the short-term. It seemed painfully obvious to us both that we had no choice but to end the relationship and split up as best we could under the circumstances.

While Gerry knew it was absolutely the right thing for us to do, he was reluctant to carry it through as he was worried and more than conscious of the fact that it was going to be another crisis to add to my other ones. Another loss to add to the loss of Bridget and Da. He didn't want to impose another loss on me. He was genuinely afraid that I wouldn't be able for it and it just might push me over the edge altogether. He did not want to be responsible for that.

To be honest, I couldn't but agree with him. The thought of another loss, another person to grieve felt as if it would shatter me altogether. It would knock me for six, especially as it was going to be coincidently trauma number 6. I did feel that it would indeed push me over the edge. It would be the icing on the cake and the last straw. I just could not, handle another loss. The thoughts of it were just intolerable. It just would not be fair or acceptable. Yet deep down in my heart of hearts, I knew it was the right thing to do. For him, for me, for both of us. I knew it was not fair to him to cause any further suffering to him. He was suffering enough as it was and he did not need this extra burden that my problems were placing on him. I cared about him too much to do that to him and it was obvious that he felt the same towards me. I did not want to be selfish.

I discussed the matter with Ann and she was immensely helpful around the whole thing. She thought it was an extraordinarily sad situation for a couple to be in. Everything that had happened between us was outside our control. It was not like we were having the normal, natural problems couples can have. Life traumas were dictating the course of our lives, not us. She felt it was a most unusual set of circumstances for a couple to be in. She pointed out that we had done well to survive as long as we had, as many couple relationships have broken down for far less reasons than what we were being faced with. She thought it was an awful, awful pity for us to have to be in this situation. Even she didn't think it was a fair one.

Her compassion and understanding were such a comfort that it helped me to go back to Gerry and have a further chat with him about it. We chatted about the things Ann had highlighted and it helped us both to feel a tiny bit better about coming to terms with what we had to do. However, it was still exceedingly difficult and we lingered a bit further before finally making the split. Even though we had been struggling dreadfully, I still missed him terribly for an awfully long time after that. We had shared our love for athletics, training and competing in races. We had both enjoyed socialising, going to the pictures, going to restaurants. Gerry and I used to visit Bridget regularly, taking her out to the theatre. She was very fond of him and her advice to me was, 'You should hang your hat on him.' He used to come to watch me playing and refereeing basketball. No longer having his companionship and support rendered me lonelier than ever. Feelings of suicide did sweep over me and kept coming and going and coming and going. If I had not had Ann as my anchor, I think I most definitely would not be here now, such was my loss.

There are no words to describe how harrowing a time this was for me. The overwhelm of six major traumas. The overwhelm of the physical and emotional pain. The overwhelm of my newly inflicted physical limitations. The overwhelm of my mental torture. The overwhelm of my losses. The overwhelm of the bitter, bitter loneliness I was swamped with. The overwhelm of my happy life as it was before these traumas occurred, now upturned into the unhappiest time in my life. The overwhelm of having everything I needed and I could possibly have asked for, to then being stripped totally of everything, everything, everything. There was nothing left. Nothing materialistic, nothing spiritual, nothing of anything. I was a big fat nothing. There was no me left; I was nothing but a bare shell. The sheer magnitude of it all. I could not stick it.

CHAPTER 36
Ann Puts The Boot In.

Ann was seriously concerned at my whole situation, my overall pain and agony and my psychological state. My feelings of suicide were frightening her because she could totally understand why I would be suicidal. As my boss John had outlined, any one of the traumas on its own would be enough to make someone want to die by suicide. I had relayed back to her what John had thought and she could completely identify with him and was in total agreement with him. She knew my feelings were not irrational or dramatic. She had known people who had died by suicide for far less than what I was enduring. It just seemed like everything was going, as they say in Dublin 'From bad to worse to worser.'

After a long time of this toing and froing, when I went in to her one day, she decided to have a serious chat with me. She decided to be brutally honest and upfront with me during this chat. She explained her concern to me and told me that we needed to do something majorly drastic to combat these unfortunate turn of events in my life. She adamantly expressed to me that in her professional opinion, there was no way I would be able to handle another trauma or another loss or blow in my life. We had to do something to avert another crisis. We had to, just had to, take radical action. I looked at her as if she had ten heads and I said, 'Are you for the birds or what? How the fuck are we supposed to do that? I hope you have some bright ideas because I certainly don't.' I mean seriously, putting all jokes aside, I thought I was hearing things. I asked her, 'Are you on drugs or what? There's some excuse for me being off my rocker, but there's none for you.' Normally she would smile at something like that, but that day she did not. She was unusually serious and deep in thought. She had a most worried serious face on her.

When I left her that day I said, 'Well good luck with your hare-brained idea. I hope you get enlightened and come up with some bright ideas.' That was the first step in Ann putting the boot in.

The next day when I came back in, she was equally as serious again and another grim and in-depth discussion took place. Apparently, she had been thinking about her last conversation with me and she had made some enquiries into some of the ideas that came into her head. She told me she would have some more information for me the next time she saw me as we needed to get cracking. 'Get cracking,' I thought. I knew I was cracking up, but it must have been contagious, because she was definitely off her rocker. 'Get cracking.' Get cracking at what? What the fuck could I get cracking at in my condition?

Sure as eggs, the next day I came in, she was more upbeat, more energetic and more alive in herself.

Mary	What's happened to you? You look like someone has put a new battery into you and ignited you.
Ann	(A weak smile on her face) I have good news for you Mary.
Mary	I don't like the sound of it. It can't be good; you're too buzzed up.
Ann	Would you lie down Mary. I have found a lovely 'Introduction to Counselling' course. It's a foundation course and I would like

431

	you to partake in it. It's not too far away, it's in the Donnybrook/Ballsbridge area. It would be ideal for you and it would get you out doing something good and get you back in to a social setting.
Mary	(Looking gobsmacked at her as if she had one hundred heads) That's it, you've finally lost it. Please tell me you are joking! You are *not* and could *not* be serious.
Ann	Oh, I am serious. I most certainly am not joking. Anyway, you've nothing to worry about and nothing to do, you just have to turn up because I have everything arranged. It starts next week, which is great timing.
Mary	Are you out of your head? How the hell can I do a course when I can't even sit down?
Ann	Oh, don't worry about that. I've spoken to the tutor and explained your circumstances to her and you can bring your mattress in and lie down because it's a big classroom and there will be plenty of room for you.
Mary	If you think I'm doing that, you have your glue! Holy shit, it's just dawning on me, you want me to become a counsellor? What kind of nutcase are you? Are you for real? How could I possibly become a counsellor with the nature of my ailments and injuries? Counsellors sit down when they are seeing their clients and you know I can't and won't be able to do that.
Ann	Well, I think you will make a very good counsellor. After what you have been through, you're the ideal person to under stand other people's troubles. As for sitting

down, you will just be different. You will be lying down and they will sit. You can set a new fashion. That's it now, off you go and we'll prepare for it in our next session.

That was it according to her, game, set and match. I left shocked, speechless with my head spinning and reeling, just like I was after the car crashes. I could not believe it. I genuinely thought she had gone berserk. I actually thought it was my fault because I had been such a difficult and problematic client to deal with. I thought I must have been the worst client that ever crossed her doorstep.

The next time I went back, after the shock had subsided, there were sparks flying between us, right, left and centre. I totally lost it with her. We had it hot and heavy. Nothing was left unsaid on my side and it was like she had a tennis racket in her hand and she was batting the ball back at me every single time. I was trying to knock her out with the ball but to no avail. She kept saying to me that she had said I needed to do something drastic and this was it. This is the first step. I made it clear I did not like her first step and definitely didn't want to see or hear about a second one, especially if it was anything like that one. I was hopping mad. I told her I was not going. There was no moving her. She assured me I would be grand about it once I'd started, but I was raging, the thoughts of going into a classroom in front of a teacher and a group of strangers and lying on the floor and everyone else in their seats. I would be mortified and embarrassed, sticking out like a sore thumb. She did that annoying thing therapists do, calmly assuring me we could work through my feelings in the following session. That was it, I exploded! Full-blown nuclear explosion! But she never wavered, she held her ground and had the gall to wish me luck with

the course and the cheek to tell me I might even enjoy it!
What do you think of that! The boot was well and truly in
and it was at least a size 20 boot.

CHAPTER 37
The Boot Pays Dividends

I do not know what made me go to the course in the end. I was furious with Ann, fuming with her. You name it and I was it. I could not understand. I went through all sorts of questioning in my head. Didn't Ann know better than anyone else, my childhood trauma stemming from being deaf and my difficulty in learning in the hearing world. Had she forgotten this? How could she forget it? Didn't she know my terror and fear in relation to learning? Surely, she realised that me doing this course was going to trigger my traumatic memories. Ann knew how insecure I was in myself, how I felt thick and stupid and how I felt I had no brains whatsoever. What was she trying to do to me?

But my questioning brought me to a whole other way of looking at it. While my utter lack of confidence might seem contradictory to my Grade 1 and FIBA achievements, for me there was a clear distinction between physical achievement versus academic achievement. This goes to show the complexity of our minds, how, while on one hand we can be extremely successful, and on the other hand we can feel like a failure. In my case, it was my unbearable conscious sense of academic failure which was the differentiator that ironically had driven me to be successful on the physical level. This had resulted in an emotional disconnection in my body between my mental and physical self. Ann's demand to do the course was going to challenge that disconnection in the hope of bringing my intellectual side and my physical side in to balance hence they would become integrated.

Maybe, underneath my ferocious fury and violent emotions, there was another part of me operating, that knew Ann had my best interests at heart. That part of me, despite my volatility, could see and hear her care for me. I had never seen Ann this determined and feisty in such a bombarding way. Usually, these characteristics of hers were more docile and laid-back while at the same time being firm. But this new experience of her made me realise the seriousness of the situation. For Ann to get up in arms like this made my alarm bells go off. Her sheer will and tenacity to steer my ship, my life, in a more productive way, with such fortitude and resolve made me sit up and take notice. It made me realise I would have to work through these emotions that resurfaced and I certainly was not looking forward to that.

Anyway, the tutor of the course was a lovely lady and the participants were amazing. While of course they wanted to know why I had to lie down and couldn't sit, they were extremely understanding and sympathetic. While I did most certainly feel like an awful eejit, felt mortified and embarrassed, it was not because of them. In no way did they make me feel like that. They were unbelievably helpful and accommodating in every possible way that they could be. It was a two-and-a-half-hour course, which gave me plenty of time to overcome my feelings and to settle into it. Believe it or not, I did actually enjoy it. The topics were interesting and the tutor was brilliant, leaving lots of room for interaction by us, the participants. The night flew in and I couldn't believe how quickly it went. The tutor explained there would be a group exercise that we would have to do at the end of the course and we would be given time every night to go into our respective groups to prepare for that. She put us into groups and my group were a lovely group.

When I went back to see Ann, I was still pissed off with her. I didn't want to let her see how much I enjoyed the course. I didn't want to give her the satisfaction of saying, 'There now, I told you, you would enjoy it.' I put on my disdainful face and tantrum head and tried to pretend it was just ok. However, Ann knew me too well to fall for that and it wasn't long before she got me out of my tantrum and into telling her the truth. Unfortunately, however, I did have to work through my feelings of mortification and embarrassment and feeling like an eejit. That was something else I can tell you!

I went on to complete the two years of the foundation course, much to my amazement. I even made friends with two of the women, Nuala and Catherine. To this day I am still friends with Nuala and her husband Ed. This foundation course, while unequivocally it had its challenges, was a turning point in dragging me out of my doldrums and depression. Meeting people and studying an interesting subject gave me the gee up that I needed. It just pointed me in a new direction.

Ann of course, was delighted but on the whole more relieved that the course caused a shift to occur in the long line of traumas and losses. While she could see that it presented me with a whole host of other challenges, she could also see that these challenges were going to be the make up of my future. Future reality was not going to be a nice thing for me. Unfortunately, reality was reality and it would have to be faced up to. She knew there would be no escaping this reality and she had the foresight to see, that I would need to get used to the new life that was going to open up to me, as a result of my injuries and limitations and the sooner I could begin to do that the better.

CHAPTER 38
Ann Forges Ahead

Well, Ann did not take her foot off the pedal. She was on a mission and nobody was going to stop her. Her determination was like my own. During this time, it was as if her placidness went out the window. She was steaming ahead, all engines and cylinders firing in full flight.

I no sooner had finished the foundation counselling course when she approached me to do the next course. It was the next level up. A proper counselling and psychotherapy course, which would entail a three-year commitment. It would be every Friday and Saturday. Once again, I thought she was off her rocker and could not see myself making such a big commitment. What about my running and my reffing, how was I going to manage these and fit those in? Of course, Ann had all the answers and had everything worked out in her head.

We had a few more barneys and screaming matches. She just would not take no for an answer. On a couple of instances, I yelled at her who did she think I was? Did she think I was Superwoman? Well, I told her that I had bad news for her that I wasn't Superwoman! Jesus, it had taken every ounce of my strength and heaven knows what to get me through the first course. This one was going to be much tougher with loads of assignments and exercises and group work, none of which was going to be easy. The sheer thoughts of it were unnerving. I hadn't gone to college, had scraped through secondary school and was in no way an academic. These assignments were going to require academic ability.

It didn't matter what battle or reasoning I put up, Ann wasn't having any of it. She kept reminding me I could not have another loss in my life, I had to keep forging ahead. Well fuck that! We had to stick to the game plan. I told her that she could stick the *we* up her arse as far as she could shove it. She could go and do the bloody course herself and she could tell me about it. I would be quite happy to listen to all her stories about it.

She just laughed and said, 'No, it will be me listening to you and your stories about it.' What do you say to that? I was at my wits end with her. She was driving me mad. What a bloody frustrating woman!!! Jesus, why couldn't she just go back to being her old good ol' placid self? I much preferred her that way. When I told her this, again she just laughed and said, 'Well there's more than one side to me.' 'Fuck that!'

I said that I didn't know what made me go to the first course in the end. Well, the same thing happened with this one. But now that I think about it, of course, I know what made me go. I was always the *good little girl* growing up and always did what I was told to do. Not because I wanted to most of the time, but because I was too afraid of my mother to do other-wise. We would be killed as children if we didn't do what we were told. The adults always knew best. You did not dare to question it, never mind dream of not doing it. As a result, I had that irritating habit which suited Ann down to the ground. On the positive side, it gave her something to work with in terms of getting me out of my stuckness and moving forward. It meant she could get me to respond to her outlandish ideas once we got the fighting and tantrums out of the way.

While I was on the course, I became friendly with a lady who was telling me about another course she had received information on called 'Dancing The Rainbow.' She asked me if I would be interested in doing it, she was thinking about doing it herself and maybe we could do it together. Foolishly and boy, what a mistake, I should have known better. I mentioned it to Ann and showed her the leaflet containing the information about it. Having read it she jumped at the idea of me doing it. She thought it was highly creative and it would bring in another interesting element which would complement the counselling and psychotherapy. I genuinely thought that she would think it was too much for me with the other one. But no! She thought it was a great idea. This was a two-year course, another big commitment. More screaming, more tantrums followed as per usual and before I knew where I was, she had me enlisting on the course. Superwoman! Superwoman! Superwoman! That was me! No bloody doubt about it! That taught me to keep my big mouth shut I can tell you. There was no end to the woman's ambitions for me, cripple or no cripple that I was, with my multiple physical ailments. I was frantically busy between the whole bloody lot which meant I had no time to give in to my pain or lick my wounds. I just had to keep forging ahead, pain or no pain. But of course, there was pain. Permanent pain. To put it mildly, it was not easy. But my mind was taken off the pain a little bit with the activity of the courses. Doing the assignments were extremely difficult because I couldn't sit down and write. I had to get help and get people to write for me while I dictated what I wanted to write to them. It was extra time consuming because I had to make extra arrangements to meet these people. I also had to spread it around to ensure that no one person was overburdened.

People, however, were incredibly good and kind to me around it and I got the help I needed. This didn't agree with me naturally, me being the extremely independent person that I was before the car crashes. These bloody car crashes were hampering and interfering with my much loved independence. I could not bear being dependent on other people, it really stuck in my craw to have to ask for help. The feeling that I was a burden to people and was putting people out, was the worst possible feeling that I had endured. It was horrendous for me! It never ceased to make me cringe! I never got used to it.

Anyhow, miraculously I managed to keep all the balls in the air. I did the two courses and got back into my running and reffing. Phenomenally, I got back to my international refereeing again, which was probably my proudest and greatest achievement. There were no two ways about it, Ann forging ahead in cracking the whip was the reason for it all. Of course, I did what I was told, responded to her challenges and did an extraordinary amount of emotional work which was the other half to her half. Ann was always very quick to point this out to me when I would thank her and give her praise. It was a 50/50 two-way process.

There were courses galore paralleling each other at the same time. They were interlinked however, despite this parallel process. I would not have thought it was possible to keep a balance in everything the way that Ann had been doing. Ann always had a belief that time stretched when you needed it to and this was a valuable lesson that she taught me. Once I was disciplined, organised and mentally focused everything seemed to fall in to place. My discipline and mental focus from my sports definitely stood to me during Ann's never-ending challenges and brainwaves.

She was extremely proud of me when I finished the two courses and we had a great celebration. The achievement was second to none, considering the severity of obstacles I had to overcome. She gave me a beautiful little symbolic ornament. It was two books on top of each other with a watch, a bottle of ink, a feather quill, a pair of glasses and a replica of the world. Her message to me from this ornament was, 'Take the time to read, learn and write so that you can see the world.' While it was only a small ornament, it is one I have always treasured. Its message was a supremely powerful one. I still have it to this day and often look at it as a reminder to myself to never let the message go. It is also a message I can share and pass on to other people.

CHAPTER 39
The Dance Door Opens

While I was taking part in the Dancing the Rainbow course, the two facilitators, Lani and Antoinette, introduced us to some circle dancing. I had never heard of it before. They taught us a few dances which were quite easy and gentle. The dances had lovely music and the steps fitted brilliantly with the music. I was unexpectedly fascinated by it and thoroughly enjoyed the overall experience. Because they thought it would help my injuries and help my mobility, they made a point of including it on the course as much as they could.

They both thought that when I had finished their course it would be a good thing for me to pursue next. They thought that the gentleness of the movement and the steps would be ideal for my broken body and might ease me nicely in to gaining back some of the original movement that I had lost. They had no circle dancing contacts unfortunately that they could pass on to me, but they told me to look out for it and do some research into it myself.

I couldn't find anything for a long time. Everyone I asked hadn't heard of it either. By chance, I was in a friend's house one day and her sister called in on a surprise visit. We were chatting in general, when out of the blue the conversation turned to the course I was doing and I told her what Lani and Antoinette had advised me to do. Lo and behold, she knew about circle dancing as she had been doing it for quite a while herself. Can you believe that? What a stroke of luck! She gave me the contact number for the woman who was running the dance workshops at the time.

I rang the woman and there was a course just about to start, but she would not let me do it because she didn't know me. I could not believe it. That had never happened before. I told Lani and Antoinette and they could not believe it either. They told me to tell her that they would give me a reference and she could ring them and talk to them. This I did, but the woman was having none of it. I explained to her about my injuries and the urgency of needing to start the dancing as soon as possible. That did not work either and she told me I would have to do her Soul Making course which also incorporated some dancing into it. I had no interest in doing this but was forced into it. Ann thought it was rather peculiar also and had never heard anything like this before. It was a two-year course and it involved travelling to different centres around the country, spending weekends in different places. This was going to be extremely difficult for me with my back and neck problems.

I had explained these complications to the woman, but she was not relenting. I had to do her course or else I could not dance. In the end, Ann thought I should try it and see how I got on. I could always stop if it was too much for my injuries. I decided to give it a try. It was an awful, awful struggle and the travelling most certainly was not good for my injuries. I had to arrange to get lifts with other people and lie down in the back of their cars to avoid sitting down. This brought on more spasm attacks which not only frightened me but frightened the other participants on the course as well.

I had to lie on a mattress for the duration of the course and the participants had to help me with feeding, showering, dressing, writing notes and all the other things that were part of it. I was lucky that the participants were kind and generous to me, otherwise I would never have managed it. I would have had to give it up in the early stages.

When this was finished the woman was inviting a dance teacher from Switzerland to do a Teacher Training course in Ireland on the Bach Flower Dances. After much ado, I was finally allowed to do this course. I didn't particularly want to be a teacher, but Ann encouraged me to do it for personal development and personal growth and also to help my injuries and try and improve my movement. This course was over two years, but it was only three full weekends in total. That wasn't too bad. I also had to travel for this, but at least it was in the same place every time and was one-and-a-half-hour drive from Dublin. While there were theory sessions and other types of sessions, at least this course had a lot of dancing on it. The movement was good for me. This was a big improvement on the other course. The facilitator, Martine, was a gorgeous lady, a caring motherly type and she had great sympathy for my injuries and the constant pain I was in. These particular dances were gentle and easy to learn.

I had never danced in my life before and I felt awkward and as if I had two left feet. The way I felt had nothing to do with my injuries, but of course, my injuries compounded everything. Martine was truly kind and helpful to me and kept encouraging me through my difficulties.

On this course I met a lady by the name of Bernadette. We warmed to each other and she and I got on like a house on fire. That made the course much more enjoyable. When the course was over, she asked me one day if I would be interested in dancing with a German dance teacher by the name of Friedel Kloke Eibl. She was the dance teacher running the course which the other lady would not allow me to attend. As I had heard her name mentioned before and her reputation preceded her, I jumped at the idea. Bernadette had found an open workshop in Germany that Friedel was organising and we ended up being accepted on that course. I felt it was the opportunity of a lifetime, which I was extremely excited about.

This course was completely different to Martine's course, it was more challenging particularly for my body and my injuries. The choreographies were much more intricate but that was my favourite part. We also had to learn a modified version of ballet training. It reminded me of Sean's complex game plays. The challenges of both were remarkably similar in nature.

CHAPTER 40
Ann Continues To Press On

It's difficult to keep track of the sequence of events during this time. With such a bucketload of things going on in tandem with each other, I honestly don't know how I managed to go to the right place at the right time. Since the courses were long-term and overlapping and the dance training was every second month, it felt like I was on a rollercoaster going from one to the other. Ann would not hear tell of me turning a course down even though I was busier than ever – she kept her foot on the pedal.

Her next brain wave was the worst one of all! She proposed that, now I had my diploma, I should do a degree in counselling and psychotherapy. Well, I know I flipped out pretty badly at her other suggestions, but this one took the biscuit. Me? Me, not only that but at the grand old age of 48, who felt she hadn't got a brain in her head, had no academic ability whatsoever and couldn't write an essay if you gave me the Lotto, do a degree! Not on your nanny! No, no, no! Not an option! Not possible!

Ann, incidentally, was highly intelligent and was extremely good at reading, writing and understanding highfalutin type stuff. That kind of thing went over my head completely. It used to take an awful lot of explanation from Ann before I could fully understand certain concepts and theories that she would try to educate me about. Her extreme patience and willingness to repeat and repeat and break it down until I finally understood it, helped me to get it in the end. Both that and I were hard work. It took a lot of energy. We always felt thrilled when I did eventually get it and that was the nice part of it. Anyway, this bloody degree! What the blazes! I knew I was fighting a losing battle trying to wheedle out of it and by making all the excuses under the sun that I could make. It wasn't the fact that I didn't want to become a counsellor in itself, it was the trauma of having to take on the academic challenges of doing the degree. Bluntly, I just said a straight black and white *No*! Sorry Missus Moo, I am *not* doing that. No! The degree involved a lot of modules and it would take approximately one and half to two years to complete it, depending on how quickly you did the modules. Each module had a written assignment which was the exam part and they were usually in the region of five thousand words, requiring lots of research to add to the misery of it. I felt I didn't have time for that.

My defiance this time was much stronger than any of the other times, although it was fairly bad for those as well. So, Ann had to change strategy with me in order to get around me. I was determined I was not budging! I was not buying any of her palaver! No, no, no! No, it was going to be and only No! It was alright for her. She was a bloody brain box. Well, I was not. I was a dumbo! My mother used to constantly tear up my homework, telling me it was useless and it was no good. She used to make me rewrite, rewrite and rewrite it until my poor hands were falling off and my fingers were numb. I sure as hell was not going through that again. I knew I would not be up to the degree standard and that was that. No two ways about it. Ann kept telling me that it would not be like that now, that she would help me and she would find someone to help me with writing the assignments. True to her word, she found a man by the name of Michael who was particularly good at helping people with learning difficulties. According to Ann, he was instinctively good at understanding people's lack of confidence and belief in themselves and he was the perfect person to help me with that end of things.

As if I did not have enough on my plate. Now she wanted me to go to someone else who was going to wreck my head as much as she did. Uh huh, oh-oh, not doing that! One of her was enough, I most certainly did not need a second one. The woman was gone pure mad in the head. That's what I thought and was convinced of.

Well, I am sure you can guess what happened in the end. She hightailed me off to Michael knowing that he too would help to persuade me to undertake the degree. Between the two of them they wrapped me around their little fingers and sent me marching off to P.C.I. College to do my degree. Ann did the emotional work with me and helped me with the academic side of it, while Michael taught me how to write in an academic fashion for the assignments. Michael was fantastic and he was great fun to work with which I was not expecting. This helped me enormously as I have a good, broad sense of humour. As a result, he was able to joke and laugh with me in such a way that it took the sting out of my traumas. Ann was delighted I got on better than she expected with Michael. It was a welcome bonus and between the two of them, they helped me through my degree.

Not only that, but I ended up getting mostly Firsts in my results. In one of the modules, I had to do a 10,000-word thesis. The college assigned me a tutor whose job it was to guide me to get the result I wanted. My tutor was a lovely woman and when I started my thesis I hadn't a chance of getting a First. She said I would have to do a serious amount of work to bring it up to that standard and she did not think it was possible. Michael and I worked extremely hard on it and I ended up surprising her by getting a double First mark in it. Because it was 10,000 words it was worth double marks.

That was the highlight of my course. Ann and Michael kept telling me how intelligent a person I was and that I had a powerfully interesting and inquiring mind. To them this was the proof and they wanted me to see that as well. It was difficult for me to see that because they had been such a help to me, I didn't think I would have got those results without them. However, they kept insisting that, while yes, they did indeed help me, it was my own ideas and hard work that I had put into the topic that was the largest part of it. They also pointed out that it was the most amazing achievement, given the obstacles of having to lie down on the course and being in permanent pain. The three of us had a lovely celebration and Ann gave me a lovely teddy bear with a black graduation hat on its head.

The graduation was an amazing experience as we had to go Middlesex University in England as they were the ones accrediting our degree. I never ever thought that I would ever see the day when I would be wearing a cap and gown and holding a scroll with a BSc on it. There was great excitement and celebrations on that day and while Ann and Michael were immensely proud of me, I must admit, I did feel proud of myself on that occasion in 2007. It was an achievement beyond my wildest dreams or imagination. A day I will always savour and remember until the day I die.

It just goes to show what's possible when you put your mind to it. It was reminiscent of my sports. When you put your mind to something, do all the necessary hard work to achieve it, have the help and support that you need and you have people who believe in you and your ability, anything is truly possible.

I had never thought that my mind had the same capacity to achieve as my body had up until that wonderful day. It was a lesson worth learning. I was thrilled I did not allow my defiance and refusal to spoil it. While it was an extremely difficult and challenging journey, it was one I will never regret. It brought my brain and body, which prior to this were separate entities, into unison with each other. This resulted in me being a more balanced and harmonised person within myself.

CHAPTER 41
Everything Comes Together

Now is probably a good time to summarise where I was at with everything at this stage. In 1998 I had completed my certificate in the Foundation in Counselling. In 1999 I was a fully qualified facilitator of the Dancing The Rainbow Training. In 2003 I had my Soul Making course completed and was fully qualified in that. Immediately after the Soul Making course, I was qualified in teaching both Bach Flower and Nature dances with a lady called Martine Winnington from Switzerland. I qualified also as a Bach Flower Practitioner that same year. A little aside: People are always curious in relation to what these dances and remedies are about. There are 38 Bach Flower Remedies. These remedies help to stabilise the electrical system in the body due to emotional imbalance. The most well known remedy is the popular Rescue Remedy commonly taken for shock and exam stress. Each remedy has its own dance to accompany it and it is considered that taking the remedy orally or dancing its dance, have the equivalent healing effect on the body.

By 2005 I had completed my diploma in Counselling and Psychotherapy and in 2007 I graduated with a BSc in Counselling and Psychotherapy. Back to the basketball, in 2000 I had also acquired my Grade 1 Licence in Basketball Coaching. Because I couldn't play basketball anymore, Ann had thought it would be a good idea to become a basketball coach. She felt that because I was such a good and competitive player that I would have a lot to offer as a coach.

Everything had finally come together. I felt real, genuine joy and a sense of accomplishment at completing each of these courses and seeing each through to its conclusion. They were two to three-year courses! It felt like a miracle that I had succeeded in acquiring these qualifications. I was immensely proud of myself that I had managed to juggle and keep all the balls in the air. An astounding achievement given my circumstances. I had surpassed my wildest dreams and expectations! In fact, as it turned out, the reality was I had slain my own dragon.

Further to these, my dance trainings with Friedel Kloke Eibl, Nanni Kloke, Saskia Kloke and Marielle Van Beek were ongoing during this time and were also brought to completion. I did, in the following years, continue with these until I completed my diplomas with all those teachers as well. As the dance teachers are always choreographing more new dances and themes, the dance training is something that is continually ongoing. If you want to keep up to date, it is important that you continue to attend these new trainings. For me this is not a burden because I enjoy them anyway and I love learning new things as well. The teachers often have trainings and go deeper into the dances and do a lot of repetition. I love these trainings due to what I learned from my sports, in relation to the importance of repetition. I do indeed find that repetition in dance is as equally important as it is in sport.

I had to stop playing basketball and competing in running races after my second car crash, which I was terribly upset about and was missing dreadfully. Just before my second car crash, I had been picked to run on the Irish Team for the Women's Veteran Championship which was being held in Russia that year. It distressed me greatly to miss this opportunity as I was in peak condition and was earmarked to do well in the competition. I was seriously heartbroken about this at the time. As I have mentioned already however, I did, amazingly, manage to keep my refereeing going at every level despite my injuries and the constant pain I was in. I can see now that that in itself, was quite remarkable. At the time I couldn't see that as I was caught up in the disappointment of the numerous losses.

The question now was what was Ann's next plan for me? I dreaded the thoughts of that one! Another Superhuman, Superwoman plan no doubt. Now that I had all these qualifications and was back running and reffing, what was I going to do with them, especially in my condition. While I was desperately struggling and desperately fighting not to give in to my injuries and limitations and let them stop me, or get the better of me while trying to bat off more losses, the reality was that I was far from ok. I was nowhere near being back to where I was before the first car crash. Every minute of every day was being spent on fighting the whole nightmare. Hours and hours of my time were being put into my rehabilitation programme both physical and emotional. While I missed work terribly, there was no way I could have even attempted the rehabilitation programme, never mind sustained it, had I been working. It was a full-time job in itself. It felt at this point that it was going to go on for the rest of my life. Despite some of my protests, I was happy to succumb to letting Ann come up with the ideas and run the show for me. My protests were forceful because I was in an unnatural amount of pain and not feeling well most of the time. These protests weren't as authentic as I was pretending they were. The truth was, I was beginning to trust Ann and I was loving the abundance of care and attention she was bestowing on me. It was a far cry from what my mother gave me when I was deaf. There was no comparison between them. If I was to be truly honest, Ann's help and care was touching me deeply on the emotional front. It was exactly what I needed. I was in such a state of chassis, that I was genuinely not capable of geeing myself up to make decisions by myself. Summoning up the strength and will, to respond to her suggestions was the most I could manage. Trying to trust and accept her help, to such an extent, was a huge challenge for me. To go from being super independent, to allowing my huge vulnerability to be seen, was frightening for me.

Where was I to go from here? How could I possibly fit anything else into my life? It just didn't seem possible. Knowing Ann, the way I did now, I knew she probably wouldn't agree with that, but it was most definitely going to take some figuring out, even for her. While she was highly creative and broad-minded in her thinking, she did also face reality and reality was most certainly not a friend of ours at that moment in time.

CHAPTER 42
The Plan Gestates, Gradually Unfolds And Develops Into Completely Unexpected Territory ... Again!

We had now reached the mid 2000's (2005 approximately) and Ann felt it was time to put our heads together and evaluate the situation. What was the next step? We had covered a lot of ground since my second car crash, Bridget and Da's deaths, the loss of my boyfriend, my job, my running and playing basketball! She was wondering how I could integrate the courses I had done into my life purposefully, taking my injuries and limitations into account, while also keeping my rehab programme going. It was not going to be an easy task and we needed some inspiration.

I wasn't of any help whatsoever, as my time and energy was going in to *doing what I was told*, living up to my *Superwoman* status and doing my rehab programme. By now I was beginning to understand the importance of *doing what I was told*. It was producing results, right, left and centre and not only that, but positive results, with positive outcomes. After all, look at what I had achieved despite my state of ill health. It was quite remarkable. Rowing in and cooperating, as opposed to being defensive and *fighting against*, was much more productive. What I actually realised in the end was, that no matter how bad a state I was in, physically or emotionally, once the trust was in place, it was much easier to do what I was told. The relief that flooded in, when someone who genuinely cared about me took charge and all I had to do was respond, was hugely liberating. It freed me up and took the pressure off which was a welcome and lovely feeling.

I knew that not being able to sit down was a big draw-back. That was scuppering everything, a right pain in the ass. Anyway, I left Ann to it. She was the brains behind the whole operation and I knew it was only a matter of time before she would come up with something, a something that I had no doubt would not be to my liking. I was quite happy for the time to drag by. I had enough on my plate as it was.

A basketball friend of mine told me about a coaching post that was coming up in one of the schools. He asked me if I would be interested in applying for it. When I told Ann, she was extremely eager about it and told me to apply. I did an interview and got selected for the post. I could not believe it. I got into an awful panic with Ann about the things I had said at the interview and what if I could not deliver on what I had said. Of course, she tut-tutted me and reassured me that I would have no problem delivering my promise, as I was more than well equipped to take on the job. Her opinion was, that the school would be not only fortunate but lucky to have someone of my calibre coaching their kids. I was exceptionally nervous however, because this was my first time to coach a team of any description and there was no guarantee that I was going to be a good coach. It was a school for foreign children and I was asked to work with the first and second year girls. They were extremely athletic, which was a bonus for me because that complemented my style of coaching. It meant I could do a lot of work with them and I was able to teach them aggressive defence which complemented their athleticism. The other advantage was that the school wanted me to train them extremely hard because they were an academic school and they needed them to get a lot of stress relief in their sports. They also wanted them to do as well in their sports as in their academics. This was right up my alley and I was only too happy to get stuck into it. We had a lot of time to prepare for the league competitions because I started coaching them in September and their matches didn't begin until January. This gave me time to get to know them, get them fit and teach them as many basketball skills as I could. This job was ideal for my injuries as it required me to be on my feet and moving nonstop.

When I was coaching the first years, my philosophy was quite simple and straightforward. I focused and concentrated on teaching them two things, lay-ups and how to play defence. The reason for this was twofold. Firstly, these are the two most important basic skills of the game to learn, secondly, the first years had a great chance of doing well in the competition over the older girls and boys, because everyone is starting from scratch. My philosophy, which was the one I had been taught myself, was what I tried my best to pass on to my students. We were always taught that it is out of playing good defence that the offence comes. Therefore, good aggressive defence, that causes steals and interceptions of the ball, both high and low, generally give rise to an unchallenged run to the basket to score a lay-up. The speed of the steal or interception leaves the opponents wrong-footed, making it impossible for them to catch up no matter how fast they run. Good strong defence with lots and lots of pressure on the ball forces the opponents to make mistakes that the defenders can capitalise on. Playing such strong defence requires a high level of fitness and strength. This is also an extremely exciting part of the game for spectators to watch.

It was great for me to get stuck in the way I did, because nowadays, I find it impossible to train kids properly with the *kosher* of *don'ts, cant's* – there is very little *dos* and *cans*. The restrictions on what you are allowed to do now is gone beyond a joke. It is no wonder that the kids are obese and lacking in fitness. I would be concerned that this could shorten the lifespan of many.

Anyway, these girls were great to work with. When the matches began, we were in a tough league with no weak teams in it. I knew the schools and teams from my refereeing. We won all our games and got to the semi-finals in three different competitions. We won the three semi-finals and went on to win the three finals. We advanced to the All-Ireland Championships for this age group and had to play in a weekend tournament. We went on to win that Championship which was a major achievement.

The girls were over the moon with themselves and the school was thrilled. I was delighted and undeniably proud of them. The only problem with the school was, that you could not progress with the same group any further, because they only came to Ireland for one year. We had a completely new group of girls each year and I had to start again from scratch. The other schools had the same players and were in an enviable position to develop them further. By the time my new group played against them, they had hugely improved. This naturally made my job much tougher.

I had such success with the girls that the school eventually asked me to coach the boys as well. They too were extremely athletic just like the girls and it was a real pleasure to coach them. Both the girls and the boys were extremely successful in their competitions for several years and the school advanced from the D Division to the A Division during my time with them. At one point we had enough girls to enter into two separate divisions. It was a great experience for me and I learnt a lot from coaching these kids, which would stand to me in the future in my coaching career.

When I started this job, Ann was delighted because it gave her the breathing space she needed to consider the next step and sure enough she came up with a plan. In the meantime, I got offered another coaching job with a special needs school. The pupils in this school had a variety of intellectual disabilities. I had refereed many matches for the school and two of the teachers, who knew very little about basketball from a coaching perspective, were coaching the kids. They were extremely enthusiastic however and gorgeous people. The girls always got to the semi-finals and got beaten every time. Therefore, they never ever progressed to the finals. There was a particular school who won the competition every single year and no one was able to beat them.

One day when I was in refereeing, they were discussing the game with me afterwards and I pointed out something to them in relation to one of the tall girls they had, who had great potential. Based on what I said, they asked me would I be interested in coming in to help them and give them some tips and advice. This I did and they asked me to coach them for the semi-finals, as tactically, I would be better at reading the game and might be able to break this almighty jinx that had plagued them for what seemed like an eternity. I agreed and the girls won the match, their first semi-final ever. Following this win, they asked me if I would coach them for the final. This I did and…. the girls won the final. They beat the unbeatable team! What a sweet, sweet victory! They could not believe it. They were thrilled skinny. There were great celebrations in the school afterwards. After this they were invited to play in the All-Ireland Championships and I was appointed coach for that. The standard in the All-Ireland of course, was much higher for this competition, because the best teams in the country were taking part. My girls were nervous as hell. It was a huge event for them. We won our pool, got to the semi-finals, where we met our old rivals from the school we had just beaten a few weeks earlier, beat them again and went on to win the final.

The two teachers were ecstatic, the girls were jumping over the moon and I was thrilled to bits for them. The kids in the team were incredibly difficult to coach and train as they were unpredictable and it was exceedingly difficult to get them to maintain focus and concentration. They were like a box of frogs, jumping and leaping all over the place, full of vim and vigour, a constant buzz of high-octane energy. It was not unusual to see them climbing the walls or trying to smash the lights in the ceilings with the basketballs. On top of that, they were also particularly moody and temperamental, highly emotionally charged and had childish behaviours and were forever taking the hump with each other. We had our hands full with them at the venue trying to keep them together. The fact that they were majorly excited, due to the occasion, did not help the situation. They were high as kites and we would have needed eyes not only in the back of our heads, but everywhere, to control and contain them. It was such a relief to get them back to the school and back in one piece.

They adored their trophies, their pride and joy. It was just gorgeous to see the smiles on their faces from ear to ear and the joy and pride that winning and owning their own trophy had on them. The trophies were like gold dust, they were not letting them out of their hands for love nor money. When it came to clapping the other teams, I could not get them to put the trophies down on the floor in front of them. They were not having any of it. They were tightly holding their trophies while trying to clap at the same time. There was a beautiful innocence about this that was quite touching.

They marched back to the schools with their heads held high singing like troopers. The school didn't know what the kafuffle was about but greeted them royally when they became aware of their success. The principal, a genuinely nice lady, came out to congratulate them when she heard the news. After that, the school officially asked me to coach them in the future. We went on to win six consecutive league finals and six All-Ireland championships (equalling the Dubs!). Given their various disabilities and behavioural problems, this was a major feat. The rival school were not happy campers to be knocked off their pedestal for those six long years.

People often asked me afterwards, what was my secret to success, particularly with the special needs team. I didn't train them in accordance to their limitations. I trained them in accordance to their athleticism. They were quite athletic and fast on their feet. I also had them doing the same drills that I had my able-bodied girls doing. I challenged them considerably on the physical and mental level despite their disabilities. The teachers used to be shocked at the drills and trainings I used to put them through. They often asked me, 'How did you get them to do that?' They thought it was incredible. The girls responded well because the sense of achievement they experienced, when they eventually suc-ceeded in completing the drills, had a profound effect on them. People with disabilities often feel they are no good at anything when they cannot do what able-bodied people can do. Many suffer with inferiority complexes, so teaching them more complex drills and being patient enough for them to succeed (because naturally it takes a longer time) gave them a sense of importance and accomplishment and raised their self-confidence and self-esteem. This in turn allowed them to feel that they were, in fact, good at something. This was one of the reasons that their trophies and medals were precious and meant the world to them. They made them feel special and good about themselves.

Another contributing factor was the fact that I didn't pander to their whims, mollycoddle them in relation to their limitations or succumb to their manipulative behaviours. I had clearly learned a lot from Sean! I didn't fall into the trap of trying to protect them through careful use of language. I named it as it was and dealt with their disabilities in a black and white and open way. I showed them that there was nothing to be ashamed of. Reality is reality and you can't do anything about that. I taught them the importance of adapting to their disabilities and making the most of it, rather than giving in to it. They did not need to limit their lives any further than it was already limited by withdrawing into themselves instead of being more proactive. I tried to meet their needs in a more adult and normal fashion, encouraging and demanding them to step-up to the level of intelligence that they actually had. I also had a good balance of being strict with them, while at the same time being caring, patient, understanding and kind. I would not let them away with things or pull stunts on me. I taught them to be accountable and to take responsibility for their actions. I didn't allow them to take their disability out on the world around them. I taught them the importance of striving to reach their own potential regardless of their limitations and to recognise and be grateful when they were able to do that. I explained to them that if they could do that and do the things with me that they did, they could also bring those skills and attributes into other areas of their lives. What I was teaching them was not only for their school but for their life in general.

Ann was bowled over by my achievements and successes with the two schools. While she had mentioned it before, she was now more convinced than ever that I should spread my wings even further and start doing some counselling and psychotherapy work with disabled people as well as able-bodied people. There was no doubt in her mind that I could improve disabled people's quality of life and increase their independence if I could work with both the physical and emotional aspects of their lives. Because of my injuries, I couldn't do too much at one time. Ann suggested I try and see one client a day for three days a week and see how it went. Maybe in time, if my situation improved, I could extend it further. She pointed me in the direction of how to start and she helped me until I found three people to work with.

CHAPTER 43
Ann's Next Step

I was nervous starting off as I didn't feel as competent as she was making me out to be and my injuries were adding to my lack of self-confidence. Anyway, as usual, I followed her instructions and tried to convince myself that she wouldn't let me loose on people if I wasn't good enough. My qualifications didn't make me feel any better because at the end of the day, as I knew from my sports, practise and experience is what matters the most and is what makes you improve.

I was lucky to have three nice people referred to me to work with by a colleague from college. Two women and one man and their issues were right up my alley. One was dealing with bereavement, one with loss and change in their job and one had a recurring sports injury that was affecting their sports performance. I took to looking after them like a duck takes to water. After the first meeting with them I settled in much better than I thought I would. My having to lie down was not a problem for them. Believe it or not, they actually didn't even notice or question me about it, they were that caught up in their own affairs. I couldn't believe it! That helped me enormously. It made me relax and forget about it myself.

I started off like every counsellor does and after one year I was able to extend my services to include creative approaches. I discovered that by taking creative approaches it was easier to work with people's defence mechanisms. My Dancing The Rainbow and my Circle Dance training helped me a lot with this. Ann suggested I do some bodywork training and trauma training which I did and these enhanced my creative approach even further. When I became more proficient, she encouraged me to do mattress work with my clients which is a form of bodywork. She used to run these sessions herself and she allowed me to observe her facilitating these as a way of increasing my learning. I enjoyed these sessions as it quickly became clear that they would fit in to my style of counselling.

These various trainings turned me in to an eclectic therapist. It was amazing how they complemented each other. It meant that I could work with a broader range of issues while specialising in certain areas that appealed to me most. This made my work more enjoyable and varied. I upped my clients to five and kept them spread out so as not to aggravate my condition.

As luck would have it, I was approached to work with a disabled lady who needed help on the physical and emotional levels. I started working with her and it was a great learning experience. You simply do not know what people have to go through, until you spend time in the person's real life. I had to see her at home because she was in a wheelchair full-time and there were no wheelchair facilities in those days in venues like there is nowadays. This transpired to be a good thing, because I was able to see with my own eyes, instead of listening to her details and try to imagine them. It's true what they say, that seeing is believing. I never would have got it right through trying to picture it in my imagination. Therefore, I was of much greater benefit to her because I was on top of things with her much more than I would have been otherwise. She had a lot of physical problems in her toileting which were causing her huge distress particularly while she was at work. With my sports knowledge and some bodywork techniques, I was able to reverse her problems, consequently she could function in a more normal way. She was delighted with this as it improved her life considerably.

At a later point, she needed an operation to address some other women problems that she had. She went to a few specialists in Ireland, who because of the level of her disability, told her they couldn't help her. I suggested that she try to find another specialist outside the country to get a second opinion. One of her P.A.'s (Personal Assistant) knew a German doctor who was located down the country here in Ireland and she went to him. He was incredibly kind and understanding towards her and went out of his way to get assistance to diagnose her properly in order to be able to help her. After some difficulty, they managed to get the diagnosis and he referred her to a Polish specialist in Germany, to have the operation. She asked me to go with her as she was terrified, not only of having the operation, but of having to go to another country where she could not speak or understand the language.

I went with her and in as short a time as five days, she had everything done to utter perfection. The specialist was out of this world and he did a complete reconstruction job on her, which also included totally curing her remaining toileting problems. I did the emotional trauma work with her every day and she sailed through the whole thing as a result of the specialist and myself. She did exceptionally well and they were able to let her travel home earlier than anticipated. She had no setbacks or negative repercussions afterwards and came home a new woman. Her aspirations at the time were to enter into a romantic relationship with a man. The difference in attitude between Ireland and abroad were unbelievable. In Ireland the specialist had passed comment on how she could possibly even think about such a thing in her condition and with her level of disability, whereas in Germany the attitude was the complete opposite. They were totally in favour of not only facilitating her but encouraging her to go for that as it would enhance her life. The specialist gave her his phone number and told her if she had any queries or problems not to hesitate to contact him, he would look after her. Fortunately however, she didn't have any complications or problems. The whole thing had gone smoothly and had been such an outstanding success that she never looked back after that.

Can you imagine the emotional and psychological effect this had on her overall wellbeing? She felt like a new person and eventually ended up in a relationship which boosted her confidence and self-esteem immensely. Something that had for so long been out of her reach was now within her grasp. She now had the possibility to at least explore and try things out, which provided her with a newfound sense of freedom and made her feel more normal in her life.

Here I was, involved in a totally new and unexpected area of work and had managed to help this woman overcome what had seemed insurmountable difficulties in her life. She managed to remove this blockage and move on with her dreams for her life – I could not believe I had been able to help her. I knew I had received enormous help from lots of people who had helped me to become a real functioning individual woman. I think back to Dr. Johnson, Sean and Bridget, just to name a few, all who helped me in vastly different ways. I was happy to be each of these three people for this woman providing her with care, support, motivation, guidance and love.

It was some time after that I had a disabled man referred to me. His disability was of a similar nature to the lady I have just described, only his was much worse because he was non-verbal and could not use either of his hands. He had a lot of what is termed as 'Spastic Involuntary Movement.' His legs and arms were constantly spasming which caused a lot of movement that he had no control over. My heart went out to this poor man the first time I met him. At first, I did not feel that I was equipped to work with him as I had never experienced such a bad disability before in my work. Ann thought I should give it a go, primarily because there were very few people who chose to work in this field for obvious reasons and she felt given time, I might be able to help him. She thought I would have to be extremely creative to come up with some viable ideas and that my sports background might indeed come in especially useful.

I decided to give it a go. On my first chat with him I was upfront with him about my inexperience and my concerns and gave him the choice whether he was willing to give it a try himself or not. I explained to him that it was going to be a long and slow process and that we would both have to be extremely patient. I also told him that it was going to take a while for both of us to get to know each other, especially under these difficult circumstances. His presenting issues were primarily in relation to his frustration at his inability to speak, communicate and express himself. He was drinking a lot which was causing him to end up in hospital on a regular basis with stomach bleeds. People had also facilitated him to take drugs which he had stopped taking just before he had met me. While he loved his food, his diet was poor due to these activities and poor organisation. He had bowel problems and suffered from constipation a lot. He was frustrated with the other problems his disability was causing him. There was no shortage of things to work on. He was a panicker and had a tendency to panic over everything and I mean everything.

He was all on for it and was eager to get started. We had to converse with each other through the aid of a machine called a Litewriter, which had a chin switch which accessed the letters to make sentences. When he was ready an automated voice would read out whatever he had typed. While this was a beneficial way of communicating, it was painfully slow and there were long silences between us during this process. The advantage was, that at least it was a clear form of communication once he used it properly. He also had a letter board attached to his table in front of his wheelchair, but this wasn't a feasible form of communication for us to use, due to the lack of mobility in his hands and my back and neck injuries. We decided to stick to the machine.

We both eventually got used to the set-up and discussed what his goals were and how he felt I could help him. As a result of the work we did, he got the use of his right arm back again which he had lost the use of a few years previously. He was ecstatic about this and was highly motivated as a result. This one improvement meant he was able to progress to an electric power wheelchair and we were able to get the settings modified to enable him to drive it himself with his right hand and arm. Before that, he was totally confined to a pushchair which he couldn't push himself, which meant he was totally dependent on people and his P.A.'s to take him everywhere. This progression now offered him independence.

It took time for him to be trained up on how to drive it and he had to learn gradually the different speeds which the chair could move at. He also had to work on his spatial awareness for guiding the chair in and out of small spaces. This was great because it challenged him mentally and got him using his brain more. I was joking with him saying that we would have to put an L-plate on his chair until he passed his driving test. He was absolutely thrilled at this new venture. He quickly learned how to use it and before long was whizzing around in it. Now he had two chairs and he could alternate between them as he needed. The electric chair wasn't suitable for everything and he had to use the pushchair as a back-up.

From here I worked with him to start engaging in more social activities. The electric chair helped a lot with this. One day I brought him to a place where he could join a team to play what was called 'Power-Chair Football.' This was quite amazing as they had special platelets they could stick on to the lower front part of the chair for them to kick the ball with. They were whizzing around in their chairs playing football no problem. I had never heard of or seen this game before. It was a great game and great for him. It increased his adeptness at spatial awareness, as he had to move at a much greater speed around the confined space of the gymnasium. It also improved his motor skills in his right arm and developed his muscular strength, as he had to manoeuvre the joystick in order to propel the chair around. This helped him to catch up on developmental skills that he would have lost out on in normal childhood play, due to his disability. As an avid football fan (Liverpool F.C. being his favourite team) and spectator, he was totally involved when watching football as if he was playing the game himself. He was now able to transfer this same immersion into his own football game. What a colossal liberating experience that was! He grew to love the game and travelled with the team to a few venues around the country to play matches. In time he became quite nifty at playing it.

His next adventure was to take up swimming every week and I found ways for him to do this. He loved the swimming as this was something he could also do with his family.

After that, I went with him to his physiotherapy sessions, to discover that the exercises he was on were surprisingly minimal, I'd even call them pathetic. After he got the use of his right arm back, the physiotherapist nearly had a hissy fit at the idea of him trying to use his arm again and pointed out to him that he could get bone contractures. This frightened him. I sent him back to ask what that meant and was it a definitive guarantee that this was going to happen. He came back with the answers and we discussed the situation. It turned out that it wasn't guaranteed that it would happen, it was only a possibility. On this basis, I pointed out to him, was it not better to have a better quality of life for whatever number of years he would get out of it, rather than being stuck in dependency. Was it not better to take a risk that could enhance his life more? I told him to think about it, that the choice was his. Due to his kamikaze nature and his thirst for thrill-seeking, it was an easy decision for him to take the risk. The confines of being in a wheelchair and the suppression of not being able to speak, probably fuelled his hunger for adventure. I really admired his feistiness.

I came up with an alternative exercise programme that was far more challenging for him, that he was well able for and slowly and gradually built him up on it. He brought it into the physiotherapist to be told 'Oh No' he couldn't do that. Again I sent him back to find out the reasons why. In the end he simply had to explain that he really wanted to do these exercises, that he found them extremely helpful and he enjoyed doing the exercise programme as it was helping his morale and confidence, for them to eventually agree to it. This meant he could now do the exercise programme both with the physio and at home. He was totally committed and dedicated to improving this aspect of his life.

This was followed by getting him to cycle a bike. We found a special stationary bike that was suitable for his needs and he started cycling every day. In a short space of time, he was able to build up to cycling 10kms. No mean feat with his level of disability. This was particularly good for him because it helped to reduce the spasming and involuntary movement in his legs a bit. This in turn made him more comfortable when sitting in his chair and gave the rest of his body a rest from the incessant jerking. It brought a sense of stillness into his body, which he had never experienced before.

Helping him to achieve these various sporting activities reminded me of how much sport had helped me to deal with the frustrations in my own life. As I look back on what I did with him, I realise I took for granted everything that I had learned as a sports woman and the skills I had developed and the understanding of what exercises could be of benefit to him, although I wasn't a physiotherapist. My sports also had helped me to direct and express my anger positively. I was hoping it would help him to do the same and give him some relief from the pent-up feelings inside himself and some expression to those untold number of words that were stuck in his head. I was also hoping it would relieve his stress and reduce his tendency to panic. Physical activity and especially intense physical activity is great for relieving tension and stress in the body. Like it did for me, I could see that the exercises improved his mood hugely as he was enjoying everything so much. He became more alive in himself and more fun.

During this time, I was running my Dancing The Rainbow workshops and doing a lot of creativity with my groups. I asked him would he be interested in joining one of the groups and trying it out. It meant a lot of reorganisation on my part as I didn't want to discommode the other group members or having them lose out due to his participation. With a lot of creative thinking and re-juggling, I was able to come up with a few ideas to accommodate him and he decided to give it a try. He absolutely loved it and it was one of the best things ever for him, as it opened up his own creative talent and gave him another form of expression which broke his internal silent world. It gave him the opportunity to interact with others and to be challenged in a way that, previous to that, he hadn't been. The *Charmer* part of his personality also got the freedom to express itself and this helped him to feel more alive and more involved in ordinary, everyday life.

At this point he was quite chuffed with himself and loving the outcomes of the work we were doing. I was constantly looking for ways to extend his independence, decrease his limitations and bring out his own hidden creativity. I'm a great believer in the saying 'Don't limit your challenges, challenge your limits.' He had written some beautiful poetry and some short stories but had stopped doing it. I encouraged him to reignite this aspect of himself as his writing was thought-provoking and meaningful. There was a depth and quality to it that was voicing his inner turmoil and pain that was quite touching.

One day I got the brainwave of getting him to paint. On the creativity courses I had dabbled in painting with him and we had tried various ways of managing it. It was incredibly hard for him to hold a paint brush never mind paint. But surprisingly with much patience, much trial and error, we succeeded in finding a way. As I didn't have any personal experience of painting, I suggested to him to join an art class. This he did and the paintings he subsequently went on to paint were amazingly beautiful. The art teacher got him to use coloured pencils and like that, came up with great ideas of how he could make some wonderful pictures. Some of them were good enough to be chosen for an art exhibition. I was proud of him and his artwork, as it took a lot of courage for him to stick with it and overcome his multitude of difficulties. This helped him to achieve it in the end.

I could personally relate a lot to him around the suppression of his creativity. Mine had been stunted due to my deafness and due to my mother's stress, which made her silence my voice and left her unavailable to help me. His was similar due to his disability and due to the patience, time and effort required to stick with something long enough to make him succeed in the end. I knew from my own experience that patience was a key element and that holding the belief in him and persevering were essential. These were the things that had helped me and I was hoping that they would help him too. Another thing we had in common was our willingness to cooperate and to respond to somebody's help and care. As I had responded to Bridget, Sean and Ann, he was responding to me.

He had a lot of disorganisation in his daily living and I helped him to straighten this out and make his home living much better. Between us we improved his P.A. service, his dietary needs and his cooking arrangements, the cleaning of his house, his grocery shopping and general shopping. I came up with a plan to reorganise the structure and layout of his house, which made it more convenient to accommodate his wheelchair and for him to get around especially for the times he was on his own. I helped him to set up rotas for his P.A.'s as a way of keeping everything in order to prevent this area of his life getting out of control again. We came up with a plan to take advantage of the P.A's strengths and limit their weaknesses. This improved his home life and his own personal general health no end, as he was now eating more healthily and living in a safer, cleaner and clutter-free environment. This also had a major positive affect on his mental and psychological wellbeing. It removed a lot of the stress he had previously experienced due to his lack of organisation. He got to a place where he could manage his P.A. service much better and could oversee the necessary paperwork in a more efficient way. This improved his relationship between his P.A.'s and himself, that hitherto, had been fraught with discontentment and frustration on both sides.

As children growing up, my brother and I had lived in a highly disorganised living environment as a result of our mother's inability to manage her and our lives. This had a very destablising effect on us both and had caused mayhem in our lives. I could see that along with the clutter in his head, the disorganisation of everything around him in his daily living was having a similar effect on him. A disordered living environment can cause a disordered mind and affect one's physical and mental health. Tackling this problem helped him to overcome his internal and external chaos, just as the structure and order of playing basketball, the training and the matches had served me.

When this was done, like Ann, I kept my foot on the pedal with him and came up with an idea to get him standing for short periods of time. Being confined to his wheelchair and stuck in the same position for hours and hours every day didn't seem like it was good for his health. I came up with creative ways of giving him breaks from sitting in his chair all day. He loved the freedom of this and was like an eager beaver, willing to experiment with my somewhat unorthodox ideas. We adopted the ones that worked and discarded the ones that didn't. Trial and error is a great thing. We shared many laughs and fun trying out the various suggestions. After a period of time, when he began to trust me and feel safe with me, my hare-brained ideas helped to improve his sense of humour. This was great because it got him laughing more and broke any nervousness that was linked with trying things out. We then developed his standing ability. I got him to check this out with the physio and of course we got the usual *No* response. He kept at her however, until he eventually got her on board and we got him a special standing machine. This was such a fantastic progression and he was mega excited about it. It meant he could stand up for as long as was comfortable for him and he could release a bar which allowed him to sit down for a rest. He could alternate between sitting and standing quite easily and comfortably.

This improved his lung function and increased the muscular power throughout his body. It reduced the involuntary movement in his arms and legs. It gave him a sense of feeling tall as he was only half his size sitting down in his chair. It helped to stretch and relax his body differently to the other exercise routines. He could even dance to some music. His morale was boosted no end by the adventure and thrill of this and his frustration with life diminished. He was now more organised, more physically active, more socially interactive, more independent and more creative in himself. This undoubtedly added a new spark to his life, opened up more opportunities, gave him a great sense of belonging, a greater and varied opportunity to express himself, increased his mobility, his self-confidence and his self-esteem. His life now had more meaning, more purpose and felt more worthwhile.

His willingness to cooperate at the physical level and to experiment and explore were a pleasure and a treasure to work with. Working with him opened up my eyes as to what is truly possible if you are willing to dare and take the risks involved. It completely validates athlete Michael Johnson's belief, that after you have stared long enough into the dragon's eyes, there's nothing left to do, but slay the dragon, which means, slaying negative thoughts and beliefs that we carry and allow to get in the way and impede us. Not only did this man stare into the dragon's eyes and slay the dragon within himself, but he also stared and we could maybe say eyeballed, the eyes of the dragons of the *Professionals* and *Experts* that were dealing with him and subsequently slayed their dragons too. All their *noes* were obliterated through his sheer determination and perseverance. Michael Johnson believes that once the dragon is slain a very rich reward is awaiting us. There is no doubt that this man got a very rich reward.

Michael Johnson believes that it is only when the dragon is slain that we can truly meet our core, our ambition and our joy, these deep vital parts of ourselves that are necessary for us to reach our potential. This man accessed those aspects of himself that Michael Johnson is talking about by facing his fears, taking risks and having the courage to trust me and himself. My vision to see past the label of his disability, combined with my unique skill set, enabled him to unlock his hidden and trapped potential. This in turn helped him to accept Michael Johnson's guidance - to follow him to the places he had gone to within a whisper of his personal perfection, to places that were sweeter because he worked so hard to arrive there, to places at the very edge of his dreams. I think it's safe to say that this man most definitely took Michael Johnson up on his offer and followed his example. We had come a long way in a short time and had achieved a phenomenal amount, despite the obstacles and limitations imposed on us by his disability.

I think back to the hard work I had done with Sean over a span of many, many years. There is no doubt that Sean's positive influence on me was passed on to this man during this time. Memories of Sean's training, attitudes and beliefs flooded into me while I was working with him. Sean's *no nonsense* approach which I somewhat adapted with him, was extremely useful in breaking down the barriers caused by his disability. It also reminded me of the hard work I had done with Ann. The combination of Sean's pragmatic and tough style combined with Ann's caring, sensitive and patient approach were a powerful combination that worked a treat with him.

Once again, Ann was bowled over with the results I achieved with him. She truly felt that there was no way she could have done that herself. He was a lucky man to have the benefit of that experience. I felt that I was lucky to have the opportunity to explore and experiment with him in the way that I did. It was a mutual effort that produced mutual results. I had no doubt that it would further enhance my work in the future. The step-by-step approach I used with him as described by Michael Johnson earlier, worked exceptionally well for this man. It was a wonderful example of creativity producing incredible outcomes, just as the elite sports athletes I have mentioned, Michael Jordan, Michael Johnson, Nadia Comaneci and the creative energy in their achievements.

CHAPTER 44
The Baby Steps Grow Up

The work I did with these clients boosted my confidence and gave me the oomph I needed to continue on. While the work was tough, I really enjoyed it. I got great satisfaction out of it and it was truly uplifting to be putting in to practise each thing that I had learned over the last number of years. It was fascinating to see how the various styles and types of models of counselling could be interwoven into my work. I was able to connect them just like putting all the pieces of a jigsaw together. I adored the creativity and the experimentation. I loved taking risks and seeing the benefit of that. It was a majorly different type of work to what I had been used to in the past and I found that exhilarating.

My next venture was to run a series of one day Dancing The Rainbow workshops but this time with a therapeutic twist to it. Combining the creative aspect of Dancing The Rainbow and the therapy turned out to be a big hit. The participants, through the dance and the creative process, were able to express themselves more freely and in a completely different way than they were able to do sitting in a chair in their one-to-one sessions. The group element facilitated them to access deeper seated emotions and blocked out memories, that may have never been unearthed in a regular one-to-one session. The group aspect also helped them to be triggered into their family of origin patterns and behaviours and to observe the family role they had taken on in relation to their parents and siblings. This was extremely helpful as these were the patterns and behaviours that were being re-enacted in their daily lives.

I encouraged them to make notes to help them to remember the material that came up for them. This was greatly beneficial because it gave them a lot to bring into their one-to-one sessions to work on. It also made it easier to track the links between one thing and another and to identify re-occurring issues. It gave them an opportunity to prioritise the important issues. They were as surprised as I was by the number of revelations. It resulted in no shortage of work for either them or me. Ann of course, helped me along the way during this series of workshops and her input was invaluable. What was great for me also was the fact that I was mostly on the move or standing which meant I didn't have to sit down. This kept me from seizing up.

The first series of workshops were such a success that everybody wanted to do a second lot. We did this and in the middle of it, Ann asked me to help her at one of her bodywork workshops as she wanted me to try out some techniques with her clients who were stuck. I was over the moon at being asked and couldn't wait to give it a whirl. I was so eager and excited. She got me to do a major piece of work with one man in particular who was extremely stuck and lo and behold after four hours we had an almighty breakthrough. While this was the highlight of the workshop for us both, I also learned an awful lot from working with the other people over the few days. It was lovely working alongside Ann in this way and we also included some of the dancing which was great for integration purposes as it was gentle and calm.

Ann suggested that I try to run a residential workshop with my clients to see how I would get on. This I did and it too just like hers, turned out to be extremely beneficial and worthwhile for everybody concerned. These ventures were taking my mind off my own pain and injuries which was helpful. They motivated me to keep my rehabilitation programme going because otherwise I couldn't have managed to run the workshops. At least now I was feeling a bit useful again, as opposed to the useless being I had become after the car crashes and my loved ones that I had lost in my life. While I still had a long, long way to go, I felt that things were looking up.

Out of the blue, a friend of mine who had been teaching Circle Dance to a group of people with physical and intellectual disabilities had to leave. I was asked to take over teaching the class. This was a new challenge for me going from individual disabled clients to a full group. Anyway, as usual, no better woman than Ann, she ordered me to give it a go. She thought it would be a great experience and an ideal situation for my injuries. The lady organising the group, Marie, was a lovely, lovely person and we hit it off immediately. She was in the process of setting up various other dance groups and, over a period of time, she asked me to take those on as well. These groups were composed primarily of people with Down's Syndrome but there were also people with other intellectual disabilities. At times I found this group demanding and challenging, but I also found the people gorgeous and incredibly funny. The people in this group loved the dancing, loved the music and loved the social interaction when we had a cup of tea and a biscuit to end off the session. Like myself, a lot of members in this group had a sweet tooth with no amount of tricks for nobbling as many biscuits as possible. We needed eyes everywhere, not just in the back of our heads.

I grew to love the people in these groups dearly and the feeling was mutual. There's many a funny story to be told.

In one of the groups one day, one of the men, who was an absolute dote, came into the class smiling from ear to ear, his face beaming, high as a kite and in great humour. I asked him what had him in such a happy mood and in such good humour? He replied, 'I flushed 42 toilets today Mary.' I laughed and said, 'My oh my, you were busy, weren't you?' He nodded his head, clapped his hands and continued grinning like a Cheshire cat. Marie explained to me afterwards, that people with Down's Syndrome can sometimes have a fascination for certain things and flushing toilets can be one of them.

One of the women had a fascination for picking things up off the floor especially if it was a carpeted floor. She would go around picking up the tiniest speck that you could see and the carpet would be cleaner than hoovering it. Everyone had a special seat and woe betide anyone who took their seat. There would be holy blue murder and all hell would break loose.

Having said this, interestingly there were some unbelievably spiritual people in the group. Even though they were challenged by their various disabilities at a physical level, there was a real beauty that was visible in the movements of their dance. It was powerful, prayerful and spiritual. I think it was because the individuals were connected deeply at a heart level to what they were doing, that it resulted in a beautiful movement despite the lack of coordination. One of the men asked me one day if I had learned the dances from a priest. He was quick to point out that these dances could be easily danced in a church. The next week he came into the class he approached me and said, 'Can I ask you a question?' I said, 'Yes of course you can.' 'Are we doing the *Prayer* dances today?' he asked. I couldn't believe it! You could have knocked me over with a feather. For a few weeks after that, he kept asking me questions about the dances, the movements and the meanings of them. He had it all worked out in his own head and his interpretation was second to none. I was flabbergasted! After responding to him he would come in again the next week, having considered and thought about my response and would have an enlightening addition to the information I had given him. He absolutely loved and adored prayer dances. The prayer dances were a more ballet type style of dance, with beautiful, graceful arm movements. Some dances had universal gestures which were prayer-like to anyone who may have come from a spiritual background.

It's no joke to say that I could have been working with able-bodied people in the same way, with the same dances and I'm not sure they would have interpreted it in the way he did. It was just fascinating to listen to him.

Everyone had their favourite dance. People were highly tuned in to each other. 'We have to do the roly-poly dance' or 'We have to do Suzi's dance.' It was lovely the way everyone made sure they got their turn to do their favourite dance. While on one hand, there could at times be killings in the group, people always got over them quickly enough to point out everyone's favourite dances. They didn't hold grudges or harbour animosity towards each other. Once it was over and people had 'Kissed and Made Up' it was genuinely over. Over and out until the next hoo-ha.

Teaching these dances were great for my injuries because I was constantly on the move and the arm movements were particularly helpful for my upper body stiffness. The coordination of the arms and legs challenged my mobility considerably. Combining the left and right sides of my brain in this way was challenging another aspect of coordination altogether, which was outside the straightforward realm. I could feel the disharmony of the movement inside myself, struggling to get the timing and synchronicity in unison. It felt like the two parts of my brain were at odds with each other. It took a lot of practise and perseverance to eventually get them to cooperate. The next element of the challenge was speed. The quicker the movement the harder it was to coordinate it. This made me feel that one part of my brain was racing ahead of the other while that other part was desperately trying to catch up with it.

These more complex coordination movements are fantastic for people with disabilities. I used a lot of them in my basketball training as I've mentioned already and now here they were present in the dancing as well. Over time, to see people improving and mastering these challenges is truly amazing. It brings an extra dimension of satisfaction to the work and makes the struggle feel worthwhile in the end.

My dance classes became as successful as my basketball coaching and I was able to achieve similar results. The same question, 'How do you get them to do all that?' arose again. The answer is the same. Although this particular dance environment is not a competitive one, we did actually have a few performances where we performed in public on certain particular celebratory occasions. Marie had organised an award ceremony for the Centre that had improved its disabilities services the most in the year. RTE's Joe Duffy was the invited guest and awards presenter for the occasion. My group were invited to dance as part of the ceremony. We did three dances in total. We prepared very well for it and the group were extremely excited about the whole thing. I was extra nervous because it was my first time to lead a dance performance. I was quaking at the idea of the group getting out of hand, in the middle of the performance, becoming emotional and fighting with each other. Marie thought it would be a good idea for the group to dress up in colourful scarves, which everyone loved doing. We decided that we would wear black and put on the different coloured scarves over the black. The group were amazing. People wanted to wear the scarves everywhere, around their heads, necks, waists, wrists and anywhere you could put one. Luckily enough, I had loads of scarves thanks to my Dancing The Rainbow collection.

While we were getting ready and I was trying to gather myself together, a woman in the group came over to me and said she wanted to go to the toilet. I pointed out the toilet to her and sent her on her way. She would not budge however and it soon became clear she wasn't going unless I went with her. I reassured her she would be fine and explained I had to get ready myself. That didn't make a blind bit of difference to her. She was not budging until I went with her. Of course, I had to succumb and go with her in the end. She insisted on me standing right outside the cubicle door that she went into. She proceeded with a litany of telling me how nervous she was and what if she forgot the steps, she was afraid she was going to forget the steps. I calmly reassured her that she would not forget the steps, she knew them better than she thought and that there was no need to be nervous, we had practised a lot and the practise was going to pay off. People coming in and out of the toilet were giving me the strangest of looks and must have thought we were as mad as two hatters. She didn't give a hoot and I was left blushing profusely. She made me promise to hold her hand and to keep nodding at her, to let her know she was doing alright. This I did which made her happy and content.

We went back in and it was just time for us to do our first dance. Well! The girls were absolutely brilliant. I couldn't believe it. Not only did the group not put a foot wrong, but they behaved like angels, as if butter wouldn't melt in anyone's mouths. Of course, while this was a great start, there were still two more dances to go. Anything could happen! It wasn't over yet! We were only one third of the way through! To my utter astonishment, the next two dances went the same way and you could hear a pin drop in the whole room. Joe Duffy remarked that he had never seen or experienced anything so peaceful and he thought it was beautiful.

The gang of course were delighted and chuffed with themselves and thought they were the bees' knees, which they were of course. Marie told everyone she was super proud of the group. I too was immensely proud of everyone but more relieved that it was over and went smoothly without any uncouth outbursts. Marie clapped me on the back and said, 'There was no need for you to be worried Mary, this group love performing.' 'Well, you could have told me that in the first place, I had no idea of that,' I retorted. But yes, I couldn't, couldn't, just couldn't believe it after everything I had gone through, every week in practise and in the class in general. It just showed us what people are capable of once they put their minds to it. Another valuable lesson and as in sport an example of when you put your mind to it and practise, it is amazing what you can achieve.

Our next few performances were as successful as that first one and the audiences were profoundly touched and amazed. People commented afterwards on the precision and the harmony of movement. They commented that they had never seen anything like it before, they were completely astounded by the whole thing. They also commented on the beauty of the choreographies and how the group got into the performance at an emotional level. They were surprised that the people in the group could engage at such a deep spiritual level, given the level of disability that they had. It was a pure eye-opener for everyone involved. The viewers were mesmerised, in awe and suitably impressed.

The group themselves were on a high for weeks afterwards and kept tormenting poor Marie about when were they going to perform again. They never laid off, they had her demented the poor thing. But Marie was well used to this, it didn't bother her, she just let it go over her head. Just as well or she would have had no hair left!!!

There was one girl who asked to join our group who had an acquired brain injury. Marie didn't know if she would be suitable or if she would be able to fit in. She was a lovely girl with a lovely caring and kind nature, but, due to her brain injury, was very disruptive and quite loud. She could not sit down or stay still for more than one minute; she was permanently running around. She had a full-time carer with her which was helpful because she knew her well and was able to explain to us things we needed to know. I said to Marie that we won't know until we try her out and we decided to give it a go. On the first day I got her to run around on the outside of the circle because she wouldn't join in and we kept dancing as normal. She was delighted to do this and after some time it seemed like she enjoyed the music. It took the others a bit of time to get used to her, but interestingly enough they eventually did. The great and lovely thing about people with Down's syndrome is that they are in no way cliquish, they are extremely inclusive of others. The fact that this girl had a different disability didn't bother anyone. She was included and made to feel welcome. This of course made a difference and we managed to get through the class and kept her involved for the whole time.

I suggested to Marie to let her come for a while because in her particular case it was going to take time, it would be a slow process. I told Marie that now that I had met her, I would think about it and see if I could come up with some ideas to help her more. The next week I did the same with her and gradually, week after week, I got her to put her hand on my shoulder sometimes while she was running around. This took a while for her to do, but she did it eventually and that was the beginning of her joining in the group and the circle itself.

Due to her brain injury, she had problems with cognition and memory. This naturally interfered with her learning capability. Patience and perseverance were required to help her and repetition was the key ingredient in the end, which helped her to have a major breakthrough. After a few months she began to remember the steps and the music and at the end of one year she was able to stay in the circle long enough to complete one whole dance. Over time, I got her sitting for short periods and we gradually built that up to where she could actually stay sitting for five whole minutes. These progressions were seriously major achievements in her development. She improved greatly and she was even able to take part in one of our performances. We couldn't believe it and she didn't cause any disruption to the group.

Marie received a lovely letter from the Acquired Brain Injury Clinic to thank us most sincerely for the wonderful work we did with her. They maintained that the dance yielded results that they would never have expected in a million years, which also helped them to help her further in the long run. It was lovely to receive an acknowledgement for our hard work and with more time, she went on to improve further.

In one of my other groups, I had a girl who was a lovely dancer and had great potential. She absolutely adored the dancing. She used to arrive early and she couldn't wait to get dancing. I always had to dance with her on her own until the others arrived. Marie thought it would be a good idea to invite her to join the other group for one of the performances. She was delighted and over the moon to do this. A few months later there was a dance competition advertised in one of the disability events and Marie entered her in it with me as her partner, as she was too shy to go by herself. I took one of the choreographies and adapted it so that we could both dance it. I structured it in such a way that it would highlight her rather than me and that her talent would be obvious and to the forefront. We practised the dance a lot until she perfected it. We had a trial run in front of another group, to give her the opportunity of practising it in front of an audience in preparation for the real thing.

When the day came, she was both nervous and excited and I reassured her that she would be fine. There were 10 competitors in the competition and she ended up winning first place. She got a beautiful trophy which she was chuffed with and it boosted her morale no end. She brought the trophy in to show her group the next week and they were delighted for her. This girl had never won anything in her life before and had always felt self-conscious as a result of her disability. She became a new woman after winning this competition and her self-esteem, her self-confidence and her mood improved enormously. She went on to get a job afterwards which was an incredible experience for her. Her dancing improved further as she was now highly motivated. For Marie and I it was lovely to see the positive changes in her and to see her grow in confidence and stature. She also grew in maturity and became more responsible as a result. Overall a fantastic outcome.

CHAPTER 45
OK! I'll Learn More About Dance.

I began to realise there were a lot of similarities between the dance and the sports. However, I didn't know anything about dance training and I thought it would be a good idea, now that I was becoming more involved in it, to try and read up a bit and educate myself on dance and dance training. Ann agreed that this would be a good idea as being able to cross-reference with my sports, might not only be useful with my dance training in general but would enhance my work in the disability field in particular. Where to start though was the question? There were a huge variety of dance forms to choose from.

After much consideration I thought that because the dance I was teaching had a ballet element to it, that to study ballet would be the best option. I had seen a programme on T.V. which was a documentary on the male ballet dancers that pioneered a major change in ballet, by bringing the male role in to an important evolution to become equal to the women. It was a fascinating documentary which highlighted the athleticism and power of the male dancers, along with the revolutionary emotive and dramatic aspect the men developed and incorporated into their choreographies. As I wanted to educate myself on both men and women, I ended up choosing Rudolph Nureyev and Margot Fonteyn as they were the indisputable champion dancing partners of their era.

It was astonishing to see the similarities between the sports I had done, the basketball and athletics heroes I have written about, the gymnastics and the dance. I could see that many of the same characteristics were present. Requirements such as commitment, dedication, perseverance, practise and repetition, love for what you're doing, not giving up, aiming for and achieving perfection, just to name a few.

In order to fully appreciate these comparisons, I would like to digress to give some background information about Rudolph Nureyev and Margot Fonteyn and their dance partnership.

CHAPTER 46
Mary Whelan Meets Rudolph Nureyev

Rudolph Nureyev is one of the most famous Russian ballet dancers of all times. He was only seven years of age when his love for dance became apparent and he knew in his heart and soul that he wanted to become a ballet dancer. However, being a man, dancing wasn't something considered suitable as a career. To Nureyev's father this was preposterous. He wanted him to become a soldier like himself. Rudolph, however, defied his father's wishes as his love for dance was like a burning flame, that grew into a fire inside him. Such was his deep-rooted passion for ballet, that he had no doubt whatsoever, that his choice to dance professionally, would be not only a perfect choice but his true heart's desire and destiny. Rather amazingly, for a child so young, his love for dance was nourished by a self-belief and unshakeable conviction, that at the age of seven, he knew that his exceptional physique and the fact that he possessed such natural gifts, would help him to make his dream come true.

When I compared myself at the age of seven to Nureyev I was flabbergasted at the depth of self-belief, self-conviction and self-awareness that he had. When I was seven, I on the other hand, was a negative image of Nureyev - no self-belief, no conviction about being good at anything and most certainly had no sense of talent. He seemed to be deeply connected to himself at a soul level. I found this fascinating. Unlike me, he was not desperately trying to prove to anyone else or himself that he was good at something. While at seven I thought I wanted to be a primary school teacher, this wasn't genuinely from the heart or coming from a deep sense of conviction. This was undoubtedly influenced by Miss O'Flynn's effect on me when I struggled as a lone, deaf child in a hearing world.

It was only when I was introduced to basketball by Sr. Patricia, that I discovered or should I say, developed such passion inside myself and, eventually considered playing basketball with the same determination and conviction that Nureyev had chosen dance. For me it was desperation that ran my show, along with my need for love and attention. I marvelled at his courage to defy his father's wishes. I was that downright afraid of my mother I didn't have the same courage that he had. Playing basketball for me was an escape from my mother and my home life, whereas dancing for him was his true heart's desire. I was taken aback by the two distinctively different entry routes into each of our careers. Nureyev's conviction was both internal and external due to the fact that his mother, having introduced him to ballet at a young age, went on to support him to pursue his dream. Mine, on the other hand, was created by the external influence of Miss O'Flynn, supported by my mother's forcefulness and drive to achieve her own self-serving goal to have her daughter attain a profession of respectable status.

In the early 1950's ballet dancing was totally dominated by women. Men were considered as assistants. Their job was to highlight the beauty and gracefulness of the women dancing. Men got no recognition whatsoever. Ballet was deemed as a highly feminised activity. Male dancers carried a stigma and were viewed as effeminate. When Rudolph Nureyev came along however, he blew that reality out of the water by dancing his way into a female world. He caused an earthquake in the ballet arena. His dancing genius led him to develop a new style of male dance that provoked a breakthrough and brought male ballet dancers the same recognition and importance as female ballet dancers.

His pure athleticism, his outstanding physical power, his incredible leaps and aesthetic qualities, his phenomenal technique as well as his artistic skills and his charisma and beauty rocked both the ballet arena and audiences the world over. He became a force to be reckoned with. Nureyev had the unique ability to dance as emotionally and as expressively as a woman. He not only stormed his ballet performances with this ability but also with his incredible virtuosity. He was also considered to be both sexually and sensually attractive to men and women alike. The magnetic combination of these skills, talents and character traits hailed him as one of the most popular male ballet dancers of those times. He had such an effect on people that the public craved to see him. He filled auditoriums everywhere he went and caused a collective sigh to rise in his audiences the minute he stepped onto the stage.

There are powerful similarities between himself, Michael Jordan, Michael Johnson and Nadia Comaneci. They too had that ability to cause audiences to sigh at their breathtaking performances. They too filled auditoriums and arenas as their reputations preceded them. Their uniqueness set them apart from their competitors. Like Nureyev, in everything about them, they were a sight to behold and people couldn't get enough of them.

Nureyev was an extremely hard worker and had a severe training regime. He never slackened off. He was a great believer in challenging himself to aim to reach his potential by going as far as possible, constantly raising the bar and pushing the limits of physical possibility. He believed in the art of perfection and he thrived on reaching perfection. He practised and practised over and over again, unrelentingly, until he could master his routines to perfection. Peter Brinson when writing about Nureyev said, 'For Nureyev dancing was a collaboration to achieve perfection.' His attention to detail and his tenacity for repetition were two of the qualities which gained him the respect and acclaim which he earned.

Nureyev possessed a curious and innovative mind. He was always on the lookout for new ideas, new forms of creativity and had a keen interest and willingness to learn and explore from others. Despite his deep belief in himself he wasn't a *know-all*. On the contrary, his enquiring mind spurred him on to learn anything he could from other dancers and his tutors.

When I examined these aspects of Nureyev's life and put them alongside Jordan, Johnson and Comaneci I can see the same work ethic among them. Relentless training sessions, relentless commitment and dedication to striving for and achieving perfection, relentless repetition, relentlessly challenging themselves to go further, relentless focus and concentration. They each embraced and learned from failure. They were willing to observe and learn from others and trust their coaches and trainers. They were incredibly creative in their thinking and their practical application.

What has been particularly significant for me about Nureyev? What is it about his approach that connected so strongly with me? I was buzzed up reading about Nureyev because I could see many striking similarities between himself and myself. While mine was at a much lower level, nevertheless, the same qualities that he possessed were also qualities I possessed. I could immediately recognise in him the deep love and passion that I felt for what I was doing, the fanaticism and the devotion to not giving up. I also had, just like these amazing athletes and Nureyev, a sincere and a deep loyalty to my passion, my coaches and my trainers. I too had the guts to put myself in a position where I took the risk to step out into the world to be seen. I wasn't only inspired by them. They clarified to me and illustrated what I too had done in my career.

All along Nureyev's path he was lucky to have his talents recognised and supported by his various teachers. He progressed to two of the most famous ballet schools in Russia, The Leningrad School of Ballet and The Kirov. In the Leningrad School of Ballet, he had the great fortune to be assigned Alexander Pushkin as his teacher. He was an extremely reputable teacher and it was he who propelled Nureyev forward into his professional dancing career. Due to the recognition, encouragement, interest and the individual attention that Pushkin gave Nureyev, it resulted in Nureyev positively responding to such an extent, that he mastered the immensely difficult dance syllabus in half the time of the other students. Pushkin was an insightful and inspirational teacher who swiftly recognised that Nureyev's mind was matched physically by a natural gift for emotional expression through the body. Pushkin rightfully identified and appreciated that this was a unique combination of talents.

Through this foresight he steered Nureyev to become the dancer he became. He drove on to build on Nureyev's strengths and improve on his weaknesses by encouraging him to perfect his technique and acrobatic feats. He fired up Nureyev's theatrical imagination which added a dramatic style to his execution of the moves and techniques. This in turn fine-tuned Nureyev's physique. The combination of these attributes, along with the hard work, time, dedication and commitment put in by Nureyev accentuated his sheer giftedness even more.

This element of Nureyev's dancing career captured my attention. Luck is a key element in a lot of things in life. He was lucky in as many ways as I was. He was lucky to have had Pushkin, I was lucky to have had Sean. He was lucky that there was a space for him to step into – breaking into that female dominated world. I was lucky that there was a space for me to step into – breaking into that male-dominated world. I guess we were both lucky with the timing involved. Any later may have been too late for us both. He was lucky that Pushkin spotted his potential. I was lucky that Sean spotted mine. He was lucky that Pushkin nurtured and developed his potential further. I was lucky that Sean did the same for me. Pushkin not only recognised and developed Nureyev's physical potential, but he also recognised his intellectual potential and united his mind and body. Sean did the exact same thing for me. My intellectual confidence in my ability was much lower than Nureyev's. Sean had a lot of work to do on that one. I was fascinated by these similarities and revelations. When I was reading about Nureyev, I realised his path described mine surprisingly well too. I would never have seen dance as a sport. I would have always viewed dance as a creative art form. Ann at one stage had pointed out to me the creative aspects of my sports. Now and it is only now, that I can see and understand better what she meant. These connections to Nureyev were a real eye-opener in that regard.

Nureyev had a strong outgoing presence and personality which attracted the media like nobody's business. He also possessed a defiant impulsive side which could surprise people and catch them off-guard. He was the type of person that caused people to comment on him and his vibrant personality warranted many vibrant responses. People's comments of him were varied and extremely descriptive. Alexander Bland writing about Nureyev described him as having 'A haunted untamable pride.' Another writer described him as a 'Comet from an empty land, blazing through the world of art and beauty,' a very poetic description I think. Margot Fonteyn said of him, 'He's not only an exceptional dancer, but also a unique personality fortified by one of the sharpest brains imaginable.'

Being the Gemini star sign that I am, I have two sides to my personality, one of which would equate to Nureyev and one that is the opposite. The opposite one when I was younger was shy, wanted to hide away, did not want to attract attention or trouble and wanted to remain secret. This side of me did not have a strong outgoing presence like Nureyev. It was quiet, meek and demure even weak and pathetic, slinking away to hide in the corner. This was my scared side, which was afraid of everything, even its own shadow. I did not want to shine or to be in the public arena.

However, I also did have a strong outgoing presence like Nureyev. In common with Nureyev, I too possessed a defiant impulsiveness which not only surprised people but at times, shocked them. This side of me was to the forefront in my basketball playing career, most definitely in my refereeing career and also in my athletics. I loved the attention, loved being seen and loved to be in the public eye. The more people watched me the greater the performance. I thrived under pressure. Like Nureyev, people used to frequently comment on me. The intensity of my training regimes always attracted comments such as, 'She trains like a man, how does she do that?', 'Look at her go, I wish I could do that' etc., etc. I could even see Nureyev's haunted untamable pride in myself which was one of the driving factors that led me to my successes. While Nureyev blazed through the world of ballet, art and beauty, in my own way I blazed through the world of basketball playing and refereeing.

It occurred to me as I wrote this that Sean too had this haunted untamable pride. Maybe this was one of the things that helped us to connect so strongly and drove both of us to raise the bar as often as we did in our training sessions together.

Nureyev had a wildness to him that he expressed freely in both his personal life and in his dancing. It not only endeared people to him it seemed to have had a contagious effect on the other dancers around him. It gave him the ability to draw the best out of others and to help them to connect to that wildness in themselves. He led by example and was therefore able to demand the same of others. He was regarded as a super role model as he walked the talk.

The wildness in me wasn't expressed freely like Nureyev's was. Mine crept out over time and had to be enticed and drawn out slowly. My wild side lacked the confidence of Nureyev's wild side. He had no inhibitions whatsoever, mine was full of inhibitions. When I was seven, I was pure terrified of the world. With time, I did *walk the walk* and was a good role model to my teammates and students.

His dancing attributes were reflected in his personality. It is said that another reason for his positive influence on other dancers was the fact that he was especially generous in sharing the knowledge that he possessed. He didn't share his knowledge by way of it being a favour. He saw it as being his responsibility and part of his job. This attitude was an extension of his commitment to perfection. There was no holding back, he gave it everything, the full 100 per cent.

Peter Brinson gave Nureyev the greatest compliment possible by saying, 'In 30 years Nureyev pushed back the boundaries of the impossible.' Thirty years is an exceptionally long time. To be able to sustain that level of performance and perfection for so many uninterrupted years must be one of the most amazing feats ever achieved in dancing history. Generally speaking, elite athletes and performers have a short lifespan at the top in their careers. Nureyev's achievement has to be one of the most phenomenal in that regard.

Looking back over my early years and throughout my career as a player and as a referee, I can confidently say that my commitment to perfection was equal to his and like him I didn't hold back. I gave it everything, the full 100 per cent. In my own small way, I too pushed back the boundaries of the impossible and like Nureyev sustained that level for my whole FIBA career. Even today I am still doing the same, thirty plus years later. This is an amazing feat, especially considering the numerous unfortunate setbacks that occurred in my life. Nureyev's story inspired me and helped me to see the parallels in my own story. It made me value and appreciate the qualities that I shared with him. It enabled me to acknowledge and honour my own achievement as being similarly phenomenal in the context of my own life. It highlighted and brought to my attention, the important aspects I needed to focus and concentrate on, in my own teaching as a dance teacher to my students.

CHAPTER 47
Margot Fonteyn - Who Never Met
Mary Whelan
But Inspired Her

Margot Fonteyn was one of the world's greatest female ballet dancers of all time. Like Nureyev, the minute she stepped onto a stage, she cast a spell on her audience. She had her worldwide audiences eating out of the palm of her hand with her amazing technique, her total musicality, her beautiful physique, her soft style of movement and her gentle loving manner. She was particularly known for her exquisite lines that made her dancing a sight to behold. Her audience adored and idolised her. She was enchanting. She had a beautiful pale face, black hair, luminous eyes and an engaging smile. Those eyes and that smile touched audiences' hearts. These trademarks were what set her apart from other dancers. Another attraction was her legendary radiance, rapture and uncanny youthful air. More than anyone of her times, she knew that an art form like ballet was larger than any individual. 'Ballet is more than a profession; it is a way of life.' True to her belief she ate, slept and drank ballet. It was her life. She became a ballerina to cherish.

When I was reading about Margot Fonteyn, like Nureyev, I became engrossed in her story and in awe of her. I didn't stop to think about my own situation regarding my own sports. Here it was under my nose and I didn't see it. I also began to learn about her development and career. I could see the parallels between the skills and qualities which she brought to her dance and what I brought to my work as a basketball player and referee. Initially it surprised me how similar these were.

Margot Fonteyn had a natural ease with her femininity which seemed to be in her from the beginning of her life. She oozed femininity, whereas it was the complete opposite for me. My mother's constant brainwashing, telling me I was ugly and that no man would be bothered with me, sealed my self-belief that what she said was true. This made me run away from the female that I was, making way for the tomboy to take over. I couldn't have protected my brother for all those years from my mother and his peers without my tomboy. I would never have been the player that I became and most certainly I would never have achieved my Grade 1 and FIBA if I had been as feminine as Fonteyn. It was my tomboy that got me through it. Margot Fonteyn was extremely comfortable being feminine and expressing her femininity. I always wanted to be a boy. I always felt that behaving in a feminine manner was a weakness that would get me into trouble with men and perhaps cause the men to take advantage of me. These were notions that had been put into my head by my mother. One thing I did have in common with Fonteyn however, was the fact that I ate, slept and drank basketball. Basketball became a way of life for me too, once I got into it and I grew to love it the way she loved her ballet.

Fonteyn was an intuitive performer as was I. The better I became at playing and refereeing basketball, the more my skills became intuitive. She studied ballet in China initially and by the young age of 21 she was the principal dancer and biggest star in the British Royal Ballet Company. Her dancing was distinguished by the perfect lines in her dance movement and by her exquisite lyricism. This made her especially stand out in lyrical roles. She rose to fame as a result of these lyrical roles and her performances in particular in Sleeping Beauty, Swan Lake and Giselle. These performances separated her from her peers and were what made her not only different but made her the greatest.

She was revered for being able to dance the most difficult choreographies with such wonderful disarming ease and with simplicity, grace and passion that she made the ballet dance look easy. In parallel, I remember Sean, when he brought back his difficult set plays for us to practise and it took us ages to get them. Other teams did remark on how easy we made the plays look, when we eventually perfected them. They couldn't fathom the plays out because we did them with such ease.

Fonteyn's ability as an actress enhanced her artistic and emotional expression which had an extra-special effect on her love scenes. In her presentation of Princess Aurora in the Sleeping Beauty, in her interpretation, she captured the essence of the role to such perfection that it was considered the ultimate interpretation of that particular role. This was an incredible achievement. She played a huge variety of roles and each were more triumphant than the previous. This made her a consistent performer which earned her constant rave reviews in the newspapers and media.

As a player and basketball referee and as an athlete, my ability to be consistent was one of my strongest qualities. Consistency is a vital component in anything that pertains to competition. It is the ability to be consistent that leads to perfection. The consistency that I developed through my hard work for my Grade 1 and FIBA exams was critically important and an integral part of my successes. It also stood to me in my athletics competitions.

Margot Fonteyn was known for the ethereal magic that surrounded her. Her softness and her deeply charismatic presence were part of this magic. Another part of this magic was the fact that when she was on stage, she was natural and spontaneous and she came across as being completely at home with herself. The stage did not frighten or daunt her. She never got the old familiar stage fright, that some people got when they were faced with huge audiences. This was one of her major strengths.

In this regard, I can identify with her very well. I would love to be able to say that I too had that ethereal magic that surrounded her. I didn't. However, my charismatic presence on the basketball court, both as a player and as a referee, were present albeit the opposite to her softness. I was hard and tough. What I did have in common with her however, was a naturalness and spontaneity from being 100 per cent at home on the basketball court. Like her, large audiences or being under public scrutiny, did not frighten or daunt me either. In fact, it helped me to thrive even more. This too was one of my strengths.

Margot Fonteyn was known and recognised for her genius, for the combination of her personal qualities and her dancing skills. In a non-egotistical fashion, she herself described it, 'Genius is another word for magic and the whole point of magic is that it is inexplicable. I explained it when I danced it.' That's it exactly. Like the other athletes, Michael Jordan, Michael Johnson and Nadia Comaneci, their genius and magic were inexplicable. They explained it when they performed their sports. It is this inexplicable magic that cast the spell on their audiences and spectators and caused them to sigh the minute they stepped onto the stage or the floor.

Fonteyn, along with her exquisite techniques, was gifted with an incredible turn of speed and versatility. Alongside her femininity she had an amazing strength which added to this versatility. This is one of the reasons why her arabesques were as straight as rectangles. These attributes were a great advantage when it came to performing tricky variations in the choreographies. Her every movement was beautifully presented, beautifully placed and beautifully executed. This was seen through every inflection of her arms which were curved and flowing. The beauty of every inclination of her head movement also flowed with what can only be described as an incredible grace, executed from the centre of her being. Another beautiful feature were her hands. They were immaculately shaped. Her head moved in unison with the rest of her body and her hands and feet were in perfect line. Her physical presence was the personification of perfection. This unison of movement also contributed to her magic. Because she was so grounded and everything stemmed from the centre of her being, her movement was like one connected whole, with her energy extending beyond the points of her fingertips and toes into the space around her. This gave the impression of a continuation at the end of the movement into something more eternal. The movement didn't come to a sudden halt or stop, it continued on. This was spectacular and magical to bear witness to. It brought a whole new level of exquisiteness to the dance and the performance and left the observer with a depth and richness in their experience.

Fonteyn's graceful and flowing movements highlighted her femininity. The purity in the refinement of her movement led to her spectacular execution. Well, it took me a while to recognise that basketball players of high skill level also have the same beauty and refinement in their movements when executing their spectacular scores. Fonteyn only had to contend with the extension of the movement in her own body. Basketball players on the other hand, also have to contend with the extension of the movement in their own body and have the added dimension of controlling the ball at the end of the movement which is travelling swiftly at high speed. This is extremely difficult to do and while good players make it look easy, I can tell you that it is far from easy. Like Fonteyn, every inflection of the basketball player's arm, strong and taut with tension, curved and flowing and every inclination of the head has an important effect on the outcome of the final part of the movement. While her hands were immaculately shaped with the energy extending beyond the tips of her fingertips, basketball hands are strong hands with firm muscles and fingers that are both strong and flexible with a widespread on the fingers to be able to balance the ball in the hand. In basketball the head also has to move in unison with the rest of the body and the hands and feet along with the ball, have to be in perfect line. Like Fonteyn, basketball players must be grounded and the movement has to stem from the centre of the player's being which requires a steady, sturdy core.

Michael Jordan too, exhibits many examples of these movements. In particular his slam-dunk specials demonstrate to perfection everything that I've just described. His leap into the air, his ability to appear to float and remain at such great height in mid-air, as part of his trajectory to the basket, where he finally slams the ball, from varying positions into the basket, at phenomenal speed, are both spectacular and magical. He demonstrates his magic when he performs these outstanding feats of athleticism. His genius is indisputably a coming together of mind and body.

It was fascinating for me to see the many links between Margot Fonteyn's dance and basketball. Never in my wildest dreams would I ever have made those connections before. If

I had been a betting person, I would have lost many a bet on it. While I adored Michael Jordan and his superb skills, I now had an even greater appreciation for him, those players who excel in basketball and indeed for myself. Looking at and breaking down the movements in a more detailed way, allowed me to see the hidden nuances which were vital components in that inexplicable magic. It helped me to value much more, the years of constantly striving for perfection when I could look back at the movement involved in my own basketball play and view it in the context of Margot Fonteyn's dancing.

Nadia Comaneci in her gymnastics most definitely had the same qualities that Margot Fonteyn had. I would say they could well have been sisters. There are many similarities between the movement in the dance and gymnastics which is quite remarkable to see. Both executed their movements to perfection and had the audiences sitting on the edge of their seats. Both exuded the same beauty, brilliance and genius. Both reached their potential and achieved the highest acclaim possible in their dance and sport respectively and despite this, they both shared Fonteyn's belief that, 'We are all happier when we are still striving for achievement than when the prize is in our hands.' Both had the same infectious effect on the media. Both were adored and idolised by their audiences and even their competitors. They both have gone down in the history books for all time.

What else made Margot Fonteyn the superb dancer that she was? She was noted for her lack of arrogance. Despite her brilliance she continually expanded her acting, her range of movement and her spatial awareness in covering the stage. She made great use of the whole stage and did not restrict herself by only using part of it. While I was confident and sure of myself in my playing and refereeing, I wasn't arrogant either. I wasn't in any way cocky in my behaviour. My behaviour stemmed from my love and passion for the game and my desire and competitiveness to win. I wanted to win for my teammates and my coach as much as for myself. People who knew Fonteyn would say that her greatest strength and attribute was her ability to recognise and deepen what she did best through being herself. I think this was something I did especially well also. The basketball court was the only place I felt safe and free to just be myself. This encouraged me to deepen what I did best in terms of my skills and training. Like Fonteyn, I used the whole stage of the basketball court, not limiting my play to a section of the court.

She had an unassuming nature, which prevented her from ever deeming herself to be above any of her fellow dancers. This particular attribute resulted in her maintaining her popularity amongst her peers and enabled her to remain a star within the ensemble of the companies she danced with. Her peers loved her as much as her audiences did and this earned her their respect. I could not say that I had an unassuming nature. My approach was much more pragmatic, black and white, down to earth. It could almost have been seen as having a maleness to it whereas her unassuming nature was part of her femininity. I felt I was better than my peers but not from a conceited place, just from a black and white place of knowing that it was because I trained much more and much harder than them, I was faster, fitter and stronger and my shooting percentages were higher. My feeling that I was better felt deserved on this practical, factual basis.

Fonteyn's giftedness was also something that she had in common with Michael Jordan, Michael Johnson and Nadia

Comaneci. So outstanding were they in their giftedness that it was impossible for their peers to be jealous or envious of them. Their teammates and competitors were able to acknowledge how much of a benefit and positive influence they were on themselves and others and appreciated the enhancement they brought to them as individuals and to their teams. This same thing happened to me in my playing career in basketball. I have mentioned already about teammates acknowledging my contribution in relation to winning trophies and medals, winning leagues, tournaments and championships. Sean and some of my other coaches were always quick to deal with any envy or jealousy amongst the players and sharply nipped it in the bud. As coaches they had a strong sense of integrity around fair play. If someone was better because they worked harder than anyone else to be better, then that person deserved the credit and the rewards for that.

At the ripe old age of 42, when Fonteyn was at the height of her career and it was expected that she would retire from professional performance what happened? Margot Fonteyn met Rudolph Nureyev. Instead of retiring she continued on, not only performing, but entering into a partnership that challenged her in a way that she had not been challenged before. They clicked together in an unimaginable way. Her partnership with Nureyev brought her to a higher level of perfection which enabled her to surpass herself. She rose to even greater heights in herself than she had thought possible. They pushed the physical boundaries way beyond anything that either of them had done before. It was hard to believe that they could inspire each other to this extent, a 42-year-old and a 23-year-old, but they did!

Margot Fonteyn continued to dance and perform for a further unbelievable 18 years with Nureyev, right up to the age of sixty. Totally and utterly unheard of in the world of ballet! Definitely a statistic for the record books. Imagine being able to sustain such a high level of performance with a man nineteen years her junior and a man of such physical power and prowess. It doesn't bear thinking about. Phenomenal!

When I look back at my own career, I can see that I was in a similar situation with Sean only the other way around. He was twenty-one years my senior but yet we pushed each other way past our physical boundaries. The mixture of age, youth and his experience challenged us both indefinitely and quite unexpectedly. We were a perfect match for each other and we clicked beautifully. He couldn't get another man to challenge him the way I did and I most certainly couldn't get another woman to challenge me the way he did. We were two sides of the same coin – inseparable. Like Nureyev and Fonteyn, we strove for perfection and kept increasing those higher levels of perfection along our own journeys. We too helped each other to surpass ourselves, our wildest dreams and our expectations. Nureyev and Fonteyn were the coming together of two great dancers. Sean and I, in the context of our lives, were the coming together of two great athletes, two great referees. Like Nureyev and Fonteyn, Sean and I remained loyal friends to each other until the end.

In her writing about Margot Fonteyn, Eileen Battersby summed up Fonteyn beautifully when she said, 'Fonteyn remains the defining untouchable, a classical artist whose elusive grace, beauty and consummate purity on stage defied technique. Nothing – neither time, nor the increasing physical vulnerability that became part of every performance and not even the emergence of a host of gifted young pretenders – could banish her it seems. She danced and danced an apparent immortal until she was 60-years of age. Night after night, in the theatres of the world, the middle-aged woman regained her youth.'

While unlike her I was forced to retire from my FIBA refereeing at the age of 50 because that's the retiring age FIBA have set for their referees, I did manage despite my injuries to continue on to that age. In Ireland and the other European countries there is no retirement age. I have also managed to continue to referee at the top-level here in Ireland right up to the same age as Fonteyn and have now passed her age and am continuing to do so. In recent years many of the younger male and female referees reported being in awe of me passing a fitness test to qualify for the top-level when they failed the test themselves.

As I get older, just like Margot Fonteyn, of course it becomes more difficult to keep going, keep training at such an intense level, keep aspiring to staying at the top and keep challenging myself to maintain my high levels and standards of fitness and refereeing. People in the basketball world who have known me for years marvel at what they consider and refer to as my eternal youth. I cannot say that I feel this myself because the effort that I have to put in and the time it takes to remain committed and dedicated is tough going. On the plus side, what makes it easier is the fact that I still love what I am doing and with the exception of my injuries have been blessed with good health to keep doing it. This motivates me to keep going.

Of course, I know full well that the time will come when I have to retire eventually, but it's nice to keep going while I can. It's also nice to be a good role model and a real inspiration for younger people. I like to give them the message, 'If I can do it, you can do it.' Look at what Rudolph Nureyev and Margot Fonteyn achieved. They broke the bounds of the impossible. I firmly believe we can all do that in our own way. I find it a pleasure to demonstrate that important message to people and especially young people in whatever way I can. I am proud of myself to realise that like Margot Fonteyn, I too am 'Breaking the bounds of the impossible.' It has felt a phenomenal achievement and I am truly grateful to everyone, Sean in particular, who helped me to get there.

CHAPTER 48
Perfect Partnerships

Rudolph Nureyev and Margot Fonteyn first met in 1961 when Nureyev was invited to an annual gala for the Royal Academy of Dance which was organised by Margot Fonteyn. This was Nureyev's debut having defected from Russia to the West. It laid the foundation for Nureyev's subsequent career and proved to be the catalyst for the perfect partnership, which saw their debut performance one year later in 1962. Their first ballet performance was *Giselle*. In that performance the chemistry, vitality, powerful energy, animation and passion which exuded between them, rendered them enormously successful.

They went on to develop and sculpt a unique partnership which spanned nearly twenty years and transpired to be the highlight of both their careers. From what I have described already in relation to them as individuals, you can see why they became so popular as a duo. Their initial meeting was quite stark. The contrast between their dancing styles was distinctive, the polarities between their ages and the fact that she was known and he was unknown, were miles apart. Fonteyn was a well known aging Prima ballerina on the verge of retirement and Nureyev was a potential young, unknown entity to western ballet audiences. At 42, she was nineteen years older than him on their first meeting and he was 23. In ballet dancing terms this was an unprecedented situation. From the outside, one could look at their profiles and wonder, how the heck would it be possible for such a pair to gel with each other. Strangely though, it was the exact opposite that happened. It was the contrast in their distinctive styles and these polarities that moulded them. The dynamic magnetism, charisma and charm that they both radiated while performing together, along with the unique talent, giftedness and emotional expression that they portrayed in their performances, is what brought them both to heightened and improved levels of performance.

At 23 Nureyev gave Fonteyn a new burst of creative energy which catapulted her in to an even more sensational second career. He also challenged her to relinquish her old formal, classical style of ballet and to step into a new innovative dance style, which had more freedom of movement and fluidity than her old rigid style. This new style was well suited to her and with practise she was able to embody it fully. Her ability and willingness to respond to Nureyev's challenges launched him on an unprecedented trajectory of fame.

Nureyev's ability to be dramatic and theatrical tapped into Fonteyn's acting ability and inspired her to reciprocate in such a way, that it enhanced their artistic expression. It created an electrical spark between them. Their work rate was second to none. They both worked harder than most to perfect their art. She overcame problems with her feet that would have ended the careers of most dancers. This incredibly intense work rate created a tension, chemistry and beauty on stage that was legendary.

Their compatibility as a duo, resulted in a special magic that no other duo ever accomplished on stage. This compatibility stirred audiences all over the world and caused them to light up the stage like no other partnership had ever done prior to this. However, it was the perfection in their performances that truly captured the hearts and minds of these audiences and it was this perfection that inspired the audiences to reward Nureyev and Fonteyn, with long repeated frenzied curtain calls and bouquet tosses after their performances.

Nureyev and Fonteyn were often questioned about the unique magical quality of their dance relationship. Nureyev said, 'We danced with one body, one soul' and Fonteyn said, 'I've found the perfect partner.'

Mary Whelan and Sean Treacy first met in 1974 you may remember, when Whelan joined Haroldites Basketball team where Treacy was coach. When Sean and I started to train we also had a special chemistry between us. It emanated from an intense passion and desire to be as physically fit as we possibly could. Whenever we trained the vitality, powerful energy and animation between us was palpable. Interestingly, once we got going, we more often than not trained in silence. This silence however, had a unique sound and language of its own. The silence spoke multitudes and spurred us on more and more. Such was the silence that we could hear each other breathing and we could practically hear each other's hearts beating. The sound of our sweat trickling down our faces and our bodies and finally plopping off us onto the ground in tiny little torrents, was barely audible due to the fierceness of the heavy breathing and the huffing and puffing sounds being expelled as we worked out.

We pumped out the exercises, one after the other, after the other, in complete synchronicity. We never faltered. Our rhythmic movement was in complete unison, complete harmony. We were like one well-oiled machine, doing what it's supposed to do, in order to keep in perfect working order. When we ran the up and down sprints, our feet and bodies were perfectly matching, step for step, running side by side, so even paced you wouldn't believe it. When we did the chair step-ups that was the same, our legs and feet touched the chair in perfect coordination, at exactly the same time. Up and down, we went like clockwork. If you couldn't see us and were outside the room, by the sound you would have heard, you would have sworn it was only one person training by themselves. Everything we did in our training was the same, the bar work, the bench-presses, the press-ups, the sit-ups, jumping on and off the benches, skipping, the weight training, everything. It was incredible how we had become so perfectly tuned in to each other.

There most definitely was a dynamic magnetism and charisma that radiated from us, as we trained our hearts out, day after day, week after week. When I look back at it now, I can see that the silence caused us to go deeper inside ourselves. It affected us in such a way, that it enabled us to dig deeper and draw from the depths of our being, that extra effort it takes, to spur one on to be the best and achieve the impossible. It is a place that overrides the very notion of giving up. It was from that deep place, that Sean and I achieved our FIBA refereeing awards.

Sean most definitely was a uniquely gifted P.E. teacher, basketball trainer and basketball referee. While Nureyev gave Fonteyn a new burst of creative energy which catapulted her forward despite her age, I was Nureyev to Sean's Fonteyn. (He would kill me if he heard me saying that). As Fonteyn and Nureyev responded to each other, Sean and I did the same. Like them, our work rate was second to none. We both worked harder than most to perfect our art.

From what I read about Nureyev in relation to working and training with Fonteyn, he was a tough taskmaster, stupendously demanding of her and extremely critical. In one sense Sean becomes Nureyev here. He was a tough taskmaster, but I think, that Sean and I were much more compatible and maybe more evenly matched as a duo. We never fought or argued in our training sessions. We just got down to business, didn't waste a minute, maximised every moment, whether training on or off the court as referees. We just did it. This kind of compatibility is quite rare. How lucky was I, just like Fonteyn, to find *the perfect partner* albeit it a much less temperamental one.

CHAPTER 49
A Plethora Of Perfect Partnerships

I realise that I have been extremely fortunate to have experienced the Perfect Partnership with numerous people in my life. Dr. Johnson was my first experience of a perfect partnership. Not only did he get me hearing again, but he seemed to connect with me as a father, beyond his doctor role. Miss O'Flynn, my primary school teacher, was constantly good humoured. She gave me my first experience of creativity and in the busy classroom never gave up on me. Sr. Cecily, who I haven't mentioned before, was my music teacher in secondary school who developed my love for music. She was a real gentle creature, passionate in an infectious way about music and wholeheartedly encouraged me, in spite of my partial deafness. Vivienne was my perfect work partner and our friendship developed into the perfect partnership. A partnership of mutual love and admiration. Bridget of course was next and how can I describe Bridget? My relationship with her had so many perfect elements to it. I suppose the constant element being our social partnership which brought great enjoyment, fun and laughter to both our lives. My aunt and godmother Bridie gave me the primary family relationship and partnership that saw me through many a tough time during my childhood. My tomboy partnership with my brother during our childhood, developed critical aspects of my personality, which were invaluable in my later years, when breaking the bounds of the impossible for women in basketball.

My perfect partnership with basketball and athletics that paved the way to me becoming outstandingly successful by breaking records, was actively the most central to moulding me into the person I am today. Then of course, Sean and I, that perfect partnership that challenged me, influenced me and my life in so many ways and was the catalyst in dispelling the negative beliefs in myself and opening the door to encouraging me to trust again.

There were also the relationships with my boyfriends, three in all, that I haven't spoken about other than Gerry, my last one. They too were fabulous partnerships that taught me a lot about love and helped me to grow up, become mature and helped me to regain my femininity.

Michael Pita, my acupuncturist, was the perfect partnership that physically got me on the road to recovery after my second car crash. Without his expertise and superb knowledge of the musculoskeletal system and the Chinese methodology, I think I would have ended up in a wheelchair had he not salvaged the detrimental damage that the orthopaedic surgeon inflicted upon me. Michael, like the others, has been extremely challenging of my condition and hence the nickname Pita. He's been a right *'Pain in the ass.'* He has a strong male, stubborn personality (just like me) which has caused us to have had many ding-dongs between us over the years. However, I have always managed to come out on the right side of them lucky enough! Michael is one of those constant thorns in my side that never gives up. But I do actually appreciate this, because I realise that I am indeed hard work – not an easy customer by any manner of means. We travelled a long, slow, hard road with my multiple injuries, constant setbacks in the initial stages and the infinite complications that unexpectedly arose along the way. But at least it was worthwhile in the end and we can both now see the benefits of his hard work. At the end of the day, I know that Michael genuinely has my best interests at heart and that he cares about me and this is something I feel lucky that I can treasure. Despite what I've said, we do have fun and laughs when I drive him mad on those testy occasions. I can let a lot of his comments go over my head and am well able to slag him back.

Virginia, the bereavement counsellor, who I have mentioned already, is one of the loveliest, kindest, gentle and nurturing people I have ever met. She was a biased fan of me as a person and my umpteen achievements. She was forever encouraging me and like Ann, felt I was capable of anything, especially if I put my mind to it and got the right help and support that I needed. Virginia is a most compassionate person and I learned a lot about the virtue of compassion from her. Her compassion was deepened by her amazing tolerance and understanding of the fragility of the human race. She also had a wonderful comprehension of people's vulnerabilities. These qualities gave her a soft, gentle countenance which allowed her to bypass my defence mechanisms quite easily, enabling me to grieve properly. She has a beautiful, charming nature, which is a natural and genuine part of her personality. Virginia is a truly authentic person. What you see is what you get. Her adorable and loving qualities made her a perfect partner for me, as she was able to reach my own compassion and my vulnerability, in a way that others could not.

There's no forgetting Ann, equally as significant a partnership as Sean and I, albeit different. Her superhuman spirit and her effervescent personality had a huge influence on me and touched me deeply. From an emotional perspective, without her therapeutic skills and expertise, I most definitely would not be alive today. Her sticking with me through thick

521

and thin, her unrelenting challenges, her infinite wisdom, care and love, her depth of courage, her indeterminable and unshakeable belief in me, her fearlessness to risk take, got me through my traumas past and present. Ann indisputably, was the most perfect therapeutic relationship for me, that has enhanced my life no end and has helped me to grow and blossom into the person I am today.

Then there is David, the wonderful therapist that Ann passed the baton on to, when she became ill and she had to cease working. David is another Ann in many ways. A loving, caring, gentle, broad-minded, extremely generous therapist and like Ann, knowledgeable and exceptionally experienced. But he is also different and has his own special qualities which are unique to him himself. He too has been a constant in my life in the latter years, an immense support on every level and is always reaffirming of me as both a therapist and a person. I often slag him saying that he, along with Virginia, is the most biased person in my favour. But truly and honestly, I really love that, because it helps me to feel good about myself.

Martin, I haven't spoken about yet. I am truly grateful that he was recommended to me to help me with my injuries. Martin is a highly qualified practitioner who has expertise in many areas. He has fully trained as a physiotherapist, osteopath, chiropractor, kinesiologist, naturopath, cranio-sacral therapist and he is an expert in the various lymphatic and drainage systems in the body. His knowledge of the musculoskeletal system is awesome. I have never had anyone work on my body the way that he does. He is most definitely unique in his approach. I always feel when he is working on me, that my body is a roadmap that he is following and he covers every inch of it every time I see him. His approach is holistic, he sees the bigger picture and he uses his diverse disciplines when he is working on me in accordance with what I need. It's fascinating to see how he integrates these disciplines into his treatments.

Martin is gifted with an unbelievable sense of intuition and incorporates this into his treatments. He has helped me no end and when I go into him with a complaint about something, I usually come out cured. He also has fantastic homeopathic remedies that he has given me from time to time, which always do the job they are supposed to do. Using his kinesiology techniques, he can test me to see if I need a remedy or not and this is very beneficial because he only prescribes what's appropriate. I feel lucky and privileged to have been introduced to another perfect partner for my physical injuries. If I had met Martin immediately after my first car crash, I have no doubt that I would have been completely cured of all my injuries in no time at all. Due to the time lapse in meeting Michael and Martin after the orthopaedic interventions, it made it more difficult for them to treat me. It's an awful pity, but 'Better late than never.' At least now I can avail of what Martin has to offer. Martin is a lovely, gentle, unassuming man. He has no airs or graces, has no arrogance whatsoever and is extremely grounded, sensible and down to earth. He does what he does expertly and to perfection. He's not afraid to admit if he doesn't know something. His use of touch is guided by his intuition and it has a quality to it which makes it powerful and trustworthy. Despite the language barrier between us, because he does not speak much English and I have no German; I always feel that I am in really safe hands. This helps me to relax and benefit more from his treatments. I try to go to him four times a year which is what he recommended to me from the start. While I might be sore sometimes after the treatment, I always feel like a new woman when the soreness wears off. This is particularly motivating for my life. Martin is a very precious physical therapist and I have the great fortune to be in, what I consider, a perfect partnership with him.

Last but not least is my perfect partnership with Michael, the man Ann encouraged me to add to my support list who I've mentioned already. What can I say about Michael? He is one of the most fantastic men I know and I feel blessed to have him in my life. He's such a breath of fresh air, generous, kind, caring and vibrant. Michael is also one of the most interesting and creative men I have ever met. He has led an amazingly interesting life, with such a great variety of experiences. He has not only been involved in helping me but has also helped a huge number of other people in their lives. Michael, as I have said already, has been instrumental in guiding me along my academic route. He has been a key contributor in writing this book. What I love about him is his unique ability to turn something that appears daunting and terrifying in to real and genuine fun. I love the way he is always on the ball about things and I adore, adore, adore his amazing sense of humour and his great knack for mimicking. I cherish the hours and hours of laughter and craic that we have had over all my years of working with him and knowing him. I just love the way he understands me and we are always on the same wavelength. I appreciate his directness, his fearlessness, his courage, his sensitivity and tenderness in dealing with me. It undoubtedly has been the perfect partnership for me in healing so many areas of my life that were badly hampered by my deafness.

Analysing my plethora of perfect partnerships has made me realise, that while it's a great thing to be independent and able to manage by myself, it doesn't compare to the benefits

I have gained from being in relationships with other people. I can categorically say that my life would not have turned out the way it did if I had stumbled along on my own. It was through forming these relationships, that I succeeded in getting through those tough times in my life, all the traumas and misfortunes and turning my negatives in to positives. Without this turnaround it would not have been possible to achieve the impossible things that I have achieved or to become as successful. The partnerships faced me with the necessary challenges that I needed to succeed. They enriched my life twofold and taught me that life is too difficult and too tough to go it alone. Everybody needs somebody, everybody needs help. I learned that the more I opened myself to the help, let the help in, embraced it, appreciated it and was grateful for it, the more successful I became and the more I changed myself and the dysfunctional patterns and behaviours in my life. This helped me to grow and blossom into a more vibrant and creative person. These partnerships reduced my fear levels, dispelled my old negative beliefs about myself and helped me to draw on my suppressed courage, to take the risks I needed to take, in order to step into myself to reach and fulfill my potential. Collectively they turned out to be a most rewarding life experience and worth all the suffering I encountered along the way.

CHAPTER 50
The Core Qualities Required
To Achieve Success,
Reach The Pinnacle Of Perfection And
Make The Impossible Possible

'Don't practice until you can get it right, practice until you can't get it wrong'

Unknown.

There are a major number of elements that determine success. The sports athletes and the dancers that I have written about and indeed myself too, shared a common goal of striving for and ultimately achieving perfection, in order to become successful in our careers. Carefully examining each of the individuals concerned, I drew from them the list of core qualities that are common to each of them. Furthermore, I realised that the application of the core qualities, requires consistency and repetition over a sustained period of time in order to reach perfection. Aristotle once said, 'We are what we repeatedly do, excellence then, is not an act, it is a habit.'

I was at a basketball referee seminar in 2017 and the presenter during his presentation informed the group that it takes 9,000 repetitions of each action to be practised, in order to get the action right and ultimately perfect. He explained the importance of getting to the point where you don't have to think about the action anymore in your head. You perfect it to the extent that it becomes automatic. Results are primarily achieved through the repetition. 'It is in the repetition that change occurs.' This quote I can definitely relate to and I totally agree with it, because that's exactly what happened to me in my athletics and in my whole basketball playing and refereeing careers and particularly in my FIBA exam, when the mechanics were totally changed.

The great thing about these core qualities is, that they do not only apply to sports people or dancers, they apply to everyone and in any situation in life. Successful business-people, entrepreneurs, academics and many other genres would also benefit from these core qualities.

Learning

'Learning is a gift, even when 'Pain' is your teacher'
Michael Jordan

'Success is no accident. It is hard work, perseverance, learning, studying, sacrifice and most of all, love of what you are doing or learning to do.'
Pele

As you know by now, learning was a very traumatic experience for me in the formative years of my childhood, those long ten years of deafness and for more years into my adulthood. I was deprived of what the Irish education system had to offer and between the jigs and the reels, when I did the sums on it, it equated to approximately one quarter of my life. A stark statistic I think you will agree! I had not realised or made this connection in relation to my learning before. We know how important learning is and what a vital role it plays in our lives. Learning is a lifelong process, the basis of development for everything in life. I think humans have a natural hunger for learning, especially if learning is encouraged. The minute we come out of the womb our learning begins. Even in the womb we learn how to take our food and nourishment from the mother in order to survive the nine months of pregnancy. It is a natural and instinctive learning process. We learn to listen to the meaning of the sounds around us and when we can see, we begin to learn by observing and absorbing everything that is going on in our world. Without it, we cannot grow into healthy intelligent beings. We learn from everyone around us, our parents, family, teachers, friends, our environment, in fact we learn from everyone and everything we do or don't do. No matter how much we know about something there is always more to learn. With every year that passes, I learn more about refereeing as it develops and evolves with time. Learning is broad and expansive. Learning can be interesting and exciting like it was for me when I was learning about athletics and basketball and especially after I met Sean. Learning stimulates curiosity which allows us to open and expand our minds and our brains. My curiosity was suppressed by the times I lived in, by my mother and from being deaf. Curiosity ensures that we question. As a child growing up, I was not allowed to question anything. Children had to be seen and not heard. Questioning is another integral part of learning, as it is through asking questions and receiving answers, that we gain an understanding of what it is that we are trying to learn about. Even though I loved Miss O'Flynn in primary school, I was still terrified to ask questions, as my mother had taught me that I was cheeky when I did and I was not allowed to be cheeky or get above myself. Being deaf always made me afraid to ask questions because I always felt stupid and thick when I did, as it exposed my ignorance due to my lack of hearing.

In general, I think there are some things we can learn quite quickly and other things can take weeks, months and years to learn. I always felt I was a slow learner, which in my case came more from being deaf than from having a problem with my brain. Learning requires an openness, exploring new ideas and a willingness and a hunger to learn from others. It was only when I could hear fully again and when I met Bridget that I developed a hunger for learning. Bridget challenged me greatly on this front and it was thanks to her that I overcame my fear and developed an openness for it. She also taught me the value of exploring new ideas and not to be afraid of asking questions. Bridget always maintained that there was no such thing as a stupid or silly question. It was more stupid and silly *not* to ask the question. Bridget also maintained, that each learning experience and each learning curve that we went through in life, were important steps on the way to reaching our potential. She always believed that making mistakes and accepting failure were especially important in any learning environment, that the most valuable learning comes from making mistakes. She had a lovely phrase that she used, 'Mistakes are vital signposts and are the arrows that point us back into the direction we need to go, in order to relearn again, whatever it is we need to learn that we didn't learn in the first place.' According to Bridget making mistakes makes us aware of our weaknesses. She pointed out to me the importance of this in relation to my sport. She was oh so right! Overcoming my weaknesses and turning my weaknesses into strengths were of critical importance in developing me into the athlete, player and referee that I eventually became. Bridget was a great fan of Carl Jung, who said, 'The gold is in the shadow,' when he was referring to dealing with the unconscious. From a learning perspective Bridget believed that the mistakes we make are the same gold.

Through Bridget, Sean, Vivienne, Virginia, David, Ann and the two Michaels, I am delighted to say I have discovered a new part of myself, that now and only now loves learning, is curious and extremely interested about learning and, wait for it…. finds learning fun and enjoyable!!! Who would have ever thought that Ann's words from all those years ago, would have ever come true! Certainly not me! It just goes to show what is possible!

I now understand how the learning process helps us to grow in our wisdom as we get older. It is the culmination of the learning from mistakes and life's experiences, that help that wisdom to grow and deepen. The Native American Indians and the indigenous tribes in Africa have a fantastic respect for their elders. They recognise the gained knowledge of their elders and draw on it to help them to deal with difficult situations in their lives. The elders are the equivalent of Carl Jung's 'Gold in the Shadow.' I don't think that in Western society we are as good at respecting and learning from our elders. We do not appreciate their life's learned wisdom in the way that we should. We do not keep the elders physically and mentally stimulated enough, to be able to interact with them and draw from their wisdom. I saw a lot of this when my aunt hit her nineties. As in those tribes, those wise people pass on their knowledge and wisdom to the younger generation and this is an ever-evolving process. I was one of the lucky ones to have the benefit of so many wise people around me. Wise people who influenced me positively and helped me to achieve the successes I achieved. What I have learned from them is, that as I get older now, it is my turn to do the same for others.

So, what have I learned about learning? I have learned many things. I have learned that people learn in different ways. Some are visual learners, they learn by watching others, some learn by listening, some learn by being shown what to do and by actively doing what they are shown, some people learn by figuring things out for themselves. I learned that disabled people, while they can use these methods too, also use their senses differently to learn. For example, a blind person will learn by listening, by smelling, by tasting and by using touch. A deaf person will use their sense of smell, their eyes and touch to learn. A person in a wheelchair, who has no use of their limbs will use their eyes and if they can their voice to learn. The guy I worked with in the wheelchair who was non-verbal used his eyes and his body language in a very expressive way to communicate which for him was the most effective way to learn given his physical limitations.

I had a lovely experience recently in relation to learning. I went to my local hairdressers to get my hair done. There was only myself and one elderly lady there at the same time. The hairdresser and the elderly lady struck up a conversation in relation to baking cakes. It transpired that they both loved baking. As the conversation progressed it became clear that they were like two peas in a pod. They were exchanging tips and information regarding the ingredients for cakes and they were talking about cakes I had never heard of, never mind tasted. The cakes sounded only gorgeous, to die for cakes! My mouth was drooling listening to them, as I love cakes and I have an extremely sweet tooth. With every ingredient talked about, my mouth was watering more and more and I noticed myself suddenly becoming hungrier and hungrier. However, I was too interested and engrossed by their exchange to pay attention to these urges and I had to put my hunger pangs on hold.

I got the distinct impression that the cakes they were talking about were old-fashioned cakes from a long time ago. I got the shock of my life when the hairdresser told me that the elderly lady was 96 years old. I nearly fell off the chair I was sitting on. I could not believe it! I am not joking; she didn't look a day of 80 never mind 96. I told her so, in no uncertain terms, that she was the freshest and most *with it* 96-year-old I had ever seen in my life. I had never, ever, met a 96-year-old who was still baking and cooking like she was, never mind turning out these spectacular sounding cakes. Not only that, here she was still baking these awesome cakes and yapping away as coherently as myself and the hairdresser, able to describe everything to perfection and remember everything from donkey's years ago to the present day, not a bother on her. She took the biscuit altogether when she told us that she had still got some rose petal jam left from last summer that she had made. She described in full-blown detail, how she made the jam with the real live petals from the roses in her garden, how it turned pink and how delicious it tasted. After she was finished, I definitely wanted some of that! Jeepers tonight! I was totally gobsmacked! What a woman! An exceedingly rare woman, particularly by Irish standards I thought!

Anyway, getting back to the learning experience. I sat back in silence at the beginning, observing them and it was a pure pleasure and joy to watch them both sharing their ideas and experiences with each other. The joy and passion that exuded from them as they compared notes and gave each other tips about this, that and the other. I saw the excitement in them both, of dying to go home and try out what the other had recommended. I saw their openness and willingness to learn from each other and neither gave the impression of knowing more than the other. The hairdresser had shown us a photo of a communion cake that she had made for her grandson and it was magnificent. It was creatively decorated which made it stunning altogether. I watched the elderly lady looking at the photo with great interest, taking in every detail of the cake in the picture and genuinely, from the heart, complimenting the hairdresser on its magnificence. Her affirmation of the hairdresser's creative ability was beautiful, tender and full of warmth. It was clear to see that she could identify with and appreciate the hard work that went in to making that special cake.

Watching how they were learning from each other was a rich experience for me. Watching the back and forth interactions that were operating with such ease between them was lovely to watch. Even though I can't bake for nuts and I'm only mediocre on the cooking front, I thoroughly enjoyed the whole affair and felt lucky to have witnessed it and been a part of it. It was a coincidence that I was there because it was only due to a last-minute cancellation that I got the call to go in. It was obviously no coincidence; I was meant to be there. I left the hairdressers feeling that what I had witnessed is exactly what learning is all about. A powerful learning experience! A 96-year-old learning from a 50-year-old and vice versa.

Competitiveness

**'Competitive sports are played mainly on a five and
half inch court,
the space between your ears'**

Bobby Jones

I have spoken a lot already about competitiveness and
its importance, not just in sport but in life. It is an inherent
part of any competition of any nature. We have seen already
how genuine and true competitiveness is one of the main
components that produces top-class and world-class athletes
and performers. Competitiveness awakens an inner fire, an
inner desire that is driven by an inner spirit to be the best,
to do one's best and to reach one's potential. The athletes
and dancers I have referred to before had that inner fire and
desire, which drove them on to be the successful athletes
and dancers that they became. Athletics highlights the competitiveness in a crystal clear manner with the visible clock
or the measure of distance and drives people on to break records and to set new and higher standards. It caused the likes
of Michael Johnson and the others to go beyond the norm,
establish greater challenges and produce and perform at an
optimum level. This is something I too had to do in order to
achieve my Grade 1 and FIBA exams.

You may well ask, what did these people do and what did
I do to supercede our competitors? Well, first and foremost,
we had to draw on our talents, giftedness, knowledge and
experience and on the hours and hours that we had practised
and trained. Secondly, we had to develop and draw on our
self-belief, our self-confidence and our wisdom, to know we
could push beyond our limits knowing there is always more.

These latter ones were extremely difficult for me. Thirdly and imperatively, we had to draw on our mental and psychological abilities, which like the physical element, had to be practised and practised.

Sean maintained that competitiveness, when innate, always remains part of a person's system. He used to tell others that this was one of the reasons I was always consistent in my performances. Sean as a coach and referee, had the ability to expose his opponents' weaknesses and take full advantage of them. He also taught us how to improve on our weaknesses and how to limit the opponents' access to those weaknesses. He taught us that these were important components of competitiveness. We saw a clear example of this when he asked his guy to train with me. This guy exposed my weaknesses quite easily, but on the other hand, it took me a long time to figure his out. Thanks to him, I eventually improved on this area of my play. While I couldn't hide them from him, I did however learn how to limit my opponents' access to these weaknesses in my matches. This was especially beneficial when I was playing matches at the different and higher levels of competition. Trying to capitalise on our opponent's weaknesses can make us appear ruthless. This sounds like a bad thing, but in competition it's not. This is, in actual fact, a normal and natural part of development. Sean's guy was totally and utterly competitive with me, respecting and allowing the male part of me to emerge in my play. This proved to be a good thing. It toughened me up no end and gave me a huge advantage when playing against the tallest women in my leagues. After all, this guy was another four to five inches taller than the tallest woman I was up against. Beating them felt easy after him. Sean was also ruthless taking his *no help* stance. That in fact helped me to build up my own confidence in my ability to figure it out.

Sean taught us, that pure competitiveness is the ability to *Dig Deep* when it seems like there is nothing left to give. Well, by golly, did he and I do that as training buddies. We became masters at it. Sean and I were able to get the results we wanted, by our willingness to push ourselves to utter collapse, through using our power to expend every last ounce of energy and by sweating blood and tears in every training session. It was a strange thing and it sounds like a contradiction, but when the training session was over, that state of utter collapse transformed us in to more energetic beings afterwards and we bounced back to normal as if we had not suffered in the first place.

Some of the things I have learned about competitiveness is, that it enables consistency, hard work and intensive longing for the next training session or the next match. You would be dying for it. A solid and permanent foundation of physical, mental, emotional and spiritual connection to a deep inner wanting is of vital importance. This wanting, to want it more than everyone else, so much so, that you will do anything and I mean anything and do things that others would shy away from in order to get it, is the key to being purely competitive in an incredibly positive way. As Sean and I were hammering out our daily training sessions, our wanting became so hard-wired and fine-tuned, it isn't any wonder that we were both able to compete and succeed in achieving our FIBA awards. An example of competitiveness at its best.

Work Ethics

**'To be a champion, I think you have to see the big picture.
It's not about winning and losing;
It's about every day hard work and about thriving on a
challenge.
It's about embracing the pain that you'll experience at the
end of a race and not being afraid'**

Summer Sanders

Working hard and hard grafting is, undoubtedly, one of the core elements of success. The top athletes of the various sports agree on one thing. It is only through devoting the time it takes to perfect and hone the skills of your sport that you will become successful. This will enable you to reach the top of your game. It is widely recognised and agreed that dedication and commitment to working hard is central to being able to sustain consistency at all levels of training and competitions. This consistency is of vital importance. One of the best examples of it, is when we see the athletes at top events in the various sports such as the World Championships and the Olympics. They have to have the fitness and endurance to compete in the various preliminary rounds of the competition in order to progress to the quarter-finals, the semi-finals and final stages. For these stages there is a huge demand on the body to be able to work hard and to sustain working hard each day. As the elimination rounds progress the lower performing athletes are eliminated at each stage with only the top-level athletes remaining. Their poor bodies have to be able to peak and peak again, at the last three stages of the competition. This makes it essential for the athletes to maintain their physical ability to do that. These training hours and repetitions play a significant role in preparing the body to perform and peak at the optimum level required, throughout those consecutive days of competition. The athletes must work hard to raise the bar every day and to step-up to the next level of challenge. The poor ol' tired and sore muscles have to return the next day and not only repeat their excellent previous performances but have to dig deep to find and induce an increased effort, as the next level of competition is elevated in its standard.

When we look at the athletes I've mentioned, we see how each one managed to do this and how they had to suffer in the process. 'No pain no gain' as they say. I remember when I used to train and run around the grass track in Trinity College at lunchtime with the lads, Noel Carroll, the famous 800 metres Irish Runner, was always saying this to us when he would pass by. We knew in no uncertain terms what he meant and we agreed with him. Everyone was working in harmony, applying a very intensive work ethic to their training session. Everyone egged everyone else on. This sense of community spirit amongst us helped to lessen the pain that we were enduring.

Likewise, when I trained with Sean, our work ethic was second to none. There was no let-up, no cheating, no shirking, no whinging or whining. We just got stuck in and let rip despite the pain. We had to have immense mental application. What I discovered with Sean was, that mental tiredness is more difficult to recover from than physical tiredness. It is not easy to relax and quieten the mind, to reduce stress and worries and to stop the mind going over and over again the routines it's been trained for. The benefit of our silence helped us to increase our mental strength, kept our minds from getting too tired and saved us from all the distractive thinking. Physical tiredness and soreness on the other hand,

I learned, could be overcome easily with a cocktail of rest, sleep, healthy eating, massage, physiotherapy, icepacks and heat lotions. The physical side surrenders more easily than the mental side.

Another element of work ethic that comes in to play and is also particularly important is the emotional side. The emotional side needs to be proficient in order to contribute to the physical and mental aspects. As we all know, our feelings and emotions can be quite intense, especially in the lead-up to competitions; when the competition is over; and also during the post-mortem phase. Therefore, it is vitally important that athletes and performers can contain, express and release their emotions in accordance with the need and demands of their performances. We saw this when the referees were shocked at the FIBA exam, when they were informed that they would have to implement the new mechanics as part of their exams. All hell broke loose for a while and they had no choice but to calm their emotions down in order to apply themselves to the task at hand.

This FIBA experience showed me the importance of the compatibility and the balance between the interrelationship of the physical, mental and emotional aspects of ourselves as whole human beings. It taught me that this interrelationship is a key factor in determining excellence in performance. It helped me to realise that when we think of hard work, we immediately think of the physical pain only and can easily overlook the others. I was lucky that Sean taught me that hard work applies to the three elements. During our training sessions and when he was coaching the team, he gave equal attention to all three. He hammered it into us that this is what brings the most positive outcomes and results when competing to win.

Nadia Comaneci hit the nail on the head when she said, 'Hard work has made it easy. This is my secret. This is why I win.' Sean and I raised our hats to her.

Passion

**'Follow your passion, be prepared to work hard and sacrifice,
and, above all, don't let anyone limit your dreams.'**
Donovan Bailey

Passion is defined in the dictionary as, 'A strong feeling or emotion' and is synonymous with, Vehement, Desire, Love, Animated and Great Enthusiasm. As a person, I am full of strong feelings and emotions and for a long time now, I have no problem expressing or reacting from them – unlike in my childhood. I think in recent years I have been making up for lost time! It has served me well in helping me to achieve in my life. My vehemence as a child sparked an unshakeable determination, not to let my mother win completely. This vehemence I applied to my sports, to be the best player I could be, to achieve my Grade 1 and FIBA and to be the best in athletics I could, given my late entry in to it. There is no doubt that my desire to be loved fuelled my desire to be in the many amazing relationships I was in, including my friendships and professional relationships. It also gave me the ammunition to go against my mother, by throwing my heart and soul into my sports. When I got into basket-ball, I just loved, loved, loved playing the game and playing matches. My love for refereeing also grew as did my love for athletics. People often reflected back to me, how animated I was when talking about anything to do with basket-ball and athletics. I always watched the Olympics with great animation and enthusiasm. I was so absorbed in them, that everything else was put on hold until they were over. Two full animated and enthusiastic weeks which I truly revelled in! I used to think I was in heaven. I always approached my training sessions and competitions with the same fierce enthusiasm even if I was a bit nervous beforehand. Despite knowing I was going to suffer with Sean I still looked forward to our training sessions. I think I can safely say that I was the most enthusiastic player on the team. Behind my back as usual, Sean always told people I was a pleasure to coach and train with because I was always so enthusiastic. He also commented on the fact that regardless of how I was feeling or if I had an injury, my enthusiasm never diminished. Apparently, he loved and admired this quality in me. Passion is a key element of creativity. Without passion creativity is impossible. Sean and I certainly didn't lack that. Sean's passion drew him to notice and observe innovative techniques and strategies which enhanced him as a trainer, referee and coach. This ignited his excitement to try them out on us. Sean used to say, 'Passion overrides the fear of failure.'

These elements have undeniably made me a passionate person. My family and friends thought I was nuts and described me as someone who 'Eats, sleeps and drinks' basketball and athletics. I can see now that I was truly living for my passion. Passion is a fiery emotion. In my case it most certainly was exactly that. It is vibrant and full of energy and creates a great feeling of aliveness in a person. I always felt alive whenever I was running, training, playing or refereeing matches. Every cell, every fibre of my being was ignited, creating the vehemence and the strong feeling of desire and emotion that continually inspired me, propelled me forward and drove me on daily. It was the driving force behind my willingness to endure and suffer, day in and day out, the relentlessly difficult training sessions and hours of repetition, to achieve my desire to be my best. Passion results in a sense of wellbeing and my passion also provided me with a great sense of satisfaction. After training sessions and competitions, I always felt enormously satisfied and delighted with myself that I had done it and completed it. The harder it was, the more satisfied I felt.

My achievements and successes were the rewards of my passion. Passion has an infectious element to it. The physiological endorphins that passion releases, are what's known as pleasant and happy ones. People like to experience them over and over again and I was one of those people. Passion is an essential element that motivates people to aspire to and perfect an art. Madhur Falladia describes it beautifully when he says, 'To be fulfilled in life, to enjoy your life, you need work that is your passion, you need to love what you do.'

Personally, I found this to be absolutely true. Without passion and love, I would not have been able to endure the pain and suffering of tough training sessions, the disappointment of losing, to overcome the fear of failure or making mistakes. I would not have found it possible to cope with adversity or cope with the stress and pressure that performing demands of us. Passion at its best, encourages us to invest time and energy in what we love doing. It becomes part of our identity and helps us to develop intrinsic motivation and respond positively to external motivation. It brings a balance of harmony into our lives and into our performance. Certainly, in my case, my passion left me with a feeling of warmth that I could feel deep inside. This warmth created a buzz of excitement that vibrated and pulsed inside me, before bursting out into constructive action. My passion was extremely important in helping me to overcome the insurmountable obstacles that occurred in my Grade 1 and FIBA exams.

The Body

'The body is a marvellous machine...a chemical laboratory, a power-house.
Every movement, voluntary or involuntary, full of secrets and marvels!'
Theodore Herzl

I love, love, love this quote. The first time I read it, I immediately felt, 'That's me! Good grief, that's me.' Throughout my athletics and basketball careers people always, always referred to my body as a machine. They didn't use the word marvellous unfortunately because they thought I was mad in the head. But I always felt that my body was the most marvellous machine on the planet. My training with Sean increased this belief even further. I would go as far as to say his body and my body were indisputably two marvellous machines, two powerhouses of the highest order. I don't know much about the details of the chemistry of the body, but our intensive training regimes without any doubt, set in hectic action the chemical laboratories that lay within our bodies.

Most of the movements involved in our training routines were, of course, voluntary - I did choose to go there! There were many equally that were involuntary. Movements that stretched us to our full capacity and movements that took months to perfect, slowly but surely, unveiled the secrets our bodies had hidden away from us. But boy oh boy, did we marvel when those secrets crept out. Chin-ups on the bar for example, were one of the things I thought I would never be able to do. I felt I would never crack it. But lo and behold, the day that I did, I marvelled at myself and Sean too marvelled at me. A joint exercise that Sean and I struggled with was sitting against the wall. The pose is that of sitting against a wall as if you are sitting on a chair, but there is no chair underneath you. It puts huge pressure primarily on your thigh muscles and is an exercise to strengthen the thigh. The longer you sit against the wall your legs begin to quiver and shake and you feel a burning sensation which makes you want to jump up as fast as you can. But you cannot do this. You have to be careful to get up gently and slowly, to avoid sending the muscles into spasm. Sean and I started doing this for one minute, increasing it every day by one minute. We eventually got the time up to sixty minutes. We voluntarily increased the time by one minute. Our legs quivered involuntarily. We voluntarily stayed with it, but involuntarily wanted to jump up and stop. We practised this both alone and together, an achievement we both marvelled at. Sean and I shared and witnessed many other marvelling moments between us. It was one of the things that brought us closer. It united our spirits.

When I was away on my FIBA International Refereeing appointments the referees always had to get up early before breakfast to go running. I was always up the front with the lads and even ahead of them. They too always marvelled at my running capabilities. Without exception, they always described me as the *Running Machine* of the referees group. As we know, everyone's bodies are different in size and shape and in how they function. The refs who were head and shoulders above me, with their longer legs, were blown away at how this 'Half-Pint' could possibly keep up with them never mind pass them out. They were visibly shocked at the powerhouse my body was. Of course, me being me, I was delighted with the positive attention that they were bestowing on me and this made me appreciate and feel even more proud of my superb little body.

Over the years, one of the most important things I have learned, is that no matter who we are, we each have to work with the body we have, in order to refine it to meet the needs and requirements of our various activities. The body is an extraordinarily complex organism with a massive amount of functioning capabilities. It has a variety of ways of operating and an instinctive way of coping with problems that arise, for instance a weakened left leg will be supported and carried by the right leg and the back until it is better. This is central to enhancing sports performance.

The body has a natural ability to heal itself. The ancient Greek physician Hippocrates, born in 460 B.C., believed that sick people would benefit from rest and time away in order to let the body heal itself. He created what is seen as the first ever 'Hospital' for this self-healing purpose. Whenever something goes wrong in the body, other organs, for example the brain, as well as the blood system, the electrical and various fluid systems, gather and work in unison to protect and fix the sick, injured or damaged parts.

It is amazing too, how the mind can influence the body even though the body is deteriorating and may be close to death. People have been known to wait until a specific family member arrives at their bedside to say goodbye to them. The mind can then say, 'It's ok to go now.'

There is no underestimating the pure steely resilience, the power and strength and the tenacity of the body. It will fight until the bitter end. It has the constitution of an ox. Its ability to realign, readjust and reorganise itself is remarkable.

However, to get to know our own body is necessary. No two bodies are alike. What works for one body may not necessarily work for another. Sean and I were a good example of this. Whatever it was about us, we were both permanently on the same page during our training regimes. Even with our many differences, we gelled together and trained like clockwork.

Training schedules often refer to the importance of listening to one's body. Knowing when to cut back or readjust training schedules, when to revert to cross-training, when to rest and recover are considered vital components to success. It is said that learning and understanding the difference between backing off for good reason and being afraid to back off for fear of this becoming a bad habit is essential. Contrary to the *no pain no gain* theory, there are some who say, that pain and fatigue are signs that something is wrong. Listening to these signals is as imperative as extending training when the body is feeling good. Sean and I didn't adhere to these principles. These are more modern ways of thinking. Perhaps it was the old-fashioned school of thought which Sean came from, a former army man, that influenced him in developing and operating his own training techniques. The mindset from Sean's era was a much tougher mindset which did not entertain wimping out by submitting to pain or fatigue. The thinking was, if you were to avoid training because you were tired or in pain, sure you would never train! It is easy to find excuses and what better excuses than pain and fatigue. Strangely enough though, Sean and I seldom got injured and when we did we just carried on. We didn't allow the injury to stop us. We found alternative methods to keep our training programmes intact. Nowadays, I am sure, the current generation would be horrified at such an approach. But I honestly have to say that it did not do us any harm. I don't think poor ol' Sean would be able to fathom out the modern mindset of today's generation. He would have been driven nuts by what he would see as a lack of commitment, dedication, 'Mollycoddling and wrapping up in cotton wool.'

When I was trying to learn more about dancing and the body, I read some articles by Stephanie Burg, a professional ballerina. She stressed the importance of fuelling the body with high quality foods, eating nutritiously and focusing on the good in ourselves. However, she told a story about herself growing up and training to become a ballerina. She spent many hours in front of the mirror every day judging and criticising everything about herself, focusing only on the negative aspects of her physique and movements. She did it to such an extent, that she realised one day, that if you stare at anything long enough you will find its flaws. This realisation suddenly made her *cop on* to herself, see her mistake and notice what she was failing to see as a result of this. Her body was a strong capable body and the beauty her body was creating through her movements was quite astonishing. By changing her thinking and focusing on the good, she was able to befriend her body in a new way, radiate more beauty through her body and bring it in to her dance performances.

I have always loved my body. I think this is due to the influence that playing sports and meeting Sean had on me. Being the tomboy and being heavily involved in sports prevented me from getting caught up in the figure consciousness, wearing make-up, wearing high heels and the *shop till you drop* syndrome that a lot of women get stuck in. The idea of Botox, lip jobs, face lifts, tummy tucks etcetera would be an absolute and utter betrayal, a rejection of the highest order to what I consider my amazing body. My body has been the most loyal and faithful body to me throughout my years and years of sport. A lifetime in fact, of the seriously challenging and sometimes impossible demands that I placed on it. The last physiological sports testing that I had a few years ago revealed that my body was sixteen years younger than its age. How could I possibly disrespect or disregard this? I would feel like a hypocrite and a traitor to myself.

While I appreciate and understand that the aging process is a difficult one, I look forward to seeing how my body copes with this process. I would hope to age in a graceful manner. I trust my body implicitly that it will be as resilient to old age as it has been during my whole life until now. The impact of the car crashes of course, will have repercussions which might make my aging process more difficult. Nevertheless, I am hopeful that my body will pass the test of this reality. I will continue to do what I have always done to assist this future process.

Although people slag me by referring to me as Superwoman, I have always been proud of my body's capabilities to earn and somehow deserve this title, even in jest. I marvel and will continue to marvel into the future at my body's capacity to deal with the effect that the car crashes have had on it. This probably has been my body's second greatest achievement after my success in athletics and my basketball playing careers and refereeing. Every day I thank my body for its many accomplishments.

Psychological Strength

**'Mental Toughness; Once an athlete has mastered all the
technical and physical qualities required to be successful
on the international circuit,
then success is 10 per cent physical and
90 per cent mental'**
Judo Training Development

It seems like everything we do is primarily on the physical level. We start our day by getting out of the bed, showering, dressing ourselves, preparing and eating our breakfast, preparing our lunch, heading off to work, some walking, cycling or running. We wave to friends, scratch our knees, pick things up off the floor and sweep it. We successfully do these things. So where does this meagre 10 per cent come from?

For those of us who do not want to get out of bed in the morning, we want to roll over for those extra five minutes of sleep when that bloomin' alarm goes off. But it is the mind that tells the body to get up, you must go to work and insists you do in spite of the mind also telling you to stay put. The mind balances one option against the other and comes to a decision. It is the mind that decides what clothes to wear, thinking about what the weather is like, what you will be doing that day, who you are going to meet, what sort of mood you are in. Your mind decides what to eat for breakfast .... and so on and so forth.

Psychology plays a constant role in our ordinary everyday life. We often do not realise the full extent of it. It is a significant part of our relationships. The mind is continuously at play in trying to figure out the other person and trying to read the other's mind. We even try to access the most convenient and best way to get around the other person, to get what we want or to get our own way!!! Some people may even go as far as creating their own alternative reality in order to avoid their discomfort with the pressure of everyday life and relationships.

Psychology in sports and performances, while active in the same way, perhaps has a more definitive role. In order to achieve the mind's long-term goals, the mind has to be more focused and more concentrated on the immediate task at hand. In both fields nowadays, it plays a different and more vital role than it did in years gone by. Its importance has only been recognised in recent years. In ancient times preceding Hippocrates, it was unheard of to pay any attention to this area. The focus was purely on physical application and training methods. In the good old times, when an athlete had true grit and determination, the ability to push themselves that extra bit in order to win an event, it was considered as part of the physical effort. There was no credit given to the strength required by the mind for this. Nowadays, due to the change in psychological thinking and knowledge, we now know that that grit and determination was, in fact, mental and emotional application, pure psychological strength. We also know now that this can be worked on and developed through exercising the mind. From physical training we know that the body has many muscles that need to be exercised, including the brain and the fact that it too responds well to exercise. Combining both enhances performances.

With the advancement in technology and psychology, a new world of possibilities for performance enhancement has opened up. It is now widely accepted amongst athletes worldwide, that connection between physical, emotional and mental aspects of a person are interlinked. The more balanced the three are, the better the results and the better it is for overall success in performance.

The athletes and dancers I have mentioned, including Sean and I, were not lucky enough to have the benefit of this psychology. We just had to muddle along in our own way as best we could and when things went against us which they did naturally, we had to carry on regardless. Whenever we fell down, we just had to pick up the pieces, get up again and carry on. The thinking was, 'Get over yourself and just get on with it.' What tough and hardy annuals we were!

It is hard to believe that nowadays everything has completely changed. Ancient athletes would not understand or recognise these changes, nor the complexity that lies behind these new theories. In those days it was black and white, extremely clear and straightforward. In order to reach optimal performance at elite level, ancient athletes would have considered the six following qualities as essential to a person's character: the ability to deal with and overcome the fear of failure; courage to take risks; the ability to respect an opponent's skills level; physical strengths while still maintaining one's own self-confidence and self-belief; the ability to identify and improve one's own weaknesses; the ability and desire to accept and step-up to challenges and raise the bar no matter how difficult the demand.

While these six qualities would still apply nowadays, there is now the extra added bonus of the current psychological research and knowledge. Significant importance on the emotional level is given to self-awareness, the importance of deciphering between being in control in general, learning to control the emotional self and learning to regulate stress levels. The same applies to staying present and focusing on the task at hand in the present moment, rather than becoming excessively concerned in achieving the end result. On the physical level it is vital to practise the basic skills and techniques repeatedly until you become adept at performing these skills and techniques instinctively. It is important to correct weaknesses and maximise strengths. On the mental level, new techniques for pre-game preparation such as using imagery skills, concentration and relaxation techniques have been devised. The idea is that these psychological tips put the onus on the athlete to take responsibility for their own performance and to accept the outcome and results.

If we compare and contrast the current tips to my olden days, I think many of them were unknowingly present but were not formulated with the consciousness of today's suite of psychological tools. The mental techniques in relation to pre-game preparation were also definitely not in vogue. However, this did not deter athletes from taking full responsibility for themselves and their performances. On the contrary, the athletes of those times, if anything, were responsible in a different way, through their grit and determination, due to the era they lived in.

I'm not sure and actually I don't know if Sean and I would have benefitted a whole lot from the current psychological inputs. Perhaps, like the other athletes I have spoken about, we were just made of 'Good Stuff.' Psychologically our mental strength was like Mt. Everest and our courage was as deep as the ocean. I distinctly remember over the years training with Sean, that my courage spurred on his courage and equally his courage spurred on mine. This was a constant process that resulted in our courage developing and growing with every year of training that passed. I must thank Sean, for the astonishing assistance he gave me, the remarkable companion he always was to me and I will be forever indebted to him.

Creativity

'Creativity is intelligence having fun'
Albert Einstein

'Creativity is like freedom: once you taste it, you cannot live without it. It is a transformative force, enhancing self-esteem and self-empowerment.'
Natalie Rogers

I love this quote by Albert Einstein. It just hits the nail on the head. The idea of intelligence having fun is a lovely idea, because more often than not, we associate intelligence with more serious things, the most common being academic intelligence. Leaving Certificate students are constantly using their intelligence in order to achieve their 600 points or as close to that as they can get in their Leaving Certificate exams. Not much fun in that!!!

Primary school children are still given a lot of permission to have fun while exploring their creativity. Children have an innate ability to be creative and like to explore new ideas. It is their way of making sense of the world. Children have vivid imaginations which they are not afraid to use. As they get older, they become the daydreamers looking out the window, their minds drifting off into some imaginary place. They can also be extra active and playful as they like to try out what their imaginations are dreaming up. They are the people in groups who don't hold back and who like taking risks trying out their ideas. You do not see these people hiding in the corner. No, they are out there quite happily trying to transfer their creativity into artistic expression in sport or dance or whatever it is they are interested in. People who retain the ability to use and apply their creativity will have an advantage over their other competitors. We saw in the Play chapter how the creativity in the various games we played as children, developed us in different ways and prepared us to become proficient sports people in later life. We saw how our imaginations got stimulated, which allowed us to invent and create new games on a regular basis. We saw how the expression of our creativity through playing our games, gave us hours and hours of great fun and enjoyment and kept our bodies and minds occupied in an extremely healthy way. Unlike the kids of today, we *never* got bored.

Michael Johnson applied innovative mental techniques to his running by creating the Zone for himself. This helped him to outwit his opponents psychologically. Michael Jordan was extremely creative in developing athletic feats that enabled him to develop new skills in jumping and twisting. This made him impossible to mark as a player and earned him the title of 'Slam-Dunk' champion on numerous occasions. Nadia Comaneci produced amazing choreographies which were novel, new and exciting to her gymnastic performances. It was these creative ideas which made her excel on the parallel bars, the beam and the floor, giving her an advantage over her fellow competitors. Without her creative passion she would never have scored the perfect 10.

Dancing is another area where creativity and artistic expression are of vital importance to outstanding performances. Margot Fonteyn and Rudolph Nureyev's creative and innovative choreographies transformed ballet in the same way that Nadia Comaneci transformed gymnastics. Nureyev, in comparison to his male contemporaries, was constantly on the lookout for new and novel ideas to include in his ballet routines in order to shock and stimulate his audiences. His observations of other people seemed to stir his own creative mind even further. It sparked in him an even greater eagerness to take risks to explore his own creativity at a much broader level. This enhanced his own dancing and his dance partnership with Fonteyn and brought an expansiveness in to their creativity as a team, that made them the unique and special duo that they became in their times.

Creativity is something that evolves from a curious mind. It sees things from different perspectives as opposed to being stuck to one thing. It creates an openness to discuss more and to play around with things in a variety of ways. Creativity can lead to innovative thinking. It is developed and stimulated by seeking new experiences as much as possible. Nureyev explored the characters of other people paying attention to everything around him - people, situations, feelings, actions and anything else he observed. This approach enabled him to stand back and notice where movements or posture for example, could be improved. Using this approach, new ideas that emerge can be worked with and tried out, not being afraid to alter and re-alter until you come up with something that is to your complete and utter satisfaction. This approach brought Nureyev's dancing to a completely new level.

This is something I did a lot as a referee as I have explained earlier, using the *buffet* idea that we were taught by FIBA. Sean did the same when he went away reffing and watched the coaches doing their training sessions with their teams. He brought it back to try it out on us – we were the guinea pigs – lucky us – though it did not feel like that to us at the time, when we were demented by the whole thing! Sean was more creative and innovative in his training sessions than I gave him credit for. It was only when Ann pointed this out to me, that I began to appreciate this aspect of Sean properly. It was through eventually appreciating this in Sean that I was able to pass it on to others myself.

Sean explained to us that creative people recognise, understand and accept that when doing anything new, everything is trial and error. It takes much time and many tries to enable ideas to develop to fruition. Each try, if unsuccessful, is not considered a failure, it is considered the route to the next try. The more you try the more likely you are to eventually succeed. He often used to tell us that if you keep catching the rebound on a missed shot for the basket and you keep throwing the ball up at the basket, the ball will eventually go in. It means that despite the bad shooting, based on the law of averages, a fluke of sorts will happen, which makes it inevitable for the ball to enter the basket.

Talent And Genetics

'Mastery is not a question of genetics, of luck,
but of following your natural inclinations
and the deep desires that stirs you from within'
Robert Greene

'A really great talent finds its happiness in execution'
Johann Wolfgang Van Goethe

Talent and genetics always pose interesting questions and provoke interesting discussions in sport. Do talent and genetics play a role in elitism in sport and dance? Are we born with talent? Is it developed by our experiences, environment and personal application? Is it nature versus nurture? Is it genetics versus environment? Does everyone have natural ability? If yes, what does it take to unveil that talent? There are a variety of schools of thought on this topic. Psychologist Drew Bailey is of the opinion that, 'Without both genes and environment there are no outcomes.'

Talent is defined as Natural Ability or Natural Aptitude or Skill. The comment 'What did you expect? He/she has talent' is often regarded as a dismissive or throwaway comment. I think that the phrase 'Hard work beats talent when talent fails to work hard' is a more accurate viewpoint. There are a lot of people who purport to have talent, but they don't do anything with it and end up wasting their talent. There is no point in having talent unless you make use of it. Rudolph Nureyev is a prime example of someone who recognised his own talent and made excellent use of it.

Usain Bolt, Olympian Gold medalist, is a typical example of this. Apparently at a young age he showed natural talent for sprinting and when he ran races, he beat a few people. He stopped trying and began losing his races. This boosted the other boys' confidence to such an extent, that not only did they beat him, but they also got to the point where they beat him easily. His lack of hard work and effort resulted in him declining further and further. It was only when he realised this, started getting serious again and started applying himself physically, mentally and emotionally to his training, that he eventually rose to the top of his field. This is a good example of 'Talent alone does not pay off or breed champions.'

Tim Stevenson, sportswriter, backs up the Usain Bolt experience. He believes that neither are solely responsible. He believes 'You have to apply yourself to training and everything else that goes with it. You have to train hard, eat well, recover effectively and surround yourself with great people. The better you can do all those things the more likely you are to be successful. If you don't have the best genetics, you are going to have to work harder than those that do, if you are lucky enough to be naturally gifted with the right body type and physiology, well you better be working hard, otherwise you might find yourself getting beaten.'

Another athlete, Andy Turner, who was a British 110 metre hurdler said of himself, that he was not the most talented or gifted athlete at the hurdles. However, he gave his training his best effort and grafted hard to achieve his dream of becoming a national champion. He was convinced that working hard helped him to maximise whatever potential he had that lay within his physiology. He knew exactly what he wanted and was determined to do whatever he could to prevent anything getting in the way of him achieving his dream. He believed that it was a futile exercise to get caught up in the ideas put forward in relation to genetics and exposure to environment. He maintained that it is only when you have maximised the opportunities presented to you that you will truly know what capabilities lie within you. He was adamant that you must be fully committed to achieving your dreams and working hard for it. But above all, he stipulated, that you have to want it – really want it.

I must say that on this topic, I readily agree with Tim Stevenson and Andy Turner. My own experience throughout my own athletics and basketball careers were exactly what they described. Like Andy, I too never considered myself to be particularly talented in relation to sports. There was certainly no genetics from my family passed on to me. When I traced back my family background there wasn't even one person who had partaken in sports, never mind achieved anything in sports. I was constantly being told that I was the *black sheep of the family,* 'I don't know where we got you from' or 'You're the odd one out.' The family genuinely had no clue whatsoever as to what the hell possessed me to take up sports.

When I started playing basketball it did seem as if I had a natural flair for it. But I think to be honest, that as I have explained already in the Play chapter, it was more to do with the fact that the games I had played as a child primed me for my transition to basketball. In the same way, I most definitely did not have a talent for athletics. Despite the athletics coach in secondary school in Eccles Street spotting me and picking me out, I always felt I laboured a lot more when running than in basketball. Maybe I did have some flair for it and I didn't see it myself, but maybe also it was the individual element to it that made it seem more of a struggle and seemed harder to me. While I always worked extremely hard in my basketball training, I always felt that the athletics training was 10 times tougher.

What else can we say about talent and genetics? Well, with the standard of competition rising every year, every two years in the World Championships and every four years in the Olympics and World Cup competitions, the bar is constantly being raised and times are becoming faster and faster. This elevation in competitive performance has been contributed to by the amount of scientific and psychological intervention that has developed over recent years but, as Michael Jordan says, 'Everybody has talent, but ability takes hard work.' This means that physical prowess, talent and genetics no longer stand alone. These interventions which are considered as extra revolutionary are undoubtedly according to reports, enhancing competition performances.

I remember when Sean and I were training, the question of talent or genetics never arose. It was all hard work, pure grafting, biting the bullet, getting stuck in and go, go, go. If we had talent, we used it. Everything was mixed in together. It was akin to baking a cake. You must mix the ingredients together in a bowl before you put the cake in the oven to bake. That's what we did. We put all our ingredients into the bowl, not always realising what ingredients we were using!!

Luck

'I'm a great believer in luck, and I find the harder I work the more I have of it'
Thomas Jefferson

'We all need a bit of luck' as people say. Some people are luckier than others. Luck can be either good or bad. Being in the right place at the right time is regarded as good fortune. Equally, being in the wrong place at the wrong time is considered to be misfortunate or bad luck and as in the case of my two car crashes, bad luck twice!!! How unlucky is that!!!

Nureyev was lucky that he managed to defect from Russia formerly known as the U.S.S.R. It wasn't easy, he made it by the skin of his teeth. However, he was also unlucky because his defection meant that he could not return to Russia to see his family until nearly 30 years later when he received a special dispensation from the authorities allowing him to return to see his dying mother. Were Nureyev and Fonteyn lucky that they met each other? Was it fate or did they meet by chance?

Some people say that we make our own luck. If luck is success, we know from the people I have spoken about that success is a result of extremely hard work. Therefore, does it follow that it is through this extremely hard work that we make our own luck? Whether it is in sport or in life in general, are we unknowingly working towards and creating our own luck?

People regularly describe meeting people in the supermarket by *chance*, meeting somebody in town by chance and 'I ran into so-and-so yesterday, by chance when I was walking in the park.' It can happen in sport, in work, through contacts, that somebody is unexpectedly seen doing something important by someone by chance. Being watched or being observed by chance can open up amazing and incredible opportunities in life for people. Chance, however, requires taking the chances that come your way in life, taking opportunities that are presented to you as opposed to rejecting those opportunities. It is important to be conscious of what's going on around you and be self-aware in order to be able to take advantage of a situation if good luck comes your way. When Michael Johnson was struck down by food poisoning a fortnight before the 1992 Olympics in Barcelona, this provided an opportunity for his opponents to take advantage of his illness. However, while we might consider that this was a stroke of luck for his opponents, which they undoubtedly must have felt, they still had to work hard to win the race by surpassing him. They had to seize the opportunity. Luck alone was not sufficient. It often happens in sport and in life that things such as illness, absence and injury can provide unexpected opportunities to others to capitalise on.

There is an amazing story about an amateur photographer called Tony Duffy, who became a multi-millionaire after capturing the one and only photograph of the American, Bob Beamon, smashing the Olympic and World Record for the long jump in the 1968 Mexico Olympics. This Olympic Record still stands to this day. Beamon's jump was a special jump in 1968 and a special jump right now. It was one of those *perfect* jumps when everything came together at the right moment. Beamon had great fortune on his side that the weather conditions for jumping were perfect for setting official records. Luck was on his side, although it was on everyone else's side too. Beamon's jump was longer than the electronic measuring device could record. The whole distance of the jump and a measuring tape had to be used for the final calculations. The World Record was obliterated by almost two feet. The matching photograph by Tony Duffy was equally astounding, as he was the only photographer to catch Beamon at peak height head-on.

The story goes.... Duffy was on holidays attending the Olympics. He decided to take a stroll one day and casually walked into the Athlete's village which was off-limits to him. During his stroll around he fell upon a group of people discussing the long jump competition, evaluating the participants and their current jumping form. They analysed all the participants and when it came to Bob Beamon, Ralph Boston, the then current co-holder of the World Record, commented on Beamon saying, 'Don't get him riled up because he's liable to jump out of the fucking pit.' Duffy immediately made a mental note of this remark thinking, 'Wow, this Beamon must be worth watching.' On the day of the competition, he sneaked into the Athlete's Village again, waved his camera at the guards and walked into the stadium alongside the competitors. The long jump was the first event on the afternoon programme and as the athletes began their warm-up routines, Duffy noticed that the stadium was slow to fill. He made his way past the security guards and sat in the front row where he could be perfectly positioned to get a head-on shot of the jumpers as they leaped towards him. Duffy had positioned himself at the prime place near a low railing and was able to aim his camera over the railing just 50 feet away from the pit. He photographed just one frame of the jump. Duffy had luck on his side as he was practically the only photographer stationed at the long jump pit because the 400 metres track finals were scheduled to begin around the same time. This is also what made the photograph extra-special because few people actually saw Bob Beamon breaking the record. Duffy's photo was named, 'The only photo that mattered.' One amateur photograph which surpassed the photographs of the professional photographers due to his superb positioning, changed the course of Tony Duffy's life forever.

Was that luck? Was it good fortune? Was it chance? Well, let us analyse the element of Tony Duffy's luck here. He most certainly was in the right place at the right time. But was it that or was it the fact that he had followed his own sense of adventure by going into the athletes' village which was off-limits, not only once but twice? Was it by chance that he was the *Bold Boy* in doing that, doing something he should not have done? Was he being guided to take this risk? We cannot deny the risk he took – twice. We often hear people saying, 'I don't know what made me do that, I just had to do it.' Was this the case? There are many people who wouldn't dare to do or dream of doing what Tony Duffy did. If he had not done this in the first place, he wouldn't have overheard that conversation about Beamon and probably, like everyone else, would have chosen the 400 metres track final instead. After all, the 400 metres track event is one of the main highlights of the Olympic Games. So, is this how Duffy made his own luck? He went on to make a mental note of the remark he overheard and followed his instinct. He trusted himself and his hunch in relation to choosing which event to photograph. How many times in life do we fail to trust ourselves, ignore our gut instinct and ignore our intuition? Tony Duffy didn't do this. Having taken the photo he had no concept of what he had photographed. It was only after he got the photo developed a couple of days later, that he realised what he had achieved was truly monumental. It turned out to be a spectacular shot, showing Beamon's amazing athleticism in the leap, the true grit and determination on his face whilst suspended as if frozen in mid-air, just as Ralph Boston prophesised jumping out of the 'Fucking Pit.' The shot was even more significant because it was captured on a standard camera as opposed to a high-tech professional camera.

Once the photo hit the media, magazines and posters throughout the world, Duffy's credentials as a photographer became acclaimed. Here he was, a simple man, out taking pictures for pleasure, never for one moment thinking or contemplating his potential as a professional photographer. Duffy's photo was a perfect example of Dorothea Lang's quote, 'Photography takes an instant out of time, altering life by holding it still.' Two lives were altered. Bob Beamon did Duffy a favour and Duffy returned the compliment. The perfect jump and the perfect shot of the perfect jump, made them both famous and successful. Tony Duffy's photo catapulted him in to a new and unexpected career, which made him so successful that he became a multi-millionaire. Not bad!

How did luck play out in my life? Well let's start with the bad luck and end on a positive note with the good luck. 'That which happens to a person' certainly happened to me in bucket loads. I probably could write a book for each of the years of my life on that score. Being born into the family I was born into certainly wasn't lucky for me. Having a mother who was not equipped mentally and emotionally to mother her children properly was most unfortunate. Having an unreliable father who shirked his responsibilities and did not take my mother to task was disastrous. Falling down the stairs and going from being able to hear to becoming deaf was a nightmare. Those formative years from 4 to 14 and the adult years that followed, which were impacted by this incident were another nightmare. Having the relationships of the two loves of my life destroyed by my mother's interference, was probably on a par with being deaf. Both of those losses changed the course of my life completely. Eventually, after picking myself up and recovering from that, to be hit with the two car crashes and the six losses that accompanied them, not to mention the serious injuries I sustained, was an inconceivable and overwhelming amount of bad luck. The misfortune after misfortune of that two-year period, felt like a lifetime of pure and utter agony. Unlucky, bad luck, misfortune do not remotely cover that horrifying list.

On the positive side, I was lucky that Dr. Johnson stayed with me throughout my years of deafness, that he cured me and that I ended up having a loving and special relationship with him. I was extremely fortunate to have a creative, patient, tolerant and kind person in Miss O'Flynn, my primary school teacher. Meeting Sr. Patricia and being introduced to the game of basketball most definitely was a pivotal turning point in my life at that vulnerable age. Continuing my basketball career in Eccles Street School and being introduced to athletics built on Sr. Patricia's foundation. Of course, being introduced to Haroldites Basketball Club and Sean, vitally cocooned me over a long period of time from many years of difficult home life. Most importantly, my training and personal relationship with Sean was one of the highlights of my life. His support and encouragement to follow my dream of becoming a Grade 1 and FIBA referee was extraordinary. His pride in me when I succeeded in making history in both was precious. That is a priceless memory I can treasure for the rest of my life.

Meeting Bridget and the 23 years of love that I experienced with her, along with her wisdom, fun and laughter was another high point in my life. My wonderful working and personal relationship with Vivienne and friendship of

45 years, has been absolutely fantastic and has taught me how to value and appreciate loyalty. My lucky introduction to Virginia, the bereavement counsellor, who was nothing less than gorgeous and who got me over the first hump in my bereavement process was inspirational. Ann, who gave me everything that nobody else could give me, was the most significant person and influence in my personal life, especially after the overwhelming amount of misfortune and bad luck in that awful two-year period. If it wasn't for her, I wouldn't be here or able to write this book today. That introduction was most definitely the luckiest one of all. Closely following Ann came David, who filled Ann's shoes beautifully. There's no doubt that Ann would have applauded David's interventions and would have regarded them as good as her own. I can't forget Michael Pita, whose incredible expertise helped me to regain my mobility and prevented me from ending up in a wheelchair after the second car crash and who continues to keep me mobile to this day. Last but not least, my great fortune in meeting Michael – the wonderful, creative, fun-loving Michael, whose support, inspiration and invaluable assistance in writing this book, has given us both many, many hours of laughter and joy.

I have been incredibly lucky in my life being blessed with a rich blend of many friends, from different walks of life, outside my sports career, whom I haven't included in this book. They too, like the other people, have had such a huge positive impact on my life. Despite my sports fanaticism and some of them thinking I was pure nuts in the head, they still valued and appreciated that aspect of me as a person. Regardless of coming from different walks of life, the one thing we all have in common is our strong sense of self and character. While I had my teammates in the basketball, these friends are my teammates in life.

Courage

'I don't run away from a challenge because I am afraid. Instead, I run toward it because the only way to escape fear is to trample it beneath your feet.'

Nadia Comaneci

The cowboy and Indian films we used to watch growing up, both in the picture house and on T.V., were stories of courage. The good cowboys and good Indians went to great lengths to demonstrate their courage in these pictures. They were the *Brave* ones, the *Heroes*. The bad guys however, were the *Cowards*, *Yellow Bellies* and were often described as having yellow streaks down their backs. The cowards were despised and nobody wanted to be associated with them.

The good guys were always trustworthy men of honour, who had integrity, always told the truth, admitted their mistakes and always put their hand up to own up whenever they did any wrong. They could look everyone straight in the eye. They were men who took responsibility for their own actions and accepted the consequences. When they got a slap on the cheek which they knew they deserved, they were able to turn the other cheek as a sign of acknowledgement that what they got was indeed what they deserved. It took courage to do this. It was considered chivalrous. The good guys had backbone and guts.

The bad guys on the other hand, were the mean, cruel, underhand guys. They always had a sneaky look around the eyes. You could not trust them as far as you could throw them and that wouldn't be far. They couldn't look anyone straight in the eye. They told lies and never took responsibility for their actions. They put the blame on everyone else and had a great knack of getting other people or at minimum trying to get other people, especially the good guys, into trouble. Selfishness, lack of honour and integrity and lack of concern for others were their character traits. They had no guts. They were spineless. While watching these guys in action in the picture, we would be squirming and coiling up in our seats looking at them. They were horribly despicable you detested everything about them. They made you cringe and you just wanted to get as far away from them as you possibly could. People watching in the picture house often got so caught up in the picture, that they would often *boo* the bad guys and clap and cheer the good guys.

I used to love the atmosphere in the picture house. It was electric because everyone took these values the characters were playing to heart. My nana used to take my brother and I to the pictures twice a week, which meant these values were instilled and drummed into us. When we would come out after the pictures were over, my nana would talk about the pictures and stress even further the importance of the morals and values that had been shown to us through the pictures. She had a big thing about not being a coward. 'Nobody likes a coward,' she would tell us. 'Cowards don't have friends and can't get jobs.' She told us that even though we might get punished for owning up and telling the truth, by God, we would be punished a hundred times more if we told a lie. Lies were despicable and intolerable. It was undeniably better to have courage and to tell the truth. Nowadays, it's not cowboy and Indian films, but the same message of good versus bad comes through in Star Wars, Harry Potter, Home Alone and countless other childrens' films.

My nana used to talk about courage to us and tell us how important it was to have courage. According to her, everything in life depended on it and the more courage you had the better your life would be. When I started playing basketball in primary school, she always affirmed my courage in this and kept encouraging me to do that. She admired my courage in standing firm in my conviction to follow my basketball vision, despite the opposition from the rest of the family. She pointed out that I would have to dig deep inside myself, to find the strength and courage to be willing to stand alone. She told me to stay true to the knowledge that what I was doing was the right thing for me. 'Don't let anyone stop you,' she said to me one day after we came out of the pictures. 'You have to have the courage to do what the good guys did in there today. Remember them and you will do it.'

As soon as I made up my mind to go for my Grade 1 and FIBA awards, I knew it was going to take a lot of courage to face and overcome the significant obstacles that were ahead of me. Training with Sean took courage too, as he was such a tough taskmaster and the fact that he practised what he preached and led by example himself, made training with him all the tougher. There was no such a thing as saying to Sean, 'Let me see you doing what you're expecting me to do. I bet you can't do that,' because of course he could always do it.

As I went up the grades in refereeing, the higher I went the more I realised that courage was an important quality to have. The referee had a responsibility to the players and to the game, to act on their integrity and make the correct calls at the correct time. Those tough calls, at the most critical stages of the games, were exceptionally important to call. There was no shirking out. You had to be the *Good Ref* just like the cowboys, which would result in one team liking you, while at the same time be despised like the *Bad Guys* by the other team for calling against them. A tricky situation to be in. You could hang up your whistle if you had a need to be liked or popular with everyone, because that was never going to happen. Behaving in such a manner would most definitely compromise your integrity. I learned many a lesson on that one from observing other people refereeing over the years.

The message from the pictures were always crystal clear. Take action and learn. This included learning from your mistakes. When you fail and have setbacks, get up and start again. Disappointments are inevitable. Personal courage and strength separate the good guys from the bad guys. In life that means it sets one apart from one's peers and competitors. Courage ensures that you get over the line just as the good guys always did by the end of the picture. Courage conquers all things. Courage can give strength to the body, motivate you to reach for the stars. We each have the potential for courage. You must tap into it by overriding the fear. Courage is something that you can work on and develop. One step of courage leads to the next step. Courage leads to victory, your victory. It effects the people around you in a positive way. The good cowboys and Indians in the pictures were good role models. They taught us the difference between bravery and cowardice. They taught us what courage is truly about. The only thing we need to do is to follow their example, take their lead and bring it in to our own lives. Then and only then can our courage touch the lives of others.

Daring Greatly

It is not the critic who counts; not the man
who points out how the strong man
stumbles, or where the doer of deeds could
have done them better. The credit belongs
to the man who is actually in the arena,
whose face is marred by dust and sweat and
blood; who strives valiantly; who errs, who
comes short again and again, because there
is no effort without error and shortcoming;
but who does actually strive to do the deeds;
who knows great enthusiasms, the great
devotions; who spends himself in a worthy
cause; who at the best, knows in the end the
triumph of high achievement, and who at
the worst, if he fails, at least fails while
daring greatly, so that his place shall never
be with those cold and timid souls who
neither know victory nor defeat.

Theodore Roosevelt
'Citizenship In A Republic'

Perseverance

'Perseverance is failing 19 times and succeeding the 20th time.'
Julie Andrews

'Patience and perseverance have a magical effect before which difficulties disappear and obstacles vanish'
John Quincy Adams

While all the core qualities are extremely important for varying reasons, perseverance is probably in some ways, the most important quality. Perseverance is the ability to keep going, no matter what difficulty or problem arises. Without perseverance the other core qualities become stuck especially for example, creativity, competitiveness, work ethic and passion. Perseverance demands us to press on, not give up, particularly in the face of challenges that seem impossible or seem insurmountable to us. While we know this is anything but easy, it is this very fact that makes the end result so precious. The years and years of hard training in my career as a basketball player were worthwhile in the end. Even today, when I look at my trophies and medals and shine them up from time to time, I can still remember winning them and feel enormously proud of myself.

Perseverance requires us to remain steadfast in our quest, approach our goals with absolute resolution. When the going gets tough and we want to give up or feel we cannot go any further or we are going to collapse, we must apply our tenacity and hold on to our determination to succeed. This requires dogged, tireless, incessant grit and endurance.

When I was preparing for my Grade 1 and FIBA referee exams my resolution, my tenacity and my will to hold on to my determination to succeed, was challenged over and over again, especially after the examiners didn't pass me the first time on my Grade 1 exam. I had to call on my doggedness and dig deep for my grit and endurance so defiantly before that second exam game.

Perseverance requires us to want it badly enough. 'The brick walls are there for a reason. The brick walls are not there to keep us out. The brick walls are there to give us a chance to show how badly we want something because the brick walls are there to stop the people who don't want it badly enough. They're there to stop the other people.' (Prof. Randy Pausch). Athletes who run the marathon often describe hitting this wall. It is the athletes who persevere and train properly that go through the wall and cross the finishing line. That feeling of wanting it badly enough, I can remember it so well. It was all the pain and suffering, all the sacrifices I had made that made me push on and refuse to give up. When I came to the brick walls, I knew in no uncertain terms, that I had only one choice and that was to go straight through them. The walls of my own limitations. The walls of the closed male-dominated world. The walls of the social norm. Just had to be knocked down.

When I was training to run my first 26-mile marathon, I had heard such ferocious stories about hitting this famous wall that I was dreading it. However, much to my surprise, it was indeed the fact that I had trained properly and prepared for that part of the race that got me across the finishing line in a relatively good state, as the course was quite a tough one. By the time I ran my second marathon, I went through the wall easier than the first time despite running faster, recording the very respectable time of 3 hours 20 minutes, smashing my first time of 3 hours 45 minutes!

Stubbornness is a quality that has a positive aspect to it in these situations. The stubbornness to continue when every single one of your muscles are screaming at you to stop can come in extremely useful here. I was always criticised by my parents for being such a stubborn and obstinate person. As I have explained already, they could never understand my obstinacy in pursuing my sports to the level of fanaticism that I did. However, l could relate to what Henry Ward Beecher put forward, 'The difference between perseverance and obstinacy, is that one comes from a strong will and the other from a strong won't.' In my case my strong *Will* to succeed and my strong *Won't* to let anyone stop me was paramount to my success. Therefore, my stubbornness and my obstinacy were, in many ways, my best friends. They got me to places where I would never have got to without them. They were key characteristics in me achieving my Grade 1 and FIBA exams and winning the extensive number of races that I ever won.

Sean used the word persistence a lot because, like the F-word, you can get your teeth stuck into it more than the word perseverance. The latter is posher and more ladylike perhaps, while the former is more aggressive in that it promotes action and gives the message to hang on at all costs, even if it is by the tips of your fingernails. The *sis* in it is like a snake hissing and encourages attack, keep attacking. We saw how the other sports people I have talked about had this quality in spades. Nureyev and Fonteyn were super role models in this regard, they both persisted until they made their dreams come true. Persistence was undoubtedly one of my strong points.

I think being deaf as a child taught me a lot about it. Trying to persevere and operate in a hearing world was extremely difficult. My deaf world was such a different world. There was no comparison between them. There were times when my deaf world seemed like a better place to be. When I was on my own, away from people, it felt much safer and much more peaceful. Being amongst hearing people was a constant struggle. Always desperately battling to make myself fit in and force myself to be included was a lot of hard work. This was one of the things I had to persevere at. I used to be totally drained from the intensity of the effort it required by the end of every day as I vied for acceptance. While I hated being deaf, there were times when I wanted to give up on everything and just surrender to my deaf world. It would probably be easier nowadays to do that because there are a lot of facilities and help available that didn't exist when I was growing up. Only for Dr. Johnson, I don't know where I would have ended up. He was my motivation for persevering through the intense torture.

Sean and I were two of a kind. Perseverance most definitely was one of his strong points too. In fact, I do not think I've ever met anyone to persevere like him. He was unbelievable. Our grit and our determination were dictated to by our perseverance. It was just unthinkable for either of us to give up. It's an interesting fact, but Sean and I never had to encourage each other not to give up. It just happened automatically between us.

When I think of the number of people in my life who I have truly helped to persevere with things rather than give up, if I had a penny for each one, I'd be a millionairess by now. When I look back, I can see that my perseverance was something I took for granted. I didn't realise that what was so natural to me was impossible for others to do. Sadly, a large percentage of people give up especially at the crucial point when they are so close to achieving their goal. I have seen it time and time again, both in sport and with my counselling clients. There they are, with the light at the end of the tunnel in front of them, their goal within their grasp and they abandon ship at the last moment, just because the last bit is the toughest bit. That last bit, that toughest bit challenges them to face the truth about themselves that perhaps they don't really want to persevere to change after all. As Jordan Peterson says, 'The truth is something that burns. It burns off dead wood. And people don't like having the dead wood burnt off, often because they're 95 percent dead wood.' It breaks my heart when this happens because the people are much stronger than they realise and, more often than not, have the ability to make it through to the other side. Just when you think you are there and the cake is in your hand ready to eat, for some peculiar reason that last effort of getting the cake from your hand into your mouth can become, for some, apparently elusive. It is particularly difficult in athletics trying to shave off that last second. In Jim Ryun's case, he persevered, he got the cake from his hand into his mouth. He shaved off that apparently elusive 0.1 of a second in his last world record. The magnitude of the effort he went through, all for that 0.1 made his perseverance worthwhile.

It is also quite common in weight loss. People often lose stones and when it comes to the last half stone or a couple of pounds they need to lose to achieve their target weight, it can take them double or treble the time to lose that last bit of weight. This is the point, just like hitting the wall, where the tension builds and builds. It becomes extremely frustrating and often causes people to throw in the towel. Managing this tension and frustration, is a skill that requires emotional development and challenges our ability to be patient. Patience is the essential key at this point.

Whenever we are on the cusp of a breakthrough, Murphy's Law steps in and makes sure everything goes against you. The breakthrough is left hanging in the air. The wind blows it and it shivers, shakes and quivers. It feels like your back is against the wall and there is no escape. This is the critical moment, the moment when you must breathe, recall your belief in yourself and hang in there no matter what. As Harriet Beecher Stowe describes it, 'When you get into a tight place and everything goes against you…never give up then, for that is just the place and time that the tide will turn.' Of course, it no more feels like the tide is going to turn than the cat. When you are in the throes of everything going against you, it is incredibly hard to hold on to this belief. However, there are many examples to draw on of this truth being the case. Jim Ryun's world records, Nadia Comaneci's perfect '10', my own examples of achieving the chin-ups with Sean and my Grade 1 and FIBA exams.

Reflecting on the core quality of perseverance I have within myself; I realise now that I totally underestimated how proficient I was in this area. It is a quality that has spanned my life from a young age, right up to the present moment. While I have often felt like running away and really wanted to run from difficulties in my life, I've always managed to not do that. Perseverance played an essential part in my overcoming the countless obstacles of my childhood, the obstacles I faced in sport and of course, my car crashes. Working with Ann I frequently just wanted to run away. The issues we were dealing with were extremely painful and I desperately wanted to run away from my pain. What I have learned however is, that running away causes much more pain than the original pain that you are running away from in the first place. Persevering and going through the pain, is far, far easier. This applies to everything in life.

So, the lesson is clear as a bell. Persevere - stay - do not run away - press on. Hang in there and get support if things become unbearable or overwhelming. Persistence pays dividends in the end. Stay positive and keep your mind on the end goal. Keep reminding yourself that not giving up will be worth it in the long run. Remember that perseverance will be your number one friend and mentor. Perseverance will bring you the success that you crave and turn you in to a formidable person in your life.

'Perseverance is the hard work you do after you get tired of doing the hard work you already did'.
Newt Gingrich.

These eleven core qualities enabled me to become a master of my sport. This meant I brought a high level of skill to what is nowadays referred to as my *Active Mindset*. This active mindset requires from a basketball player a multitude of skills and actions they need to constantly hold in their awareness throughout the entire game. For example, while dribbling the ball, the play-maker needs to be looking to see what the opposition defence is doing, so that they can call the right play to beat the defence and not just keep their eyes on the ball. The active mindset for a referee of course, calls for different but equally multitudinous skills and actions to manage and control the game. For example, while managing their primary area of responsibility they also must use their peripheral vision and their positioning to keep all the players in sight, while working in conjunction with their co-official. The core qualities develop the level of skills in the players and the referees to be able to function with proficiency from the lowest level to the highest level in their game.

It is fascinating looking back, how I managed to hold each one of the core qualities, use them succinctly and dip back in as required, without even being aware that I was doing this. It says there is something natural in this, that the practise and the repetition, the being in the Zone enables this. These core qualities became the fundamental foundation of my belief system in striving for success, providing me with a unique and condensed framework to achieve my goals. From the time I started playing in St. Clare's Primary School, I brought these burgeoning qualities to my game, unaware that they had been gathering in me, taking root, as I grew up through the many experiences, good and bad, that my life had presented me with and through the multitude of choices I had made. Maybe if you look at any young passionate sports person and observe their enthusiasm and love of the sport, you are ob-serving the beginnings of these core qualities?

CHAPTER 51
Reaching Your Potential Through The Lens of Perfection

'Always dream and shoot higher than you know you can do. Don't bother just to be better than your contemporaries or predecessors. Try to be better than yourself.'

William Faulkner

This chapter, perhaps, summarises what this entire book is about. It is unfortunately, also the most difficult one to write. What I am describing in words is, essentially, an experience. Words won't quite describe it. However, I will do my best to get the message across.

I was recently recommended to watch a documentary entitled 'In The Realm Of Perfection', about John McEnroe, the American tennis player ranked the World's no. 1 in 1981, 1982, 1983 and 1984. The camera totally focused on McEnroe and McEnroe alone, during all his matches throughout the 1984 French Open tournament. It was a point-by-point portraiture of McEnroe. He was the hot favourite to win the tournament, as he was unbeaten on the world circuit up to that point. This tournament was a pivotal one, as he was aiming to reach perfection, having in essence already assembled a perfect season to date. He was on course to becoming the first tennis player to win all the tournaments in the Grand Slam for that year. It was only in the fractious tournament Final, 10th June 1984 that the documentary included footage of his opponent, the Czech player, Ivan Lendl. Lendl was considered to be the underdog, as he successfully reached finals but never won the prize. It was anticipated that McEnroe was going to obliterate him in under two hours, making it a quick match. The camera work turned out to be crucial, as it captured the monumental collapse of the world's number No. 1. The documentary is the opposite of everything I have written about in this book. It is a great example of what *not* to do.

The analysis of John McEnroe's technique and style as a player and his strengths and weaknesses, were shown in a most finely tuned manner due to the cameraman and his complete focus and attention to detail in his observations of McEnroe. On the physical front, the analysis highlighted McEnroe's presence, his talent and giftedness as a technical player, his agility and speed in approaching the net and most importantly, his spatial awareness in his ability to place the ball, particularly his drop shots, consistently in the correct place to win his points. It also highlighted his unpredictability as a player and his ability to make his opponent feel insecure. The cameraman's focus on McEnroe meant he could break down McEnroe's movement to such an extent, that it allowed him to see what the eyes cannot see. It was amazing to see this on screen, as it produced an in-depth insight, which provided a lot more information.

On the psychological side however, McEnroe was an extremely temperamental and angry player, constantly arguing and fighting with the umpires over their decisions. His favourite plea, whine and demand was, 'Show me the mark, I want to see the mark.' These demands were in response to the umpires calling the ball in or out on the court lines. He contested these decisions in a vicious manner, not on rare occasions, but on many, many occasions, holding the game up and bringing the game to a stop for indeterminable lengths of time. In attacking them, his comments to the umpires were nasty and personal. He also had major reactions to the cameramen and to the noise that the cameras were making when filming. On numerous occasions he came across as a spoilt little brat, a child throwing tantrums right, left and centre and a pouting child who was going to burst into tears at any minute. This is an example of the behaviour that earned him the title/nicknames *Superbrat* and *McNasty* early in his career. The media described him in 1979 at the age of twenty as follows: 'He is the most vain, ill-tempered, petulant loudmouth that the game of tennis has ever known.' The psychological assessment in the documentary stated that his anger, his reactions to a sense of injustice and his obnoxious behaviour, made him the player that he was. It stated that he could only play well when he felt everyone was against him and hostile towards him. His internal torture and the raging wild animal inside him, had to be projected on to the umpires, cameramen, spectators and everyone around him. He was not happy until he turned people against him. It also stated that it was unusual for this type of destructive behaviour to yield positive results.

I disagree with this final statement in the documentary. In my humble opinion, he got away with murder in relation to his behaviour because of his natural talent and giftedness.

Why is the information in the documentary so important? Because it breaks down in psychological terms, how he himself dismantled his concentration and focus. He did not remain in the 'Zone.' In my opinion, on that fateful day, when he failed to reach the perfection he was striving for, it was because this critically important skill of remaining in the zone was lacking. He was romping ahead in the French Open Final by two sets to nil, 6-3 and 6-2. In tennis, just as in basketball where it was considered a mortal sin to miss a lay-up at the crunch time in a game, losing a game in tennis when you are two sets up, is a *mortaler* of equal dimensions. If you do that in basketball you can hang up your boots, the equivalent in tennis is hanging up your racquet and tennis shoes. The turning point of the match came in the third set. McEnroe was becoming increasingly agitated by a cameraman whose headset was emitting noise that sparked the American's quick temper. His failure and inability to stay in the *Zone* and instead, resort to his agitated behaviour, categorically caused him to lose that fateful match. Lendl took advantage of McEnroe's weakness, his game grew in strength as his ground strokes became menacing, while McEnroe's game, on the other hand, became weaker and weaker, including his serve faltering. By the time he regained his composure it was too late. He could not claw his way back into the match despite making several desperate attempts to get himself back on track. Lendl's courage came to the fore as he battled on to eventually win the match, nail bitingly and unexpectedly in a time of 4 hours and 8 minutes. A far cry from the original time anticipated. Without a doubt, an epic match. The underdog coming out on top.

The documentary shows, step by step, the roll out of McEnroe's disintegration. He could not contain his negative emotions, nor could he channel his anger in a constructive way. By stepping out of the zone, he gave away his power and his energy on something that didn't matter. It was all so pointless. Those calls by the umpires didn't matter in the least and had no bearing or relevance whatsoever on the outcome of the game, because he was generally speaking, way ahead in his matches. All that arguing, fighting and unsportsmanlike behaviour was futile. Umpires, 99.9 per cent of the time, are not going to change their minds. You have to know that. But the problem with his behaviour was, that when it came to the crunch time in this vitally important match, he couldn't hold it together mentally. When your back is to the wall, that is when you need the spectators on your side more than ever. The spectators support switched over completely from the favourite to the underdog Lendl. Therefore, when the pressure increased, he found himself completely alone and he fell apart altogether. This one match was the ruination of his future tennis career, as it was a once off opportunity to make the history books. Considering the fact that 1984 was his most spectacular year, it transpired that the tennis great would never find his way to these heights again. This one match epitomises the saying 'One man's loss is another's man's gain.' McEnroe's career plummeted; Lendl's career rose. Lendl went on to become the World's No. 1 ranked tennis player for the next 3 successive years.

Watching the documentary and thinking about what Sean had taught us, made me realise that I had the great fortune to have had the positive outcome that McEnroe sadly missed out on that day, not only once but twice in my life. The documentary touched me emotionally and while I felt sorry for him and his loss on the one hand, I have to be honest and say that he didn't deserve to win either. He threw the match away, when it was right in the palm of his hand, by letting his destructive behaviour get the better of him. His natural talent and giftedness were of no use to him. They could not save him on that fateful day. He was left a disgusted, raging, bitterly, bitterly disappointed man. He said afterwards, that to this day, he has sleepless nights over that one match. He also described being haunted by that dreaded reality of being only as good as your last match. This reality truly hit him and plagued him for many years afterwards. John McEnroe missed out on the feeling that I am about to try and describe. The feeling that he desperately, desperately wanted to experience. The feeling he strived hard for, for many years can only be experienced through the achievement of perfection. It was right there, within his grasp, until he blew it! He could not get that cake from his hand into his mouth! What a pity! That's what made his feelings of disgust, rage and disappointment worse. He was haunted by the fact that he knew in his heart and soul that he had nobody to blame but himself.

When Sean was coaching us, he always taught us, that the referees calls and decisions don't lose the game. It is *You*, meaning us the team, through our own mistakes that cause us to lose the game. 'How many lay-ups and free-throws did we miss as a team?' he would question. 'That's not the referee's fault, that's your fault.' He often yelled at us, 'Don't question or argue with the referee, that's my job.' He would insistently point out that it was our job to focus and concentrate on playing the game, give the game our total attention. He vehemently harped on at us about the vital, vital importance of not allowing ourselves to get sidetracked by anything and that meant literally anything, going on around us, especially the decisions of the referees. Woe betide anyone on our team who got sanctioned by a referee during a match. The consequences were horrific, so much so, that Sean only had to apply them once to get his point across. 'You can't play the game and referee at the same time,' he would roar at us from the sideline. 'Focus, concentrate and play the game, just play the bloody game.' His bellow would rock the gymnasium to such an extent, that even the people sitting in the stands would quiver in their boots, almost pleading with us to, 'Do what you're told and play the bloody game.'

Heaven only knows what Sean would have yelled at John McEnroe. We were mild in our questioning in comparison to McEnroe's outbursts. I would have loved, loved, loved to have seen that one! The sparks would surely have been flying between them. No doubt about it!!! Destructive behaviour was not an option, from Sean's perspective. Definitely not allowed. How right Sean was!

How lucky was I? I was grateful beyond words that I didn't do what McEnroe did and that everything worked out in my favour. In comparison to him, I reached my potential through persistently aiming for perfection on my two crowning occasions. I experienced that wonderfully, incredible, amazing and energising feeling that John McEnroe missed out on that day in Paris.

So now, how do I describe this feeling? Well here goes… You will have to bear with me… Let's see if I can do it justice.

After I refereed that *perfect* match for that first Grade 1 exam, I felt on such a high. I was high as a kite. I was ecstatic beyond ecstatic. I truly felt the euphoria of my achievement. My stomach, which had been in knots from the prematch nervousness and tension, was now gurgling like mad. The knots were gone and were replaced by a churning, just like a washing machine that is spinning the clothes dry. While this may not sound very enticing, I can assure you it was the most wonderful feeling in the world. The sheer delight of my achievement was spinning and spinning inside me. I could not stop it. I did not want to stop it. It just kept going, spinning and spinning. It felt like a happy stream, gurgling its way towards the river. It was delightfully and happily gurgling and spinning around inside me. It was a sensation I had never felt before in my whole life. I was more than happy to hold on to it. The happiness and joy I felt was electric.

My body felt like it had undergone an electric shock. But it was a good shock. It was as if the electrical circuits in my body had blasted into a frenzy of fireworks, exploding and sparking everywhere. My body was vibrating with the force of this current.

As people came over to congratulate me and clap me on the back, the feeling travelled up my body and my whole body from my head right down to my toes was tingling with pure and utter joy. When it reached my head, I felt a bit dizzy and both my head and my tummy were spinning. It wasn't a sensation that made me feel as if I was going to faint. Instead, it was a fuzzy-wuzzy feeling that made me feel I was going to fly. What was extra-special about it, was the fact that I was totally conscious throughout the whole experience. I could feel everything that was happening to me crystal clear. The claps on my back were reverberating through my whole body, adding to this amazing sensation that I was already feeling. Everyone else's excitement for me was amplifying my own excitement and delight which was coursing through me. Within the consciousness of it there was also a surrealness that seemed to lift it up to an extra dimension. Some people might describe it as a spiritual experience or transcendental. I don't know. It did seem however, to be outside the normal realm of experiences. I had never known anything like it before. But what I do know is, that it felt as if there was no other experience in the whole wide world that could outclass this multitude of feelings.

I was acutely aware that what I was feeling was the euphoria of the result of reaching my pinnacle of perfection, the perfection I had so resolutely strived for. It was pulsing through my veins. The decades of hard work and the torturous, unrelenting grafting had suddenly come together and culminated in reaching this point. In that euphoric moment of realisation, everything felt worthwhile. Everything. There were no regrets for all the sacrifices made, for all the time, the blood, sweat and tears and the hours and hours of commitment and dedication. This euphoric moment seemed like the longest moment of my life. It felt eternal. It expanded and stretched like a piece of elastic. But the elastic did not snap and break, it just kept expanding and stretching. The most incredible feeling. My emotions and feelings were expanding with it. I felt as if I was 10' tall – imagine. It was the most glorious, glorious feeling.

This feeling has a rare quality to it. It is not a feeling that comes from the competitiveness of trying to beat your opponent. It is a feeling that is developed from respecting the talent, the hard work, the commitment, dedication, passion and perseverance that your opponent has courageously, ardently and gallantly strived for, in order to be as good as they are. Then with that respect and admiration for them in mind, trying to figure out or question, what is it going to take to surpass that and put into action what is required to achieve it. While the moment eventually ends and the feelings peter out and you have to come down to earth again, the feeling remains firmly planted internally, never ever to be dislodged.

From what I've described, you would think that this feeling would have a major anticlimax to it. But, surprisingly, it doesn't. It was only when I was preparing for my FIBA exam that I discovered this. I was able to draw on the memory of the feeling again and again during my preparations on that gruelling week in Dortmund and the exam itself. The anticipation of this feeling awaiting me should I pass the FIBA exam, was an extra motivation and a key factor in spurring me on. It ensured that I did not give up and encouraged me to dig deeper for that vital second time. It was a formidable discovery that dawned on me. I did not think it was possible to have that feeling again. It had felt particularly unique and precious that very first time.

After that fated phone call informing me that I had passed my FIBA exam, I was proven wrong, very wrong. The feeling resurfaced and reemerged with such a force and a bang! I will never forget it. It was doubled, unbelievably doubled. This achievement was far higher than the first one. I hadn't expected this. In hindsight however, I can now see that of course it was only natural that this would be the case. I unequivocally cannot describe this second feeling in words, but you can double the description of the first one to get some idea of it.

Reflecting on everything afterwards, it became clear to me that the striving for perfection is what brought me to reach my potential. It dragged every last ounce of ability out of me. It would not take no for an answer. It pushed and pushed me, demanding me to go further, aim higher, keep striving for the *more,* that indisputable *there's always more* concept, until I eventually succumbed and surrendered to its demand.

What I learned from these two incredible experiences was, the higher the achievement, the higher the feeling. These feelings are extra-special. They cannot be felt in the humdrum of ordinary, everyday life. It is only through the course of challenging ourselves, seriously challenging ourselves, that makes this experience possible. As we all know, there is nothing free in life. Everything comes at a cost and a price. These experiences are the same, but by golly, the rewards are far more fruitful than anything you could ever imagine or dream of. While they don't last forever in the physical moment, they last forever in a much more meaningful and important way. They are something you can draw on for the rest of your life. There is no greater feeling of satisfaction and joy in striving, achieving your goals, reaching your potential and making your dreams come true. Through embracing perfection and allowing it to fully extract every ounce of your potential, you will reach far greater heights in yourself than you ever thought possible. After my own experiences, I can honestly say that I would thoroughly recommend it.

EPILOGUE

Delving into the background of the sports people and dancers I have referred to, began to shine a light on my own background which has allowed me to value and appreciate my
own journey. Throughout my life it seems that everything I
did was on a purely automatic basis. I always felt I just put my
head down and bulldozed my way through everything. I never gave myself enough credit for my perseverance and hard
work in overcoming my pain and suffering and the mind-bog-
gling obstacles that I had to overcome to achieve my own
successes and to make history the way I did. The significance
of my integrity, my morals, my values, my principles and my
ethical standpoint never dawned on me. I never for one moment realised that these attributes were universal amongst the
top achievers in the world. I underestimated the invaluable
lessons that Bridget, Sean, Ann and everyone else had taught
me. I never realised that each of them were, in their different
ways, encouraging me to step in to myself.

It was when I looked into the sports lives of Michael Jordan, Michael Johnson, Nadia Comaneci and the dance lives
of Rudolph Nureyev and Margot Fonteyn that I realised the
same criteria applied to all of them. In essence, there was
no difference between them. It became apparent to me too,
that the path I had taken at my level, was the same as theirs.
I was shocked to make this discovery and at the same time
delighted. When I looked back at my life, it brought to my
attention the importance of proper role modelling and its
effect on others. Each and every one of these people were
sending out the same message of inspiration, 'If I can do it,
you can do it. You too, can push back the boundaries of the

impossible in your life.' In my own small way, I had done the same thing as these people, without realising it or honouring myself for it.

I realise the rewards far outweigh what seem like the torture. The culmination of all the hard work, blood, sweat and tears suddenly comes together to bear fruit. The long periods of waiting, waiting and more waiting, become worthwhile. The torture of all the waiting transforms into a pure joy. Applying, developing and nurturing the *Core Qualities* into the whole of our being guarantees a profound personal growth in our characters and personalities. This growth rewards us, not only with a sense of immense satisfaction, but with an informed conviction of the true power and strength that lies within us. This leads us to recognise the undeniable reality in our unshakeable abilities and authentic potential. It dangles the carrot in front of us that invites us to make the impossible possible. It waves the flag that says, 'Chase your dreams and make them come true.'

The sweetness of success and achievement is sweeter than the sweetest cake you could ever eat. Striving for perfection yields the greatest reward you could ever imagine. It takes you towards the pinnacle of your potential. It is here that you can truly savour the taste of that success, an everlasting taste that will never leave your tongue. The euphoric moment that occurs at the height of the achievement is a moment that is everlasting until the day you die. No one can take it away from you. It is a moment you can draw on to carry you through the tough times in life. You need perseverance, patience and the courage to risk going after it. But it is there for everyone to choose. When you have it, you have it and it has a special resting place in your heart where it will stay forever.

Now it has become clear. Life is not easy. Life is tough. Reaching our potential is not easy. It is in fact as tough as life is. However, with the right attitude, the proper role models, the help and support of the right people and the combination of the Core Qualities, it **is** possible to achieve your life aspirations and make all your dreams come true. Michael Jordan, Michael Johnson, Nadia Comaneci, Rudolph Nureyev and Margot Fonteyn clearly demonstrated that to us. In all that I have done from the very start, from my engagement with Dr. Johnson, the deep connection I made to Miss O'Flynn, my treasured sporting journey with Sean, the whole way through what really has been a difficult path, I too have shown that to myself. I hope that my story inspires you to do the same.

Little Mary and Doctor Johnson

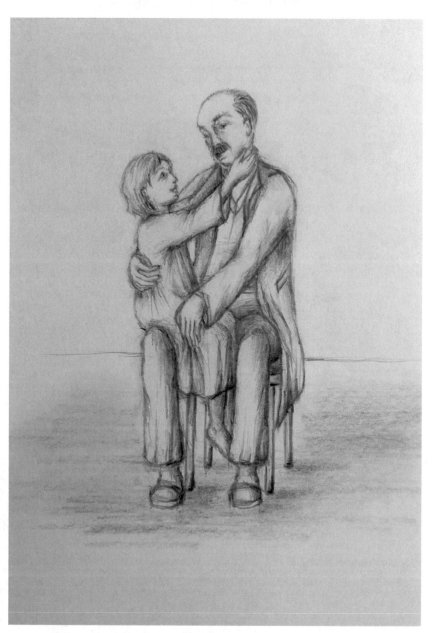

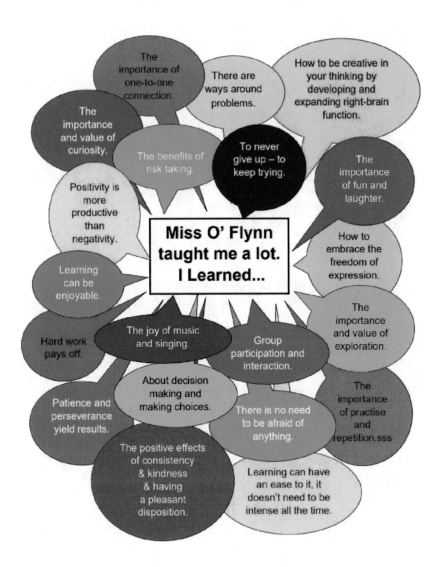

My Father

Bill's Al Jolson Act

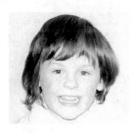

"Baby Face, You've Got the Cutest Little Baby Face"

My Brother,
The Cutest Baby Ever!

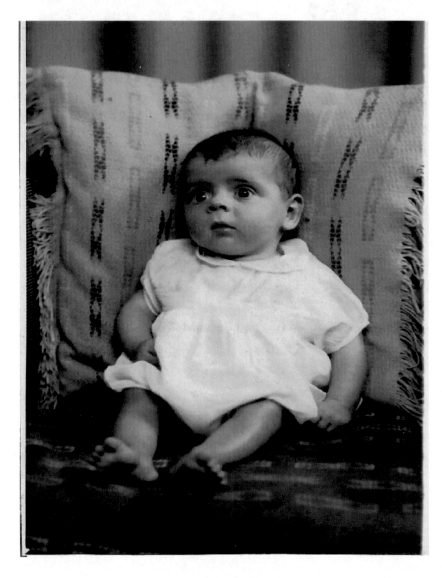

Mary running a half marathon

Mary & Sean

 **Mary racing to victory!**

Mary playing basketball with Meteors

Mary playing basketball

Mary takes control of the court

Mary with her beloved basketball

Sean

Mary refereeing a match showing the "Power of the Whistle"

40

FOX

Mary's Da

Bridget and Da

Little Mary

Mary takes a breather from her basketball

I did it! Mary's graduation

Mary

Mary's Dance Teachers

The Core Qualities Required To Achieve Success, Reach The Pinnacle Of Perfection And Make The Impossible Possible

ACKNOWLEDGEMENTS

Writing this book has been a dream come true for me. It would never have been written and most certainly the subject matter I'd never have chosen if it wasn't for Maurice Curtis. It was Maurice whose idea it was and who inspired me with absolute adamancy to write about myself and my history making and highlighted the importance of sharing and leaving behind a legacy when I die of valuable information for the generations to come. Thank you so, so much Maurice because I'm delighted I stepped up to your challenge. It was one of the most enjoyable and memorable experiences of my life and one I will treasure until the day I die.

There are many people who have helped and encouraged me throughout the process and unfortunately too many to mention individually but you all know who you are because we will celebrate in person together.

I would sincerely like to thank my publishing company Europe Books U.K. and each and every one of the publishing team for their amazing contributions, for accommodating my requests, for respecting my work and for making my publishing journey a pleasurable, special and unique venture.

I would especially like to thank Marialaura who chose my manuscript in the first place and spotted its potential and whose feedback was encouraging and uplifting. I truly felt that Marialaura genuinely understood and connected with the message the book is conveying in all its aspects and in particular at the emotional level. This was lovely to experience.

I would like to thank my editor Alessia for finding my book fascinating, for her efficiency, flexibility, patience, encouragement and all her hard work in making the editing process a smooth, collaborative and pleasant experience. I would especially like to thank her for respecting the integrity of my voice and ensuring it remained authentic and in its true form.

I would also like to thank Elisa, Head of Production, Simone from the graphic design team and the promotion team for their much appreciated hard work, effort and assistance in making this possible and giving me the opportunity to make my dream come true and pass it on to others. I thank you all from the bottom of my heart.

I would like to reiterate my thanks to the people I have mentioned in Chapter 49, Michael Pita, Virginia, Ann, David, Martin and Michael. An extra special word of thanks to Michael who without his help this book would most definitely not have been written.

To Ela for her beautiful illustrations. To Deirdre for her unwavering support, encouragement and continuous affirmation throughout this journey. To Ray from Sportsfile for his photographic contributions. To Cheryl for her invaluable input and creative talent in helping me to design my graphics. To my friend Karen and my two cheerleaders Ann and Adelle for their enthusiasm, avid faith and ardent belief in me and being so proud of my achievement. To my brother Paddy, my friends Edser, Marie, Gerald and all my many other friends who are too numerous to mention, for their continuous support, infectious enthusiasm and excitement and the chats over the cuppas and goodies. Last but not least, Siobhán and Rebecca for their long and faithful involvement with the typing and the graphics, the collaborative process of thrashing out questions and ideas and being a real case of three heads are better than one. For their patience and endurance and hanging in there when the going got tough from the beginning to the end and especially when the deadline was looming. Thank you both for all the fun, laughter and slagging, the dinners and chocolate that sustained us all.